Lionel James Trotter

The life of John Nicholson, soldier and administrator

Based on private and hitherto unpublished documents

Lionel James Trotter

The life of John Nicholson, soldier and administrator
Based on private and hitherto unpublished documents

ISBN/EAN: 9783337305895

Printed in Europe, USA, Canada, Australia, Japan

Cover: Foto ©Raphael Reischuk / pixelio.de

More available books at **www.hansebooks.com**

THE LIFE

OF

JOHN NICHOLSON

SOLDIER AND ADMINISTRATOR

BASED ON
PRIVATE AND HITHERTO UNPUBLISHED DOCUMENTS

BY

CAPTAIN LIONEL J. TROTTER

AUTHOR OF

'A LIFE OF WARREN HASTINGS,' 'A HISTORY OF INDIA UNDER VICTORIA,' ETC.

WITH PORTRAITS AND MAPS

THIRD EDITION

LONDON

JOHN MURRAY, ALBEMARLE STREET

1898

TO THE

SURVIVING COMRADES, FRIENDS, AND RELATIVES

OF THE HEROIC

JOHN NICHOLSON

THIS VOLUME IS DEDICATED

BY

THE AUTHOR

PREFACE

—•—

FORTY years ago Brigadier-General John Nicholson vanished like a meteor from the scene of his gloriously brief career. Since then his heroic figure has marched across many a page of commemorative print, from the careful narratives of Cave-Browne and Kaye down to the most brilliant of Mrs. Steele's romances. 'The heroic Nicholson' is the title by which the men of his own generation love to speak of the young soldier-statesman who led his stormers against fearful odds into the central stronghold of the great Sepoy rebellion in 1857.

History, gossip, and prose-fiction have busied themselves with the deeds and character of John Nicholson; and numerous legends, well invented but more or less untrue, have grown up around his name. How is it, by the way, that no English poet of any mark has commemorated the fall of Delhi, that master-incident in the story of the great Mutiny? Tennyson has glorified the defence of Lucknow, and Gerald Massey has sung of Havelock's march and Sir William Peel. But the siege and storming of Delhi have remained unsung, except by Mr. Charles Kelly of the Indian Civil Service, and one or two other forgotten poets.

a 3

Up to this time the only authentic record of Nicholson's life and work is the admirable sketch which Sir John Kaye contributed more than thirty years since to *Good Words*, and afterwards republished in his *Lives of Indian Officers*. As a short and appreciative memoir based on original documents, it left for the moment little to desire; but as a final presentment of its subject, it was necessarily incomplete, and on points of detail not always accurate. To fill up the gaps and remove the inaccuracies in Kaye's narrative, to offer fresh illustrations of my hero's character, habits, faculties, and methods of work, and to sift the wheat from the chaff of the stories current about Nicholson during the last thirty years, has been my purpose in writing the present volume. How far I have succeeded will be seen from the frequent references in the text or the footnotes to new or recent sources of information, whether in print or manuscript.

That I have had to work upon a limited store of new materials is due, I am told, to the fact that most of the papers entrusted to Kaye by Mrs. Nicholson and others were destroyed by a fire in Kaye's rooms. Happily the loss of these documents has to a large extent been made good by the readiness with which many of John Nicholson's friends and relatives have responded to my appeal for help. Some two dozen of Nicholson's autograph letters have thus come into my hands, besides a large stock of manuscript notes, reminiscences, letters, and commentaries, which have been turned, I trust, to good account.

For some years past death has been busy among John Nicholson's friends and contemporaries, and two of my

most valued contributors have lately 'joined the majority.'
To one of these, the late Sir James Abbott, K.C.B., I am
indebted for a detailed and correct account of his young
comrade's little campaign in the hills of Hazàra and Rawal
Pindi, during the second Sikh War. To the many who
happily still survive, whose names are mentioned in the
following pages, I offer my grateful acknowledgements for
all the help they have rendered me towards making this
memoir as full and trustworthy as circumstances allowed.
I only hope that nothing here written will cause any
of them to regret their generous reliance on my good
intentions. I have tried at least, with their help, to reproduce for the readers of to-day as much as possible of the
impression which Nicholson made upon his contemporaries,
as a man who ' nothing common did or mean '; as a leader
who chained victory to his standard, whose iron will and
stern sense of duty overlay the tenderness of a woman
and the thoughtful kindliness of a true gentleman; as
a magistrate terrible to evil-doers, and prompt to punish
convicted criminals, but careful to investigate every charge,
and merciful to offenders whom want or bad example had
led astray.

I may add that this volume contains no anecdote concerning John Nicholson which is either in itself incredible
or lacks sufficient voucher for its truth.

L. J. T.

Eastbourne,
Oct. 26. 1897.

CONTENTS

LIST OF MAPS AND ILLUSTRATIONS

'Then from city to city, from cantonment to cantonment, went the chequered tidings; Delhi had fallen, the king was a captive—but John Nicholson was dead.'-- KAYE, *Sepoy War*, vol. iii.

> 'He is gone who seemed so great.—
> Gone; but nothing can bereave him
> Of the force he made his own
> Being here.'
>
> TENNYSON, *Ode on the Duke of Wellington*.

LIFE OF JOHN NICHOLSON

CHAPTER I

FROM BIRTH TO ADOLESCENCE, 1822–1839

In the days of our Tudor sovereigns the family of which John Nicholson was to be the bright particular star had made their home in the border county of Cumberland. 'Our tradition,' writes Mr. Henry Nicholson of Cranagill in Armagh, 'is that the first who came over [to Ireland] was a Rev. William Nicholson, M.A., who arrived in 1589, and was married to a Lady Elizabeth Percy. This Rev. William Nicholson was, by tradition, the Rector of that portion of the country in which Cran-na-gael—the " oak-tree of the Gael "—now corrupted into Cranagill, was situated. We find as a fact, that in a visitation of the Archbishop of Armagh in 1623, he was enrolled as Rector of Derry-brughas, with a curate named O'Gill at Killyman. This parish was partly in the counties Tyrone and Armagh; and the parish church was at Mullenakill—" the Hill of the Church "—now in the demesne of Churchill, the seat of the late Sir William Verner, Bart.'

A tradition common to many Anglo-Irish families tells how two brothers followed or accompanied William Nicholson to Ireland. One of them settled in Derry, and the other in Dublin, from which latter the Nicholsons of Balrath descend. Of the Derry branch my kind informant can discover no recent trace. His researches, however, make it clear that, some time before 1632, Cran-na-gael had passed by purchase into the family of the William Nicholson aforesaid.

The fortunes of William's family came very near to utter overthrow by McGuire's rebellion in 1641. His son's wife and her infant boy were the only two in Cran-na-gael who escaped the common massacre, by hiding, with the aid of a faithful servant, behind some brushwood. In their wanderings thence they fell in with a party of loyalist soldiers, who escorted them safely to Dromore, whence they made their way across sea to the widow's former home at Whitehaven. Here they seem to have remained throughout the troublous years that followed the outbreak of the great Civil War.

What became of this poor lady does not appear. Her son William, during his sojourn in Cumberland, had become a Quaker, perhaps, says Mr. H. Nicholson, through being brought into contact with the founder of that sect, the quaint, soul-stirring George Fox. In due time he returned to Cranagill, and had three sons, one of whom died childless during the siege of Derry in 1688. From William, the eldest, our John Nicholson was directly descended[1].

Of John's own father, Dr. Alexander Nicholson, I learn from John's nephew, Dr. Theodore Maxwell, that he was one of sixteen children borne by Isabella Wakefield to John Nicholson of Stramore House, Gilford, in County Down. Among this large family Alexander, the eldest son, came third in order of time. From school he went on

[1] Letter from H. J. Nicholson, Esq.

to Trinity College, Dublin, where he afterwards took his doctor's degree. In his twenty-seventh year he married, in 1820, Clara Hogg of Lisburn, the daughter of an Ulster merchant who had ruined himself in the process of founding the linen industries of his native town [1].

The Hoggs, like the Nicholsons, had some noble blood in their veins, if it be true that the first of them who settled in Ulster in the seventeenth century had run off with a daughter, or some near relative, of the Duke of Hamilton. Be that as it may, the fortunes of the family now represented by the second Lord Magheramorne had sunk very low indeed, when Clara Hogg's father died, leaving her and her brother Charles to the care of their widowed mother and her eldest son James.

Happily for them all, young James Hogg proved splendidly equal to so imperious a need. He had just passed with high honours out of Dublin University. In 1809, at the age of nineteen, he went forth armed with a passport from the Duke of Buckingham, to seek his fortune in the dominions of the East India Company, which still looked askance on all unlicensed 'interlopers.' On his way round the Cape, his vessel was chased by a French cruiser, and only escaped by running up the Mozambique Channel. At Calcutta he had to borrow, at exorbitant rates of interest, the means of supporting the dear ones left at home.

By his own merits and the knowledge he had gained in the Law Schools of Dublin, James Hogg soon made his mark at the Calcutta Bar. In five years he fairly distanced all his rivals, and at the end of five more he was making £15,000 a year. From 1825 to 1833 he held the lucrative

---

[1] Clara's mother was sister to James Dickey, Esq., of Rendlestown, co. Antrim.

post of Registrar to the Supreme Court at Calcutta. His
return to England in 1834 heralded his entrance on
a wider and more ambitious career, as an eloquent speaker
in the House of Commons, a leading Director of the East
India Company, and in 1858, an influential member of the
Queen's Indian Council. In 1846, while serving as Chairman of the Court of Directors, James Weir Hogg was
rewarded with a baronetcy for his great political services
to the Ministry of Sir Robert Peel [1].

To return from John Nicholson's uncle to his father:
Dr. Nicholson, a Quaker by long descent, had been guilty
of marrying a lady who belonged to another church. For
this act of contumacy he was at once expelled from the
Quaker brotherhood. The blow fell harmlessly on a young
husband happy in the love of a true God-fearing wife, and
resolute to make his way in the career of his own choosing.
Soon after his marriage he obtained the post of Assistant
Physician to the Lying-in Hospital at Dublin. His practice
in the Irish capital increased with his increasing family;
and in ten years he had gained no mean repute for skill
and experience in medical treatment.

In the course of those ten years Dr. Nicholson had seven
children, two girls and five boys. His eldest boy, John
Nicholson, was born at Lisburn on December 11, 1822.
Sir John Kaye describes him as 'a precocious boy, almost
from his cradle; thoughtful, studious, of an inquiring
nature; and he had the ineffable benefit of good parental
teaching of the best kind. In his young mind the seeds
of Christian piety were early sown and took deep root.'
The parents were earnest, upright, Bible-reading Pro-

---

[1] For the account of Sir J. Hogg's antecedents and his Indian career I am
indebted to his son, Mr. Quintin Hogg.

testants, of a type still common in the north of Ireland. One day Mrs. Nicholson found her little three-year-old son furiously flicking a knotted handkerchief at some invisible object. 'What are you doing, John?' was her wondering question. 'Oh, mother dear,' he gravely answered, 'I'm trying to get a blow at the Devil. He is wanting to make me bad. If I could get him down, I'd kill him [1].'

The little fellow was quick at learning, and at four years of age could read and even write well. He had hardly entered upon his ninth year when, at the close of 1830, his father died, at the age of thirty-seven, from a fever caught in the discharge of his professional duties. The widowed wife and her seven small children returned to Lisburn, where old Mrs. Hogg still lived to welcome her kinsfolk into their future home.

About a year later John Nicholson was sent to a private school at Delgany, in County Wicklow. In his twelfth year he was transferred to the Royal School at Dungannon in County Tyrone, of which Dr. Darley, afterwards Bishop of Kilmore, was then headmaster. A glimpse or two of the boy's character at this period is all that I am able to supply.

With five boys to bring up on a slender income, Mrs. Nicholson would sometimes betray in her sad countenance the cares that harassed her mind. If little Master John happened to notice one of these passing shadows, he would go up to his mother, and say, with a comforting kiss, 'Don't fret, mamma dear; when I'm a big man, I'll make

---

[1] Kaye, *Lives of Indian Officers*, vol. ii. Kaye has given 1821 as the year of John's birth. This is a manifest error, for John's elder sister, Mary, was born in October of that year.

plenty of money, and give it all to you [1].' How loyally
he kept his promise will appear in later pages of this story.
His cousin, the dowager Lady Tweedmouth, remembers
having heard, when she was about six years old, how
John Nicholson ' was always leader in games at the boy's
school, and *never* was known to tell a lie. Quite a hero
from the first.'

At Dungannon the boy remained to the close of his
sixteenth year, working, idling, joining in every boyish
game, and fighting any boy who tried to bully him, or
whom he caught maltreating a smaller boy. His fiery
temper, for he certainly had a very fiery temper, was
especially roused by anything which offended his strong
sense of justice, or his hatred of mean or cowardly practices.
Among his schoolfellows were several whose names have
since stood high in the honour-lists of the British Army.
One of them, Major-General R. N. Lowry, C.B., who was
in the form below him, speaks of him in 1838 as a fine
manly fellow, of a firm, but open, generous disposition; and
he has ' just a dim remembrance ' of John's cool, resolute
bearing in a fight he had with another boy.

The boy who gets on best with his schoolfellows is not
always a favourite with his masters. This, however, was
not the case with young Nicholson. A brother-in-law of
Dr. Darley assures me that the good bishop ' always spoke
most enthusiastically ' of his former pupil. Beyond this
general statement Mr. Richard Greene's memory fails to
carry him; but it may at least be inferred that young
Nicholson's finer qualities had won their way into the
heart of his admiring preceptor. The boy spent his
holidays in the old home at Lisburn. On one of these

[1] Kaye, *Indian Officers.*

occasions, for which no date can be given, he met with an accident which went near to blind him for life. He was playing one day with gunpowder, some of which blew up in his face and half blinded him. Covering his face with his hands, he made his way into his mother's room, and told her what had happened. When he removed his hands ' it was seen,' says Kaye, ' that his face was a blackened mass; his eyes were completely closed, and the blood was trickling down his cheeks. For ten days, during which he never murmured, nor expressed any concern, except for his mother, he lay in a state of total darkness.' At the end of that time the bandages were removed, and lo! as if in answer to the widow's prayers, her boy's sight had been wholly restored to him [1].

In December, 1838, young Nicholson bade a last farewell to Dungannon. No records of the school as it was in the time of Dr. Darley are now extant; so I have been told by its present headmaster, Mr. R. Dill. If John had been careful not to injure his health by overwork, he had at least received what was known as a liberal education, which seemed usually to mean a moderate supply of Greek and Latin, with a slight infusion of mathematics. As he journeyed homewards, he was already on the eve of entering another kind of school than that which he had just quitted. His good uncle, James Hogg, had returned in 1834 from India, a rich man and the father of a family, to become the member for Beverley and a leading proprietor of East India Stock. To make one of the twenty-four directors who sat for business at the old India House in Leadenhall Street, was in those days an object well worthy of any man's ambition. In the winter of 1838

---

[1] Kaye.

Mr. Hogg was pretty sure of his election into that power-ful body. He had some good friends upon the Board, and he wanted to help his widowed sister in securing an honourable livelihood for her eldest boy. Through one of those friends he now obtained for his nephew a cadetship in the Bengal Infantry.

A 'direct' cadet had to go through none of the special training provided at a certain cost by the Company's Military College at Addiscombe. It was enough for him to produce a good character from his last school, and a medical certificate of his soundness in wind and limb. Early in 1839, at the age of sixteen, John Nicholson received his mother's farewell blessing, exchanged some loving words with the rest of the home circle, and made all haste to join his Uncle Hogg in London.

His days in the great city were chiefly spent in prepar-ations for the long sea-voyage, the cost of which, as well as that of his regular outfit, the same kind uncle had promised to defray. More than one visit of inspection was paid to the ship in which he and several other youngsters, bound on the same errand, were about to sail. Under his uncle's escort he appeared one day before the India House mag-nates, to take the necessary oath of allegiance to his future masters. From time to time his uncle gave him some helpful advice, or pointed some wise moral drawn from his own experiences in the far East.

At last, by the end of February, 1839, the good ship *Camden* passed through the Straits of Dover on her way to the scene of John Nicholson's future achievements and glorious death.

CHAPTER II

NOTHING unusual seems to have happened during the months which our young cadet passed on board the *Camden*. We may take it for certain that the vessel touched at St. Helena, and had a fairly good run from the Cape into the Bay of Bengal. According to Kaye, young Nicholson kept very much aloof from the other youngsters on board, whom he described as, 'for the most part, of a noisy and riotous kind.' Good health, high spirits, and sudden freedom from the restraints of school, probably accounted for most of the pranks played by these careless roysterers. He himself spent much of his time in reading the books he had brought out with him, or could borrow from the ship's small library. We can well believe in the 'favourable impression' which John Nicholson's quiet, steady behaviour made upon the captain of the ship.

About the middle of July, 1839, in the height of the monsoon rains, young Nicholson landed in Calcutta, where he spent a few weeks with his uncle's friend, Mr. Theodore Dickens of the Calcutta Bar. At that time the Governor-General, Lord Auckland, was far away at Simla, watching the development of his grand scheme for re-establishing the futile Shah Shuja upon the throne of his fathers at Kâbul. The storming of Ghazni by Keane's troops on July 23 sealed for a time the fate of the masterful Dost Muhammad, and cleared the road to Kábul for his thrice-rejected rival. On August 12, before Calcutta had heard of the Shah's triumphant return to the Bala Hissar, our young cadet took leave of his kindly host, and embarked in the steamer which was to bear him up the Ganges to Benares, where he had been ordered to do duty for a time with the 41st Sepoys.

Landing at Benares early in September, he became for three weeks the guest of Dr. Lindsay, the Civil Surgeon, to whose good offices an introductory letter from Mr. Dickens had commended him. After that he tenanted a small bungalow in the cantonments, that lay beyond the picturesque and populous city where the minarets of Aurangzeb's mosque tower above a confused mass of ghâts, groves, and stately buildings, interspersed with hundreds of Hindu pagodas. To live there 'all alone,' as he tells his mother on October 13, 'is not the most agreeable thing in the world, when you have servants who cannot speak one word of English, and you yourself are master of about fifty Hindustani ones.' A new experience, in the shape of a severe bilious attack, did not tend to raise his drooping spirits. 'I do not know,' he writes, 'what I should have done, had not Uncle Richardson most luckily happened to be here in Benares at this time. He very kindly came over very often, and saw I had everything I required [1]. He has made me a present of a horse. Uncle James [Hogg] told me I should not keep a horse for the first three or four years. Now I could not do without one. A civilian

---

[1] This Richardson Nicholson was a younger brother of Dr. Nicholson. He had been mate of an East Indiaman before he obtained a post in the Company's Opium Department at Mirzapur, where he lived to a hale old age, many years after the Mutiny.

might; but I could not walk about in the sun to courts-martial, parades,' &c., &c.[1]

Our young ensign proceeds to tell his mother how he is 'getting on.' He pays 40 rupees a month for his bungalow, 30 for his food, 45 for servants, none of whom he is obliged to 'keep'; 17 to military funds, 7 for his horse's food, and 12 for 'ale.' 'Then there are clothing, postage, and other minor expenses. I am now living within my pay, and can do very nicely. But I am not yet permanently posted, and I may be ordered to-morrow to join a corps some hundreds of miles up country; then I have to buy a tent, to hire camels, &c., so that if I was to remain always in one station, I could save money. But I must incur heavy expenses: a tent costs 400 rupees, which it would take me a year to pay up; if I am ordered to march to-morrow, I have not 400 rupees to buy one, for I have been only two months receiving pay. However, I am very well off, and have no reason to complain. On the contrary, I am thankful for having got such a good appointment. I am getting very steady, and am beginning to learn the language.'

The youthful writer of these simple utterances then asks for a full account of everything that goes on at home, how they all are: 'Is Alexander fit for College? What is Mary doing? How is Lily getting on, also Master James, William and Charles?' As some new regiments are about to be formed, he may become a lieutenant in twelve months. 'I go to church,' he continues, 'every Sunday, and read my chapter every day, as you advised me. I find dear Mary's Bible very useful.' Among the friends to whom

---

[1] MS. Letters preserved by Rev. E. Maxwell.

he would be kindly remembered is Mr. Gregg, the future
Bishop of Cork and father of the late Primate of Ireland.
He finds Miss Walker's *Book-keeping* ' very useful in keeping my accounts,' and he 'would give anything' to have
learned French instead of Latin and Greek. His heart is
full of home-yearnings. 'Tell me,' he repeats, 'how you
and the children are. . . . Has Alex been at dear Castle
Blaney this summer? Is Charles behaving well? I hope he
is. Whenever I get an opportunity I will send home some
Indian curiosities, which here may be purchased very cheap.
. . . I often, when I am sitting alone here in the evening,
think of you all at home, and say to myself, there is no
place like *home.*'

When he had duly learned his drill under the adjutant
and the serjeant-major, John Nicholson took his part as
a company officer in the usual cold-weather parades and
other regimental duties. How he got on with his brother
officers, and what part he played in the social life of an
important civil and military station, I cannot say. From
his silence on these points it may be inferred that he did
not care to spend upon social pleasures the money that he
would rather save for his dear ones at home. At the
mess dinners he probably talked little, drank no wine, and
retired early to indulge, as we have seen, in lonely musings
about past days and absent friends.

Before the year's end Nicholson was permanently posted
to the 27th Native Infantry, quartered at the new frontier
station of Firozpur on the Satlaj, which then divided the
North-West Provinces from the Punjàb. In December,
1839, he informs his mother of his intention to set out for
his new station at the beginning of the next year. The
march thither would be a long one. 'I am afraid it will

prove a very unpleasant march to me, as I go alone and am unacquainted with the language and country.'

Travelling by way of Meerut and Karnâl, he reached his journey's end on March 23, 1840, safe in person, but not without sad loss of property. At Meerut one of his own servants robbed him of his forks and spoons. 'At Karnâl my tent was cut open at night by practised thieves; and a small trunk in which were my pistols, my dressing-case which belonged to my poor father, about £10 in money, and various other articles, were carried off. As usual, all attempts to discover the thieves proved of no avail.'

Another incident, of which Nicholson makes no mention in his letters home, appears to have happened during his halt at Karnâl. Among his few failings was a hasty temper which, even in after years, he could not always keep under control. When Dr. J. Campbell Brown was surgeon at Karnâl, he met John Nicholson for the first time as a youngster just arrived in company with another officer named Rattray, of the 2nd Native Infantry, brother of him who afterwards did good service at the head of 'Rattray's Sikhs.' The two young officers, so the story runs, had brought a Sepoy detachment thus far up the country; and Nicholson, who was Rattray's junior only by a few months, had fallen out with his senior officer for presuming to teach him his duty. He told Dr. Brown of his grievance, and asked him to carry a challenge to the offender. This the doctor declined to do, and treated his young friend's proposal as a jest. But Nicholson's wrath still blazed. Another gentleman was requested to go upon the same errand, but he too declined to act. By that time the fiery youngster was cooling down, and the quarrel which had threatened to become so deadly closed in a mutual shaking of hands.

Such in effect was the story which Doctor--afterwards Sir—John C. Brown told to an officer, who, noting it down in his own diary, has kindly furnished me with a transcript from the same. Of its substantial truth there need be no question. The doubting reader must bear in mind that duelling had not then wholly died out in England, and in India was still a not uncommon mode of seeking redress for some personal wrong. Even as late as 1852 three officers out of four concerned in one particular duel were dismissed the service; while the fourth, who had given the challenge, was left unpunished, because of the gross provocations which had driven him to defy the law [1]. A youth of Nicholson's proud spirit and fiery temper would easily in those days be tempted to assert his wounded dignity at the pistol's mouth. If his letter of March 30 from Firozpur says not a word about any companions met on the road, his silence makes nothing against the truth of Dr. Brown's story. In all likelihood he had fallen in with Rattray at Cawnpore or Meerut, and parted from him at Karnâl. A sense of shame at his own folly, mingled with a tender regard for his mother's feelings, would have prompted so reticent a youth as John Nicholson to keep the whole matter within his own breast.

I may add that Dr. Campbell Brown had an excellent memory and took an admiring interest in our hero's subsequent career. In 1842 after the surrender of Ghazni by Colonel Palmer, he heard much about Nicholson's heroic courage during the siege from a high-caste native apothecary

---

[1] See Mawson, *Records of Sir C. J. Napier's Indian Command.*

who had obtained his post through the doctor's influence. This man's reports were full of Nicholson's splendid daring, and he declared that if all the other officers had behaved like this one, there would have been no surrender, nor any talk of it, for ' he would have driven the Afghans from the place and neighbourhood [1].'

To return to Nicholson at Firozpur in 1840. Owing to political and strategic requirements, Lord Auckland's government had decided to form cantonments for a strong brigade on the sandy treeless plain near the Satlaj and the old town of Firozpur. The 27th Native Infantry was one of three Sepoy regiments which had been ordered to provide themselves with winter hutting. ' Officers and men,' writes Nicholson, ' immediately commenced making some kind of habitable buildings ; but from the haste with which they were necessarily constructed, they are very ugly and badly planned.' He himself, poor fellow, is sharing a stable with a brother officer, until he can build himself ' something better.' He is determined that his own bungalow shall not cost him more than £40. Even that sum, which then represented two months of an ensign's pay, will put him to ' some inconvenience for a few months.'

Of his new station he remarks curtly after a week's trial, ' I do not like it.' But he likes very much what he has seen of his brother-officers ; and ' the corps is con-sidered a first-rate one.' The letters from home which greeted his arrival fill him with delight at the good news they bring of all he holds dearest. A parcel from Lisburn, containing some pretty and useful gifts from his mother

---

[1] Letter from Major W. Broadfoot, R.E.

and sisters, receives warm appreciation. Lily Anna, he thinks, 'has become a first-rate needle-woman,' while Mary 'continues to work worsted as well as ever.'

Uncle Hogg had offered Alexander a cadetship, if the Nicholson family would pay for his outfit. 'I am sure they would not,' he says, 'and asking would only irritate them. I do not besides think Alexander at all fitted for it. . . . A cadetship would do for James, when he is sixteen, much better, and I think that by that time I might be able to pay his outfit and passage; I mean if I am at all fortunate as far as promotion goes.' Why he should have spoken so positively about Alexander's unfitness for the army, does not appear. At any rate he was one of two brothers who went out in due course to India, from whence neither was fated to return[1].

The young soldier's fine sense of family honour comes out towards the close of this letter. He is very sorry to hear of his mother's annoyance in the matter of rents, &c., and hopes that affairs have meanwhile been settled to her satisfaction. 'But, my dear mother, I never would (as long as there was the remotest probability of matters being amicably settled) expose one of my own relations in a law-suit[2].'

Writing to Uncle Hogg on April 6, Nicholson says, 'We are on the *qui vive* for intelligence from the frontier. Kàbul by all accounts is quite quiet, and has almost ceased to afford us any interest. On my way up here I passed through Ludhiana. Whilst there I was introduced to Colonel Wade, the great political agent in this part of the

---

[1] James himself died in March, 1840, at the age of fourteen.
[2] MS. Letters.

country. He was very kind to me, and gave me a Perwannah to the Jemadars of all the villages I should pass through on my way, ordering them to supply me with everything necessary, on my paying for it. However, at several of these villages (which are in the Punjàb) the Jemadars desired the people to give me nothing, adding, ' What do we care for Colonel Wade ? We are Sikhs. You may [go hang] unless you bring an order from ———— [1] or Nao Nihal Singh.' Fortunately I had a Naik's (corporal's) escort with me, and by threatening these refractory Sikhs with a good flogging, I managed to procure enough to eat. It is reported here that we cannot keep on good terms with the Lahore Court much longer ; and what I have just mentioned shows, I think, that they do not like us.'

At Benares he had been able to study the languages, but ' the heat in this stable is so great, that until I can get into a house, I must leave it off.' By that time the hot weather had set in, and the fiery winds from the western deserts had probably begun to blow, so that life in a stable without a punkah must have sorely tried the endurance even of so brave a youth as John Nicholson. No wonder that a few weeks later he was down with a severe attack of fever, which temperance and a good constitution carried him safely through. ' You have no idea,' he presently wrote to his mother, ' how the hot weather enervates the body, and, if you do not take special care, the mind also.'

Of Firozpur and its surroundings, in June, he gives a faithful picture, in a letter quoted by Sir John Kaye. ' This station is a perfect wilderness : there is not a tree or a blade of grass within miles of us ; and as to the tigers,

---

[1] Some of the words are effaced or torn out in the original. Nao Nihal Singh was Ranjit's grandson.

there are two or three killed in the neighbouring jungle every day. I intend in the cold weather to have a shot at them ; but at present it is dangerous work, from the great heat.' About this time he was reading, with much interest, Faber's *Fulfilment of the Scriptural Prophecies*, a work which he strongly recommends his mother to read, if she has not done so already. He reports himself as now nearly six feet high, and likely to grow three or four inches taller yet ; 'but I think I am thinner even than I was at home.' A few years later the expected inches had been added to our hero's stature.

Not long after he had removed from the stable into his new house, the 27th Native Infantry were ordered to relieve another regiment then serving in Afghanistan. Instead of shooting tigers in the cold weather, John Nicholson was marching, in November, across the Punjâb to Peshâwar and the far-famed Khaibar Pass. At Peshâwar the officers were hospitably welcomed by General Avitabile, the Italian who had made his name and fortune in the service of Ranjit Singh. Thanks to the suasive influence of British gold, the Afridi guardians of the Khaibar Hills still kept their passes open for the use of our troops and convoys ; and early in 1841 the 27th Sepoys arrived safely at the Afghan city of Jalalabad, where Shah Shuja himself was passing the winter, while Dost Muhammad, a self-sur-rendered captive, was journeying under a British escort towards the Satlaj.

CHAPTER III

JALALABAD TO GHAZNI

Soon after reaching his new station, John Nicholson learned that his brother Alexander would probably come out to India as a cadet in the spring. So he sat down, on Feb. 19, to write his brother ' a few words of advice, which I am sure you will take, as I mean them, in good part.' He is sorry to hear that Alexander has been rather idle, and earnestly exhorts him to make the best use of his time on the voyage out. 'On board ship you will have little to do. If you borrow a Strarth's _Fortification_[1] from one of the Addiscombe cadets on board, and study it well, you may find a knowledge of fortification of great advantage to you hereafter. You should also endeavour to improve your manners on the passage, as without good manners you can never advance yourself. Be reserved and prudent in your communications with your fellow-passengers, and those with whom you may be associated on your arrival in this country.'

The province of Kâbul he describes as ' a dreary tract of country,' and hopes that his brother will not be ordered there. 'We go out the day after to-morrow, to reduce

---

[1] A text-book well known to all Addiscombe men of the days before the Mutiny.

some small but strong hill-forts at a place called Peish-Kotah, and there is no saying how long we shall be out. How do you like England? [The Nicholsons had gone for the winter to Torquay.] Not so well as Ireland, I suppose. . . . Have you grown very tall? I hope to pass my examination in the native languages. I should have done so months ago, were it not for this marching continually. Let me hear from you before you leave home.'

Ere long the little fort was taken, and blown up by our engineers; its defenders having stolen away by night else whither. But Nicholson's study of the native languages was doomed to further interruption. In May his regiment formed part of a column ordered down to Peshâwar, to assist a convoy marching towards the Khaibar under the bold and resourceful Captain George Broadfoot. The Sikh troops in the Peshâwar valley were in open mutiny, and threatened to attack the approaching convoy, which included 600 ladies of Shah Shuja's harem, with all their baggage and a long train of camp-followers; the whole escorted by a regiment of sappers, whom Broadfoot had just been raising for service with the Shah. For two days the convoy halted beyond the Indus, within a few miles of four or five thousand mutineers who, with their two guns, blocked the road to Peshâwar. Broadfoot's cool courage, aided by news of Brigadier Shelton's rapid advance to his rescue, sent the Sikhs flying in the nick of time across the Indus; and the convoy marched on unhindered to Peshâwar. By the beginning of July Broadfoot's difficult task had been accomplished, and the ladies of his convoy were safely lodged in the Bala Hissar, or citadel of Kâbul [1].

---

[1] Major W. Broadfoot, *Career of Major George Broadfoot, C.B.*

Nicholson's regiment was one of those which went on to Kâbul with Broadfoot's party. But his wanderings did not end even there. 'We suffered a good deal from the heat,' he writes in July to his uncle Hogg, 'on our return to Jalalabad, and without halting there continued our march to Kâbul, where the other corps remained; but we proceeded to relieve the 16th at Ghazni, and are now comfortably settled there.' At this moment all Afghanistan seemed to be settling down into that state of outward calm which led our envoy at Kâbul, Sir W. Macnaghten, to declare that all was 'perfectly quiet from Dan to Beersheba,' and that Europeans were everywhere received 'with respect, attention, and welcome.' It was not long before the fires that smouldered beneath those deceitful ashes burst forth to his undoing, and to the ignominious collapse of the policy he had done so much to further.

Before the 16th Native Infantry marched off from Ghazni for Kandahar, John Nicholson had gained a friend in Neville Chamberlain, then a subaltern in that regiment, and his senior by about two years. 'He was then,' says Sir N. Chamberlain, 'a tall, strong, slender youth, with regular features, and a quiet, reserved manner. We became friends at first sight, as is common with youth, and we were constantly together during the short time that intervened between his regiment taking over the fort and my regiment leaving for Kandahar. After my arrival at that place occasional correspondence passed between us, but neither of us was given to letter-writing, and what most occupied our minds was the events taking place in our respective neighbourhoods; for there were already signs that our occupation of the country was resented by the people [1].'

<hr>

[1] Sir N. Chamberlain's MS. notes.

For a few months, however, Nicholson was free to resume his study of the languages, in order to qualify himself for some post either in the Shah's service or in the Company's. The Shah's army, he wrote in August, ' is officered by Europeans, who receive a much larger salary than they do when serving with their regiments. However, I shall soon pass in the language, and perhaps, through my uncle's interest, may obtain some appointment in Hindustan better worth having[1].'

But all hopes of quickly bettering himself, for the sake, in part, of others, were soon to be brushed aside by fears and anxieties for the fate of our garrisons in northern Afghanistan. In September, 1841, the first murmurs of coming storm might be heard by thoughtful men in the Kàbul cantonment. Lord Auckland had just decreed from Calcutta that no more subsidies should be paid from the Indian Treasury for the free passage of convoys and merchants through the Ghilzai country. Macnaghten had to obey his master's reiterated orders; and the chiefs were bidden to look thenceforward to the Shah for payment of their subsidies on a reduced scale. The chiefs replied by plundering a caravan and blocking up the passes between Kàbul and Jalalabad.

Macnaghten spoke lightly of an outbreak which was really the prelude to a widespread revolt against Shah Shuja and his English protectors. In the latter part of October Sale's brigade was fighting its way from Kàbul to the valley of Gandamak. The murder of Burnes and his companions in open day at Kàbul, on November 2, marked the first stage in a series of disasters leading up

---

[1] Kaye, *Lives of Indian Officers*, vol. ii.

to the great catastrophe of the following January, when 4,000 British troops, with thrice as many camp-followers, perished amid the blood-stained snows of grim Afghan passes, in the vain attempt to reach Jalalabad.

About 85 miles south-westward of Kâbul lay the hill from which rose the walls and bastions of Ghazni, then garrisoned by one weak regiment of Sepoys under Colonel Palmer. Nothing had been done to repair the defences of a place which our troops had captured two years before; nor had Colonel Palmer been allowed by the men in power at Kâbul to lay in a sufficient stock of supplies. There were guns about the citadel, but no gunners, and little ammunition. Too late for any practical purpose, Palmer took the question of supplies into his own hands. By November 20 Ghazni was surrounded by swarms of Afghans, armed with their long *jezails* or matchlocks against which the smooth-bore muskets of our Sepoys were of little use. The first snows of an Afghan winter already covered the ground. A week later the enemy had disappeared, on hearing that Maclaren's brigade was approaching Ghazni on its way from Kandahar to Kâbul. It proved to be a false alarm; for the snow about Kalat-i-Ghilzai forced Maclaren to fall back betimes on Kandahar. Meanwhile our Sepoys had time to destroy the villages within musket-shot of the walls, while their officers amused themselves with skating on the moat.

On December 7 the enemy reappeared in greater force than before. Motives of humanity, quickened by a rash belief in the good will of the townspeople, had dissuaded Palmer from turning them out of his stronghold. On the night of the 16th thousands of Afghans poured into the city through an opening dug for them by their friends inside.

After many hours of hard fighting, our men were driven to retreat within the citadel.

By this time the winter had fairly set in, a winter as intense as that of Canada. The fortress itself stood nearly 8,000 feet above sea-level, and the frequent snow-storms that swept across it were remarkable for their destructive fury. The thermometer would often mark from ten to twenty degrees below zero. So scanty was the supply of fuel, that the shivering Sepoys had barely enough to cook their half-rations of 'bad flour and raw grain.' Whenever they wanted water from the wells, they had to break the ice for it. The officers fared little better than the men; but at least they had come from a climate far colder than the plains of Hindustan. Every man in the garrison was on duty eight hours out of the twenty-four. So sharp and deadly was the fire from the enemy's marksmen in the city, that no one could show his head for a moment above the walls. The Sepoys, says an eye-witness, 'constantly soaked and unable to dry themselves, got sickly; and the hospital was crowded with men whose feet had ulcerated from frost-bites.' The Afghan bullets added their daily quota to the losses of Palmer's garrison from cold and sickness.

So things went on to the middle of January, 1842, when the enemy declared a truce, pending the arrival of Shamsuddin Khan from Kâbul with orders from General Elphinstone for the surrender of Ghazni. Similar orders were sent to Nott at Kandahar, and to Sale at Jalalabad; but neither of them would obey the terms of a convention extorted by Afghan cunning from British helplessness. Palmer's position, however, was far more desperate than either Sale's or Nott's. His provisions were nearly exhausted, and melted snow had to serve the garrison for water. If he could hold out for three months longer, Nott might send a force to his relief; but how, without food or water, could he hold out so long ?

Shamsuddin did not arrive before the middle of February. For the rest of that month Palmer, still hoping against hope, contrived to prolong negotiations with the Afghan leaders. At last they threatened to renew the siege. By that time the snow had disappeared. The garrison had no water, and starvation stared them in the face. Palmer proceeded to make the best terms he could with men whose good faith he must take for granted. The chiefs swore solemnly upon the Kurán that Colonel Palmer and his garrison should march out with all the honours of war, and be escorted safely to Peshàwar, as soon as the passes became quite clear of snow. On March 6 the wasted garrison moved down from the citadel with colours flying to the quarters prepared for them within the city.

At noon of the following day, while the soldiers were busy cooking their midday meal, a crowd of yelling Ghazi fanatics rushed upon their lines, and stormed the house in which Lieut. Crawford's native troopers had found shelter. In the next house Crawford himself was sharing a room with Burnett of the 54th and Nicholson of the 27th. From the roof he saw the wild work of slaughter and havoc among his own men. The bullets flew thick around him, and Burnett was shot down by his side. For two days Crawford and John Nicholson, aided by two companies of Sepoys, fought on for their lives in a building set on fire by savages thirsting for infidel blood. Driven from one blazing room after another, they proceeded on the second night to dig a hole with their bayonets through the back wall of their ruined post. It was hard work for tired men who had eaten and drunk nothing for the last two days. But the hole was dug, and dropping through it one by one into the street below, Crawford's party made good their way to one of the houses still held by their surviving comrades.

By the 10th all who had escaped death from Afghan knives or bullets were crowded into the two houses held by Colonel Palmer and the head-quarters of the 27th Native Infantry. 'You cannot picture to yourself,' says Crawford, 'the scene these two houses presented. Every room was crammed, not only with Sepoys, but camp-followers—men, women, and children; and it is astonishing the slaughter among them was not greater, seeing that the guns of the citadel sent round-shot crashing through and through the walls[1].' These were the very guns which, in our possession, had been useless throughout the winter for want of skilled hands to work them. Had gun-drill been taught in those days to our infantry soldiers, Ghazni would not have fallen.

After some days of unspeakable suffering—Crawford saw high-caste natives groping in the mud for pieces of ice to moisten their parched throats, while the officers were burning the regimental colours and preparing, each in his own way, for certain death—the enemy ceased firing, and the faithless Shamsuddin Khan invited the English officers to yield themselves up as prisoners into his safe keeping. They would not listen to any offers which abandoned the helpless Sepoys to their fate. It soon became clear, however, that the Sepoys were determined to make their own way with or without their officers to Peshâwar, which to their wild

---

[1] Crawford's *Narrative*, printed in the *Bombay Courier*.

imaginings was only fifty or sixty miles off. Meanwhile the Ghazis were once more howling for the blood of the Farangi Kaffirs. Then followed fresh overtures, which Palmer, in his dire extremity, could not but accept. The Afghan chiefs, says Crawford, 'swore by all that was holy that, if we laid down our arms, we should be honourably treated, and sent to Kàbul to the Shah as soon as possible.'

On the night of March 20 the remnants of Palmer's garrison laid down their arms. It is said that young Nicholson thrice drove the Afghan guard before him at the point of the bayonet, before he bade his company give up their arms to men whom he abhorred for their treachery and despised for their cowardice[1]. Tears of grief and rage stood in his honest eyes as he flung his own sword at the feet of his captors. During that night Palmer and his surviving officers were safely lodged, by Shamsuddin's advice, within the citadel. As for the Sepoys whom they left behind, most of them stole away in the darkness, bent upon trying to gain Peshàwar by a short cut across the mountains : they lost their way through the falling snow ; and next morning were all either slain or captured by their merciless foes, to be sold as slaves in the adjacent villages.

For a few days Palmer and his fellow-captives were 'treated pretty tolerably.' Shamsuddin and his brother, says Crawford, 'used to visit and condole with us on the change of fortune we had experienced,' and they regretted that the violence of their fanatic followers had prevented a strict observance of the previous treaty. 'But gradually they discontinued their visits ; every little thing we had managed to secure, such as watches, penknives, money, &c.,

---

[1] Kaye, *War in Afghanistan*, vol. iii.

was taken from us, and we were strictly confined to a small room 18 feet by 13. In it there were ten of us. . . . When we lay down at night we exactly occupied the whole floor, and when we wanted to take a little exercise, we were obliged to walk up and down (six paces) in turns. Few of us had a change of linen, and the consequence was that we were soon swarming with vermin, the catching of which afforded us an hour's employment every morning. I wore my solitary shirt for five weeks, till it became literally black and rotten; and I am really surprised that none of us contracted any loathsome disease from the state of filth we were compelled to live in[1].'

It is worth noting by the way that one officer at least was not stripped of everything that could be turned into money. Writing to his mother from Meerut in April, 1843, Nicholson says: 'I do not know whether I mentioned to you that I had managed to preserve the little locket with your hair in it. It was the only thing worth a shilling that was kept by any of us; and I was allowed to keep it because, when ordered to give it up, I lost my temper and threw it at the sirdar's head, which was certainly a thoughtless and head-endangering act. However, he seemed to like it, for he gave strict orders that the locket was not to be taken from me.'

On April 7 they heard that Shah Shuja had been slain at Kâbul by the son of a rival chief. From that day, continues Crawford, 'the severities of our confinement were redoubled; they shut and darkened the solitary window from which we had hitherto derived light and air, and they also kept the door of our room constantly closed, so that the air we breathed became perfectly pestiferous.'

[1] Crawford's *Narrative*.

On the 21st Colonel Palmer was so cruelly tortured with a tent-peg and a rope before all his comrades, that it was 'wonderful he ever recovered the use of his foot.' The process was likened by Crawford to that of the Scotch boot described in *Old Mortality*. The rest of the party were threatened with similar tortures, unless they revealed the spot where, in Afghan fancy, they had buried four lakhs of rupees, then equivalent to £40,000. In case of further obstinacy, they were all to be blown away from guns. This, adds Crawford, 'was a pleasant sort of life to lead, never being certain of that life for twenty-four hours together.'

No doubt the Afghan jailers hugely enjoyed the grim joke of keeping their prisoners in a state of prolonged mental torture as to the doom which hung over them. And no wonder that some of the victims would have liked to apply a similar experience to certain critics in the Anglo-Indian press, who denounced the surrender of Ghazni as a military crime. Nor were harsh and hasty judgements confined to critics in the local newspapers. The new Governor-General, Lord Ellenborough, writing in April to the Queen, spoke of the 'premature surrender of Ghazni' in language at least as premature; and the old Duke of Wellington, some months later, was still of opinion that Palmer yielded sooner than he need have done.

Nicholson hotly resented all such imputations against the soldiership of his chief. Writing to his aunt Hogg in May, 1843, he avers that the Duke's speech, as reported by the last overland mail [1], 'deals hardly with us poor unfortunates who were in Ghazni. He says, "Ghazni was surrendered

---

[1] The P. and O. Company had lately begun carrying the Indian mails across the Isthmus of Suez.

without any pressure." That his Grace is a high military authority is beyond a doubt; but the want of water, or I should rather say of snow—for we never had any water—would by most military men, I imagine, be considered rather a severe pressure; and when his Grace discovers his error, which he doubtless will when the papers concerning our commandant's court-martial reach home, it is to be hoped that he will make the *amende honorable*.'

Our hero was not the man to take too lenient a view of his colonel's conduct; and I may add here that Palmer's acquittal was entirely confirmed by his commander-in-chief, Sir Jasper Nicolls, who held that the circumstances leading to his surrender of so strong a post 'were such as he could neither alter nor alleviate[1].' The Duke's strictures fell in fact on the wrong shoulders. With the help of a few score sappers and artillerymen, Palmer's garrison could have held their own until Nott or Pollock came to their relief. Craigie at Kalat-i-Ghilzai showed what might have been done under like conditions at Ghazni.

---

[1] *Afghan Blue Book*, 1843.

CHAPTER IV

THE CAPTIVES OF GHAZNI

RETURN we now to the tale of suffering at Ghazni in April, 1842. By the end of that month, says Crawford, 'our guards suddenly became particularly civil to us for a few days; and we found out they had a report of the advance of our troops.' Pollock's army in fact had lately forced the Khaibar, and joined hands with Sale at Jalalabad. 'Indeed, on to the period of our actual release, we could always form a pretty shrewd guess of what our troops were about, by the treatment we experienced at the hands of our captors. If there was any forward movement among our people, any arrival of reinforcements at Jalalabad or Kandahar, &c., then we were treated well for a few days, and we got better food. But if our people appeared to be idle, and things remained *in statu quo* for a week, then our guards taunted us on the unwarlike spirit of Farangi armies, and boasted how they would exterminate them if they advanced.'

On May 12 our countrymen were permitted for the first time to take an hour's walk on the terrace of the citadel. This indulgence was repeated every Friday, when Shamsuddin made 'a kind of religious picnic to a neighbouring shrine.' The prisoners anxiously counted the days and hours between each recurring Friday; so keen was their delight in the fresh air and fields of young wheat and clover that met their hungering gaze. In the middle of June their number was reduced by the death of Lieut. Davies from typhus fever. One of them read the burial service over his body before consigning it to the guard. What became of it Crawford could not tell.

On the next day another delightful change befell the survivors. They were removed to another building, where they had three or four rooms to themselves and a court-yard to walk about in. The old guard, too, was 'replaced by a more civil set,' and though their new quarters swarmed with vermin, they could at least roam the courtyard by day and sleep in it by night, with sheepskin for their sole covering. From that time also Shamsuddin's bearing became less ungracious. He often went to see his prisoners, with whom he 'chatted in a kind manner,' bidding them hope for speedy release in exchange for Dost Muhammad. But as the weeks passed and deliverance seemed no nearer, they began once more to despair.

On the night of August 19 they were all hurried off to Kàbul in *kajawahs*, or square panniers slung across the backs of camels. We may imagine the delight with which they looked their last upon the place they had entered with eager hopefulness thirteen months before. Three days' fast travelling brought them to Kâbul, where the bold and able son of Dost Muhammad ruled as Wazir in the name of his absent father.

Muhammad Akbar received them all with kindness in the Bala Hissar. Crawford could not bring himself to believe that 'the stout, good-humoured, open-hearted looking young man, who was making such kind inquiries after our health, and how we had borne the fatigues of the journey, could be the murderer of Macnaghten and the leader of the massacre of our troops.' After his late experience of such contrasts between Afghan manners and Afghan deeds, one would hardly have expected our honest Englishmen to feel surprised at anything. In justice to Akbar however, we must bear in mind that he shot our envoy in a fit of wild passion, and that he certainly tried to mitigate the horrors which he was powerless to avert. Some scores of English men and women owed their lives to his intervention at times when the fury of his Ghilzai followers burst all bounds.

Assuring his new captives that he would treat them like officers and gentlemen, Akbar invited them all to dinner. Two of his chief hostages, Troup and Pottinger, the hero of Herât, were sent to see them in the meantime. They all sat down with Muhammad Akbar and his sirdars to 'the best meal I had had for many months.' During the meal Akbar 'chatted and joked away on ordinary subjects'; and on taking leave of his new guests, he consigned them for that night to the care of Pottinger and Troup.

About that dinner Nicholson afterwards wrote to his mother that he 'never was in the company of more gentlemanlike, well-bred men. They were strikingly handsome, as the Afghan sirdars always are.' Just opposite him sat Sultan Jan, 'the handsomest man I ever saw in my life, and with a great deal of dignity in his manner. He had with his own hand murdered poor Captain Trevor in the preceding winter; but that was nothing. As I looked round the circle I saw both parricides and regicides, whilst the murderer of our envoy was perhaps the least blood-stained of the party.'　While bitter experience led him to regard the Afghans as ' the most bloodthirsty and treacherous race in existence,' he held that they had ' more natural innate politeness than any other people I have ever seen [1].'　Next morning, after an excellent breakfast, the whole party, under Akbar's escort, rode out a few miles to the fort where his other prisoners were confined, amongst whom were Lady Sale and her daughter Mrs. Sturt.　The new-comers found themselves in what appeared to them ' a small paradise.'　Their countrymen had ' comfortable quarters, servants, money, and no little baggage, and a beautiful garden to walk about in [2].'

This garden, or rather vineyard and orchard, Lady Sale herself regarded as ' a great luxury: we walk in it every evening for an hour or two.'

A strong Afghan guard was always present on such occasions, but seldom annoyed our people by dogging their steps.　She, too, admits that her party on the whole were ' well treated [3].'

The arrival of the Ghazni prisoners on August 23 was an agreeable surprise to their fellow-captives.　' Their joy at getting among us,' writes Sir George Lawrence, ' was very great. . . . Although lean and hungry-looking, they were all in good health.　Their treatment had been very different from ours, which was soon exemplified by their amazement at seeing me suddenly rush downstairs, and summarily eject from the square sundry of the guards who had followed them inside the building.　" Why," said they, " if we had even asked them to go out, instead of pushing them as you have done, we should have been killed on the

---

[1] Kaye, *Lives of Indian Officers.*　　　　　[2] Crawford's *Narrative.*
[3] Lady Sale's *Journal.*

spot."' The guards themselves seemed rather astonished at Lawrence's action, but walked off without a word [1].

Here too it was that John Nicholson once more enjoyed the luxury of a clean shirt. In after years he used to say, according to Sir Herbert Edwardes, 'that he never could forget the feeling of gratitude he experienced when George Lawrence received a small box of clothes from Henry, and immediately on opening it gave a shirt to Nicholson—the first he had had for months [2].' The acquaintance thus begun between the grave young subaltern and the light-hearted captain of horse soon ripened into a lasting friendship, fruitful of good to the worldly prospects of the younger man.

In this Elysium, whither they had been transferred in Shamsuddin's absence by his kindly brother Ghulam Muhammad, the new-comers were not to tarry long. Akbar's efforts to treat with Pollock for the withdrawal of our troops from his country had all failed, while Pollock and Nott were already marching in concert upon his capital. Rather than yield up his prisoners unconditionally, Muhammad Akbar decided to send them off, men, women, and children, beyond the Hindu Kush, while he himself made ready for one last stand against the invaders of his father's realm. Accordingly on the night of August 25 nearly all the prisoners then in the fort began their march towards Bamiân, under the charge of a strong escort commanded by Salah Muhammad, one of Akbar's most trusted officers.

---

[1] Lawrence, *Forty-three Years in India.* The Ghazni prisoners were Colonel Palmer, Captains Alston and Poett, Lieutenants Harris, Nicholson, and Williams, all of the 27th Native Infantry; Captain Burnett and Lieutenant Crawford of the Shah's service, and Dr. Thompson.

[2] *Life of Sir Henry Lawrence.*

The brave Lady Sale and most of the gentlemen rode on horseback, while the rest of their party were carried in *kajawahs*. This, says Sir G. Lawrence, ' was the most mournful of all our moves, and many of our number were quite despondent, and abandoned all hope for the future.' They were journeying along that very road which Lawrence and Outram had traversed three years before in hot though vain pursuit of Dost Muhammad and his son. Every night's march— for they rested during the heat of the day—seemed to bear the prisoners so much further away from the chance of a timely rescue by our troops. Once beyond the lofty passes of the Hindu Kush, they might end their days in hopeless bondage among the bleak highlands of Turkistan.

Help, however, was not very far off, and it came from an unexpected quarter. Lawrence recognized in Salah Muhammad a deserter from one of Shah Shuja's regiments. If this man had played one master false, might he not be induced to turn against another? Treachery was a leading trait in the Afghan character, and almost every Afghan had his price. On August 27, when the party had struck the road to Ghazni, Lawrence and two of his comrades ' tried to induce Salah Muhammad to make short marches, so as to allow Nott's force to come up and rescue us.' To this end they promised him a large sum of money, to which every prisoner would contribute his proper share. The Afghan ' affected to be very angry at such a proposal, and refused to listen to us[1].' The time for listening to such overtures was not quite ripe, for Nott had still to fight his way to Ghazni, while Akbar was preparing to bar Pollock's advance on Kâbul.

On September 1 the prisoners crossed the Hindu

---

[1] Lawrence, *Forty-three Years in India.*

Kush and encamped next morning at Bamiàn, famous for its caves and colossal images carved out of the adjacent cliffs[1]. On the 9th they found a sorry shelter in one of the forts that studded the Bamiàn valley. A day or two of terrible suspense ensued. Their head jailer had just received his master's orders to carry them off into the wilds of Kulum in the event of an Afghan defeat. But Salah Muhammad knew that Nott was already master of Ghazni, and that Pollock was timing his forward movements by those of Nott. His duty to Akbar must not prevail over a timely regard for his own interests. On the 11th he told Major Pottinger, who had acted as our envoy on the death of Macnaghten, that he was now ready to listen to the overtures he had once declined.

Pottinger flew to acquaint George Lawrence with this glad news. At Lawrence's request Lady Sale gave up her best room, in a mere outhouse, for the conference which was to decide the fate of more than a hundred men, women, and children. A Persian emissary from Kàbul accompanied Salah Muhammad to the place of meeting. Beside Pottinger and Lawrence sat Captains Johnson, Webb, and Colin Mackenzie, all men of good repute. 'After some discussion, we agreed,' says Lawrence, 'to guarantee to Salah Muhammad a pension for life of Rs. 1000 per month, with Rs. 20,000 to be paid on our arrival at Kàbul.' A bond to this effect was at once drawn up by the Persian emissary, and signed by all five officers ' in the presence of God and of Jesus Christ.' Captain Johnson then drew up another paper, in which all the captives promised to make good the guaranteed payments, if the British Govern-

---

[1] For a good account of these huge figures and of the ruined city of Galgula, see Vincent Eyre's *Journal*, fifth edition.

ment should fail to do so. This paper was eagerly signed by all to whom it was presented. It need hardly be added that the Government duly honoured their servants' bond [1].

Next morning Salah Muhammad's 'flag of defiance' waved above the fort. At Pottinger's suggestion a new governor was set up over the Bamiân district. Two of the Hazâra chiefs tendered their allegiance to the new rule. Salah's colleague, the Mir Akhor, or Master of the Horse, withdrew betimes with his followers from a scene in which he found himself superfluous. The want of money for their immediate needs was in part supplied by a raid upon a passing caravan. A few more chiefs then joined the new revolt against Muhammad Akbar. Pottinger himself was an active leader in this bold enterprise, and kept Pollock duly informed of all that was going on.

By September 15 it was known at Bamiân that Akbar's army had been scattered at Tazin, that Pollock and Nott were both within a march or two of Kâbul, and that Richmond Shakespeare was about to start for the rescue of his countrymen. There was no more talk now about holding the fort. Early on the next morning the whole party under Salah Muhammad were on their way to the foot of the Kalu Pass. Next day they marched across the Hindu Kush, and halted for a while below its southern slopes. Presently a cloud of dust rose up from the further side of the valley. It proved to be Sir Richmond Shakespeare at the head of 600 Kazilbash horsemen. Soon Shakespeare himself galloped forward to exchange greetings with the rescued party. It was a proud moment for the man who had but lately escorted another

<hr>

[1] Lawrence; Vincent Eyre; Lady Sale's *Journal.*

body of rescued captives from Khiva to Orenburg. Lawrence shook his old friend warmly by the hand, while Lady Sale and some of her companions welcomed his approach with happy cheers. For many others the joy of that meeting was too deep to find expression in vocal sounds. Turning presently to Salah Muhammad, Sir Richmond warmly thanked him for his services to our countrymen, and taking off his own turban, placed it in Eastern fashion upon that worthy's head [1]. Salah Muhammad felt that he was not forgotten amid the general rejoicing.

Next morning, at daybreak, the combined forces resumed their march towards Kâbul, where Nott and Pollock had now joined hands. On the 20th all fears of attack from Akbar's horsemen were dispelled by the advance of Sale's column from Argandab. Sale himself rode on ahead to meet the brave wife and widowed daughter from whom he had been parted for ten anxious months; and with him rode Henry Lawrence, a political officer of high promise, whose Sikhs had lately been doing soldierly service with Pollock's force. The old soldier's beaming face as he bent over his dear ones was a thing to remember. Sale's own regiment, the 13th Light Infantry, lined the crest of the Safed Koh, and cheered the ladies as they passed by; Broadfoot's Sappers took up the stirring welcome; the mountain guns under Captain Backhouse then fired a royal salute, and the whole party marched on to Sale's camp at Argandab.

Next day, the 21st, as the rescued prisoners passed near the camping-ground of Nott's force, officers and men turned out with one accord to welcome the survivors of so many perilous adventures and hairbreadth escapes. Marching

---

[1] Eyre's *Journal.*

on later through the Great Bazâr of Kâbul, past the spot where Burnes's house had once stood, Sale's brigade with their precious convoy arrived at sunset in General Pollock's camp on the eastern side of the city. 'Again,' says Vincent Eyre, ' the artillery uttered its boisterous notes of welcome, and old friends crowded round us with warm congratulations. For the present our cup of joy was full.' The few whom they had left behind in the fort near Kâbul had already been set free, and a few days later Captain Bygrave, for whom Akbar had a special liking, was allowed to rejoin his anxious friends.

Nicholson, like most of his fellow-captives, was dressed as an Afghan at the time of his deliverance. 'Shortly afterwards,' says Sir Neville Chamberlain, ' as I was passing, not far from a tent apparently surrounded by Afghans, I was struck by a stone. I put my hand to my sword, and approached the man, who was stooping to pick up another stone, when to my surprise who should my assailant prove to be but John Nicholson, surrounded by other rescued officers, dressed in their Afghan prisoner's dress, when of course we both burst out laughing, and shook hands heartily. We naturally saw a good deal of each other whilst the combined divisions remained at Kâbul.'

It was a happy day for John Nicholson when he clasped hands again with his old friend and fellow-countryman, Richard Olpherts, of the 40th Foot. Olpherts, he afterwards wrote, ' was very kind to me. Indeed, but for his kindness, I don't know what I should have done. He supplied me with clothes and other necessaries, and I lived with him till we reached Peshâwar.' From this it is evident that our youthful hero of less than twenty years was now attached to Nott's division of the Avenging Army, for

Olpherts' regiment had borne its part in that great leader's defence of Kandahar, and in his triumphant march from Kandahar to Kàbul. From Ghazni, also, Nott had brought away some 300 of Palmer's Sepoys, who had been working as slaves in that neighbourhood. As many of them as were fit for duty now took their turn of it with the rest of Nott's force.

CHAPTER V

FROM KÂBUL TO MEERUT AND MORADABAD, 1842-1845

THE departure of our victorious troops from Kâbul was heralded by the destruction of the Great Bazâr, where Macnaghten's mangled body had been exposed before a mob of exulting fanatics. Nott would rather have blown up the Bala Hissar, as he had blown up the citadel of Ghazni; but Pollock and the politicals ruled otherwise. This act of public vengeance was followed by a general and unauthorized pillage of the city itself. On October 12 the united armies began their homeward march, Pollock's own troops leading, while Nott's veterans brought up the rear.

The long procession of troops, non-combatants, baggage, and captured trophies wound its way with much toil and some few mishaps among the frowning passes that marked the road to Gandamak. On the 22nd our sappers blew up the defences of Jalalabad, which Sale's garrison had held so stoutly during the past winter. On November 1, at Dhaka, the Afghan mouth of the Khaibar Pass, Nicholson had the delight of meeting his brother Alexander, who had but lately come out to India, and been posted to a regiment in Pollock's force. ' You may imagine,' the elder wrote to his mother, 'we were both happy at meeting after so long a separation. Three days after I placed him in his grave; but it is a consolation to me that he met a glorious death. He was killed in action near Ali Masjid on the night of the 3rd inst.' The robber clans of the Khaibar had attacked our pickets, and the poor young fellow was among the few slain. 'He was a great favourite with the officers of his corps, who all spoke in high terms of his courage and amiable qualities. Indeed, I never saw a boy more improved than he was, and deeply do I feel his loss. It will be a consolation to you to know that he was buried by a clergyman of the Church of England: few have been who have perished in this country.'

The shock to John Nicholson must have been all the greater for the manner in which he first became aware of his brother's death. He was riding on rear-guard down the pass, in company with Ensign J. B. Dennys of the 38th Bengal Native Infantry—one of Nott's 'beautiful regiments'—when they espied what seemed to be the naked body of a European gleaming to the right, some way off the line of march. Cantering up to the spot, heedless of danger and of their chief's orders against leaving the line of march, they found the corpse of a white man stripped of everything save a mere fragment of the shirt, and fearfully mutilated in true Afghan fashion about the base of the trunk. Dennys, who had been first to dismount, remarked to his companion that the texture of the shirt was too fine for a private soldier. Nicholson gazed at the dead man, and, 'for the moment,' says Dennys, 'he could not speak.' He had recognized the features of his own brother.

The poor boy's remains were borne off in a dhoolie to

the next camping-ground. After solemn burial, Dennys
had a large bonfire lighted over the grave, ' leaving only the
ashes, so that the Afghans might suspect nothing, as they
were very fond of disinterring our dead and heaping
indignities on the bodies. Poor Nicholson felt it deeply,
and the tears coursed down his cheeks[1].'

In his letter, written from Peshâwar on November 8,
Nicholson entreats his mother to bear her loss 'with Christian
resignation and fortitude, and sorrow not for him that is
gone as one without hope, but rejoice rather that it has
pleased God to remove him from this world of sorrow and
temptation.'   Such was the first piece of news which Nicholson had to send home after a silence of more than a twelvemonth.   He is ' keeping some little things ' to send to his
mother by Lieutenant Olpherts, who is going home soon.
There were many subjects which he had intended to write
about, but he is ' not in spirits to write about anything at
present.'   This sudden blow, coming on the top of all he
had suffered during the past twelvemonth, seemed almost
more than he could bear.

With a heavy heart he accompanied his comrades in
Pollock's leisurely march across the Land of the Five
Rivers to Firozpur, where another army under Sir Jasper
Nicolls was drawn up to receive them with all the honours
of successful war.   Our conquering heroes were all in good
time to take part in the festive gatherings of that historic
Christmas.   As a fitting close to the series of pageants
designed by Lord Ellenborough himself, the assembled
armies—40,000 strong, with 100 guns—were manœuvred
by Nicolls on the wide Firozpur plain, before the delighted

---

[1] The officer to whom I am indebted for these sad details is now a full
general on the Supernumerary List.

Governor-General and a brilliant group of visitors from many lands.

At the age of twenty Nicholson had served a very rough apprenticeship in the school of war. He had encountered many of the worst hardships and confronted some of the sharpest perils that could fall to a soldier's lot. He had come out of his fiery ordeal hardened in body, and perhaps a little in mind ; a tried soldier and a capable leader of men. Nor need we wonder that a man of his strong sincere nature brought away with him a fierce undying hatred of the Afghans and all their works. Of his inner life during the past year we know nothing, except that he looked upon the escape of his party from Ghazni as ' little less than a miracle. I certainly never expected it, and to God alone thanks are due.' As for the Afghans, he 'cannot describe their character in language sufficiently strong. . . . From the highest to the lowest, every man of them would *sell* both country and relations. In fact, our politicals found out latterly that the surest mode of apprehending a criminal was to tamper with his nearest friends and relations [1].'

Meanwhile Dost Muhammad and his fellow-captives had all been set free. The great Barakzai chief returned to Kábul, where his faithful son Akbar was guarding on his behalf the throne whence we had driven him in 1839. The war was over, and the lesson which events had taught us was carefully remembered by our countrymen for many years to come. We had burned our fingers badly in the fire of our own lighting, and for a whole generation no sane English statesman dreamed of meddling with the domestic affairs of Afghanistan.

[1] Kaye, *Lives of Indian Officers.*

In the course of January, 1843, the army on the frontier was broken up, and Nicholson's regiment marched down to Meerut, where Colonel Palmer was tried by court-martial, and acquitted, as we have seen, of the offences laid to his charge. It comforted Nicholson to learn that his mother ' had been enabled to bear up so well against the shock of poor Alexander's death.' Mrs. Nicholson asks for full details of the past year, to which her son replies on April 18: 'I sent you from Firozpur a newspaper containing a brief but well-written account of the siege of Ghazni and our imprisonment, after which nothing of any interest occurred.' Instead of going into those personal details for which his family were longing, he dwells with scornful bitterness on the ' ideas of people at home ' concerning the the late war. ' One would imagine that the Afghans, instead of being the most vicious and bloodthirsty race in existence, who fight merely for the love of bloodshed and plunder, were noble-minded patriots. The stories told, too, of the excesses committed by our troops are false or greatly exaggerated. The villages or forts of only such people were destroyed as had signalized themselves by their treachery and hostility towards the force of 1841 : Kâbul itself, for instance ; Charikar, where a whole regiment was destroyed without pity ; Saidabad, where an officer and 100 men were murdered in cold blood, as the Afghans always do commit murders.'

For his own part, he thinks that the retribution was not heavy enough ; and he was ' sorry to leave Kâbul while one stone of it remained on another.' Here indeed, as in some later passages of his career, the natural man in John Nicholson kicked against the more merciful teaching of the Sermon on the Mount. It must be allowed, however, that the actual provocations went far to excuse the worst excesses committed by our troops, European as well as native. The sight, for instance, of those shrivelled corpses piled up so thickly along the Jagdalak Pass could have been hardly less maddening than the sight in after years of those human shambles at Cawnpore.

'You will have heard,' he continues, 'of Sir C. Napier's two victories, the last of which seems so decisive that no more fighting is expected in that quarter.' Miani had been fought on February 15, and Haidarabad on March 24: both battles brilliantly won against heavy odds by the best English general of his day. Sind became a British province, ruled for some years by Napier himself with a firm, light, and skilful hand. In the same letter Nicholson reports an armed rising in Kaithal, a small frontier state which had lately passed under our rule on the death of its heirless Rajah. 'A cavalry regiment left this yesterday by forced marches, and a European one will probably follow. Our friends the Sikhs are believed to be assisting the old lady [the Rajah's widow] in an underhand manner.' The prompt dispatch of troops from the nearest stations soon quelled an outbreak which had been fomented by the Rani herself in concert with several of the protected Sikh princes of Sirhind[1].

Olpherts and his sister, Mrs. Dunkin, are now at Meerut. Nicholson sees them frequently, and likes both 'exceedingly.' He will write to his sister Mary next month, for he 'cannot, being a very bad letter-writer, fill up two overland letters at once.'

On May 8 he writes to his aunt Hogg, 'I am now study-ing as diligently as I can; but to study at all, with the

---

[1] See Sir Lepel Griffin, *Rajas of the Punjaub.*

thermometer at 90°, I do not find easy. However, I have no doubt of passing at the next public examination, which will take place in November.' Meanwhile he began to fret under the forced inaction to which life in cantonments during the hot and rainy seasons condemned the subaltern who sought to live within his pay, and kept aloof from the social gaieties which satisfied other men. Like young Charles Metcalfe, he pined after the home and friends of his boyhood. In June he writes to his mother: 'I dislike India and its inhabitants more every day, and would rather go home on £200 a year than live like a prince here. At the same time I have so much reason to be thankful, that I do not grumble at my lot being cast in this country.'

He was living at this time in the same bungalow with Dennys, who had been drawn more and more towards him since the day when they stood together beside the dead body in the Khaibar Pass. 'In general,' says that officer, 'he was reserved almost to moroseness in those days, and I was one of the very few who were in any way intimate with him. He made me feel that he had probably in him what must make him a man of mark. Fear of any kind seemed unknown to him, and one could see that there was a great depth behind his reserved and at times almost boorish manner. I never met him again after those days.'

It was not long before brighter prospects rose into view. His colonel offered him the adjutancy of his regiment. For some time he hesitated to accept the offer. The military secretary held out to him hopes of 'a better appointment' if he passed the next examination. 'However, before it was too late,' he says, 'I discovered that he was not to be depended upon, and accepted the adjutancy, for which I am indebted to no one.' For the next two months the new adjutant found so much to do that he was 'obliged to give up studying' until August saw his regiment settled down at Moradabad, within view of the towering Himalayas. 'I have only just commenced again,' he writes on the 7th, 'but cannot give so much time to it as formerly.'

In the same letter Nicholson remarks how greatly his mother erred in assuming that he must be saving money out of the sum drawn by him for arrears of lieutenant's pay and allowances. For the six months of his imprisonment he drew only the bare pay of his rank, and his claim to compensation for the loss of all his property was disallowed. And so, instead of putting by anything, he had been thrown into debt, he said, through no fault of his own. An adjutant, of course, gets larger allowances than a mere lieutenant; but then, as Nicholson reminds his mother, he 'has to keep up a charger and a writer, or clerk. I have just paid 600 rupees for the former. In six months I have every reason to believe that I shall be out of debt, after which it is my intention to remit home £100 yearly.'

In giving these details his sole object was to show that he had been neither careless nor extravagant. 'I know,' he adds, 'many people at home labour under the delusion that poor subalterns in this country live luxuriously. Half the time I was in Afghanistan I paid 150 rupees a month, and upwards, for camel hire; and that when my pay was 195 rupees—great luxury!'

After thanking his sisters for their letters, and congratulating Charles on his rapid progress at school—'he will find the advantage of being diligent while young hereafter'—he replies to Mrs. Nicholson's questions about the Afghans. 'They are Muhammadans, as I thought was well known at home; and they themselves claim descent from Saul, which

I think not unlikely to be the case. You say nothing in your letter about the probability of a rebellion in Ireland, though the papers are full of it. The knowledge that you are in one of the most loyal parts of Protestant Ulster makes me feel less uneasy about you than I otherwise should. Young Stannus is in the 5th Light Cavalry, and not in any Dragoon regiment, as you mentioned in your letter. The only Dragoons in India belong to Her Majesty [1].'

This young officer, a cornet of 1840, was to bear his part before the year's end in one of the two battles which brought the Maratha kingdom of Gwalior into closer dependence on the paramount power. The 5th Light Cavalry won fresh honour in all the hard fighting of the two great Sikh wars. At Gujarât Stannus was in command of Lord Gough's escort, when a troop of Sikh horsemen made a sudden dash at the point where Gough sat his horse, watching the progress of the fight. Stannus saw the danger, and saved his chief by a brilliant charge which nearly annihilated the whole band.

In his letter of January 18, 1844, Nicholson expresses his disappointment at having received no letters by the last two mails. He feels sure that the letters were written, and lays the blame for their miscarriage upon the Bombay Post Office, 'in which great carelessness and irregularity exist.'

He has been thinking that his brother Charles must now be old enough to go to Addiscombe. 'If so, in my opinion, the sooner he goes the better; for though more expensive than a direct appointment, it is worth the money: that is, the education he may receive there, if diligent, is worth the expense, which, as I before said, I will defray.

[1] MS. Letters supplied by Mr. Maxwell.

Young men who come out to India with direct appointments have no knowledge of their profession whatever, either practical or theoretical, and are sometimes very shortly after their arrival placed in responsible situations (as many subalterns were in Afghanistan the other day), where a military education would be of invaluable advantage to them. I took my accounts this morning, and I believe that, please God, I shall be able to send you £100 by the mail which leaves Bombay on June 1, which ought to pay Charles' expenses for nearly a year at least at Addiscombe; and I believe I can manage to remit a similar sum in a twelvemonth afterwards.'

Then follows a passing reference to the fighting in Gwalior, where Richard Olpherts' regiment 'suffered severely. He will be much vexed that he was not present at it.'

By this time the proceeds of poor Alexander's estate had been handed over to the Registrar of the Supreme Court. Nicholson tells his mother that he is going to write that day to his uncle Charles Hogg, who is in Calcutta, 'and ask him, if possible, to get the amount without delay remitted to you. Uncle James, who was some years ago registrar himself, can tell you that great delay frequently occurs in the adjustment of deceased officers' estates.'

He had written during the previous month to his sister Mary. ' But I fear my epistle was a very brief one, as I had no news to communicate, and I always find great difficulty in filling up a letter unless I have.' When he has no news to communicate, he seldom fails to fill up his square sheet of thin paper with kindly references to absent friends. In this very letter, for instance, he is 'surprised and disappointed to hear from Aunt Bellingham' so sad a report of his uncle Robert's health. 'She said truly that he was very amiable, and more free from imperfections than mortals usually are. I trust the change of air at Stanmore and careful nursing may yet prove of use to him.'

During the year 1844 nothing of special interest seems to have ruffled the quiet tenor of John Nicholson's life and work at Moradabad. The discipline and smartness of a native regiment depended mainly on its adjutant; and Nicholson had all the zeal and energy which enabled him to turn his professional knowledge and his soldierly instincts to the best account. His new duties seem to have delayed the progress of those linguistic studies which he had lately resumed. At any rate it was not till November, 1845, that he passed the examination which qualified him for a post on the General Staff.

Meanwhile a new Governor-General, the brave Sir Henry Hardinge, had come out in the room of Lord Ellenborough, recalled by the offended Court of Directors. Nicholson rejoiced to hear that the heroic George Broadfoot had replaced an older and weaker man as political agent for the north-west frontier, at a critical moment in our relations with the Punjàb. He rejoiced still more to learn a few months later that his sister Mary was about to be married to the Rev. Edward Maxwell.

The marriage took place in February 1845, about which time Mr. Maxwell exchanged his curacy at Leeds for the spiritual charge of a poor and populous district, owning neither church, school, nor parsonage, in the busy manufacturing town of Barnsley.

CHAPTER VI

THE SATLAJ CAMPAIGN: JAMMU AND KASHMIR, 1845–1846

HARDLY had Nicholson passed his examination at Umballa, when the thunderclouds which had long been overhanging the Satlaj valley burst with fateful violence on the British side of that river.

The likelihood of a collision with our turbulent Sikh neighbours had of late been growing into a certainty. Ranjit Singh had left no fit successor to govern the kingdom which his own strong arm had carved for itself out of the wrecks of Mughal and Afghan rule. The ill-will of his proud Khâlsa soldiery towards a Power which had curbed their ambition, underrated their military worth, and used their country as a highway into Afghanistan, had since been inflamed by the conquest of Sind and the gathering of British troops along their frontiers. For some months past Sir Henry Hardinge had been carefully increasing the strength of all his garrisons from Firozpur to Meerut, while Napier's army seemed ready at any moment to cross the southern frontier of the Punjâb.

On November 17, 1845, the Lahore Council declared war. On December 11 a large Sikh army crossed the Satlaj. Declining Littler's bold challenge in front of

Firozpur, the Sikh leaders marched off to entrench them-selves at the village of Firozshah, and to bar Sir Hugh Gough's advance on Mudki.   On the afternoon of the 18th Gough's tired and thirsty soldiers—they had been marching twenty-five miles a day for a week past—fought and won at Mudki the first of those battles which taught us to respect the prowess of our Sikh foes, and to admire the sturdy courage with which they fought their guns. Three days later began, at Firozshah, that long, changeful, and bloody fight, on which for many hours the fate of India may be said to have hung.

At this momentous battle, which lasted far into the next day, Nicholson was present in his new character of com-missariat officer.   This appointment, which in India was always held by an army officer, he had just obtained through his uncle's good friend, Colonel Stuart, then mili-tary secretary to the Indian Government.   'It scarcely gives me any increase of pay at present,' he tells his mother, 'but will do so after I have served a few years in the department.'   In Gough's camp he could see something of his old hero, George Broadfoot, whose timely warning saved Gough from the trap prepared for him by the Sikhs at Mudki.   Three days later Broadfoot himself died the soldier's death at Firozshah.   Of all our losses on that hard-won field, this was accounted by all who knew him, from the Governor-General downwards, the heaviest and most untimely.   Nicholson, for one, could never speak too warmly in his praise.   'Let us think how Broadfoot would have acted in the present case,' he would say years after-wards to his friend Herbert Edwardes, whenever things looked blacker than usual for our countrymen in the Punjâb.

So doubtful had seemed the issue of the first day's fighting, that, during the night of the 21st, Sir H. Hardinge, who had led the centre of Gough's line, sent orders to his chief secretary, Mr. Frederick Currie, for the destruction of all State papers left in his charge at Mudki, in the event of final disaster to our arms. Even in England the first news of actual victory was received by some of our leading statesmen with more of consternation than rejoicing. Peel himself was among the croakers at a council-meeting in which the old Duke of Wellington had been taking a somewhat listless part. At Peel's reference to our Pyrrhic victory and the perils which beset our Indian empire, the old warrior flashed out: 'Make it a victory; fire a salute, and ring the bells. Gough has lost a good many men; but what of that? You must lose officers and men if you have to fight a great battle. At Assaye I lost a third of my force [1].'

For more than a month Gough's soldiers rested on their arms, while Hardinge and his subalterns were straining every nerve to collect supplies and bring up reinforcements of men and guns from Meerut and Delhi. There was plenty of work for the commissariat, to which Nicholson contributed his full share. Meanwhile the anxious Governor-General had been looking towards a secluded valley in the mountains of Nipal for a meet successor to George Broadfoot. In answer to the summons of his brave old chief, Henry Lawrence, then British Resident at Khatmandu, hurried off towards the seat of war, in time to rejoice over the rout of a Sikh army at Aliwal, and to take part in the crowning victory of Subraon, won by Gough on

---

[1] Trotter, *Life of Lord Dalhousie.*

February 10, 1846, after six hours of deadly struggle with a powerful and determined foe. On that day the Satlaj was choked with the corpses and red with the blood of Sikhs drowned or slaughtered in their vain attempts to reach the opposite bank.

'We are encamped,' writes Nicholson on the 27th, 'at the capital of the Punjáb, without having fired a shot since we crossed the Satlaj on the 10th instant—a proof how completely the Sikh army has been humbled and its strength and confidence lessened. Our loss since the commencement of the war has—though heavy—been nothing in comparison with theirs. It is believed that at least half the force they had in the field at Subraon on the 10th perished; and our trophies are 230 guns, innumerable standards, arms of every description, and nearly all the camp equipage they brought across the river with them[1].'

A week before this letter was written Gough's army was encamped under the walls of Lahore, and on the 22nd a British regiment occupied the citadel; and so ended the First Sikh War[2].

It was not Hardinge's policy to annex the whole of Ranjit Singh's dominions. The arguments against such a course at such a moment were in truth exceedingly strong. So he contented himself with annexing the Jalandhar province and the hill-tracts adjacent, and with selling Kashmir to Guláb Singh, the wily Rajah of Jammu, for the million sterling which the Lahore treasury could not pay towards the cost of the war. The intriguing mother of little Dulip Singh was still to be the nominal head of

---

[1] Kaye, *Lives of Indian Officers.*
[2] Cunningham, *History of the Sikhs*; Sir H. Lawrence, *Essays*; Marshman, *Life of Havelock*; Keene, *History of India,* &c.

the Lahore Darbar, or Council of State, with Lâl Singh
for her vizier; while Colonel Henry Lawrence, as British
Resident at Lahore, was to inspire the Darbar with
a growing sense of public duty, and to guide, coax, or
gently push the Sikh leaders along the new paths pre-
scribed for them by the treaty of March 9. A strong
British garrison remained for the present at Lahore, in
compliance with the wishes of the Sikh ministers. John
Lawrence, Henry's civilian brother, was called by Hardinge,
in return for his helpful services at Delhi, to fill the post
of commissioner for Jalandhar.

About this time the new ruler of Kashmir was asking
for the loan of a few English officers competent to drill his
wild Dogra troops after the best European methods. The
two officers whom Hardinge selected for that purpose
were Captain Broome of the Bengal Artillery, and Lieutenant Nicholson, of the commissariat. Broome's memory
lives still in his great, though unfinished, work on the
history of the Bengal Army. Both men owed their
appointments to Henry Lawrence, who was himself
a captain of artillery, proud of the part which that arm
had played in our Indian wars; and who knew that
Nicholson had been an adjutant before he became an
assistant-commissary.

Lawrence and Nicholson had first known each other at
Kâbul in September, 1842, when George Lawrence had
introduced his young friend and fellow-captive to his
brother Henry. The acquaintance soon ripened into
mutual esteem. 'To such a man as Henry Lawrence,'
remarks Sir John Kaye, 'the character and disposition
of young Nicholson were sure to recommend him as one
to be regarded with great hope and tender affection.'

Nor was the younger man slow to recognize a sympathetic spirit in the frank, courteous, high-toned, tender-hearted soldier, who had calmly proposed to change places with his captive brother at Kábul [1], and to whose resourceful energy Pollock's timely forcing of the Khaibar was largely due.

When the two met again, three years later, on the banks of the Satlaj, their mutual liking grew with closer intercourse. Lawrence's place in the Governor-General's counsels enabled him to hold out to younger men of approved worth or manifest promise that helping hand, for want of which they might else have failed to rise above the level of ordinary achievement. He could see that Nicholson was fitted for higher things than commissariat duties. One day in March John Nicholson was summoned to an interview with Lord Hardinge, who in the kindliest possible terms offered him the post for which Lawrence had recommended him. 'I accepted it gladly,' he wrote to his mother, 'on the condition that if on trial I did not like it, I might fall back upon my old commissariat office.' He deemed it best to have a second string for his bow. As things happened, however, there was little need for such a precaution while his good friend Henry Lawrence was at hand to furnish him with a second string.

On April 2 he arrived at Jammu in company with Maharajah Guláb Singh. 'Since then,' he wrote in May, 'I have been leading the most monotonous life you can well imagine. I have no duties of any kind to perform,

---

[1] George Lawrence had been sent by Akbar to Jalalabad with certain overtures for General Pollock. When the mission proved a failure, his brother Henry offered to take his place at Kábul, as he had but one child, while George had four. The offer was of course declined.—G. Lawrence, *Reminiscences.*

and am quite shut out from the civilized world.' For his own part, he had never believed that Gulâb Singh was 'really desirous of having our system of discipline introduced into his army'; and now it 'has turned out he merely asked for two European officers, because he was aware of the moral effect their presence would have at his Darbar, in showing the terms of intimacy he was on with the British Government, and made the wish to have his army disciplined a pretence.' Nicholson thinks that his new appointment cannot prove a permanent one, because Gulâb Singh will soon become tired of paying his and Broome's staff salary. 'Hitherto,' he adds, 'we have both received every civility from him, and as long as he considers it his interest to treat us well he will doubtless do so. The Maharajah talks of going to Kashmir next month, and taking me with him. I look forward with great pleasure to a trip to this beautiful valley (albeit in such company), believed by natives to have been the earthly Paradise.'

Clearly Nicholson had no great love for his new employer, whom Lawrence's close friend and trusty follower, Herbert Edwardes, described as 'the worst native he ever came in contact with,' and of whom Lawrence himself could only say that morally he was no worse than many other native princes, while in intellect he was 'vastly the superior of all [1].'

Yet even in such company would John Nicholson gladly have gone any whither, to escape from the depressing thraldom of those 'merely nominal duties' for which the Maharajah was paying so liberally. 'After the busy life I have led for the last three years,' he writes in June, ' and

[1] Merivale, *Sir H. Lawrence*; Lawrence, *Essays*.

the excitement of the late campaign, my present want of
employment renders my exile from the civilized world
irksome to a degree; so much so, that, should this state
of things last much longer, I shall very likely throw the
appointment up, and fall back on the commissariat, though
it is a department I am not very partial to [1].'

This state of things was not to last much longer. Towards
the end of July, 1846, Gulâb Singh, escorted by a body of
his own troops, and attended by his two English officers,
began his march across the mountains which divided
Jammu from his new kingdom of Kashmir. On August 12
he entered his future capital of Srinagar, past which the
river Jhilam winds through 'the loveliest valley in the world.'
Nicholson was 'much pleased with the beautiful scenery
and fine climate of the mountain-range which we crossed
to get into the valley.' But about the valley itself, whose
praises were sung so tunefully by the author of *Lalla Rookh*,
he is curiously silent. This valley was soon to become the
scene of an armed insurrection against the new rule. 'We
had not been many days in the city,' wrote Nicholson,
'before we learnt that the governor had made up his mind
to drive Gulâb Singh's small force out of the valley and
seize us. We had great difficulty in effecting our escape,
which we did just in time to avoid capture.' Marching
off by one of the southern passes, Broome and Nicholson
rejoined the Maharajah at Jammu about September 20.
Meanwhile Gulâb Singh's troops in the Kashmir valley had
been heavily defeated by the insurgent forces. The survivors threw themselves into the fort of Hari Parbat, where
they might hold out until relief should come.

---

[1] Kaye, *Indian Officers*.

The report of this outbreak found Lord Hardinge at Simla, where Colonel Lawrence also was taking a little rest after many months of anxious, hard, and incessant labour. Both of them saw the need for prompt and vigorous action. Wheeler's brigade in Jalandhar was ordered off at once to protect Jammu; while Henry Lawrence, hurrying back to Lahore, marched towards the scene of danger at the head of some ten thousand of those very Sikhs who had fought against us at Firozshah and Subraon. He had reason to believe that the rebellious governor, Shaikh Imâm-ud-din, had been egged on by the treacherous vizier, Lâl Singh; and John Lawrence, who took his brother's place at Lahore, was instructed to seize and imprison the traitor, in the event of harm befalling the British Resident.

Then for the first time was seen the extraordinary spectacle, to use Lawrence's own words, ' of half a dozen foreigners taking up a lately subdued mutinous army through as difficult a country as there is in the world, to put the chief, formerly their commander, now in their minds a rebel, in possession of the brightest gem of their land [1].'

Among the few Englishmen who accompanied Lawrence on this truly hazardous errand was his new friend William Hodson, the future leader of ' Hodson's Horse,' while Herbert Edwardes went off to Jammu, as political adviser to Gulâb Singh. Henry Lawrence knew well what risks he was incurring. But he knew also that in such crises boldness and promptitude were the best cards for an Englishman to play. He had acquainted Lâl Singh's vakil, or agent, with the instructions given to his brother John. He trusted something, of course, to the magic of his own

---

[1] Lawrence, *Essays.*

fine personal influence over the Sikh commanders, and yet more perhaps to the restraining potency of a British force advancing in their rear.

Fortune on this occasion stood by the brave. By the end of October Imâm-ud-din had ridden across the mountains and yielded himself up to the safe keeping of Captain Edwardes, who on November 1 conducted his penitent captive to the tent of Colonel Lawrence, at the foot of the pass leading into the Kashmir valley.

Lower down the Thana valley were encamped, in picturesque confusion and motley garb, the combined forces of Jammu and Lahore. It was here, no doubt, that Nicholson and Hodson first came together ; and during the next fortnight they must have learned to know each other as worthy rivals in the school of their common friend and master, Henry Lawrence.

While Herbert Edwardes, at Lawrence's request, was escorting Imâm-ud-din down to Lahore, Gulâb Singh entered, under Lawrence's careful leadership, into peaceful and secure possession of his new kingdom. Hodson describes the new sovereign as 'a fine, tall, portly man, with a splendid expressive face and most gentlemanly, pleasing manner, and fine-toned voice . . . to all appearance the gentlest of the gentle, and the most sincere and truthful character in the world ; and in his habits he is certainly exemplary ; but he is the cleverest hypocrite in existence, as sharp and acute as possible, devoured by avarice and ambition, and when roused horribly cruel. . . . Yet he is not a bit worse, and in many ways infinitely better, than most native princes [1].'

_____

[1] *Hodson of Hodson's Horse.*

Such a character reminds one of Byron's Lambro—

> 'The mildest-manner'd man
> That ever scuttled ship, or cut a throat.'

And yet this man, who had thought nothing of flaying people alive, still less of cutting off their noses, ears, and hands, consented, at Lawrence's pleading, to abolish slavery, *suttee*, and infanticide throughout his dominions.

On November 16, as we learn from Nicholson's letter to his brother Charles, Lawrence, Broome, and the others turned their backs upon the far-famed valley, leaving Nicholson there 'quite alone.' Charles Nicholson had come out that year to India as a direct cadet of infantry, and was on his way to join the 31st Native Infantry at Almorah. John himself on November 23 was just recovering from a severe attack of fever and ague, which had laid him up for a fortnight past.

'But living in an open house,' he adds, 'I dread a relapse, as the weather is very raw and cold.' Kashmir to him at that season, as he told his mother a few days before, was 'anything but a terrestrial Paradise. My fingers are so cold that I can scarcely hold the pen; and glazed windows are unknown here.'

His utter loneliness, 'without a European within scores of miles' of him, weighed the more heavily on spirits weakened by bodily suffering. 'I have suffered so much from ill-health within the last eight months,' he tells his brother, 'that, unless some improvement takes place, I fear I shall be obliged to go out of India somewhere on sick certificate before long. I have had more sickness within this twelvemonth than in the previous six years and a half; and I sometimes fear that my constitution is going. Nothing brings " home " to a man's mind more readily in

India than illness; he then thinks of the nursing and grateful acts of attention he would receive, were he among his own friends. Here I have not even the sight of a white face to cheer me. May you be never in a like predicament!'

This despondency was no doubt a passing mood. The 'something better' which Lord Hardinge had virtually promised Nicholson on the eve of his mission to Kashmir was already coming into view. Before leaving Kashmir Henry Lawrence had given him an acting appointment in the North-West Frontier Agency. Lord Hardinge was not slow to grant the formal sanction for which Lawrence applied; and a few weeks later Lieutenant John Nicholson was duly gazetted an assistant to the Resident at Lahore. For him there was no more question now of falling back on the commissariat, or of going somewhere out of India on sick leave.

While Nicholson was yet wavering between hope and fear for his immediate future, a timely Nemesis overtook the real authors of the rising in Kashmir. As soon as Henry Lawrence had reached Lahore, a commission of five British officers, civil and military, sat in judgement upon the treacherous vizier whose secret orders to Shaikh Imâm-ud-din had provoked the rebellion against Gulâb Singh. Lâl Singh's guilt was proved beyond question before a large audience of Sikh sirdars. By Lord Hardinge's order the Queen-Regent's worthless paramour was deposed from his office, and sent off a State prisoner to the Fort of Agra. His crafty mistress likewise ceased to have any voice in public affairs. By the Treaty of Bhairowal a Council of Regency, composed of eight sirdars, guided and controlled by Henry Lawrence, was now appointed to govern the Punjàb in the name of its child-sovereign, Dulip Singh. The Resident's powers were to 'extend over every department, and to any extent.' In plain fact, from those last days of 1846, Colonel Henry Lawrence, still a captain of Bengal Artillery, became, by consent of all his Sikh colleagues, sole Regent of the Punjàb.

CHAPTER VII

THE PUNJÂB IN 1847

JOHN NICHOLSON entered upon his new career at an auspicious moment, for all associated with Henry Lawrence in the work of teaching Sikh and Muhammadan officers some plain, elementary lessons of good government.

The men designed for that mission were all picked men, taken from the Company's service; men who were destined to leave some mark on the pages of Anglo-Indian history. Well might Lawrence, writing afterwards to Kaye, account himself fortunate in such assistants as George Lawrence, Edwardes, Nicholson, Reynell Taylor, Harry Lumsden, Lake, James Abbott, Cocks, Hodson, Pollock, Bowring, 'all of whom,' he adds, 'were my friends, and almost every one of whom was introduced into the Punjâb through me. . . . Each was a good man; the most were excellent officers. My chief help, however, was in my brother John, without whom I should have had difficulty in carrying on.' It was John indeed who, during Henry's absence at Simla, had compelled the reluctant Lahore *Darbar* to provide the troops which his brother led into Kashmir[1]. On more

[1] Kaye, *Indian Officers*; Bosworth Smith, *Life of Lord Lawrence.*

than one occasion afterwards John was to fill his brother's place at Lahore, as ably as he filled his own at Jalandhar. In short, as Henry himself declared, 'in various ways John Lawrence was most useful, and gave me always such help as only a brother could.'

On February 7, 1847, Nicholson left Kashmir, 'crossing 8½ feet of snow in the Pûnch Pass.' On his arrival at Ramnagar, a town on the Chinâb river within six marches of Lahore, he received instructions from the Resident to proceed to Multân, and thence to Dera Ghazi Khan on the right bank of the Indus. During this journey, which extended over two months, he reported to his chief on the state of the country he passed through. So much at least we have a right to infer from Lord Hardinge's letter of April 16 to Henry Lawrence, in which he says: 'Edwardes, Nicholson, and your brother [George], each in the districts he has visited, give a wretched account of the natural impediments which must, under any government, however ably administered, render the Punjâb a poverty-stricken acquisition [1].'

On the morning of April 20 Nicholson reached his journey's end, and, after a hearty breakfast, set out to look for his brother Charles, whom he had last seen as a child of ten. It was a meeting to which he had been looking forward for months past. But he was hardly prepared for the change which eight years had wrought in the outward form and features of both. 'Fancy neither of us recognizing the other!' he wrote to Mrs. Nicholson. 'I actually talked to him half an hour before I could persuade myself of his identity. He is as tall, if not taller than I am, and will, I hope, be much stouter and stronger in the course of

[1] Kaye ; Merivale, *Life of Sir H. Lawrence.*

another year or two. Our joy at meeting you will understand, without my attempting to describe it to you.'

By this time Nicholson had begun to find a compensating charm in the solitude of which he had so often complained.

'You may remember,' he says in the same letter, 'my writing to you, some time ago, that the want of society rendered me low-spirited. Well, I have within the last few months become so reconciled to living alone, that really, were not Charles here, I should wish myself away again in the Kashmir hills or the Jammu forests[1].'

A few days later our young political set off for Lahore, where he spent some hot but happy weeks of May and June under the same roof with his friend and master, Henry Lawrence. From daily intercourse with his hard-working chief he learned some fruitful lessons of unsparing labour and self-denying zeal for the welfare of a people who had never yet tasted the blessings of a just, merciful, well-ordered rule. He could see how bravely Lawrence plunged into the difficult task of managing 'a venal and selfish Darbar,' and thwarting the daily intrigues of an ambitious Queen-Mother, of employing turbulent sirdars in unaccustomed duties, turning disbanded soldiers into peaceful husbandmen and traders, and of setting a number of village headmen to draw up 'a very simple code of laws, founded on the Sikh customs, and administered by the most respectable men from their own ranks[2].' And he learned, too, what great things Herbert Edwardes was already doing among the fierce Pathán tribesmen of Bannu, and how strenuously George Lawrence was upholding the cause of peace and civil order throughout the valley of Peshâwar.

---

[1] Kaye.   [2] Ibid.

It was Lawrence's custom to send out some of his officers ' on visits of a week or a month to different quarters,' in order, as he said, that ' we may help the executive as well as protect the people.'

Early in June Nicholson was dispatched on a special mission to Amritsar, the Holy City of the Sikhs, for the twofold purpose of inspecting the adjacent fortress of Govindgarh, and of inquiring into the general management of the Amritsar district. So well did he discharge his errand, that, by the end of June, 1847, Lawrence entrusted him with full political control over the Sind-Sàgar Doàb, the broad tract of land between the Jhilam and the Indus.

Nicholson was instructed to cultivate the acquaintance of the two nazims or governors, as also of their deputies, and ' all respectable kardars.' Much might be done ' by cordiality, by supporting their just authority, attending to their moderate wishes and even whims, and by those small courtesies that natives look to, even more than they do to more important matters.' His first duty would be to protect the people from the oppression of the kardars, or revenue officers; his next to keep up an efficient and disciplined army. ' Without allowing the troops to be unduly harassed, see that parades and drills are attended to. I insist upon insubordination and plunder being promptly punished ; and bring to my notice any particular instances of good conduct. Avoid as far as possible any military movement during the next three months; but, should serious disturbance arise, act energetically [1].'

In the last days of July, however, serious disturbances did arise, not in his own district, but in the neighbouring glens of Hazàra, where the chivalrous Captain James

[1] Kaye.

Abbott was trying to restore order out of long-existing chaos. Abbott had summoned certain chiefs of Simalkhand to answer before him for 'the most dastardly and deliberate murder of women and children at Bakkar.' The chiefs laughed at his messengers, and defied his threats. Turning for help to his nearest colleague, Abbott begged Nicholson to march his men up to Hazru, on the Rawal Pindi border, whence they could act in timely concert with his own troops. Nicholson moved his troops to a point still more advanced than Hazru. On the night of August 2 three different columns marched from three different points upon the rebel stronghold at Simalkhand. Nicholson's force was the first to approach that place on the following morning. But by that time the enemy had slipped away, and Nicholson took possession of an empty fort.

A little later in the same month Lawrence found himself compelled to remove the little Maharajah Dulip Singh from all intercourse with his pernicious mother, whose arts had taught him publicly to insult the worthy president of his council, the new-made Rajah Tej Singh.

That Hindu Messalina was promptly escorted, with Lord Hardinge's sanction, to the guarded privacy of a fort at Shaikopura, a quiet place about twenty-five miles from Lahore. That business ended, and matters looking peaceful throughout the country, Henry Lawrence felt himself free to recruit his shattered health and rest his tired brain among the pines and deodars of Simla; while his brother John once more took his place at the Sikh capital.

In the latter part of October Henry was back again for a few weeks at the Residency, winding up his official affairs, taking his last walk with John, exchanging farewells with Sikh and Muhammadan friends, and preparing for his journey home on sick leave, in company with his attached friend and like-minded leader, Lord Hardinge, who in the following January made over his viceregal charge to the young and promising Earl of Dalhousie.

Meanwhile, John Nicholson was carrying out his chief's instructions with a zeal, energy, and resourceful boldness, which none of his compeers could have surpassed. The country he had been sent to govern was mostly wild, rugged, and thinly peopled by men of diverse races, customs, and callings, from the warlike Ghakkars, Pathâns, and Rajputs, to the cattle-lifting Gujars and the peaceful Jats, who tilled the terraced slopes of the Rawal Pindi highlands. From the banks of the Jhilam to Attock on the Indus spread a rough sea of fort-crowned hills, with only a few strips of level plain between them.

Under Sikh rule violence and plunder were the usual methods of enforcing payment of arrears due to the Sikh soldiery, or of taxes required by the State. Nicholson set his face sternly against all kinds of lawlessness and wrong-doing. The Sikh sirdars and officers, with whom he often rode out hawking in the cold weather, soon discovered the fearless strength of purpose that lay beneath the quiet courtesy of his manner. The village people found in him an upright judge and a powerful protector in time of need. The troops refrained from their usual excesses at the mere bidding of one who seemed to them more like a demi-god than a man. Everywhere among all classes, the new Sahib's orders were accepted as decrees of Fate, which none could defy and live.

In his *Forty-three Years in India*, Sir George Lawrence gives a significant picture of the evils which our political agents had to cope with in almost every part of the

Punjâb. At Hasan Abdâl, on his way to Peshâwar, he gave audience to a number of notorious freebooters—'no petty robbers, but heads of clans, who kept in their pay large bodies of Sikhs, Afghans, and Hindustanis,' and levied blackmail from the Margalla Pass to the Attock, 'acknowledging no authority unless supported by regular troops.' They agreed to ' cease from all acts of violence and depredation,' pending a reply from Lahore to the agent's representations on their behalf.

At Peshâwar he was beset by crowds of noisy supplicants, ' many of them carrying fire on their heads, as illustrative of their extreme misery and grief.' All alike complained of ' the unchecked rapacity and violence of the soldiery, of the grinding extortion practised by the kardars, and the heavy and incessant fines levied upon them on all pretexts and occasions.' As for the troops and their mutinous excesses, it had ever been the custom to give them orders for their pay on the revenue collectors; ' which amounted, of course, to allowing the soldiery to live at free quarters on the country, and enforce their own demands.' Regular pay and severity tempered by redress of real grievances were found to be the best medicines for this particular evil.

Then there were several heads of clans and villages, who proved so backward in paying their revenue, that George Lawrence had to ' make an example of them for the intimidation of the rest.' Thanks to the prompt and rapid movements of Lumsden's little force, the Khan of Mashu Khail was speedily brought to reason ; and several other malcontents ceased from defying the agent's commands.

Before the close of 1847, Nicholson was able to report

to the Resident at Lahore, that ' the country round Hasan
Abdâl and Rawal Pindi, hitherto more or less disturbed, is
perfectly quiet, and the kardars, for the first time for years,
move about without guards [1].'   Similar tidings reached the
Residency from all the other districts in the Punjâb.   It
seemed as if Lord Hardinge's efforts to breathe new life
into the death-stricken body of Sikh rule were already
reaping their full reward.   So bright and peaceful was the
prospect even in the long-troubled Peshâwar valley, at the
end of October, that the chief mullah, or Muhammadan
high-priest of Peshâwar, offered up a public thanksgiving ;
and Major George Lawrence felt himself justified in paying
a farewell visit to his brother Henry at Lahore.

When George Lawrence returned to Peshâwar at the end
of January, 1848, so profound, he wrote, ' was the tran-
quillity prevailing there and throughout the entire Punjâb,
and so complete the absence of all causes of alarm, that
I was accompanied by my wife and children.   Sir Frederick
Currie had joined his appointment as Resident during my
brother Henry's absence in England ; and my brother
John . . . had resumed his old duties as Commissioner of
the Jalandhar Doâb.'   Even in the hills and glens of Bannu
the genius of Herbert Edwardes had wrought miracles of
peace, order, and well-doing among tribes for whom
fighting and plunder had always been as the breath of
their nostrils [2].

[1] *Punjâb Blue Book*, 1847–49.
[2] Kaye ; G. Lawrence ; *Life of Sir H. Edwardes.*

CHAPTER VIII

FOR the first three months of 1848 the peace of the Punjâb was ruffled only by a successful raid against a gang of Thugs, who had robbed and strangled peaceful travellers between Umballa and Lahore; or by the mad outbreak of a Sikh fanatic, who, with the help of a few followers, held a tower near the great Tank of Amritsar for three days against a whole company of British troops. Lord Hardinge had just predicted that the peace of India would remain unbroken for the next seven years. *The Friend of India*, then edited by John Marshman, spoke of Dalhousie's arrival at a moment when ' the last obstacle to the complete, and apparently the final, pacification of India has been removed. . . . Not a shot is fired from the Indus to Cape Comorin against our will.' ' India,' said the London *Morning Herald*, ' is in the full enjoyment of a peace which, humanly speaking, there seems nothing to disturb.' Dalhousie himself was content to forward home, without comment, the official reports addressed to him by Sir Frederick Currie, as acting Resident at Lahore.

From this feeling of unwonted calm—' the torrent's smoothness ere it dash below '—all India was soon to be roughly awakened by tidings of unforeseen disaster in the southernmost province of the Punjâb. Before the end of

April the thunderbolt had fallen out of a blue sky. On the 20th of that month two of our politicals, Agnew and Anderson, were cruelly murdered on a peaceful and friendly mission to Mulraj, the Governor of Multàn. They had been sent from Lahore to establish a new diwàn, or governor, in the room of Mulraj, who had lately obtained the Resident's permission to resign his post. Mulraj himself was not slow in marking his approval of the crime he had made no effort to avert. He proclaimed a holy war against the English, brought his own family and treasures into the citadel, and set about strengthening the defences of a stronghold which had thrice defied Ranjit Singh himself.

Agnew's urgent note to Edwardes, written the day before his own death, met with a response as prompt and bold as it was fruitless for the purpose of saving two valuable lives. The keen-witted subaltern of Bengal Fusiliers at once realized the need of quelling a local outbreak before it blossomed into a national revolt. In a few weeks, with help from Colonel Cortlandt and the loyal Khan of Bhawalpur, Edwardes got together an army which, by July 2, had thrice routed the troops of Mulraj, and sent their leader flying back to the safe shelter of his own capital.

Had men like John Lawrence and Herbert Edwardes had their own way, the army which General Whish arrayed before Multàn in September would have come into touch with Edwardes early in June. To such men the hazards of a hot-weather campaign seemed as nothing in comparison with the dangers of delay and the moral effects of prompt, bold, and resolute action against an Indian foe. By July 2 Edwardes and his few comrades had done all that brave men could do, with slender resources, to keep rebellion confined to a corner of the Punjáb. There was no one at hand to reap the fruits of their labours; and in September it was too late to make up for past shortcomings, when the whole country from Multán to Pesháwar was bursting into revolt. And Lord Dalhousie was too late when he granted Currie in July the free hand which Currie had asked for at the end of April.

In fact some echoes of the Multán explosion were felt at Pesháwar as early as the month of May. By that time Lumsden had returned on special duty to Lahore, and John Nicholson had taken his place as chief assistant to George Lawrence. 'The district,' says Lawrence, ' began to be disturbed, and several murders were committed in different parts.' Six men and a woman were murdered in one village alone. Nicholson was dispatched with a body of Sikhs to 'seize the murderers and punish the headmen.' Surrounding the village before the maliks, or headmen, had prepared for resistance, he succeeded in bringing away not only the murderers, but a quantity of arms and ammunition stored up in the place.

Emissaries from Mulraj were already tampering with the Sikh troops in the Pesháwar valley, and Sikh fanatics in the city were heard exhorting the soldiery to rise against the Farangi and wipe out the disgrace of Subraon; which, adds Lawrence, ' I well knew they were burning to do.' Gladly therefore did he avail himself of the Resident's permission to raise a corps of Muhammadan Patháns, ' as a counterpoise to the Sikh element.' No two men had clearer eyes than George Lawrence and Nicholson for the perils which surrounded them, or could have striven more manfully to put off the evil day which Sikh treachery and British procrastination were surely bringing about.

Nicholson at this time was in frequent correspondence with the wise and resourceful Deputy-Commissioner of Hazâra.   On June 27 he writes to James Abbott [1], whose forecasts of coming danger had found no favour at Lahore :

My dear Abbott,

   I this morning received yours of the 24th, returning Taylor's letters.   Lawrence and I agree entirely with all you write ; indeed, no one who even slightly knows you will suspect that your motive in addressing the Resident as you did were other than unselfish and disinterested.   I enclose a letter this moment received from Edwardes.   May his shadow never be less !   It is getting late, so good-bye, with kind regards.

Yours very sincerely,

J. NICHOLSON.

In his letter of July 1 [1] John Nicholson has a hearty fling at the well-meaning but slow-sighted Resident of Lahore, the ' rosy one ' of his tale :

My dear Abbott,

   I received yours of the 28th this morning.   It is impossible ever to fathom the Rosy One's real intentions, but I fear he can, with some degree of plausibility, decline your mediation with the Kurna chiefs, on the ground of their long recusancy.   I am sorry to hear so bad an account of Boodh Singh's corps, but it was scarcely to be expected that, amidst the general rottenness, it would remain sound.   We are without further news from Multân or Lahore, save that the Resident talks of the success of *his* ' Muhammadan combinations ' and of the way in which *he* ' hum-bugged the Khâlsa.'   This is remotely verging upon the extreme confines of coolness !   I imagine he will make a favourable report of E. for so well carrying out *his* plans and instructions.   I will get Lawrence to send you a letter he had from him yesterday, an amusing but disgusting production.   I return Inglis's letter with thanks.   With kind regards to you and your circle.

Yours very sincerely,

J. NICHOLSON.

[1] Letters supplied by Mr. Raymond Abbott.

Towards the end of July one of Mulraj's emissaries, a fakir, was handed over to Major Lawrence by a faithful Yusafzai chief, who had caught him in the act of urging the men of Yusafzai to rise against the English in concert with the Sikhs of Peshâwar. This man had just returned from a similar errand to our ancient foe Dost Muhammad, who declined his offers and refused to see him again. With Currie's sanction the fakir was duly hanged on August 8, in view of ' a large concourse of people, who evinced no sympathy whatever with his fate [1].'

By this time, however, troubles were coming up, not single spies, but in battalions. One of the nazims, whose acquaintance Nicholson had been advised to cultivate, was the Sikh sirdar, Chatar Singh, Governor of Hazâra, and lord of large estates in Rawal Pindi. This old chieftain's intrigues among the Sikh troops quartered in Hazâra had of late been giving James Abbott food for much anxious pondering. By August 9 Lawrence learned that a faithful colonel of Sikh artillery had been cut down beside his guns by some of Chatar Singh's followers, and that Chatar Singh himself was calling upon the Sikhs in Hazâra and the neighbouring districts to rise and join him in a march upon Lahore.

The wily old traitor had at length thrown off the mask which Abbott alone among our politicals had learned to see through. For some months before the murder of Colonel Canora, Captain Abbott had been quietly watching the movements of Chatar Singh, and searching out the evidence of his complicity in a widespread plot for restoring the queen-mother to her palace at Lahore and expelling the English from the Punjâb. Meanwhile he had been careful

[1] Sir G. Lawrence, *Forty-three Years in India.*

to hide his own feelings and to treat the sirdar with all the
courtesy due to the nazim, or ruler, of a Sikh province.
The outbreak at Haripur gave him the open challenge for
which he had long been waiting. The armed peasantry
of Hazâra, mostly Muhammadans, rallied like faithful clansmen round their white protector, and enabled him for
several weeks to arrest the forward march of the Pakli
brigade [1].

Hastening to confer with Nicholson over the unwelcome
news from Haripur, George Lawrence found his subaltern
ill in bed from a sharp attack of fever. Telling his sick
friend all that he had heard, he went on to express his
deep anxiety to forestall the movements of the rebel leader,
by sending a body of trustworthy troops to save the important fortress of Attock from falling into the enemy's hands.
' Had you been fit for the work,' he added, ' I should have
wished to send you ; but that is out of the question. Herbert
or Bowie must go in your place.' Nicholson insisted upon
going himself : ' Never mind the fever ; I will start to-night.'
It was arranged that Nicholson should start that evening at
the head of sixty Pathân horse and two companies of foot,
to be followed next day by some Muhammadan levies which
our Yusafzai friends had placed at Lawrence's disposal [2].

It was now that Nicholson's true character first revealed
itself to an admiring comrade, who watched him making the
needful preparations for his momentous journey. ' Never
shall I forget him,' he afterwards wrote to Kaye, ' as he
prepared for his start, full of that noble reliance in the
presence and protection of God which, added to his unusual
share of physical courage, rendered him almost invincible.'

[1] *Punjâb Blue Book*; Abbott's *MS. Narrative.*
[2] Kaye ; Sir G. Lawrence.

At the hour appointed Nicholson rode off on his long night-march as eagerly as if August was the coolest month in the year, and he himself but a few hours ago had not been tossing helplessly on a couch of fever. During that night he covered the fifty miles that lay between Peshâwar and the rocky ramparts of the Indus opposite Attock. On the morning of the 10th he crossed the river and rode up to the gate of the fortress just in time to prevent the plotters inside from closing it against him. At that moment, as he wrote to his chief, 'I had not more than thirty men with me,' so fast was the pace at which he had travelled. 'The infantry which should have been in by noon did not arrive till midnight.'

Once inside the fort with his few troopers, John Nicholson lost not a moment in following up his first success. His bold words and haughty bearing won the bulk of the garrison over to his side. When the Sikh guard at one of the gates showed signs of resistance, he stalked among them like an avenging deity, dared them to lift a finger against him, and forced them to arrest their own leaders. Ere long the mutinous Sikh company was marching sullenly out of the fort. 'That I was able to effect this,' he wrote, 'is owing to the staunchness of the irregulars, whom I harangued with happy effect, notwithstanding the efforts of the regulars to mislead them.'

Before the arrival of his infantry, Nicholson had set about collecting supplies, ordering reconnaissances, and opening communications with Captain Abbott[1]. On the following day he left the fortress in charge of a loyal commandant, and rode away with his Pathân troopers and forty footmen towards Hasan Abdâl, on the road to Rawal Pindi, where

---

[1] *Punjâb Blue Book*; Kaye.

a body of Sikh horse had risen against their commander for refusing to join Chatar Singh in Hazâra.

Writing to Currie on August 12, Nicholson relates how he 'paraded the party, and dismissed and confined the ringleaders on the spot. The remainder begged to be forgiven; and having some reason to believe them sincere, and wishing to show that I was not entirely without confidence in Sikhs, I granted it. I shall of course keep a sharp lookout on them in future.' He was just then raising a local militia for the protection of the Rawal Pindi district, and felt, as George Lawrence also did, the urgent need of support at such a crisis from regular troops. 'A single brigade with a nine-pounder battery would be ample, with the aid which Captain Abbott and myself would be able to render. Delay will have a bad effect in every way, and may afford the mutineers an opportunity of tampering with the Peshâwar force.'

Sir F. Currie agreed on the whole with the views expressed by his three lieutenants. But Lord Gough and the Governor-General ruled otherwise, pleading the disturbed condition of the whole kingdom as sufficient reason for doing nothing in one particular direction. It seemed as if they were waiting only for a decent excuse to set aside the Treaty of Bhairowal and reduce the Punjâb to a British province. For Chatar Singh was not yet in avowed rebellion, George Lawrence still held his own at Peshâwar, and the timely presence of a strong British brigade in Rawal Pindi would have enabled Nicholson and Abbott to deal effectually with the mischief brewing in Hazâra [1].

Hardly had Nicholson sent off his letter to Currie, when

---

[1] Kaye; Sir G. Lawrence; Abbott's *Narrative*; *Punjâb Blue Book.*

he learned that a mutinous Sikh regiment had reached Rawal Pindi, with two guns, on its way to join the Hazâra force. He immediately ordered his own levies to concentrate at Margalla, the point where he intended to bar the advance of the mutineers. He himself rode thither the next morning—August 13—to survey the ground, which, though of no great strength, he found entirely suitable for his purpose.

'I trust,' he writes to Currie, 'I shall be able to hold it, though my levies are not very warlike; were they Afghans or Hazâra men, I should have no doubts. The regiment did not attempt to cross to-day, but I hear they purpose doing so to-morrow.'

In spite of the heavy work which now fell upon his shoulders, he still found time to write daily a brief and pithy letter to his official chief at Lahore. 'This constant knocking about,' he explains on August 14, 'prevents my writing as clearly or carefully as I could wish. I am from ten to fourteen hours every day in the saddle, though not very strong, and though the heat is great.' Instead of returning, as he had hoped that morning, to its duty, the mutinous Sikh regiment 'has advanced to Jani-ka Sang, within three miles of Margalla. . . . I shall employ all fair means to induce it to return to its duty, but will forcibly resist its advance beyond Jani-ka Sang, as I consider it of great consequence that it should not be allowed to form a junction with the Hazâra force.' If the Sikh troops in Hazâra were under the control of their officers there would, he thinks, be 'no difficulty; but, as usual in the Sikh army, few or none of the officers have any influence with the men.'

Nicholson was still seeking to 'frighten or coax the

Karara regiment' back to the path of duty, when disquiet-
ing news from Hazâra compelled instant recourse to more
coercive measures. Before daybreak of the 15th he drew
up his little force of 700 matchlock-men behind some jungle
in front of the Sikh position at Jani-ka Sang. Summon-
ing before him the colonel of the offending regiment,
Nicholson bade him tell his officers and men that the terms
already offered were still open to them. If these were
accepted within half an hour, he would rejoice; otherwise
he would be compelled to treat them as open mutineers.
'If they do not return to their duty,' he added, taking out
his watch, 'at the end of half an hour I will attack them.'

It was a desperate game which Nicholson was playing.
A strong regiment of disciplined infantry with two light
guns lay within the walls of a Muhammadan cemetery,
with open ground beyond, across which a few hundred ill-
armed, untrained peasants, however brave and bravely led,
would have very small chance of making a successful dash.
But Nicholson knew how to dare greatly for great and
noble ends. His name was a word of fear throughout the
district, and the malcontent soldiery believed that whatever
he threatened he would certainly, if need were, perform.

Fortune, as usual, smiled upon the brave. After a warm
debate the counsels of peace and prudence gained the
mastery. In the nick of time the Sikh colonel 'came out,
begged pardon on his own behalf and that of his men,
and declared their willingness to march whithersoever
I directed them. I accordingly saw them *en route* to
Rawal Pindi before leaving the ground. The debate between the peace and war parties was a stormy one, the
former being in a very small majority[1].'

---

[1] *Punjâb Blue Book*; Abbott's *Narrative*.

The letter which records this splendid piece of 'bluffing' was written by Nicholson from Hasan Abdál, after he had been fifteen hours in the saddle. How nearly his success had hovered on the brink of failure, we learn from his letter of the next day; 'a force from Haripur having actually been told off to assist' the advance of their fellow-mutineers. At this time Sir F. Currie at Lahore, still blind to the true meaning of Chatar Singh's revolt, had requested Nicholson to act as peace-maker between that worthy and Captain Abbott. To his thinking the wily Sikh sirdar, Dulip Singh's destined father-in-law, was a harmless old gentleman of infirm health, who had been frightened into evil courses by Abbott's seeming discourtesy and unconcealed distrust. Nicholson's views on this subject tended at first to agree with Currie's, but his eyes were sooner opened to the truth.

Even in his letter of August 16, Nicholson states the case against Chatar Singh's conduct after the outbreak as strongly as Abbott himself had done. 'I consider the restoration of amicable arrangements a matter of no difficulty, if the sirdar's conduct in tampering with the troops throughout the country, cutting off Captain Abbott's *dáks*, sending agents to raise the labouring population of this and the adjoining districts, ordering kardars out of his jurisdiction to send him their treasuries, and writing to Maharajah Guláb Singh for armed aid, can be overlooked; for all this can be proved against him[1].' To patch up a quarrel which had gone such lengths as these in a single week was a task achievable on no conditions short of a free pardon for the self-convicted traitor. 'If you are not prepared to grant this,' writes Nicholson, 'I would

---

[1] *Punjáb Blue Book.*

respectfully but earnestly recommend that a force of one European and two Native regiments of infantry, with two troops or batteries (for he is strong in guns and mortars), be immediately dispatched from Lahore ; as the people of this country are fickle, and very likely to change sides in the course of a week or two, if they do not hear of aid being dispatched from Lahore.'

The troops were not sent, and the negotiations fell through ; for a free pardon was out of the question, and the scheming sirdar of Haripur had no thought of visiting the Sikh capital except as the leader of a powerful army.

While Sir F. Currie was penning words of unstinted praise for all that his heroic subaltern had done since his timely appearance in Attock, and Nicholson himself was striving hourly, in loyal concert with Abbott and George Lawrence, to avert or mitigate the worst issues of a dangerous crisis, Chatar Singh was at last emerging from the dusk of underhand intrigue into the full light of open revolt. About August 20 it was known that he had raised the standard of rebellion, ' devoting his head to the Gods and his arms to the Khâlsa.' Hearing from John Nicholson that Chatar Singh was marching southwards with the whole Sikh force in Hazâra, James Abbott hastened with the bulk of his faithful mountaineers from the Silhad Pass to aid his younger colleague in opposing the sirdar's advance.

Had these two bold, eager, and resourceful comrades been free to take their own line, the whole Sikh brigade in Hazâra would have had to choose between timely submission and death by famine or the sword. But their hands were still tied by orders from Lahore, and their movements were delayed by the need of listening to delusive overtures from Chatar Singh. While these were under debate in Nicholson's camp on August 26, Abbott's telescope ere long revealed to him the real purport of the sirdar's last move. The Sikh camp was packed ready for marching, while a body of horse were galloping towards the very point of vantage from which, during the parley, Abbott had reluctantly agreed to fall back. His men, worn down with two long marches under a fierce August sun, and most of them weak from the day-long fasts observed by all good Musalmans during the month of Ramzân, had little heart left for attacking regular troops covered by the fire from several guns. After some feeble skirmishing in the dark, Abbott withdrew his men about midnight from the ravine they had been holding, and, joining forces with Nicholson, retired next morning to Hasan Abdàl[1].

It was arranged between the two friends that Abbott should return to Hazâra, while Nicholson took care for the safeguarding of Attock. Amidst the toils, worries, and distractions of the past fortnight, Nicholson had managed to pay some hurried visits to the great river-stronghold which had become his especial charge. Day after day during the fast of Ramzân, when no Muhammadan may taste even a drop of water between sunrise and sunset, his improvised troops had made long and rapid marches to and fro, under a leader who never spared himself, who feared no mortal foe, and seemed to have more than mortal powers of endurance.

Do what such a leader might, however, he knew himself powerless to cope with trained battalions in the open field. For a moment he thought of throwing himself into Attock and there awaiting the course of events. But on second

---

[1] *Punjâb Blue Book.* Abbott.

thoughts 'he was of opinion,' as he wrote to Currie on the 28th, 'that if Major Lawrence can secure the fort without me, I could be more profitably employed outside, in harassing the Sikh camp, stopping supplies, cutting off their communications, and preventing risings in other parts of the country in the sirdar's favour.' Writing some hours later on the same day, he says, 'The intelligence of the arrival of a single brigade on the Chinâb now would get me over half the army and keep my levies staunch.' And again on the 29th he affirms that, 'if another week be allowed to elapse without the dispatch of troops from Lahore, the whole of Sind-Sâgar will declare for Chatar Singh, and very likely the Peshâwar force also.'

Chatar Singh was now making straight for Hasan Abdâl. Withdrawing his own men betimes from that place, Nicholson left them to watch the enemy's movements, while he himself with a few horsemen rode off to Attock, to make all safe there against foes without and possible treachery within. On the last day of August he writes to George Lawrence asking for more men from Peshâwar. 'Six hundred more are required for the fort if I am still to keep the field. I have not yet turned out the Singhs [Sikhs], but don't really see how I can avoid it; the risk of keeping them is so very great. I have mentioned that Abbas Khan has not half *jee* [spirit], or intelligence, enough for a situation of trust. . . . Cannot Bowie or Herbert be spared? I have not let in Dunraj's men; he seems to have some doubts of them himself[1].'

Loyally and promptly did Major Lawrence respond to his subaltern's call for help. A second letter from

[1] *Punjab Blue Book.*

Nicholson reached him at 11 p.m. By that time he had sent off to Attock, as commander of the garrison, Muhammad Usman Khan, the Afghan chief who had befriended us at Kábul in the dark days of 1841. He now proceeded to rouse up Herbert, who 'started in an hour with two hundred men, and reached Attock in the morning,' when Nicholson made over to him charge of the fort [1]. Further reinforcements from Peshâwar now raised the strength of the garrison to nearly 1,000 Musalmans, whom Lawrence considered staunch, with eight guns which Nicholson had already placed in position, plenty of ammunition, and at least three months' supplies of food which Nicholson's forethought had laid in. On September 1, after giving Herbert his last instructions, and sending off to Peshâwar his latest news of the enemy's movements, Nicholson sped away from Attock to rejoin his levies at Gondul and try his best, in conjunction with Abbott, to thwart or hinder the designs of Chatar Singh.

His levies in the field amounted to 300 horse and 700 foot. No increase of their numbers, he wrote to Currie, would enable him 'to oppose successfully in the field four regular regiments of infantry and eight guns, besides irregulars.' So long as the sirdar 'remains inactive, doing no mischief, I cannot do better than follow his example, keeping of course a sharp watch upon his movements.' Nicholson's last ride to Attock had in fact forestalled the hatching of another plot between the sirdar and the Sikhs who formed a part of the garrison. Attock therefore was safe from any serious danger, so long as Abbott's levies could prevent the junction of the Pakli brigade with a Sikh force encamped about Hasan Abdâl.

[1] Sir G. Lawrence.

It was not many days, however, before Nicholson recurred to his original purpose of annoying the enemy by means of an active guerilla warfare. While a son of the rebel Sikh sirdar was gathering recruits for the force he commanded at Rawal Pindi, the arch traitor himself was marching to and fro between Hasan Abdâl and Hazâra, in order to effect his junction with the Pakli brigade, which Abbott's vigilance still held in check.

On September 27 Nicholson tells his mother that he is leading 'a very guerilla sort of life, with seven hundred horse and foot hastily raised among the people of the country. Chatar Singh and his son, who are in rebellion, have eight regular regiments and sixteen guns, so that I am unable to meet them openly in the field. I received a slight hurt from a stone in a skirmish in the hills a week or two ago.' He had often had ' a worse one when a boy at school,' and he mentions this only because he was reported to have been seriously hurt, and ' feared lest the report should reach and cause you anxiety.'

The skirmish to which he refers so casually took place nine days before in the Margalla Pass, which cuts through the rugged limestone ridge that rises across the road from Hasan Abdâl to Rawal Pindi. The pass was commanded by a *burj*, or tower, of huge stones piled up without mortar. Held by a dozen bold marksmen, the Margalla Tower might greatly hinder the march of a whole brigade, such as Utar Singh was. leading to the support of his father, Chatar Singh. Nicholson hoped by a swift and timely rush at the tower to keep the two forces apart for some time longer.

The tower, as Nicholson too late discovered, had no door; it could be entered only through an opening ten or twelve feet above the ground, by means of a ladder which the defenders drew up after them. Scaling-ladders he had none, for want of skilled workmen in his little force; nor was there a man among them, says Abbott, 'who could handle a powder-bag.' Having quietly brought his men within easy reach of the little stronghold and its small garrison, he gave the order for a charge. He himself led the way, closely followed by a dozen of his trusty chiefs and *maliks* [heads of villages]. His tall figure and European dress made him a mark for many bullets, but he reached the tower unscathed by a fire which had slain several of his bravest followers.

At that moment Nicholson discovered that the tower had no door, and that none of his matchlock-men was anywhere in sight. They had simply stayed behind as soon as their commander turned his back upon them and his face towards the foe; for they argued, says Abbott, 'that he being ahead could not possibly see who mis-behaved.' Had they followed him as they were bidden, Nicholson might have forced the garrison to surrender by means of blazing brushwood piled below their tower.

He was not yet, however, at the end of his resources. The little party who had struggled up to the foot of the tower 'found some respite from the fire of the garrison, who were too timid to expose themselves by leaning over the parapet far enough to hit them.' Meanwhile their fiery leader worked might and main to tear some blocks of stone out of the uncemented wall. But the men above him were now hurling large stones upon their assailants, and one of these struck Nicholson badly in the face. By that time a body of Utar Singh's troops was seen marching up to the tower; and Nicholson reluctantly withdrew his little band from a struggle which had already cost them dear. To his good friend James Abbott, it seemed marvellous that Nicholson returned alive. No doubt the awe which his presence inspired among a superstitious soldiery went far to impair their steadiness of aim [1].

One of the chiefs who fell by their leader's side in that daringly futile scrimmage was the gallant Yusafzai, Fathi Khan. He left behind him a little son, upon whom Nicholson, says Abbott, 'lavished much care and attention.' One day the boy, then about seven years old, asked his kind protector to grant him a special favour. ' Tell me first,' said Nicholson, ' what you want.' ' Only your permission, sahib, to go and kill my cousins, the children of your and my deadly enemy, Fathi Khan ; ' for his uncle, like his father, was so named. ' To kill your cousins ? ' asked his guardian, mistrusting his own ears. ' Yes, sahib, to kill all the boys while they are young ; it is quite easy now.' ' You little monster ! ' exclaimed Nicholson ; ' would you murder your own cousins ? ' ' Yes, sahib ; for if I don't, they will certainly murder me.' This would have been quite in keeping with Pathàn usage ; and the little fellow thought it hard that any one should prevent his taking so simple a precaution [2].

Nicholson found his levies near the spot where they had left him so shamelessly in the lurch. Utar Singh now marched on unmolested to Hasan Abdàl. A day or two later he and his father were speeding back to Hazàra, to bring off the Sikh troops still pent up at Pakli and

---

[1] Abbott's *Narrative*. The Margalla or Cut-throat Pass was so called because it cut through the western end of the rocky ridge which runs eastward to the Jhilam.

[2] Abbott's *Narrative*.

Nowashir. Divining their purpose, Nicholson hoped to
defeat it by outmarching the enemy, and seizing the pass
which commanded the fertile valley of Damtur.

This time at least his levies did not fail him. Before
Chatar Singh could get near them, they were safely
posted about the Damtur Pass. The further success of
their leader's plans depended mainly upon the people
of the Damtur valley, of whose character for fickleness
and treachery Nicholson was unaware. In spite of his
just forebodings on this point, Abbott hastened at the
head of his own levies to his friend's support. It soon
became clear to both that they could expect no help,
but rather active hindrance from the men of Damtur,
who refused to sell food to Nicholson's tired and famishing
soldiers, and declined to fight the Sikhs unless they were
posted in the front line of battle. The true motive for
this bravado was explained to Nicholson by his own men,
and the sequel proved the soundness of their inferences.

As things now stood, neither Abbott nor Nicholson
felt hopeful of ultimate success. But of two evils they
chose the lesser, resolving to make as sturdy a fight as
possible rather than abandon their strong position without
a blow. Treachery, however, worked against them from
the outset. The enemy's skirmishers were seen swarming
up a steep hill on which Nicholson the day before had
placed a strong picket. Leading a hundred of his men
to the support of their comrades, he found no one there.
The picket had in fact been treacherously withdrawn during
the night by an order purporting to come from himself.
Leaving the new-comers to hold the post, he galloped back
for fresh reinforcements. The sight of their bold leader
flying, as it seemed, before the foe, struck the whole of his

levies with dismay, and became the signal for their rapid disappearance. For a time the picket left on the hill held their ground stubbornly, in hopes of timely aid, but were driven back at last by overpowering numbers.

The men of Damtur had been the first to scuttle on seeing Nicholson dash down the hill, and his own levies naturally followed their example. The Sikh columns pushed on unhindered into the valley, where they came under the fire of Abbott's matchlock-men posted on the spur of a mountain which jutted out into the plain. These kept up a telling fire on the enemy below, whose shot and shells generally fell short of their mark. But all Abbott's endeavours to retrieve a miscarriage due to the treachery of the Damtur contingent and the panic thereby caused among Nicholson's men, were of no avail. While Nicholson was searching for his vanished levies, Chatar Singh held his way past Abbott's post on the Sirbhum mountain to the town of Damtur. Robinson, the engineer officer who had been keeping guard over the Pakli brigade, was ordered by Abbott to withdraw his men from a duty no longer feasible. Abbott himself fell back upon Nara at the foot of the Gandgarh Range, and Nicholson returned to the neighbourhood of Hasan Abdâl[1].

In the last week of September the tireless Nicholson was off again upon another bold but fruitless errand. On the 21st George Lawrence at Peshâwar learned the news of Sher Singh's sudden defection with all his troops from the allied armies and the consequent raising of the siege of Multân. Not a moment was lost in sending off Mrs. Lawrence and her two little children by way of Kohat towards Lahore, under an escort furnished by the Afghan Sultan

[1] Abbott's *Narrative.*

Muhammad Khan. This man, a brother of the re-nowned Amir of Kábul, and a debtor for his lands and life to the good offices of Henry Lawrence, was in fact what Currie denoted him, 'the most treacherous and intriguing of a race and family notorious for treachery and intrigue[1].' In spite of his own suspicions, George Lawrence could not help trusting on this occasion a gentleman who 'took the most solemn oaths on the Korán to protect my family, and see them himself safe across the Indus.'

When the party from Peshâwar arrived at Chakuwal, sixty miles south of Attock, they were met by alarming reports of a large body of cavalry sent down by Chatar Singh to intercept them on their way to the Jhilam. The officer in command, a son of Sultan Muhammad, at once decided on retreating across the Indus to his father's castle at Kohat.

This movement, whether born of treachery or timidity, filled Mrs. Lawrence with natural dismay. She had written to Nicholson from Chakuwal, telling him of her danger, and entreating his speedy help. Nicholson, who was then at Jhang, not far from Hasan Abdál, watching for any sign of a hostile march towards Attock, set off at once with a body of horsemen to succour his friend's wife and children in their distress. On nearing Chakuwal, and learning what had happened, he tried hard to overtake the party before they recrossed the Indus; but in vain. Nearly six months were to elapse before the lady and her little ones found rest and shelter among their own people at Lahore.

Halting at Chakuwal, our disappointed hero caught and punished some of those who had been most active

---

[1] *Punjáb Blue Book.*

in arresting the progress of Mrs. Lawrence's party. The whole country between the Indus and the Jhilam was now seething with disorder. The officials of the Lahore Government were flying from their posts, or casting in their lot with the Sikh insurgents. Nicholson's daily letters to the Resident had to travel by new and round-about roads; for the rebels were guarding all the passes across the Salt Range. Hearing of a plot to seize the treasure in the fort of Pind Dadan Khan, near the Jhilam on the southern side of the Salt Range, Nicholson fought his way through one of the passes, and 'marching day and night,' says Currie, 'reached Pind Dadan Khan a few hours only after it was, through the treachery of the garrison, occupied by the insurgents [1].' After driving a body of insurgents out of the town into the fort, he went on to the riverside, seized every boat he found there, and kept his men at the Ghàt for several days, in the hope of reinforcements which never came. It was another of the lost opportunities which marked the progress of the second Sikh war.

It soon became a question for Nicholson what should be his next move. To return to the neighbourhood of Hasan Abdâl was no longer possible. To stay where he was with no prospect of help from any quarter, with enemies gathering fast around him, would be courting inevitable disaster. It was near the middle of October, and scarcely a regiment of Lord Gough's army had yet got so far as Firozpur, while Sher Singh's army was in full march northwards from Multàn. He resolved therefore to cross the Jhilam and make his way to some point commanding the road from Multân to Lahore.

[1] *Punjáb Blue Book.*

After a sharp but successful brush with the rebels on the other side of the Jhilam, he carried his little force by one long night march across the country to the town of Ramnagar on the left bank of the Chináb. Here he was promptly reinforced with men, arms, and ammunition by Sir F. Currie, whose letters to the Governor-General teemed with the heartiest praise of his bold, capable, and trusty subaltern. In helping Nicholson to ' hold his own at Ramnagar ' as long as he safely could, the Resident hoped to save the districts whence our army would draw the bulk of its supplies from the ravages of insurgent bands, pending the march of a British brigade across the Rávi.

But all Currie's efforts to secure for Nicholson the support he needed were baffled by the blind inertness of our military chiefs. ' The distressing delay,' as Currie put it, in the dispatch of troops from Firozpur was already working grave mischief. On October 21 Nicholson reported that Sher Singh's advanced guard was so dangerously near Ramnagar that, in view of coming contingencies, he would fall back that night upon Gujranwála. ' The non-advance of our troops,' he remarks, ' has disheartened all our well-wishers (and they were few enough), and proportionately inspirited our many secret enemies.' It had also increased the despondency already prevailing among his own levies, so that the little confidence he once had in them was now entirely lost [1].

At Gujranwála, midway between Ramnagar and Lahore, Nicholson halted, waiting for further news or orders from Lahore. The country around him swarmed with rebels, a body of whom, on the night of the 23rd, attacked the

[1] *Punjáb Blue Book.*

native guard at the bridge of boats on the Râvi opposite Lahore, burned one of the boats, and carried off a number of *zamboorahs*, or camel-guns. An imperative summons from Currie brought Nicholson into Lahore on the 28th, the day on which Godby's infantry brigade of the advancing army crossed the Râvi, to open the campaign against Sher Singh. A few days later Cureton's cavalry marched out towards Gujranwàla, with Captain Nicholson as political officer to the whole force.

CHAPTER IX

THE PUNJÂB CAMPAIGN, 1848–1849

WHILE George Lawrence and his helpmates were struggling heroically against adverse fortune in the north-western districts of the Punjâb, Sher Singh's sudden defection on September 14 from the camp before Multân revealed to the blindest of our countrymen in India the full significance of past and passing events in the Land of the Five Rivers. Our professed allies the Sikhs had now become open and determined foes.

The siege of Multân had to be suspended for many weeks pending the arrival of strong reinforcements from Bombay.

Hardly had Reynell Taylor set out from Bannu on the extreme western frontier to join the British camp at Surajkhund, when the Bannu troops, the flower of the Sikh army, broke out in fierce revolt, slew one of their own colonels and the loyal commandant of Edwardes's new fort Dulipgarh, and marched off across the Indus to the camp of Chatar Singh. As Sher Singh moved northwards along the Chinâb, the disbanded veterans of 1846 everywhere flocked to the standard of a leader who raised once more the old Khâlsa war-cry of *Guru-ji-ke-fatha*, 'Victory for the Guru,' against the cow-killing infidels who had come betwixt the wind and Sikh nobility, and sat in the high places once reserved for the barons and councillors of Ranjit Singh [1].

If a strong British garrison watched over the safety of Lahore, the Sikh troops, who held the important fort of Govindgarh, were ripe for revolt at the first opportunity. But Hodson was ready to disappoint them.

A hundred of his Guides got into the place on September 21, on pretence of escorting some State prisoners. They took possession of the gateway, says Hodson, 'despite the scowls and threats, and all but open resistance, of the Sikh garrison.' Next day a British regiment marched from Lahore to relieve the Guides, and make our hold upon Ranjit's treasure-fort doubly sure. Earlier in the same month the flame of rebellion had reached Jalandhar, where a few Sikh fanatics strove to rouse the people against their new masters. But the plotters reckoned without John Lawrence and the civil officers under his command. With the aid of a few troops supplied by Brigadier Wheeler, the September rising was speedily quelled.

Two months later the bold commissioner led his own levies into the field against yet larger bodies of insurgents. Ably seconded by Barnes and Saunders, and with little help from regular troops, a brief but brilliant campaign sufficed to put down a dangerous outbreak in a province unaccustomed to its new yoke. 'Within thirteen days,'

---

[1] *Guru*, or 'master,' was the name applied to Nanak, the Hindu reformer of the sixteenth century, who founded the brotherhood of Sikhs, or 'disciples.' The tenth of his successors, Guru Govind, in the eighteenth century transformed the religious sect into a fighting community, the Khâlsa, which throve upon the ruins of the Mughal Empire, and finally, under Ranjit, conquered the whole Punjâb.

John Lawrence wrote to Currie, ' peace and order have been restored throughout the territory by the capture or dispersion of the insurgents. This result has been effected with little loss of life, and hardly any expense to Government. Had we not thus promptly acted, I am convinced that the rebellion would have assumed a formidable aspect, and have cost blood and treasure to suppress [1].'

Down to the last week of October the energy, tact, and cool courage of George Lawrence at Peshâwar held back from open mutiny the strong Sikh garrison of the great frontier post below the Khaibar mountains. But the Bannu regiments were near at hand ; Sher Singh was moving northwards as if to join his father ; and the Amir of Kâbul, who in July had declined to war against us, was now casting in his lot with the insurgent leaders, who pledged themselves to restore him his long-lost province of Peshâwar. On October 24 the mutineers turned their guns upon the Residency.

The Muhammadan troops could no longer be trusted, except a few score Pathâns, who, with the Sikh governor, remained true to their salt. That night Lawrence, Bowie, and Thompson, the medical officer, rode away with their Pathân escort just in time to escape certain capture, if not a violent death.

As the road to Attock was already closed against them, they made their way to Kohat, where Mrs. Lawrence and her children, some weeks before, had found shelter with the family of Sultan Muhammad after their vain attempt to reach Lahore. But there was no safety for the fugitives at Kohat in a castle belonging to the man who had sworn so solemnly to protect them ; the man whom Henry

[1] *Punjâb Blue Book.*

Lawrence had so greatly befriended in his hour of need. With the proverbial treachery of his race, this man was now arranging, for his own ambitious ends, to deliver up to Chatar Singh the refugees who were enjoying his fatal hospitality. Early in November George Lawrence was conducted by his Afghan guards into the camp of Chatar Singh near Peshâwar.

The brave old chief received his noble captive with all the honours due to a princely guest. But the whilom prisoner of Muhammad Akbar was not again to become his own master until some days after the great Sikh over-throw at Gujarât[1].

Before the close of November Herbert was shut up in Attock by the combined forces of Dost Muhammad and Chatar Singh. Abbott withdrew his troops from the open country into the heart of the Hazâra hills, and defied his enemies from the walls of Srikòt. Nicholson meanwhile rode off with a troop of his Pathâns to place himself at the disposal of Sir F. Currie and Lord Gough. Reynell Taylor was back again in Bannu, eager to assert the power of our arms against Sikh rebels and Afghan invaders. The siege and capture of Lakki, a strong little fort on a branch of the Indus, formed one of the most romantic episodes in the whole story of the second Sikh war. Dalhousie himself joined in the chorus of praise, led by Herbert Edwardes, for a feat of arms which saved the Derajât from passing into Afghan hands[2].

Lakki surrendered after a month's siege on January 11, 1849. By that time many things had happened which made the hearts of our countrymen in India swell or sink by turns within them. In the first days of November,

<hr>

[1] Sir G. Lawrence.   [2] Parry, *Reynell Taylor*.

just before Nicholson turned his back on the Lahore Residency, the leading brigades of the Army of the Punjâb had crossed the Râvi, and were soon to make their presence felt in the country beyond. On November 21 they were encamped ten miles from Ramnagar and Sher Singh's outposts on the left bank of the Chinâb. Sher Singh's main army lay entrenched along the opposite bank. In the dark of the next morning Gough himself led out a compact and eager force of all arms on a strong reconnaissance to his front. Ere long the Sikhs about Ramnagar were driven back upon the river before the advance of Cureton's fine cavalry and the quick fire from Lane's guns. So far all had gone well. But the headlong valour of Havelock's dragoons brought the day's work to a disastrous ending, and filled the camp with sorrow for the loss of many brave officers and men ; above all, of the illustrious Cureton.

On December 1 Sir Joseph Thackwell, at the head of 8,000 good troops, set out from Ramnagar to execute the turning movement which formed part of ' the extensive combinations ' described in Lord Gough's magniloquent dispatch on the fight at Sadulapur. The ford by which he had hoped to cross the river and fall betimes upon the enemy's left flank was found or considered impracticable for his heavy guns. But Nicholson was there to aid him, and his Pathâns were guarding the ford at Wazirabad, some twelve miles higher up stream. By means of the boats which they had collected, and of the help which Nicholson afforded him in various ways, Thackwell was enabled to cross the river at Wazirabad, and march the next afternoon along the right bank. But instead of surprising the enemy, Thackwell himself was to be taken by surprise.

On the morning of the 3rd, while his troops were halted outside the village of Sadulapur, awaiting the approach of a fresh brigade from Ramnagar, a few shots from an unseen battery told him that a force of unknown strength was in his front, behind three hamlets which he had neglected to occupy, or even to reconnoitre. Then followed a long and distant cannonade, varied by vain attempts to turn both flanks of Thackwell's line. About 4 p.m. the enemy's guns ceased firing. At that moment a timely charge of our ' brave and ardent infantry [1],' even though the day was fast declining, might have turned the repulse into utter rout. Our men were burning to be up and at their opponents who had been pitching long shots among them as they lay for hours on the grass.

Both Nicholson and Sir Henry Lawrence were strongly of opinion that Thackwell missed a great opportunity when he decided to attempt no forward movement until the morrow. They felt sure that the force opposed to him did not greatly outnumber his own, nor include any of the best troops in the old Khàlsa army [2].

Whatever might have been the issue of a prompt attack at so late an hour, it is perfectly clear that both Gough and Thackwell were out-generalled and befooled by the Sikh commanders.

When the morrow dawned, Thackwell's assailants were miles away from Sadulapur, on their way towards the ravines and jungles bordering the Jhilam.

On the same day Sher Singh and his main army had vanished, none knew whither, from their entrenchments on the right bank of the Chinâb.

---

[1] Sir J. Thackwell's Dispatch.
[2] Arnold, *Administration of Lord Dalhousie.*

Lord Gough's 'extensive combinations' had thus resolved themselves into a strange succession of blunders, relieved only by a lame conclusion at Sadulapur.

The British commander's Te Deum over the strategy that led up to ' the defeat and dispersion of the Sikh force,' might have been applied by Frenchmen with equal truth to Wellington's retreat upon the lines of Torres Vedras. In plain English, the Sikh leader had the best of the game thus far. While one wing of his army was holding Thackwell in check, Sher Singh was quietly but swiftly drawing off the other wing from one strong position upon the Chinâb to another yet stronger upon the Jhilam, where he could safely await a junction with his father, Chatar Singh [1].

Amidst the many fictions contained in Gough's dispatch of December 7, it is pleasant to light upon a brief but truthful reference to the service rendered by ' Lieutenant Nicholson, a most energetic assistant to the Resident at Lahore.' His energy indeed was not confined to the provision of boats for the use of Thackwell's column; for he was active in scouring the country for commissariat supplies, and in forwarding early intelligence of the enemy's movements to Lahore and Ramnagar.

At this time Mrs. George Lawrence, her children, and Mr. and Mrs. Thompson were confined in the hill-fort of Sakku, beyond the Jhilam. They were kindly treated; but Mrs. Lawrence had not yet been allowed to see her husband, who was lodged in another fort twenty miles away.

Always ready for bold and hazardous enterprises, Nicholson volunteered to make a dash across the Jhilam with his

[1] Trotter, *India under Victoria* ; Lawrence Archer, *Commentaries.*

trusty Pathâns, and attempt the rescue of his imprisoned friends. ' The plan,' says Kaye, ' excited the admiration of Lord Dalhousie,' who had lately hurried up from Calcutta to overlook and control, from the banks of the Satlaj, the movements of his Commander-in-Chief. Rightly or wrongly, so bold a project was pronounced to be too hazardous even for a leader of Nicholson's quality, and he had to fall back upon the regular duties of a ' political ' serving with an army in the field.

Meanwhile for several weeks after Sadulapur that army was destined to remain idle in the open country between the Chinâb and the jungles near the Jhilam. Such was the will of the imperious Governor-General, who held the poorest opinion of Gough and his commanders, and kept all his attention fixed upon Multân. It was only in the last days of December that the siege of that stronghold was renewed by Whish's reinforced army. The city itself was carried by storm on January 2, 1849; and the first news of its capture was brought to Dalhousie by Sir Henry Lawrence himself, who had hastened back to India in time to share in the labours of the siege.

Early in the same month Herbert fled from Attock, driven by the sudden defection of his garrison from the post he had so stoutly defended for seven weeks. The river-fortress opened its gates to Chatar Singh, among whose captives Herbert also was speedily numbered. Making Attock over to his Afghan allies, the old Sikh warrior was free at last to march towards the Jhilam and join forces with his expectant son. In order to forestall that junction, Gough also was now set free—' if he felt strong enough '—to move forwards, and do his worst upon Sher Singh.

What use the brave but blundering veteran made of his

chief's permission was shown on January 13 in the hard-fought and only half-won battle of Chilianwâla, one of the bloodiest records in the history of our Indian wars. The Sikhs, as Hodson wrote to his brother, ' though beaten, seem to have had every advantage given away to them. Our loss has been severe, and the mismanagement very disgraceful; yet it will be called a victory, and lauded accordingly. Oh, for one month of Sir Charles Napier!'

The enemy outnumbered us by more than two to one. They had sixty-two guns in position, and their front was covered by a belt of thorn-jungle about a mile deep. It was nearly three o'clock on a winter afternoon when their first shots were answered by the fire from our heavy guns. Only half an hour later our brave infantry were launched into a thorny wilderness of whose nature and extent their leaders knew nothing, in order to carry the batteries in their front. One brigade advanced with unloaded muskets, without a field-gun in support. The 24th Foot, outstripping their native comrades, reached the batteries only to be driven back with terrible slaughter by bodies of Sikh horse and foot.

Things went better in other parts of the field, where our infantry advanced firing, with guns on their flanks. But the cavalry on the right of our line got perplexed in the dense jungle, mistook one order for another, and finally fled helter-skelter before a few hundred Sikh horse. Their flight exposed the nearest brigades of infantry to imminent danger, and caused the loss of four horse-artillery guns. Several of our colours were also missing on that day of carnage. Before nightfall, however, Gough's troops were masters of the open ground beyond the jungle and of forty Sikh guns, while Sher Singh's shattered forces had withdrawn to their entrenched camp on the banks of the Jhilam.

In its results, however, Chilianwâla seemed less of a victory than a drawn battle. When Lord Gough that evening decided against his own judgement and the protests of Sir Henry Lawrence to fall back at once upon the village of Chilianwâla, he would have done well to leave a few squadrons of his fine irregular horse on the battle-field where some of our wounded soldiers were still lying, as well as most of the captured guns. For as soon as the enemy learned how things stood, parties of Sikh gunners and camp-followers came down in the dead of the night, carried off some twenty-eight guns, and murdered every man they found alive. Three days later Sher Singh was firing a grand salute in honour of the powerful reinforcements which his father had just brought with him from the Indus into the Sikh camp on the heights of Rasúl.

Both Henry Lawrence and John Nicholson were engaged throughout the battle in carrying orders from the Commander-in-Chief to the commanders of divisions and brigades, and in keeping him acquainted with what was going on outside the range of his own observation. These services were duly acknowledged in Gough's dispatch. But Nicholson's duties as aide-de-camp did not prevent him from doing a characteristic stroke of business on his own account.

A well-informed and able writer in an Indian magazine tells us how he ' was seen to give proof of that uncompromising contemptuousness from which meaner natures suffered so much in him. Seeing an English officer not so forward in attack as he thought proper, our Irish paladin —who was over six feet two, and strong in proportion—

caught the defaulter by the shoulders, and literally kicked him into the hottest of the firing [1].'

Twenty days after the fall of Multán city the defenders of the battered citadel surrendered at discretion to General Whish. To Herbert Edwardes was assigned the honour of forwarding Mulraj himself a close prisoner to Lahore, while the British general sent off three of his brigades in turn towards the camp of the Commander-in-Chief. Meanwhile the two armies stood fast upon the ground to which each had retired after their last encounter. Gough was compelled to wait for reinforcements; the Sikh leaders were making overtures of submission on terms which Dalhousie would not concede. He would have nothing short of unconditional surrender. In view of late events the old Khálsa pride could not yet bring itself to stoop so low. Even the advice of so kindly a friend as Henry Lawrence failed to reconcile Sher and Chatar Singh to the Governor-General's hard Roman conditions. They would try the chance of one more grapple with the victors of Subraon.

They certainly made a bold stroke for victory. On the night of February 12 the whole Sikh army marched quietly round Gough's right and rear towards the Chináb near Wazirabad, in hopes of intercepting Gough's reinforcements and cutting his communications with Lahore. Baffled by rain-swollen fords and British vigilance in their attempts to cross the Chináb, the Sikh leaders began to mass their forces around the walled city of Gujarát, near the Chináb, some miles northward of Wazirabad. Religious as well as

---

[1] *The Chameleon*, Mirzapore, 1873. The same story was told by an eye-witness, Major H. O. Mayne of the Body Guard, to a distinguished member of the Indian Civil Service.

military reasons inspired their choice of a position which covered the direct road from Attock to Lahore.

On February 15 Gough turned back from Chilianwâla in leisurely pursuit of the enemy who had once more outmanœuvred him.

On the 20th the last of his reinforcements came into line at Shadiwal, about three miles from the Sikh position, making up his whole strength to twenty-three thousand men and ninety guns. The hosts arrayed under Sher and Chatar Singh numbered fifty thousand horse and foot, with sixty guns.

On the eventful February 21, 1849, Lord Gough fought and won ' his last battle and his best,' as he rightly called it in a private letter to the Chairman of the India Board. For once the fiery old warrior gave his powerful artillery full play. A few days before the fight Sher Singh, conversing freely with his prisoner, George Lawrence, had ' expressed his great surprise that we did not make much more use of our splendid artillery than hitherto, instead of depending so entirely as we seemed to do upon our infantry, which he let us know his soldiers had much less dread of than our guns.' About 8.30 a.m. our eighteen heavy guns began to speak, and the lighter batteries soon took up the dreadful chorus.

The cannonade, wrote Gough, ' was the most magnificent I ever witnessed, and as terrible in its effect.' In spite of their relative weakness, the Sikh gunners fought on heroically for nearly three hours. When at last they could make no further reply, and the two villages on our right front had been stormed by our infantry, the long lines of British horse, foot, and guns swept forward to complete the discomfiture of a beaten foe.

By 1 p.m. the shattered remnants of Sher Singh's army were in swift retreat, which our cavalry and horse artillery soon turned into a murderous rout. The whole of their standing-camp, their baggage, ordnance stores, and fifty-three guns fell that day into the victors' hands. Our own loss in killed and wounded amounted only to 806; a small price to pay for a victory which decided, once for all, the question of Sikh or British rule in the Land of the Five Rivers.

CHAPTER X

THE CONQUEST OF THE PUNJÂB

AS one of the politicals attached to the headquarters camp, Nicholson bore his part in the battle of Gujarât, receiving his meed of thanks from the Commander-in-Chief for his 'valuable assistance both in the field and throughout the operations.'

In the case of such men as Arthur Cocks, John Nicholson, Henry Lumsden, and William Hodson, such an acknowledgement was no mere empty form.

Conspicuous for feats of swordsmanship in that day's fighting was Nicholson's friend Neville Chamberlain, whom Brigadier Hearsey could not praise too much for ' the example he set in several hand-to-hand affairs with a furious and exasperated enemy during the pursuit.' Chamberlain's name as a skilful swordsman and a daring leader of irregular horse had already begun *virûm volitare per ora* in Gough's camp.

Nicholson's services at this period were of a kind less brilliant, but more widely useful. During the long pause after Chilianwâla he was in the saddle day after day, leading his troop on reconnoitring errands, exploring the country for commissariat supplies, or striving to protect the peaceful villagers from the raids of numberless camp-followers who never thought of paying for what they could pilfer or take by force. He had reason to believe that some of Gough's soldiers were concerned in these outrages, which shocked alike his stern sense of discipline and his generous sympathy with the victims of injustice. He never could bring himself to see a wrong done without raising his voice against the wrong-doer. Nor did he fail to resent ' the moral wrong of plundering like so many bandits.' All persons caught in the act of plundering or ill-treating the people were handed over to the provost-marshal, who had them soundly flogged. But Nicholson found that flogging was of no avail for checking plunder, and in February he applied to Lord Gough for leave to exercise the powers of a provost-marshal. ' If I get them,' he writes to Sir Henry Lawrence, ' rely on my bringing the army to its senses within two days [1].' Had his prayer been granted, he would certainly have proved as good as his word.

Amidst these and other occupations Nicholson found time to exchange greetings with various friends in camp, especially with Chamberlain whom he had not seen for six years past, and to talk over more private affairs with his brother Charles, whose regiment, the 31st Native Infantry, bore its part with much credit in all the rough work of that campaign. No one who saw these two together at this period could doubt the closeness of their relationship. In form, feature, gait, and bearing, the younger man might have passed for a faithful copy of what the elder had been a few years before. They were nearly of the same height and build of body, and each held his head aloft with the air of what in Gough's camp was commonly called ' a stuck-up political.' In their case, however, this was only the natural expression of a lofty nature ' commercing with the

[1] Kaye.

skies,' and caring naught for the more trivial concerns of ordinary mortals.

Meanwhile another of the Nicholson brethren had been noting John's movements with brotherly interest from his post of regimental duty in Western India. William Maxwell Nicholson was older than Charles, but went out to India more than a year later, in 1847, as a cadet in the Bombay Army. His regiment was at Belgaum in 1848, when the storm-clouds were lowering over the Punjâb. His letters to his mother during the latter half of that year show how tenderly he strove to allay her fears for the safety of her eldest son. 'I do not think,' he writes on August 24, 'that he can be exposed at present to any danger. ... Perhaps you may not have heard that he has got his company, though only nine years in the service.' This was certainly rapid promotion for a Company's officer in the days when subalterns of twenty years' standing were not unknown.

From Vingorla William writes again on October 11 : 'Pray do not be alarmed about John. ... Uncle James [Hogg] would, I am sure, write and tell you what he knows. In camp I saw the paper most to be depended on, and it said that Nicholson was shut up in Attock . . . with a strong garrison of 1,000 men, whose fidelity was to be relied on (a great point now), and that the place was provisioned for three months, also that a regiment of 500 men are marching towards it.' Evidently William was not then aware that his brother had marched off from Attock in the first days of September, leaving Herbert in charge of that fortress, while he himself gave all his energies to the task of harassing and hindering the enemy's movements in the open field.

From Vingorla William's regiment marched on northwards to Bombay, whence he wrote on November 15, 'You will be very glad to hear, no doubt, that John is at present in Lahore, and out of the reach of every danger. He was ordered to return there by the Resident, but on what account has not yet clearly transpired. His services are likely to be again very soon in requisition, for they have been already very valuable to the Government, so the papers say.'

The next letter in which William refers to his brother is dated December 26, from Karáchi, where his regiment had lately landed on its way up the Indus valley to its destined halting-place at Sakkar. 'You will see from the *Delhi Gazette*,' he writes, 'that Lord Gough has highly complimented John for the energy and decision which he displayed in procuring boats for the passage of the river [Chináb]. I cannot give you any particulars, as John and I never correspond. . . . I sometimes hear John spoken of, and always in terms of the highest praise and commendation, which he certainly well deserves.'

Poor William Nicholson did not live to write many more letters home. He died at Sakkar on June 1, 1849, at the age of twenty. He had suffered greatly for some weeks past from the heat of one of the hottest stations in all India. A certain mystery hung over his untimely death. One morning near the end of May he was absent from parade. Those who looked for him found him in bed with two ribs broken, and many bruises about his head and body. The only account which the poor sufferer could give of himself was that he had been dreaming of a fall from a great height. From that time until his death, a day or two later, he remained unconscious. The officer who wrote to tell

Mrs. Nicholson of her loss could only suggest that her son had walked out of the window in his sleep, had fallen from the verandah down a cliff, and then crawled back somehow to his bed.

This conjecture, however plausible, still left something to explain. Local opinion at any rate took another and a darker view. When, years afterwards, Charles Nicholson visited his brother's grave, he found that the house in which he died had ever since remained untenanted, no native caring to live in what was popularly known as 'Murder House.' For all those years it had stood—

> 'A dwelling-place,—and yet no habitation;
> A house—but under some prodigious ban
> Of excommunication [1].'

To return to the main stream of this narrative. On the very day of Gough's crowning victory at Gujarât, a general order issued by Lord Dalhousie had declared that the war 'must be prosecuted now to the entire defeat and dispersion of all who are in arms against us, whether Sikhs or Afghans.' Before Gujarât was fought and won, he had already planned the quick march that was to carry Gilbert's flying column across 200 miles of difficult country up to the mouth of the Khaibar Pass. On the morning after the battle, while some of Gough's brigades began to scour the country to the north and west of Gujarât, 'the flying general,' Sir Walter Gilbert, was leading a picked force of 10,000 men, with eighteen guns, in pursuit of a beaten but still unconquered foe.

On the evening of February 22 Nicholson himself rode out with his Pathâns in quest of some guns which the

---

[1] Letters, &c., preserved by the Rev. Edward Maxwell.

enemy were said to have abandoned, some twenty-five miles off, on the road to Bhimbar. After a search of many hours he succeeded in securing nine guns, which brought the number then captured up to fifty-three. 'I hope,' he adds, in his letter to Sir Henry Lawrence, who had lately returned as Resident to Lahore, 'you will get me sent on with Gilbert.' The hope was speedily fulfilled. Before the close of February he had joined Gilbert's head-quarters beyond the broad, swift-flowing Jhilam, the 'storied Hydaspes,' which Alexander had once crossed on his way to fight and scatter the hosts of Indian Porus.

Besides the capture of the guns near Bhimbar, Nicholson had lately done a noteworthy piece of work by releasing several hundred prisoners taken during the rout of Gujarát, and letting them 'go quietly to their homes. I hope,' he said, in his report to Henry Lawrence, 'you approve of this.' He contended that 'we should hold all guiltless whom the force of circumstances compelled to join the rebels. I mean all who did not join Chatar Singh till he became the paramount power in the Sind-Ságar Doáb.' Those who joined him ' at the very outset ' should forfeit their grants of land ; while those who 'stood well by us,' even when our cause looked gloomy, are entitled to have their losses made good to them, and receive some reward in addition [1].' Such sentiments did credit to the humanity of him who uttered them. But to address them to such a man as Henry Lawrence seems much like the proverbial carrying of coals to Newcastle. On March 1 Lumsden and Nicholson, with a party of irregular horse, rode on a march ahead of Gilbert's column to occupy the stately hill-fortress of Rhotás, which the enemy had just

---

[1] Kaye, *Indian Officers.*

abandoned, in the hope of making a better stand at the top of the long, steep, winding Bakràla Pass [1].

It was said in Gilbert's camp that Mrs. Lawrence and her fellow-captives had been carried off from Sakku towards Rawal Pindi. Nicholson longed to attempt their rescue. On the very day when he crossed the Jhilam, he would have set off at the head of a thousand volunteers ; ' but my offer,' he writes, ' was not accepted.'

Again, on March 3 he proposed to Major Mackeson, his political chief in camp, to ' make a dash at Margalla with 1,500 volunteers, and to endeavour to prevent the prisoners being carried further off' ; if only he might count upon being supported by some portion of Gilbert's force. In spite of Lumsden's hearty concurrence the scheme fell through, for Gilbert was just then running short of supplies and ammunition. Nicholson, however, writing on March 4 to Sir Henry Lawrence, has ' great hopes that Chatar Singh will ere long be glad to make terms for himself and family by the surrender of the captives.' Hearing that many of the Sikh soldiers were ' very anxious to be allowed to go quietly to their homes,' he had already ' prevailed on Mackeson to issue a proclamation permitting them to do so after first laying down their arms.'

When Gilbert's troops were struggling up the steep gorges of the Bakràla Pass, they found no enemy to dispute their progress. Parties of Sikhs were already coming in to lay down their arms, and take the rupee which British clemency held out to every Sikh soldier who cared to claim it. As for their leaders, they too began to come in

---

[1] One of the passes through the Salt Range, which bisects the Sind-Sàgar Doàb.

as soon as they had ascertained from Lawrence and Mackeson the real meaning of Dalhousie's demand for unconditional surrender.

On March 7 many an English heart was gladdened by the news of Sher Singh's appearance with all his captives in Gilbert's camp. That evening Nicholson wrote to his friend and fellow-worker, Arthur Cocks, at Ramnagar, ' Hurrah ! the prisoners are all in ; as is Sher Singh, who is now closeted with Mackeson, and I hope the Singhs will have laid down their arms by to-morrow morning. Show this to Lord Gough, and forward it sharp to the Resident [1].'

On the following day he writes to Sir H. Lawrence that ' Sher Singh and Lâl Singh Moraria have this morning agreed that all the guns and arms shall be surrendered; so I hope our war with the Khâlsa may now be considered at an end.'

The same day several hundred of Sher Singh's retainers laid down their arms. At every stage of Gilbert's advance fresh bands of war-worn Sikhs were brought into camp by their sirdars. Many a grey-bearded veteran paused reluctantly before the pile of weapons to which he must now add his own, as the price of his promised freedom. After parting with their dearest treasures, some of them would stalk away unmindful of the proffered rupee; and one sad-eyed warrior was heard to say, like another Othello, ' My occupation 's gone [2] ! '

Meanwhile Sher Singh himself had returned to his

---

[1] Arthur Cocks, of the Bengal Civil Service, another of Lawrence's politicals, had been wounded at Gujarât in repelling a sudden attack made by a party of Sikh horsemen upon Lord Gough and his escort.

[2] *Mera kâm hogaya* = my work is over.

father's camp at Rawal Pindi, to prepare his troops—still nearly 20,000 strong—for the final surrender of all their arms and guns. As the two Sikh leaders, accompanied by George Lawrence, passed down the ranks of an army still hungering for one more fight, they were assailed with loud reproaches for selling their faithful soldiers to the Farangi[1]. Their fate, however, was already sealed. Next morning, March 11, the two sirdars with all their chief officers gave up their swords to General Gilbert in his camp at Hurmak. On the same evening the remainder of the Sikh guns, forty in number, including those we had lost at Chilianwála, had been brought in by Sikh artillery-men, and during the next day more than 3,000 Sikh infantry laid down their arms[2].

On March 14 Gilbert's troops were drawn up in fighting order on the green sunlit plain of Rawal Pindi. But Abbott's levies were posted about Margalla; and all doubt as to what might follow was quickly dispelled by the manner in which the remnant of the great Sikh army marched out from camp to lay down their arms at the feet of 'the flying general,' attended by his chief officers and a numerous staff. George Lawrence stood by Gilbert's side, as regiment after regiment halted before them, while every officer gave up his sword, and 16,000 good soldiers laid down their arms.

On this occasion John Nicholson, who never forgot a face he had once seen, recognized one poor fellow passing on to the tent in which he had to lay down his arms. 'How is this, friend?' he exclaimed. 'Did you not say you would drive us all into the sea? Your guru [pastor] should have advised you better.' 'Ah! sahib,' replied

[1] Sir G. Lawrence.   [2] Kaye, Sandford's *Journal*.

the Sikh, looking heartily ashamed of himself, 'there's no striving against Fate. There's no fighting upon a diet of cabbage. Just you try it yourself, sahib.' What else indeed than timely submission remained to men who had been living for two months upon half-raw carrots, cabbages, and turnips [1]?

This final act of surrender proved the death-blow to Sikh dominion in the Land of the Five Rivers. But Gilbert's work was not yet over. He had still to lead his staunch soldiers up and down hill, and across the Indus to the mouth of the Khaibar Pass, in close pursuit of Dost Muhammad's Afghans, who had made themselves masters of Peshâwar and Attock, and had fought against us at Gujarât. On the morning of the 17th he himself, with his cavalry and light guns, reached the Indus at Attock just in time to catch the Afghans in the act of burning the bridge of boats. The sight of Chamberlain's horsemen and Fordyce's guns sent them flying. 'We have the fort and twelve boats,' writes Nicholson the same day, ' and the Duranis have fallen back from the right bank. As we came up this morning they evacuated the fort and broke up the bridge consisting of sixteen boats, four of which they burned.' That same afternoon one of Gilbert's infantry brigades marched into camp, having covered the seventy miles between Rawal Pindi and Attock in less than three days [2].

After a day's halt to repair the bridge and rest his horses and men, Gilbert sped on with the Bengal troops in chase of his nimble foe. Knocking five marches into three, he reached Peshâwar on March 21, within a week of his starting from Rawal Pindi. He had not run down all his game, but he had fulfilled the task assigned him by chasing

---

[1] Abbott, *Narrative.*   [2] Kaye.

the Afghan intruders back, like frightened deer, into their native hills. He could say with truth in his dispatch to the Commander-in-Chief, that ' the Sikhs have been humbled and their power crushed; the British prisoners released from an irksome captivity; and the rich province of Peshâwar freed from its Muhammadan invaders.' Nor did he fail to honour with just praise the troops whose ' cheerful endurance of fatigues and privations,' on their march from the Jhilam to Peshâwar, had enabled him to achieve ' these glorious results.'

On March 30, 1849, Dalhousie issued the fateful proclamation which dethroned the child-sovereign of Ranjit's realm, and turned the Punjâb into a province of British India.

What Ranjit himself foresaw, as he scanned a coloured map of the Company's possessions, had come to pass within ten years after his death. All India, from Peshâwar to Cape Comorin, had ' become red.'

Writing to Henry Lawrence from Rawal Pindi on March 29, the very day on which Dulip Singh was signing at Lahore the document which transformed him into a throneless pensioner of the Indian Government, John Nicholson is ' not surprised to hear that the country is to be annexed. No fear of any one in this quarter getting up a row about it. All regard it as annexed already.' No other course indeed was possible after the experience of the past three years. There was hardly an Anglo-Indian, except Henry Lawrence, who did not own that annexation had become as necessary as even Lawrence allowed it to be just.

Lord Hardinge had long since foreseen the failure of his efforts to build up a strong Sikh government at Lahore.

For the great mass of Punjàbis, who were neither Sikhs nor pure Hindus, annexation meant only a change of masters, a change that might be for the better, and certainly could not be for the worse if the promises of the proclamation were faithfully carried out.

After the annexation, most of Lawrence's politicals returned with new titles and enlarged powers to their former posts. George Lawrence became, for instance, deputy commissioner in Peshâwar, Abbott in Hazâra, Nicholson in Rawal Pindi, Reynell Taylor in Bannu; while Herbert Edwardes remained with his beloved master at Lahore. In a characteristic letter to Sir H. Lawrence, the new President of the Lahore Board, Nicholson claims compensation for 'property lost at Peshâwar, Attock, and Hasan Abdâl,' which he estimates, moderately enough, at 1,000 rupees. 'I also rode a horse, worth 400 rupees, to death on Government service—not running away[1].'

---

[1] His death had been recorded by Nicholson in the following letter:—

'Daybreak. Paorie, 25th August, 1848.

'MY DEAR ABBOTT,

'A letter came last night from Chatar Sing to Jhanda Singh saying that the soldiery had prevented Utar Singh's leaving; but that he certainly would be with me to-day. I do not believe it. And I hear Partab Singh's corps has actually advanced from Rawal Pindi. I intended writing you at the time; but sleep overpowered me, before the writing materials came.

'My fine chestnut died during the night, of the effects of a gallop to Margalla and back again. Yours very sincerely,

'J. NICHOLSON.'

CHAPTER XI

IN planning his scheme of government for the Punjàb, Lord Dalhousie sought to reconcile the paramount claims of Sir Henry Lawrence with the duty which he himself owed alike to his new subjects and his honourable masters at the India House. How to make the best use of Sir Henry's fine qualities, rare experience, and strong personal magic, without harm or hindrance to the material development of the conquered province, was a problem which the shrewd young Governor-General did his best to solve aright. He had come to regard his fiery old subaltern as a sort of wild elephant, whose movements must be regulated by a tame elephant placed on either side of him. In spite of his own dislike for government by Boards, Dalhousie now established a Board of Administration in which Henry Lawrence, as president, was to be aided and kept in order by two civilian colleagues, John Lawrence and Charles Mansel, both men of pre-eminent fitness for the task that lay before them.

To each member of the Board was assigned his proper sphere of duty in a system, writes Kaye, ' of divided labour and common responsibility.' The president himself was to conduct all the political business, which included the disarming of the people, the raising of new regiments in place of the old, negotiations with feudatory and border chiefs, and the work of general peace-maker between his Government and the old ruling classes in the Punjâb. To John Lawrence was entrusted the great department of revenue and finance; while Mansel, presently succeeded by Robert Montgomery, directed all matters of police and public justice.

Over each 'division,' or shire, of the Punjâb, which once more included Jalandhar, was placed a commissioner, aided by a deputy commissioner, with one or more assistants for each district. The duties of these subalterns, nearly half of whom belonged to the Indian army, were even more multifarious than those discharged by a district officer in the North-West Provinces. They had to act, in Kaye's words, as 'judges, revenue collectors, thief catchers, diplomatists, conservancy officers, and sometimes as recruiting sergeants and chaplains, all in one[1].' Not a few of them were Henry Lawrence's men, who had already proved their fitness for any task of difficulty or danger.

By this admixture of soldiers and civilians on the Punjâb Commission, Dalhousie secured the cheap yet efficient administration of a province which needed the best men of both classes to clear away the wreckage of fallen dynasties, and evolve new forms of social order and civil progress out of the chaos which followed on the death of Ranjit Singh. Happily for those who first entered upon this work, the mass of the people were quite prepared to welcome a change of masters which promised to deliver them from the curse of military lawlessness and religious intolerance. For the Khâlsa yoke had pressed upon the Muhammadans,

[1] Kaye, *Sepoy War*, vol. i.

who outnumbered the Sikhs by six to one, almost as heavily as our English yoke once pressed upon the Catholic Celts of Ireland.

As for the Sikh chiefs and soldiery, they submitted on the whole with a cheerful grace to the rule of a conqueror whose prowess they had learned to respect, and whose clemency to a vanquished foe seemed to their eyes embodied in the person of their old friend and patron, Sir Henry Lawrence. Only a few of the more restless spirits, headed by Chatar Singh, presently renewed their plots against the English, and paid with prolonged imprisonment the penalty of their wanton breach of faith.

As a deputy commissioner under the new Board, Captain Nicholson resumed charge of the district where he had striven so manfully against the flowing tide of Sikh rebellion. He himself was received with open arms by the mass of his new subjects, who had already learned to note the contrast between a grinding Sikh tyranny and the strong yet upright, even-handed sway of an English sahib. The name of this particular sahib was in every mouth ; and local rumour already magnified him into the foremost hero of the late campaign ; the great warrior whose arms had routed the hosts of Sher Singh, and delivered the Punjâb from its Sikh oppressors [1].

It was not long before the Nicholson legend entered upon a still more remarkable phase. The transformation of a hero into a god is a natural process among people who already believe in a plurality of gods, or in an ordered

---

[1] So strongly had his fiery courage seized upon the popular fancy, that, in the words of his loyal comrade, the late Sir James Abbott, ' anything great or gallant achieved by our arms was ascribed to Nicholson.'—Abbott, *MS. Narrative.*

hierarchy of heavenly beings.   In this year 1849, a certain
Gosain, or Hindu devotee, discovered in the popular hero
a new Avatar, or incarnation of the Brahmanic godhead.
Impelled by whatever motive, he began to preach at Hasan
Abdál the worship of his new god Nikalsain.   Five or
six of his brother Gosains embraced the new creed, and
the sect of Nikalsainis became an historical fact.

Nicholson treated this kind of apotheosis with unexpected vigour of speech and arm.   Driven from his presence
by repeated threats and blows, the founder of the new sect
retired to Hazára, where James Abbott was now ruling over
a tranquil country and a contented people.   Squatting in
front of Abbott's bungalow, the fakir might be heard at
daybreak chanting sonorous prayers to his adopted deity.
At first Abbott was amused at this evidence of his friend's
popularity.   But the daily recurrence of that ' matutinal
din ' became unbearable.   The fakir could not be persuaded to return whence he had come.   A hut to shelter
him was not easy to find at a time when fugitives from
Sikh oppression were thronging back to their ancestral
homes.

The Gosain, however, had other things in hand besides
the worship of Nikalsain.   Abbott wondered why this
holy man was continually pressing him for the gift of an
old beaver hat which he could not then spare.   After a while
he learned that a similar gift had been bestowed upon the
suppliant by a gentleman at Rawal Pindi.   But of what use
could an English *topee* be to a ragged Hindu fakir ?   At
last the mystery revealed itself.   One day a shopkeeper of
Haripur rushed into Abbott's cutcherry, or office, to lodge
a complaint against the Nikalsaini priest.   This man, it
seems, had asked him for alms, and on his refusal, says

Abbott, ' had set upon the ground, right in his path, the hat aforesaid ; daring him to advance and outrage the *sahib lôg* by treading upon it. Rather than do this, the shop-keeper had given in to the fakir's demand, and paid him a rupee.'

After this revelation of the holy man's practices, Major Abbott felt that Hazâra could do without the ministrations of so masterful a preacher. With a stern courtesy which took no denial, he ' recommended ' the fakir to return home, ' wherever that might be.' The man obeyed without further argument. In the course of time he ' resorted to Nicholson, who was then in the Derajât, and made a second attempt to propitiate his deity. But his god gave him so many more kicks than halfpence, that he retired crestfallen to Hasan Abdâl, where with much zeal he renewed his worship of his impracticable divinity.'

When last he heard of the sect, adds Abbott, ' it was flourishing and increasing. Many a demigod has attained to his apotheosis upon merits more questionable than Nicholson's[1].' In one respect at least the Nikalsainis differed from the votaries of any other creed : their only persecutor was the divinity whom they adored. Flogging and imprisonment were all the reward which Nicholson bestowed upon his intrusive worshippers. But they took their punishment like martyrs, and the more they suffered at his hands, the louder would they chant their hymns in honour of the mighty Nikalsain.

In the middle of April, 1849, while Nicholson was settling down to his work in the Sind-Sâgar province, he received from Sir Henry Lawrence a kindly letter, exhorting him to curb his temper. ' Fear and forbear with natives and

---

[1] Abbott, *MS. Narrative.*

Europeans, and you will be as distinguished as a civilian as you are as a soldier.   Don't think it is necessary to say all you think to every one.   The world would be a mass of tumult if we all gave *candid* opinions of each other. I admire your sincerity as much as any man can do, but say thus much as a general warning.'

Nicholson is not to think that Sir Henry alludes to 'any specific act.   On the contrary, from what I saw in camp, I think you have done much towards conquering yourself, and I hope to see the conquest completed.'

Nicholson's reply opens with 'very many thanks' for the friendly advice contained in the letter.   'I am not ignorant of the faults of my temper, and you are right in supposing that I do endeavour to overcome them—I hope with increasing success.'   He still, however, held himself 'excusable' for the plain speaking which had made him 'very unpopular with a large portion of the officers in the Army of the Punjàb,' whom he had accused of winking at, if they did not absolutely sanction, the plundering of the peasantry in the late campaign.   'I knew from the first,' he says, 'that I was giving great offence by speaking my mind strongly on this subject ; but I felt that I should be greatly wanting in my duty, both to the people and to the army, if I did not to the best of my ability raise my voice against so crying an evil.   For the rest, I readily admit that my temper is a very excitable one, and wants a good deal of curbing. A knowledge of the disease is said to be half the cure, and I trust the remaining half will not be long before it is effected [1].'

From his long and frequent rides on public business, John Nicholson would return at intervals to the pleasant

[1] Kaye, *Indian Officers.*

valley of Hasan Abdâl, once a country-seat of the great Akbar, and still beautiful in its decay. It was here that, shortly before the second Sikh war, James Abbott came from Hazâra to visit his young friend, who had spent the previous Christmas with him in his capital of Haripur. He found Nicholson seated in a tent pitched on a wooden platform over a streamlet which his friend, reminiscent doubtless of Tom Moore, had christened the Bendemeer [1]. And here in the summer of 1849, with the murmur of running water in his ears, John Nicholson could ponder sadly or hopefully many things; among others, the mysterious death of his brother William at Sakkar, and the question of returning home on the furlough to which he was now entitled.

In those days no Company's officer might claim his turn of furlough to Europe until he had served ten years in the East. Grief for his brother's untimely end, and the desire to comfort his bereaved mother, sharpened Nicholson's natural longing to revisit the scenes of his youth, and to look once more upon the faces he loved best. There was no war on hand or in prospect, and the Punjàb seemed as tranquil as Bengal or Madras. If he went home now, he would lose his appointment. But he tells Mrs. Nicholson that he can no longer restrain his inclination to return home, and that the kindness of Sir H. Lawrence will no doubt find another post for him in the Punjàb when he goes back to India.

Sir Henry himself, writing in October, sets his subaltern's mind at rest upon this point. 'One line to say how sorry I am to have missed you. To-morrow we shall be at Damtur, the scene of your gallant attempt to help Abbott. But what corner of the Punjàb is not witness to your

---

[1] Abbott, *Narrative.*

K

gallantry ?   Get married, and come back soon ; and if I am alive and in office, it shall not be my fault if you do not find employment here [1].'

November passed away before John Nicholson found himself free to quit the scene of those brilliant services which had won for him the brevet rank of major in the Bengal Army.   India, he wrote, was ' like a rat-trap, easier to get into than out of.'   Early in December he reached Lahore, where Herbert Edwardes, the hero of Multân, was preparing for his own return to England, in charge of John Lawrence's two little girls.   The two friends readily agreed to travel together as far as their roads lay in the same direction.   From Firozpur they were to go by boat down the Satlaj and the Indus to Karâchi, and thence by steamer to Bombay.   At the western capital they hoped to catch, writes Nicholson, ' the second January steamer to Kosseir, where I purpose disembarking and marching across to the ruins of Thebes, the oldest and greatest of cities.   Thence I shall drop down the Nile by boat to Cairo and the Pyramids.'   Of his further movements he cannot speak with certainty, but thinks of taking Constantinople on his way home.

[1] Kaye.

CHAPTER XII

ON FURLOUGH, 1850–1851

A LONG river voyage, as made by two men in a rude
Indian house-boat, is one of those ordeals which test the
strength of human friendship. With two such men, however, as John Nicholson and Herbert Edwardes the days
flowed by in the easy intercourse of two fine noble spirits
bound together by common aims, sympathies, experiences,
and by a certain lack in each of that which the other could
best supply. Both men were deeply religious, each in his
own way; and both had sat to good purpose at the feet
of their Gamaliel, Henry Lawrence. In the sunshine of
the elder man's cheery nature and bright, trenchant, easy-
flowing talk, Nicholson's heart grew lighter, his countenance less stern, and his tongue found readier utterance
for the thoughts that filled his brain. Edwardes, too,
knew how to hold his tongue on fit occasion, and to
serve his friend by the silence that is often more eloquent
than any words.

Every evening during the river voyage to Karâchi, their
'budgerow' was made fast to the river bank, in order that
the boatmen might cook their simple dinner, and smoke
their hubble-bubbles after the day's work. At such times
the two friends also would sally forth, taking the Lawrence

K 2

children for a run on land, or to search for a tiger's foot-prints on the sandy shore [1].

Other incidents of this voyage remain matters for guess-work.   When our travellers halted at Sakkar on the right bank of the Indus, did John Nicholson find time to visit the still fresh grave of his brother William Maxwell?   And before leaving Haidarabad, did he and Edwardes explore the field of Napier's crowning victory over the Sind Amirs? To such questions no certain answer can now be given. One fact, however, stands out beyond dispute.   From that time the friendship born of mutual esteem and admiration struck wider and deeper root.   Edwardes and Nicholson became, in the words of Lady Edwardes, 'more than brothers in the tenderness of their whole lives henceforth, and the fame and interests of each other were dearer to them both than their own.'

In January, 1850, they reached Bombay, in time to go on by the same steamer with the brave and popular Lord Gough, whose place at the head of the Indian army was now filled by the keen-witted, fiery-tongued Sir Charles Napier.   The courteous old Irishman was not slow to renew acquaintance with the two young men whose achieve-ments in the late war had won his hearty admiration. However cheaply they might rate the generalship of their old leader, they knew him at any rate for a stout soldier and a true-hearted gentleman, to converse with whom was at once a privilege and a pleasure.

The two friends parted company at Cairo, to meet again a few months later in England.   While Edwardes with his little charges accompanied Lord Gough to Southampton, John Nicholson made the best of his way towards Con-

---

[1] Lady Edwardes, *Life of Sir Herbert Edwardes.*

stantinople.   The following letter, preserved by the Rev. Edward Maxwell, may be given here by way of preface to the strange story told by Kaye :—

H. M. STEAMSHIP 'PORCUPINE,'
Off the Piraeus, March 20, 1850.

MY DEAREST MOTHER,

My hands are so numb and there is so much motion, owing to a heavy sea, that you must not be disappointed at getting a very short letter. I reached Constantinople on the 26th ultimo, and left on the 15th in the French steamer *Lycurge*. Why I remained three weeks instead of only one as I had intended, I will tell you when we meet, and you will not disapprove of my motives. On the morning of the 16th we ran aground in a snowstorm in the Dardanelles, and failing to get off again, the *Porcupine* took us up yesterday on her way to the Piraeus with dispatches.

I shall not remain more than a week at Athens, and shall thence go direct to Trieste. I hope to be in London by the middle of April.

With love to all friends, and hoping to see you well ere the close of next month.

Believe me, my dear mother,

Your affec^te son,

J. NICHOLSON.

It was not until the last week of April, 1850, that mother and son met again for the first time since 1839, and that Clara Nicholson heard from John's own lips the reason of his prolonged stay in the Turkish capital. When the Hungarian revolt of 1848 had been crushed by the united arms of Austria and Russia, some of its leaders, notably Louis Kossuth, found an asylum on Turkish soil. The Turkish Government, backed by the whole force of British sympathy, refused to surrender the fugitive from Austrian vengeance. But by way of a compromise, Kossuth himself, the eloquent mouthpiece of the Hungarian cause, was detained in easy and honourable arrest at a fort in Asia

Minor. His daily rides were attended by a Turkish escort, and each day the direction of the ride was changed. Some of his friends and well-wishers in Constantinople had formed a plot for his deliverance and escape to the shelter of an American frigate. Shortly after Nicholson's arrival, one of the plotters, an Englishman who had served in the Hungarian army, persuaded him to take part in an enterprise which appealed so powerfully to his generous impulses.

A day was fixed, upon which Kossuth was to ride in a given direction towards the coast. At a certain point he would come upon the rescuing party who, after overpowering the guard, would carry him off by boat to the safe shelter of the Stars and Stripes. But the plotters had reckoned without the ladies who had been let into their secret. One of the party, an American, revealed the plot in the strictest confidence to his wife. She in her turn imparted the joyful news to her dearest female friend under the most solemn pledge of secrecy. The vows were soon broken with the best intentions. At last the plot became known to high Austrian officials, to whose demand for prompt interference the Porte had to lend a compliant ear. And so the plot fell through just as the rescuing party were about to start on their chivalrous errand.

In a yet more romantic adventure Nicholson was now to play a more prominent and successful part. The same Englishman who had asked his aid in the abortive plot had a wife confined in an Austrian fortress, where she languished in utter ignorance of her husband's fate. She knew that the Austrians would show no mercy, if they caught him, to an officer of the Austrian Army who had since joined the ranks of the Hungarian rebels. She herself

was a brave Hungarian lady, whose only crime had been
her unswerving loyalty to a losing cause. Her husband
had made good his escape from imminent capture ; but
no tidings from the outer world were allowed to enter
her prison cell.

At General G.'s entreaty, Nicholson readily undertook
to carry a letter from him to his suffering wife. What
else indeed could have been expected from the man who
had once dared so much in the hope of rescuing the wife
of his friend, George Lawrence? On approaching the
fortress where Madame G. was immured, Nicholson ' saw
at a glance,' says Kaye, ' that there was no getting in without leave.' Walking up to the guard at the gate, he asked
for an interview with the officer on duty. When the two
were alone together, he at once declared himself to be an
English officer who would be very thankful for permission
to see Madame G. alone for a few minutes.

The Austrian officer took a few minutes to consider his
answer to so bold a request. But he was a gentleman
with something of a heart ; and there may have been
that in the stranger's voice, look, and bearing, which went
far to reassure him. He gave orders that the English
officer should be allowed to speak with the lady alone for
the space of five minutes.

In another minute the door of her cell was opened, and
John Nicholson stood alone before the fair captive. After
a few words of explanation and apology, he proceeded
to pull off one of his boots, out of which he drew forth
the hidden letter from General G. ' You have just five
minutes to read it,' he said, ' and to give any message in
return for your husband.' With eager haste Madame G.
read the lines which assured her of the writer's safety,

and of his longing for some news of herself. Looking all the gratitude which she had no time or power to express, she gave her visitor a few hurried messages of love and comfort for his friend. She had hardly said all that was in her mind, when 'the door opened, the sentry reappeared, and John Nicholson departed with a few words of courtesy and thanks to the officer at the gate [1].'

Such in effect was the story told by Nicholson to his mother, and afterwards by her retold to Sir John Kaye. The sympathetic reader would like to know in what fortress the poor lady was confined, how long she was fated to languish there, what was her husband's full name, and whether he and his noble wife ever tasted the joys of reunion upon this side the grave. The story however, even as it stands, shows clearly forth the romantic tenderness which dared do all that might become a man on behalf of a sorely distressed lady; the tenderness which, seven years later, blazed out into almost savage fury at the sufferings inflicted on English women and children by the Delhi Princes and the fiendish Rajah of Bithur.

That Nicholson carried away with him some bright and fruitful memories of the week he spent at Athens, and of his subsequent journey home, the reader must take for granted in default of documentary proof. His quick eye and trained intelligence, aided by the knowledge gathered in past years, were sure to serve him well as he moved among scenes of living interest or old historical renown. He had left Athens about the end of March, but so leisurely were his movements, by way of Vienna and Berlin, that April was nearly over before he found himself once more in London, bending over the mother from whom he had

[1] Kaye.

parted in 1839. All through May the London season went gaily forward. The great city was thronged with sight-seers and pleasure-seekers from all parts of the kingdom, while not the least notable of its foreign visitors was Jung Bahâdur, the Prime Minister and virtual ruler of Nipal.

Herbert Edwardes and John Nicholson, their figures contrasting as markedly as the rival towers of Merton and Magdalen Colleges, might be seen at times walking arm-in-arm along Piccadilly, or watching the brilliant stream of carriages in Hyde Park. One evening the two friends dined at the Mansion House as guests of the Lord Mayor. At the same table sat the old Duke of Wellington and other distinguished officers. It fell to Major Edwardes to respond to the toast of the Indian Army. In the course of his speech Edwardes turned towards Nicholson and said, ' Here, gentlemen, here is the real author of half the exploits which you have been kind enough to attribute to me.'

Mrs. Nicholson was staying at this time in Grosvenor Square, at the house of her brother Sir James Hogg, M.P. for Honiton, who had, in 1846, been made a baronet by Sir Robert Peel for his services at the East India Board and in the House of Commons. Sir James felt a just pride in the handsome soldier-like nephew whom he had started on his Indian career, and in whose welfare he had always shown a fatherly interest. Needless to say that Nicholson met with a cordial welcome from Sir James and Lady Hogg, and was bidden to make their house his home so long as he cared to stay in London. He may have attended a levée at St. James's, and listened to a debate in the House of Commons. He certainly paid one visit to the Italian Opera at Covent Garden, where Grisi and

Mario, Alboni and Lablache, were the reigning favourites,
and the ballet was a thing of joy for all lovers of graceful
and fantastic dancing. To Nicholson, however, who had
been bred in a straiter and more ascetic school, this new
experience was not so delightful. What he thought of it
may be seen from the letter in which Lady Lawrence thus
speaks for Sir Henry as well as herself: ' I must not forget
to say that we were *delighted* with your verdict on the
Opera. In like manner, when we were in town, we went
once, and like you said, " We have nothing so bad in India." '
Some of us may smile both at the verdict and the comparison; but tastes will differ to the end of time, and a
pious prejudice honestly held can neither be reasoned nor
laughed away.

' Did not London,' proceeds Lady Lawrence, ' fill you
with the bewildering sight of such luxury as we in the
jungles had forgotten could exist, and of vice and misery
which, except in a year of war or famine, could not be
equalled here?' And she thinks that Jung Bahâdur, ' if
he is dazzled at the splendour he sees, must be equally
astonished at the wretchedness. I do not believe that in
Nipal one man out of a thousand lies down at night
hungry, or rises without knowing where he will get his
day's food.' The same letter reveals the deep interest and
anxiety felt by wife and husband as to the result of Nicholson's ' projected deed of chivalry ' at Constantinople.
' When I read of your plan, my first thought was about
your mother, mingled with the feeling that I would not
grudge my own son in such a cause.'

With the little folk who came across him John Nicholson
was always on the friendliest terms. Mr. J. Quintin Hogg,

<hr>

¹ Kaye.

a younger brother of the late Lord Magheramorne, can well remember how, as a child of five years, he used to sit upon his big cousin's knee and listen open-mouthed to some story of Indian adventure. He can still show the presents which Nicholson gave him. At Christmas of that year Nicholson was again enjoying his uncle's hospitality, for Mr. Quintin Hogg retains a lively remembrance of his cousin's intense amusement at his enthusiastic praise of a little girl who had sat next to him that evening at a Christmas party.

The same informant recalls to mind another incident of that period, which betokens the range and clearness of his kinsman's judgement on matters of prime military importance. 'I remember furthermore,' says Mr. Quintin Hogg, ' that John Nicholson, just about that time, paid a visit to Russia, and was present at a review of Russian troops: and it must have been, I think, shortly after this, that I remember sitting playing with my child's bricks on the floor while John Nicholson was talking to my mother, and expressing to her his conviction that the British Army was in a most terribly backward condition compared with those on the Continent, and that there would be a general breakdown in army administration if we were put to the test. A prophecy very fully borne out during the Crimean War.'

From the visit to St. Petersburg, where he saw the stately and ill-starred Emperor Nicholas putting 12,000 of his best troops through their field-manœuvres, Nicholson brought away the impression that the Imperial Guard surpassed our own Guardsmen in mere *physique*, as much as these surpass our soldiers of the line. On this point however his friend James Abbott, who had also in his time visited the Russian capital, could not be brought to agree with him [1].   Who shall decide when two such critics disagree on a matter so trifling?   For both men knew that mere bigness counts for little towards the making of an efficient soldier.

In the first year of his furlough Nicholson had visited all the chief cities of continental Europe, had studied the military systems of all the great European Powers—Italy was still a mere geographical expression—and had witnessed reviews of French, Prussian, Austrian, and Russian troops, on a scale at that time unknown in England.   The summer of that year, 1850, was spent by him in revisiting his mother's home at Lisburn, and renewing his acquaintance with old familiar faces and places in the north of Ireland.   On such occasions he was often accompanied by one or both of his sisters; for Mrs. Maxwell had come over from Barnsley to stay a few weeks among her own people.

On July 9, before leaving England, John Nicholson had accompanied Herbert Edwardes, as his 'best man' to the church at Petersham, near Richmond, where the happy bridegroom was married to Emma Sidney, youngest daughter of James Sidney, Esq., of Richmond Hill.   It was a real union of two brave, loyal, pious hearts, in whose happiness Nicholson also was one day to find his own.

In the spring of 1851 he was staying with Mr. and Mrs. Maxwell at Barnsley.   Their son Theodore—now Dr. Maxwell of Woolwich—then only four years old, tells how his uncle used to try his courage ' by setting me on top

---

[1] In 1840 Captain Abbott set out from Herât on that 'chivalrous and romantic journey' to Khiva, and thence to St. Petersburg, which resulted in the release of 400 Russian subjects, whom the man-stealing Turkmans of Khiva had caught and sold into slavery.

of the door, and holding me over the banisters, and I must confess he found me greatly wanting in heroism. He used to chaff me,' continues Dr. Maxwell, ' for liking sweet things and assured me that if I would come to Bannu with him, I should have butter on one side of my bread and sugar on the other; which was the way they always lived there. I meekly remonstrated that I shouldn't like to go there, because there were sure to be lions and tigers. To which he replied that he would write to Uncle Charles to have them all killed.'

At last one morning little Theodore was sent off to spend the day with ' some ladies who had a peacock.' When he returned home ' full of the peacock and other wonders ' of which he was longing to tell his parents, ' lo! and behold! they were gone. Uncle had taken them to London to see the Exhibition.' This was the memorable World-Fair of 1851, projected by Prince Albert, and worthily enshrined in those long, spacious ' halls of glass ' which the genius of Paxton reared among the elms of Hyde Park. Mrs. Nicholson and her younger daughter Lily also formed part of the family group which, under Nicholson's guidance, swelled the number of daily visitors to that fairy-like Palace of Art and Industry which seemed to many a sanguine spirit to inaugurate a new and long reign of universal peace and progress in all kinds of peaceful achievements.

Nicholson was certainly not one of those vain dreamers. At Berlin he had seen, handled, and brought away with him one of those new needle-muskets which, sixteen years later, were to make Prussia the paramount power in Germany. And among the many attractions of the Hyde Park show, he turned with especial interest to a choice collection of firearms great and small, the best of which had been devised by foreign brains, and fashioned forth in foreign workshops. These were the kind of peacemakers by which he set most store. One of the first Englishmen to grasp the virtues of the Prussian needle-gun, he tried in vain to stir up our War Office people to the duty of replacing the old short-winded smooth-bore 'Brown Bess,' with a light quick-firing breechloader, capable of killing at 500 yards. Economy was still the order of the day, as decreed by Hume and Cobden; our army was officered by scions of rich or noble families; and the absurd incoherences of our military system had yet to reap their natural harvest in the disasters that marked the long Crimean winter of 1854–55.

Nicholson used to speak regretfully of the time he had wasted at school in learning Greek and Latin, instead of knowledge more clearly befitting the needs of a budding soldier. This conviction, so dear to a large class of thinkers, his recent visit to Russia had done much to confirm; for one day at Barnsley he told his sister, Mrs. Maxwell, of the remark made to him by a Russian gentleman, that 'in his country they were more careful to teach their children modern languages than ancient ones.'

The time was now approaching for his return to India, whither Herbert Edwardes had preceded him earlier in the same year. On March 20, 1851, Edwardes had written to his friend a farewell letter from Southampton. 'Good-bye!' it began, 'we sail to-day. May you have a *séjour* in Europe as pleasant as I know you will make it profitable. If possible, take our station [Jalandhar] on your way through the Punjâb.'

With regard to the post which George Lawrence had just resigned at Peshâwar, the writer says, ' If Lumsden

has it not, *you* ought to get it. Perhaps there may be some prejudice against married men in my exclusion. [He was taking out with him his lately wedded wife.] If you return a bachelor, this may be in your favour ; but if your heart meets one worthy of it, *return not alone.* I cannot tell you how good it is for our best purposes to be *helped* by a noble wife, who loves you better than all men and women, but God better than you [1].' John Nicholson did not follow his friend's example. Perhaps he loved his profession better than any woman he had yet seen ; or perhaps his heart, for all its tenderness, was less inflammable than his temper. Be that as it may, he set forth alone that autumn on his last journey through Europe, and, early in the next year, found himself once more chatting with Neville Chamberlain in the verandah of a bungalow outside Lahore.

One of his last acts before leaving England was to have his likeness taken—in daguerreotype—by Mr. Kilburn, the well-known photographer of Regent Street. John Nicholson, says Lady Edwardes, ' had a very tender heart, and a keen love for his mother, whom he always greatly honoured and respected.' After taking leave of her at Lisburn, he remembered, with shame, how often she had asked him to give her a photograph of himself. It was not yet too late, as he afterwards told my kind informant, to ' do the one thing which his mother had so often asked of him.' He presented himself in Kilburn's studio with the clean-shaven face and bright young countenance which the daguerreotype was so faithfully to reproduce. 'And this,' remarks Lady Edwardes, ' accounts for the contrast between this picture of John Nicholson, and all the others taken with beard and whiskers.'

[1] *Life of Sir Herbert Edwardes.*

CHAPTER XIII

THE DEPUTY COMMISSIONER OF BANNU, 1852–1854

AT the time when John Nicholson returned to India, the railway across the Isthmus of Suez had hardly been begun, and the traveller had still to make his slow way by canal from Alexandria to Atfeh, and thence by steamer up the Nile to Cairo. From Cairo to Suez lay seventy miles of sandy boulder-strewn desert, over which he was jolted for many hours in a sort of van slung upon two high wheels, and drawn by four ill-broken horses or mules, who often gave the driver no end of trouble at first starting. Once fairly started, they would tear along over eight or nine miles of ground hardly practicable for any other kind of vehicle than that which swayed, tossed, and bumped behind them.

On his way up the country from Bombay, Nicholson paid a brief but welcome visit to Herbert Edwardes, at Jalandhar, where he held the post of Deputy Commissioner. Here the new comer made further acquaintance with the future Lady Edwardes, an acquaintance which was soon to ripen into a sincere and loyal friendship. There was much talk at that time of the coming war with Burmah, in which Edwardes's regiment would have to bear its part.

He himself was ready of course, as a good soldier, to go wherever duty and the public need might call him. But Henry Lawrence and his colleagues on the Lahore Board could ill spare the services of one of their ablest civil officers, and the Indian Government decreed that Major Edwardes should remain at his new post.

Arriving at Lahore in the spring of 1852, Nicholson exchanged a hearty greeting with his old comrade Neville Chamberlain, who had just been appointed Military Secretary to the Lahore Board. Showing his friend the needle-musket which he had brought away from Berlin, Nicholson descanted lovingly upon its peculiar merits, and spoke strongly of the imperative need for its introduction into the British Army.

'He was also full,' writes Sir Neville Chamberlain, ' of the iniquity of Bourbon rule in Italy, and was desirous of joining in any steps taken to overthrow that dynasty. He spoke warmly against the conduct of our ambassador [at Naples], and was indignant that he would not receive him when desirous of making some political representations.' Before he left home all England had been deeply stirred by Mr. Gladstone's eloquent exposure of the cruelties practised under the wretched King 'Bomba' against political prisoners, whose only crime was their peaceful resistance to a lawless tyranny. The name of Poerio, the noblest victim of Bourbon treachery, had become a household word with the countrymen of John Hampden. Nicholson himself on his way through Italy must have seen and heard many things which appealed strongly to his passionate hatred of all injustice, falsehood, and evil-doing. Had he lived long enough, we can imagine how anxiously his thoughts would have accompanied the march of that heroic band which

Garibaldi led in triumph to the capital of the fugitive King Ferdinand.

As for his grievances against the ambassador, we must bear in mind that the diplomatist may have been merely seeking to obey Lord Palmerston's orders, which forbade all open interference with Neapolitan affairs.

At the time of Nicholson's reappearance in Lahore, Lord Dalhousie's scheme of government for the Punjâb was bearing rich fruit in all directions. Within three years after the great surrender of Rawal Pindi, Ranjit's crude kingdom had been transformed, as if by magic, into one of the most thriving, best-ordered provinces of British India. Three years of just, wise, unflaggingly provident rule, aided by a series of favouring seasons, had raised the youngest of our Indian possessions to a level with Bombay or Bengal. Thanks to the tireless zeal of Dalhousie himself and all who worked under him, from the Lawrence brothers down to the youngest member of the Punjâb Commission, the Lahore Board could already declare that 'in no part of India had there been more perfect quiet, than in the territories lately annexed.' Never had the world seen such a record of good administrative work done in so short a period as the official report which Sir H. Lawrence and his two colleagues presented to the Governor-General in the spring of 1852.

Even on its financial side the new *Râj* had scored a substantial success. In forwarding the Board's report to the Court of Directors, Dalhousie pointed with just complacency to a state of things which belied their previous misgivings. In those three years the Punjâb had yielded to the Indian Exchequer a net surplus of about £400,000 a year.

On taking his furlough Nicholson had, as a thing of course, to resign his place in the Punjâb Commission. He had gone home as a simple captain of Bengal Sepoys; and his return to India meant a return to regimental duty, unless it should please the Governor-General to require his services elsewhere. Happily his old patron, Sir Henry Lawrence, still held his place of power, and he was not the man to forget a promise once made to any of his subalterns. There was for the moment no befitting vacancy in the list of deputy commissioners. But the high-souled Reynell Taylor, who had done much civilizing work in Bannu during the past three years, was bent upon taking his well-earned furlough while his father was yet alive. Sir Henry caught at such an opportunity for serving his favourite pupil; and early in May, 1852, Nicholson found himself appointed Deputy Commissioner for Bannu in the room of Reynell Taylor.

The name of the border district which he was now to govern had of late become familiar to all readers of Herbert Edwardes's '*Year on the Punjâb Frontier*.' It was in Bannu that Edwardes had proved his mastery in the art of governing a fierce and lawless people, most of whom, in his own words, were 'bad specimens of Afghans: could worse be said of any human race?' The Bannu of those days comprised so much of the present districts of Bannu and Dera Ismail Khan, as lay between the Indus and the Suliman Mountains. This strip of border country stretched 160 miles southward from the Khatak Hills of Kohat, covering an area of 6,500 square miles, or not much less than the whole of Wales[1].

In the northern half of the district lay the smiling Bannu

---

[1] Thorburn, *Bannu*.

Valley wellnigh encircled by ranges of rugged limestone hills, which rose on its western border to a height of 5,000 or 6,000 feet above the sea. On its northern slope stood the town of Bannu, whose name some years later was to be changed to Edwardesabad; and down nearly its whole length of sixty miles raced the waters of the Kurram river, on their way to join the broad-breasted Indus a little below the town of Lakki. It was a land of fruits and flowers and foliage, of green pastures and bounteous harvests; a land where 'every prospect pleases, and man alone is vile.' Degrees of vileness, however, could be noticed even among Edwardes's black sheep. The Marwats, for instance, who gave their name to the southern and less fertile part of the valley, were finer specimens, physically and mentally, of Afghan manhood than the mean and wizened Bannuchi clansmen of the north.

During the four years of Taylor's just but gentle government the peace of the district had been broken only by the raids of Umarzai Wazirs from the hills beyond its western border. The leaders of these raids had been called upon by Taylor to pay up arrears of revenue for the lands they held in a Bannuchi village. Instead of paying, they had gone off to the hills, whence from time to time they and their clansmen swooped down in hundreds with fire and sword upon the peaceful villages in the plain. 'They kept the border in a ferment,' says Mr. Thorburn, 'for over two years; raiding, robbing, and murdering whenever opportunity offered.'

Such was the state of things on the Bannu border when the rulership of the district passed from the 'Bayard of the Punjáb' into the hands of John Nicholson.

Towards the end of April, 1852, he set out from Lahore

to exchange some last words with Taylor at Bannu, and to learn from his old colleague exactly how things stood in that wild border district. Taylor was accompanied by his able assistant, Lieutenant—now Sir Richard Pollock, K.C.B.

' The circumstances of my first meeting with Nicholson,' writes Sir Richard, ' quite naturally prejudiced me against him, for he was succeeding one of my dearest friends—then and till his death. I rode out from Bannu with Reynell Taylor, who was making over charge to Nicholson. Taylor was—and I am not given to exaggerated phrases—just a saint on earth. Duty and religion were stamped on all he did from hour to hour, and day to day; and any one who knew him intimately would certainly endorse this very strong sentiment. Taylor was as keen to bring about reforms as Nicholson. Both worked so hard that neither could have any advantage unless he could add an hour to the twenty-four that were available. Taylor worked slowly and over-conscientiously, and would in five years have done less than Nicholson did in two, and their methods were absolutely different—one was all action, looking or fighting for quick results, the other over-elaborated.

' It was difficult to hear the first conversation of these two, as to what had been done, and what had to be done, without more or less resenting the confident tone of the new arrival, who, unconsciously overrode the explanations of the officer who had toiled so hard with great self-sacrifice, and from the moment of his arrival to take charge, could only speak of what he hoped, or rather *meant* to do to carry out reforms. The result soon justified all this, but one could not at the time foresee.'

' It should be added that Nicholson *did* ask for notes for his guidance—notes which came full, and admirable and pointed ; but not till Nicholson had discovered for himself all that Taylor had recorded.'

' Taylor, like Colonel John Becher, another excellent administrator, could never satisfy himself as to his work, and such a feeling makes quick work impossible, and *only* quick work enables one in a place like India, to get through all that has to be done in the day.'

It was not long before the new Warden of the Marches was devising his measures for bringing these ruffian raiders upon their knees. With the first breath of autumn he set out from Bannu at the head of 1,500 mounted police, in quest of an enemy who deemed himself secure within his native hills. Nicholson, however, had nothing to learn in the school of mountain warfare ; and the troops that followed him were not the raw levies of 1848. 'Three columns,' says Sir R. Pollock, ' moved against the Umarzai Wazirs, and by reason of the long distances to be traversed, the difficult nature of the country, the trying season, &c., but little punishment was inflicted as regards killed and wounded. But the *purdah* (veil) had been lifted, and they saw their country was accessible.

' When we returned a blockade was established, which helped to bring serious pressure and inconvenience and loss on the tribe. Soon the headmen came into Bannu, submitted and asked for terms. Nicholson's answer was prompt and short, " Pay a rupee a head (quite nominal) and behave well in future." He knew they had learnt their lesson.'

' When first I joined at Bannu,' says Sir R. Pollock, ' night thefts in the cantonment were often attempted. Thieves, well armed, came in from across the border, and we found that their common method was to sneak up the dry beds of the larger irrigation channels. Police were secreted in these, and soon had an opportunity of engaging a party of Wazirs, several of whom were wounded or killed. The leader turned out to be a Waziri Malik, or headman of a village just inside the Gumatti Pass, which held lands inside and beyond the border. By day this man was a respectable, responsible person—by night a thief; he was killed in the fight. It happened that the following morning was the market day, and Nicholson had the body exposed in the market-place, as a stoat might be on a barn-door.'

'When I returned to Bannu as commissioner twelve years later, I was gravely told that Nicholson had seized this Malik and had him cut to pieces in open market[1]!!'

In the first days of 1853 Nicholson learned by a note from Sir H. Lawrence himself, that his dear old friend and master was about to leave the Punjáb, and take up the duties of Agent for the Governor-General in Rajputána. This was bad news indeed for our deputy commissioner. ' I have just got your express of the 1st,' he writes three days later, ' and am sorry for the country's sake to hear you are going; and also not a little selfishly sorry on my own account, for I don't know how I shall get on when you are gone. If there is any work in Rajputána I am fit for, I wish you would take me with you. I certainly won't stay on the border in your absence. If you can't take me away, I shall apply for some quiet internal district like Shahpur. I don't think either Taylor or Lumsden will return to the Punjáb. And I am afraid poor little Abbott will soon be driven out of it. I will keep the secret.'

On January 30 he tells Sir Henry of a letter received

---

[1] Sir R. Pollock's MS. Memoranda.

from his brother John, who ' said that he hoped to prove as staunch a friend to me as you had ever been. I cannot but feel obliged to him ; but I know that, as a considerate and kind patron you are not to be replaced. I would indeed gladly go with you even on reduced allowances. I feel that I am little fit for regulation work, and I can never sacrifice common sense and justice, or the interests of a people or country to red tape. A clever fellow like old Edwardes can manage both, but it is beyond me. It would do your heart good to hear how the Sikhs in the posts along the border talk of you. Surely in their gratitude and esteem ' you have your reward [1].'

Sir Henry indeed was going, and, a few days after this mournful outburst, many a heart in the Punjàb was cast down at the thought of losing so wise and noble a master, so tireless a benefactor, so loyal a friend. To the hard-working Colonel Robert Napier of the Bengal Engineers it was ' a severe blow and totally unexpected.' He too, like some of his fellow-workers, cried out against the seeming injustice of Sir Henry's removal from a post which none other could have filled so worthily or with so much success. But Dalhousie had his reasons for the step which Sir Henry regarded as a personal affront. For some months past the friction between Sir Henry and John Lawrence on certain points of public policy had hindered the course of public business at Lahore. Henry's sympathies, roughly speaking, were all on the side of the old aristocracy, while John was equally zealous on behalf of the masses who lived by the labour of their own hands and brains.

The differences between the two brothers who dearly loved each other, grew at last to such a head, that each

' [1] H. Merivale, *Life of Sir Henry Lawrence.*

wrote to Lord Dalhousie offering to resign his post. The Governor-General, whose own views and sympathies were in close agreement with those of the younger and more practical brother, caught at so fair an opportunity of completing his own handiwork. In those four years the Lahore Board with its Rule of Three had splendidly fulfilled its framer's purpose, as the best possible means of bringing a newly conquered province into line with the rest of British India. So long as the President cared to hold office, Dalhousie was content to wait. Sir Henry had given himself away. The Governor-General took him at his word, offered him the political charge of Rajputâna at his present salary, and declared that the time had come for placing the Punjâb under a single chief commissioner, who should also be 'a thoroughly trained and experienced civil officer.' All this was gall and wormwood to the toil-worn soldier who, in the last twenty years, had undergone, he pleaded, a thorough training for any kind of civil work. Sir Henry felt 'deeply mortified' at Dalhousie's readiness to do without him in the Punjâb, although he admitted that, next to himself, his brother John was by far the fittest man in all India for the post which Dalhousie had resolved to offer him.

In February, 1853, John Lawrence saw himself gazetted Chief Commissioner for the Punjâb in the room of the defunct Board of Administration. One of his late colleagues, Robert Montgomery, reappeared as Judicial Commissioner, while the gentle Donald Macleod was set over the Department of Revenue and Finance. A few days later Sir Henry's haggard face and gaunt figure had passed away for ever from Lahore. The general sense of a great personal loss for those he left behind him expressed itself in the words of the *Lahore Chronicle*: 'Sir Henry Lawrence's successor can never be to the Punjâb what Sir Henry Lawrence was.'

In justice to Lord Dalhousie it must be allowed that a Governor-General who sought to make the Punjâb not only a model province, but a paying investment, could not have acted otherwise than he did. He had to choose between two lieutenants, each of whom had offered to retire. He could see how the public business lagged, through their very anxiety to keep clear of all strife-provoking matters. Sir Henry himself admitted that the two could no longer work together, that the time had come when one or the other must go away. In that case what else remained for Lord Dalhousie than to accept the issue thus forced upon him, and replace the old triumvirate by that one of its members who had worked the hardest in honest, able, and zealous furtherance of the policy sketched out by Dalhousie himself?

It must be remembered too that in those four years the Governor-General had borne from Sir Henry Lawrence much more than he would have borne from any other man in India. Ill health and a keenly sensitive nature had so embittered Sir Henry's feelings towards his chief, that nothing which the latter could say or do seemed right or friendly in his lieutenant's eyes. Sir Henry, in his biographer's words, 'had long regarded Lord Dalhousie as his enemy ; ' and Lord Dalhousie, with the best intentions, had failed to win him into a more neutral frame of mind.

Nicholson's passionate longing to follow his beloved master out of the Punjâb, cooled down betimes under the fatherly dissuasions of Henry Lawrence himself, and the lively remonstrances of 'old Edwardes,' who had not the least desire to follow his kind patron into another province. As for the chief commissioner, Nicholson knew that Sir Henry's brother might be trusted to look well after the interests of Sir Henry's particular friends, especially of one whom that brother himself had found worthy of all esteem and honour.

Hardly had Nicholson made up his mind to work on in Bannu, when he heard that Edwardes had been summoned from his pleasant home at Jalandhar to undertake the government of Hazára, in the room of Colonel James Abbott, transferred to the Gun Foundry at Ishapur, near Calcutta. About seven months later, in October, 1853, the death of Colonel Mackeson by the knife of an Afghan fanatic at Peshâwar opened for Edwardes the door to yet higher preferment. Lord Dalhousie at once invited him to 'fill the very important office' of Commissioner of Peshâwar—'the outpost of Indian empire[1].'

No one rejoiced more heartily than John Nicholson over the honour thus paid to the most deserving by the head of the Indian Government, a ruler not given to strewing compliments broadcast. There was comfort also for himself in the thought that Peshâwar was only sixty miles from Bannu, and that he might snatch a day or two, now and again, from his multifarious duties for a gallop along the new Kohat road and a few hours of refreshing talk with Edwardes and his wife in the Residency below the Khaibar hills. Lady Edwardes tells me that, on such occasions, her husband would lay out his own horses half way; so that his friend might make the whole journey in one ride.

'When the autumn of 1853 arrived,' to quote again from Sir R. Pollock, 'Nicholson, rather to my surprise, said, "You

---

[1] Lady Edwardes, *Life of Sir H. Edwardes.*

will be wanting to go home in a year or two, and you should see Kashmir first; apply for two months' privilege leave." I disliked adding to his work, and pointed out how difficult it would be to get a *locum tenens*; but he declared he would not ask for one, and pressed me to take a holiday, and I reluctantly did so. He gave me a letter of introduction to Maharajah Gulàb Singh, which was most useful; and he told me a characteristic anecdote of the old monster, which helped one to believe the tradition, that he used to employ men to bury his treasure, and then murdered them to make all safe. In conversation with Nicholson, he mentioned that on one occasion his cook had been found out in an attempt to poison him, " And what did you do?" said Nicholson. " I had him brought before me, and I ordered my people to separate the skin of the head from the neck behind, to the throat, then to flay the head, then to put up the skin over the skull." " Did he die?" said Nicholson. " Oh dear no, he lived for weeks!"'

At Christmas of this year Nicholson took a longer holiday, and passed a whole happy week in the Peshâwar Residency. 'We generally had,' writes Lady Edwardes, 'a number of the frontier officers into Peshâwar to pass the Christmas week with us,' and none of them was so warmly welcomed as the Deputy Commissioner of Bannu'.

Writing to his mother from Kohat on April 13, 1854, he has something to tell about a visit to the Edwardeses, with whom he has just been 'spending a few days.' He speaks of certain preparations for establishing a Christian Mission at Peshâwar. 'I have given 500 rupees towards it on your account; but my name will not appear on the subscription list, as for certain reasons I have preferred

' Letter from Lady Edwardes.

subscribing anonymously.' It was in fact against all rules of discipline and decency, for a Company's officer to take any forward or open part in missionary work among the Company's Indian subjects, and of this fact Mrs. Nicholson must have been aware.

He is glad to hear that Mrs. Nicholson and Lily have been enjoying themselves at Cheltenham. 'If you have not yet received any rent from the C——s, I would ask you not to take any. It would seem to me inconsistent with the friendly relations which I believe exist between you, to take rent for accommodation which one friend should be happy to have an opportunity of affording another. . . . Where do you think of spending the coming summer? I hope you will go to the seaside: sea-bathing always seems to agree so well with you and Lily. Charles has not quite made up his mind whether he will visit Kashmir or not. By the new furlough rules all leave counts alike, whether at home or in India; so that any one intending to avail himself of European furlough would be unwise to take leave in India [1].'

His generous sentiments are never, like those of Joseph Surface, confined to mere words. 'I have nothing to say this mail,' he writes on September 28, 'and only write to enclose the third of a bill for £185 7s. 2d., the first and second of which have been already dispatched. The weather has begun to get cool, and we to feel a little more alive than during the last four months.' For some four months of the year Bannu was about the hottest district in the Punjàb; and day after day the English *Hákim* had to sit for hours together in his darkened cutcherry, or court-house, hearing complaints, trying causes, issuing

[1] Letters preserved by Rev. E. Maxwell.

decrees, administering in short a rough but even-handed justice to all who came or were dragged before him. With the return of cooler weather Nicholson returned to the active, joyous, open-air life of tent, gun, and saddle, which made the frontier officer so great and wide-felt a power for good among the people whom he had to govern.

CHAPTER XIV

WE have seen how the new ruler of the Punjâb pro-mised to be as true a friend to Nicholson as his brother Henry had ever been. This promise he loyally fulfilled, in a manner not always palatable to its impatient holder. It was not so much the fault as the misfortune of John Lawrence, that some of his friendliest utterances were to be received with an ill-grace by the subaltern whom Henry Lawrence had managed so easily. In all his letters to the deputy commissioner he said nothing at which that officer ought to have taken offence, nothing half so un-pleasant as some things which his brother had said to his favourite pupil. Many of his letters to Lord Dalhousie glowed with the heartiest praise of John Nicholson. He spoke of Nicholson's presence among the wild men of Bannu as 'well worth the wing of a regiment.' He had told Nicholson himself how great a value he set upon his ' zeal, energy, and administrative powers.' ' You may rest assured,' he added, ' of my support and goodwill in all your labours.'

Nothing, too, could have been more kindly worded than the advice which followed this assurance. ' You may depend upon it that order, rule, and law are good in the hands of those who understand them, and know how to apply their knowledge. They increase tenfold the power of work in an able man. I hope you will try and assess all the rent of Bannu this cold weather. It will save you much future trouble.' He exhorted Nicholson to ' assess low, leaving a fair and liberal margin to the occupiers of the soil '; and to eschew middlemen, who were ' the curses of the country everywhere [1].'

Do what John Lawrence might, however, to prove his friendly interest in his brother's friend—and for that end he strove with heroic patience—he never became to his wayward subaltern all that his brother Henry had been. Nicholson might hold him in deserved esteem ; but the strange personal magic which had bound him to Sir Henry was somehow wanting here. His heart would not go out to the new mentor as it had gone out to the old. It was clearly one of those cases in which instinct or prejudice got the mastery over reason.

As early indeed as August, 1853, John Lawrence reported to Dalhousie that he looked on Major Nicholson ' as the best district officer on the frontier. He possesses great courage, much force of character, and is at the same time shrewd and intelligent. He is well worth the wing of a regiment on the border, as his *prestige* with the people, both on the hills and plains, is very great. He is also a very fair civil officer, and has done a good deal to put things straight in his district [2].'

Meanwhile John Lawrence was engaged in teaching Nicholson one of those lessons which a civil officer was, in his opinion, bound to learn. ' I know,' wrote Dalhousie, ' that Nicholson is a first-rate guerilla leader ; but we don't want a guerilla policy.' The conqueror of the Umarzais now sought to deal in like guerilla fashion with the Sheorâni hillmen, who had raided across the border and burnt a village or two which they had plundered. With his usual contempt for red tape, he proposed to lead against them a body of frontier troops selected by himself, without references to the views or purposes of the brigadier commanding. Thanks to the outspoken but kindly remonstrances of the chief commissioner, who urged him to get the brigadier's sanction to his measures, and pointed out the mischief that might ensue if a district officer of such eminence were to lose his life needlessly in such an enterprise, Nicholson was at last persuaded to leave 'the Sheorâni business' in Brigadier Hodgson's hands. The punitive expedition came off, after some strange delay on Hodgson's part, with consequent murmurs from Nicholson, and resulted in the punishment of the offending tribe[1].

In the course of this affair, John Lawrence begged his subaltern to 'report officially all incursions. I shall get into trouble if you don't. The Governor-General insists on knowing all that goes on, and not unreasonably; but I can't tell him this if I don't hear details.' Nicholson never took kindly to his pen, whether for private or official purposes, and his letters were more remarkable for brevity of statement than for amplitude of details.

And his summary method of dealing with criminals did not quite accord with the chief commissioner's conceptions of administrative decency. 'Don't send up any more men to be hanged direct,' writes John Lawrence in July, 1853, 'unless the case is very urgent; and when

[1] Bosworth Smith.

you do, send an abstract of the evidence in English, and send it through the commissioner [1].' Nicholson, indeed, was apt to discharge his public duties in the way that seemed best, not to his official superiors, but to himself. A year later an intimate friend of his found him sitting in his office with a bundle of government regulations before him. 'This is the way I treat these things,' he remarked laughingly, and proceeded to kick them across the floor.

In October, 1853, John Lawrence marched up the Punjàb towards Peshàwar, on a tour of inspection, conference, and supervision which lasted even to the following April. After some busy weeks at Peshàwar, in the course of which he planned a successful raid against the Bori Afridis, he travelled southwards to Multàn. Then crossing the Indus to Dera Ghazi Khan, he turned northwards, and passed along the whole of the Punjàb frontier, visiting every outpost by the way. The Derajàt, in which lay a part of Nicholson's district, seemed to him 'a wretched country,' but Marwat 'looked pretty well,' and Bannu itself he called 'a garden of Eden adjoining a wilderness.' In February, 1854, the travellers—for Mrs. Lawrence and her youngest child were of the party—received a hospitable welcome from Nicholson himself, who helped them over the rough places in his district, conducted them to Kohat, and won the hearts of both parents by his tender concern for the comfort of their little babe, the last of their children then left to them in India. The pleasure which they both derived from their host's companionship remains for one of them a gracious memory; while the good chief commissioner felt proud of the subaltern who

[1] Bosworth Smith.

had already done much for the cause of peace and order among the people entrusted to his charge [1].

According to Mr. S. Thorburn, who served as settlement officer in the remodelled Bannu of a later day, John Nicholson, 'though the mirror of chivalry himself, lacked that kindly gentleness of manner and laborious painstakingness in work' for which Reynell Taylor had been so remarkable. At first the people of the district regarded their new *Hâkim* as a ' hard-hearted, self-willed tyrant to be feared and disliked. But by degrees, as his self-abnegation, his wonderful feats of daring, the swift and stern justice which he meted out to all alike, became known, this impression gave way to a feeling of awe and admiration ; and the people, both within and beyond the border, became so cowed, that during Nicholson's last year of office raids, robberies, and murders were almost entirely unknown ; a happy state of things which has never occurred since [2].'

When Mr. Thorburn was in his cutcherry ' puzzled to decide which party in a suit was lying the less,' he would sometimes amuse himself by letting them both talk away for a few minutes against each other. As the disputants warmed to their work, one of them would say, ' Turn your back to the sahib, and he will see it still waled from the whipping which Nicholson gave you.' To which the other would retort, ' You need not talk, for your back is well scored also.' Flogging was still the cheapest method of punishing malefactors too poor for a fine, and too petty for a course of hard labour in a central jail.

In the matter of flogging, John Nicholson, as we have

---

[1] Bosworth Smith.   [2] Thorburn, *Bannu, or Our Afghan Frontier.*

seen in a former chapter, did not spare even the pious idiots who persisted in grovelling at his feet and worshipping him as the great god Nikalsain. They took their punishment like martyrs, and repeated their offence. 'On the last whipping,' wrote Herbert Edwardes, 'John Nicholson released them on the condition that they should transfer their adoration to John Becher [who replaced Edwardes in Hazára towards the close of 1853]. But arrived at their monastery . . . they once more resumed their worship of the relentless Nikalsain [1].' Some years later Edwardes learned that the last of the Nikalsaini fakirs dug his own grave near Haripur, and was found dead there not long after Nicholson himself had fallen at Delhi.

In the course of this year, 1854, Nicholson completed that summary settlement of the land-revenue, to which John Lawrence in the previous year had called his early attention. And, emulous of Taylor's good example, he reclaimed a large tract of waste land, called Landidāk, by carrying through it a canal direct from the Kurram river.

Before the end of January, 1854, he was grieved to hear that the noble-hearted wife and faithful helpmate of Sir Henry Lawrence had breathed her last after a lingering illness of several months. In the previous September, as she lay battling for life on her bed of pain, Honoria Lawrence had sent Nicholson, through her husband, a tender message of love and pious counsel. 'Tell him I love him dearly as if he were my son, I know that he is noble and pure to his fellow-men, that he thinks not of himself; but tell him that he is a sinner, that one day he will be as weak and as near death as I am now.' She ended by begging

---

[1] This account does not quite tally with that given in Chapter XI, but it is probably the more correct.

him to 'read but a few verses of the Bible daily,' and to say the Collect for the second Sunday in Advent. After her death Sir Henry sent him a New Testament inscribed with his wife's name [1].

By this time our country was fast drifting into that war with Russia which led up to the famous siege of Sebastopol by the allied armies, English, French, and Turk. Nicholson watched with eager interest the varying fortunes of a struggle in which he would gladly have taken part. Even before his return to India he had serious thoughts, as he tells Sir H. Lawrence in May, 1853, of getting his furlough extended to three years, with a view to 'learning Turkish, and making myself acquainted with the principal localities (in a military point of view) in Turkey and Egypt, from a conviction that we must one day have to oppose Russia in the former, and France in the latter country, and that an English officer with some active experience and a knowledge of the country and language, would have a fine field open to him.'

Both Sir James Hogg and Lord Hardinge had then 'thought the contingency too remote.' I begin, however, to suspect that it is not so.' And he goes on to argue the probable success of a French invasion of Egypt on a large scale, in the event of our fleet being too weak or too ill-informed to prevent it. 'I am convinced,' he adds, 'that any European force which surprised Alexandria would find the whole country at its feet immediately, and from the natural and artificial strength of the position have little difficulty in holding it against any *second comer* [2].'

In the same letter Nicholson is so sure that Sir Henry and

---

[1] Kaye, *Indian Officers.*   [2] Merivale, *Sir Henry Lawrence.*

Lady Lawrence are 'much better off personally' at Mount Abu in Rajputána than at Lahore, 'with its bad climate, and the over-work and various disagreeabilities attaching to Sir Henry's position there,' that he feels it would be selfish to wish them back again. 'We shall all then try to console ourselves for your loss by rejoicing in the manifest change for the better you have made. John has been very forbearing, and I am sure puts up with much from me on your account.'

This was a long letter for John Nicholson. When he began it he 'had no idea of writing such a yarn; and all this,' he modestly adds, about France and Russia, 'may be great nonsense. It would be very satisfactory to me to have it demonstrated that it is so.' There was little nonsense, indeed, in his forecast of England's action on behalf of Turkey; and only one error in his calculations regarding Egypt. It was left for England, not France, to demonstrate many years afterwards, the powerlessness of Egypt against the captors of Alexandria.

As the war-clouds darkened over the Black Sea and the Danube, Nicholson's regret for a lost opportunity seemed to grow keener. 'I feel I missed the tide of my fortune,' he writes in February, 1854, to a friend at Peshâwar, 'when I gave up the idea of learning Turkish at home [1].' We may imagine what great things he might have done in the Crimea or elsewhere, to what splendid uses he might have turned his genius for war and leadership, his resolute daring and shrewd resourcefulness, his zeal, pluck, energy, experience, if the authorities at home had given him a free hand. But would they, as things were, have given a free hand to a Company's officer whose

[1] Kaye.

rank was not yet officially recognized in his own country by the servants of the Crown [1]?

Another passage in the same letter is worth quoting, as evidence of the writer's habitual candour in disclaiming credit for any higher motive than that which had really impelled him. 'I wish your mission at Peshàwar every success; but you require skilful and practical men as well as good men. I will send you 500 rupees; and as I don't want to get credit from you for better motives than really actuated me, I will tell you the truth, that I give it because I know it will gratify my mother to see my name in the subscription list. . . . On second thoughts I won't have my name in the mission subscription list. Write me down " Anonymous." I can tell my mother it is I [2].' And he did tell her, as we saw in the last chapter.

The Christian Mission thus referred to was started by the pious zeal of Colonel Martin, then commanding the 9th Bengal Sepoys at Peshàwar. His success was only made possible by the open and cordial support of the new commissioner, Colonel Edwardes, whose eloquence and example gave due play to the zeal and abilities of two such missioners as Dr. Pfander and Robert Clark [3].

About this time Herbert Edwardes had begun to feel his way towards a friendly understanding with Dost Muhammad, the Amir of Kàbul, whom we had left severely alone ever since the failure of his last inroad into the Peshàwar valley. John Lawrence, Abbott, Nicholson, and Outram were all against Edwardes in this matter; but Lord Dal-

---

[1] It was not till the last days of the Crimean campaign that Company's officers were allowed to rank at home with their equals in the Queen's army.

[2] Kaye.　　　　　　　　　　　[3] Lady Edwardes.

housie, looking to the likelihood of a collision with Persia, gave his foremost warden of the marches leave to follow up the overtures which the Afghan Amir was already making on his own account. ' How progress negotiations with the Dost ?' writes Nicholson to Edwardes in May, 1854. ' In dealing with the Afghans I hope you will never forget that their *name is faithlessness*, even among themselves. What then can strangers expect ? I have always hopes of a people, however barbarous in their hospitality, who appreciate and practise good faith among themselves, the Wazirs for instance, but in Afghanistan son betrays father, and brother brother, without remorse. I would not take the trouble to tell you all this, which no doubt you know already; but I cannot help remembering how even the most experienced and astute of our political officers in Afghanistan were deceived by that winning and imposing frankness of manner, which it has pleased Providence to give to the Afghans, as it did to the first serpent for its own purposes[1].'

Such a warning from the whilom prisoner of Ghazni served at least to impress upon his more sanguine friend the need of walking warily towards the goal of his diplomatic efforts. On March 20, 1855, at the mouth of the Khaibar Pass, was signed by John Lawrence and a son of Dost Muhammad Khan the treaty of peace and friendship between the Company and the Amir, which owed its origin to the foresight, and its happy execution to the skill, caution, and patient energy of Herbert Edwardes alone[2]. The treaty by which Dost Muhammad now became the friend of our friends and the enemy of our enemies, turned the key, for a time at least, upon the old meddling policy

---

[1] Kaye.   [2] Lady Edwardes.

of Lord Auckland's day, and left the door open for a closer alliance whenever circumstances might seem to call for it. And the circumstances, as we shall presently see, were not far off.

Among the wilder people of his district Nicholson came across some startling specimens of childish depravity. 'Fancy,' he writes to Edwardes in June, 1854, 'fancy a wretched little Waziri child who had been put up to poison food, on my asking him if he knew it was wrong to kill people, saying it was wrong to kill with a knife or a sword. I asked him why, and he said, "Because *the blood left marks*." It ended in my ordering him to be taken away from his own relatives (who ill-used him as much as they ill-taught him) and made over to some respectable man, who would engage to treat and bring him up well. The little chap heard the order given, and called out "Oh! there is such a good man in the Míri Tappahs; please send me to him." I asked him how he knew the man he named was good, and he said, " He never gives any one bread *without ghee on it*[1]." I found on inquiry that the man in question was a good man in other respects; and, he agreeing, I made the little fellow over to him. I have seldom seen anything more touching than their mutual adoption of each other as father and son; the child clasping the man's beard, and the man with his hands on the child's head.'

'Well!' adds Nicholson, 'this is a long story for me, and all grown out of a humming-top!' He had in fact begun his letter by asking Edwardes to send him from Peshàwar a few humming-tops, Jew's-harps, 'or other toys suitable for Waziri children. I won't ask for peg-tops, as I suppose

---

[1] *Ghee*, or clarified butter.

I should have to teach how to use them, which would be an undignified proceeding on the part of a district officer.'

The letter closes with a story of 'the last Bannuchi murder, which is so horribly characteristic of the blood-thirstiness and bigotry of their dispositions. The murderer killed his brother near Goriwâla, and was brought in to me on a frightfully hot evening, looking dreadfully parched and exhausted. "Why," said I, "is it possible that you have walked in fasting on a day like this?" "Thank God!" said he, "I am a regular faster." "Why have you killed your brother?" "I saw a fowl killed last night, and the sight of the blood put the devil into me." He had chopped up his brother, stood a long chase, and been marched in here; *but he was keeping the fast*[1].'

[1] Kaye.

CHAPTER XV

TOWARDS the close of 1854 the command of the Punjàb Frontier Force fell vacant. It was one of the prizes most coveted by officers of the Indian Army, and Nicholson at once applied for a post which no man in India was better qualified to fill. But when he heard that Colonel Neville Chamberlain, who had just returned from a year's leave to the Cape, had been offered the command by Dalhousie himself, Nicholson withdrew his own application, and wrote his old friend a letter frankly acknowledging his superior claims, and heartily wishing him success. Chamberlain got the appointment, but failed to acknowledge his friend's letter, which in truth he had never received. Nicholson fretted long and bitterly over his friend's unwitting silence ; for

> 'To be wroth with those we love
> Doth work like madness in the brain.'

And an incident which happened early in the following year did not tend to allay the wound that rankled in our hero's heart.

In a raid across the border a body of Masúd Wazirs had surprised and slain one of Nicholson's trustiest Khans in the rear of a frontier post, whose garrison had somehow failed to render him timely succour. Nicholson complained bitterly to the chief commissioner of such untoward carelessness on the part of troops placed under Brigadier Chamberlain's direct command. Chamberlain hotly resented the slur thus cast through his officers on himself. For some months the two disputants fired away at each other in letters addressed to John Lawrence, whose tact, temper, and goodwill were tasked to the verge of endurance before he succeeded in composing the strife. ' You know old " Nick," ' he wrote privately to a mutual friend, ' what a stern, uncompromising chap he is. He was frightfully aggravated at the death of Zamân Khan, and spoke out plainly, too plainly, about the cavalry at the posts,' who were not to blame, he added, in this particular case. ' But the fact is that the detachments in the posts have done little or no good in the Derajât. . . . I did not tell Chamberlain one tenth of what Nicholson said, and much of which seemed to me to be true. . . . The detachments at the outposts do not effectually guard the border. This is the *gravamen* of Nicholson's charge.' Writing to Chamberlain in May, 1855, John Lawrence told him how readily Nicholson had acknowledged his superior fitness for the frontier command ; with what pleasure and confidence he had looked forward to Chamberlain's return as brigader to the Punjâb. Had either Lawrence or Chamberlain but known then of the missing letter which Nicholson had written and Chamberlain never received !

To Nicholson the chief commissioner wrote a day later, saying that Chamberlain talked of resigning unless the *amende* were made. ' I think he is somewhat unreasonable. Nevertheless his resignation would be a public loss, and bring much obloquy. I hope therefore that you will write and express your regret at having led me to conclude that the detachment in the post had received notice of the affair. I have written to you two or three times officially to send me the precise facts and dates of the four raids to which you alluded in reporting Zamân Khan's death. Pray send this without further delay, and in it express your regret for the mistake which occurred [1].'

But Nicholson was very stubborn in defence of what seemed to him right and just. His first attempt at an apology proved a failure, for which, according to John Lawrence, the most just of men and the most assiduous of peacemakers, Nicholson was not to blame. Some months later, when Neville Chamberlain was coming graciously forward, 'Nick' the uncompromising held sternly back. In his earnest appeal of December 2 to the latter, John Lawrence quotes the message of peace and amity sent by Chamberlain to himself :—' I shall be happy to receive him with the same feeling of respect and admiration which I have always borne towards him. He has only to come within reach for me to extend both hands towards him ; and in doing so I shall be doubly glad, for I shall know that the government of which we are the common servants, will be the gainer.'

Well might the true-hearted chief commissioner hold that such sentiments did honour to Chamberlain, and earnestly did he plead with Nicholson for that final reconciliation of which he had nearly come to despair. ' Two such soldiers,' he urged, ' ought not to be in a state of antagonism. . . . Chamberlain is a fine fellow, and it is much to be regretted that we have not more men of his stamp in our army. . . . His good qualities far outshine his faults.

[1] Bosworth Smith, *Lord Lawrence.*

I pray you to consider what I say, for you have not a better friend or a more sincere advocate than myself[1].'

This last appeal to Nicholson's best feelings was not made in vain. Thanks to their persistent intercessor, the late antagonists once more became fast friends ; the Punjáb retained them within its borders until the day came when their services were to be sorely needed elsewhere ; and after John Nicholson received his death-wound in the storming of Delhi, ' it was Neville Chamberlain,' in the words of John Lawrence's biographer, ' who tended and nursed him during the last terrible days of suffering with more than a brother's care.'

In the explanations which followed the first meeting of the reconciled friends, Nicholson was shocked to learn how cruelly he had misjudged Chamberlain's silence regarding the letter which had never come into Chamberlain's hands. It was touching to witness the shame which suffused his honest countenance, which choked his voice, and made him hang the head he usually held so high. His sensitive nature had been wounded in its tenderest point, his hatred of injustice, and he was too honest to hide the pain. For months past he had smarted under the sense of a fancied wrong ; and now he discovered that the wrong was really of his own doing against one who had been and was still his friend. With him, however, the acknowledgement of his error tended only to bind him closer to the friend he had so rashly misjudged.

During the controversy thus happily ended Nicholson sought relief from passing worries in restless longings after a change of scene. At one time his thoughts turned to Rajputána and the dear companionship of Sir Henry

<hr>

[1] Bosworth Smith.

Lawrence, as a haven of rest for his troubled spirit. At another he begged John Lawrence to place him under Herbert Edwardes at Peshâwar, for with the Edwardeses he always found himself a happier and better man. But Henry Lawrence loved him too well to hear of his leaving the Punjâb, and John Lawrence strongly objected to having 'two top-sawyers in one place [1].'

If Nicholson could not go where he wished in India, he would try to join his countrymen in the camp before Sebastopol. 'I have asked Lord Hardinge,' he writes to Edwardes in September, 1855, 'to give me something to do in the Crimea. I think, with our reputation, and perhaps our destiny as a nation trembling in the balance, every man (without encumbrance) who thinks he can be of the slightest use, ought to go there.' Again, however, Sir Henry Lawrence, on learning his intention, stepped in to dissuade him from going on what would have been a fool's errand. He set before his friend, in the latter's own words to Edwardes, 'the prospects which I give up here, and the annoyance and opposition which, as a Company's officer, I am sure to encounter there.' 'All this,' says Nicholson, 'I had fully considered before I acted;' but he held that, under the circumstances, he was only doing what was right. 'I trust to have an opportunity of doing the State some service, the feeling of which will compensate me for the worldly advantages which I forgo [2].' But before his letter had reached Lord Hardinge, events in the Crimea were already working to frustrate his purpose. The Russian retreat from the south side of Sebastopol in the middle of September became the prelude to negotiations which resulted in the peace of the following April.

---

[1] Letter from Lady Edwardes.　　　　[2] Kaye.

How free from any taint of jealousy had been Nicholson's part in the long dispute with Chamberlain may be clearly seen from an incident recorded in the private journals of General Dennys, who in 1855 was one of Henry Lawrence's politicals in Rajputàna. Dennys and his chief were on their way by boat down the Chambal towards Kotah, the capital of a small Rajput state bordering on Gwalior. Sir Henry seemed 'awfully vexed' about a letter which he had received from their mutual friend John Nicholson. Telling his companion how dearly he loved the writer, he put the letter into Dennys's hands, saying, 'Read that, and tell me if he is not a noble fellow.'

The purport of the letter was that Nicholson begged Sir Henry to get him away from the Punjâb to Rajputàna, because he was not getting on well with Neville Chamberlain. He knew, indeed, that the fault was all his own, and declared that, although his own claims clashed with Chamberlain's, the latter's were far superior to his, and that Chamberlain was all round by far the better and abler man. He thought that the public interests would be best served by his own removal, and gladly would he come and serve under Sir Henry Lawrence at any loss to himself.

'As to Nicholson,' writes John Lawrence to Edwardes in the following January, 'I will never help him to leave the Punjâb, though I will never oppose his going. I feel very sore about him. You might as well run rusty as he should. By-the-by, he shot a man the other day who went at him with a drawn sword [1].'

The incident thus casually mentioned had been reported quite as briefly and in much the same words by the laconic

[1] Bosworth Smith.

Nicholson to his chief. To Edwardes, however, he wrote far more circumstantially on January 21, 1856, two days after his narrow escape from assassination. 'I was standing at the gate of my garden at noon, with Sladen and Cadell, and four or five chuprassies [1], when a man with a sword drawn rushed suddenly up and called out for me. I had on a long fur pelisse of native make, which I fancy prevented his recognizing me at first. This gave time for the only chuprassie who had a sword to get between us, to whom he called out contemptuously to stand aside, saying he had come to kill me, and did not want to hurt a common soldier. The relief sentry for the one in front happening to pass opportunely behind me at this time, I snatched his musket, and presenting it at the would-be assassin, told him I would fire if he did not put down his sword and surrender. He replied that either he or I must die. So I had no alternative, and shot him through the heart, the ball passing through a religious book which he had tied on his chest, apparently as a charm. The poor wretch turns out to be a Marwati who has been religiously mad for some time. He disposed of all his property in charity the day before he set out for Bannu. I am sorry to say that his spiritual instructor has disappeared mysteriously, and I am afraid got into the hills. I believe I owe my safety to the fur *chogah* [2], for I should have been helpless had he rushed straight on.'

The chuprassie's answer to his cry for Nicholson's blood was, 'All our names are Nikalsain here.' The faithful fellow might have got the better of such an opponent; but, says Nicholson, 'I should not have been justified in allow-

---

[1] Native orderlies, with brass badges on their breasts.

[2] The Afghan equivalent for our modern 'ulster.'

ing the man to risk his life, when I had such a sure weapon
as a loaded musket and bayonet in my hand. I am sorry
for this occurrence; but it was quite an exceptional one,
and has not altered my opinion of the settled peaceful
state of this portion of the district.' On this point, indeed,
the facts were all in his favour. 'Making out the criminal
returns for 1855 the other day, I found that we had not had
a single murder or highway robbery, or attempt at either,
in Bannu throughout the year. The crime has all gone
down to the southern end of the district [Dera Ismail
Khan], where I am not allowed to interfere[1].' Such
a veto on the powers of so capable a district officer will
account for much of that friction between Nicholson and
John Lawrence, to which Lady Edwardes and Mr. Bosworth
Smith alike refer in their respective biographies.

It was about this time that Edwardes wrote for Mr. Charles
Raikes, the Commissioner of Jalandhar, that racy character-
sketch of John Nicholson, some part of which may be aptly
quoted here.

'Of what class is John Nicholson the type? Of none;
for truly he stands alone. But he belongs essentially to
the school of Henry Lawrence. I only knocked down the
walls of the Bannu *forts*, John Nicholson has since reduced
the *people*—the most ignorant, depraved, and blood-thirsty
in the Punjàb—to such a state of good order and respect
for the laws that, in the last year of his charge, not only
was there no murder, burglary, or highway robbery, but
not even an *attempt* at any of those crimes. The Bannuchis, reflecting on their own metamorphosis, in the
village gatherings under the vines, by the streams they
once delighted to fight for, have come to the conclusion

[1] Kaye.

that the good Muhammadans of historic ages must have been like *Nikalsain*. They emphatically approve him as every inch a hâkim (master or lord). And so he is. It is difficult to describe him. He must be seen. Lord Dalhousie—no mean judge—perhaps best summed up his high military and administrative qualities when he called him "a tower of strength." I can only say that I think him equally fit to be commissioner of a division or general of an army[1].'

By this time Nicholson had quite lost the boyish look of the daguerreotype taken in 1851. 'As he grew older,' writes Sir Neville Chamberlain, 'his features became more marked in character, and a very dark brown beard and moustache, almost approaching to black, added to his manly appearance. He always held his head high in the air, and carried it as if he could not see the ground before him. His step was vigorous and firm ; and any one seeing him could not fail to notice the man.' His pale, stern face now seldomer relaxed into a smile, except when he strolled among the village children, or exchanged intimate talk with such friends as Colonel and Mrs. Edwardes. 'Strong and masterful as he was,' writes General Younghusband, who did good service under him in those years, 'at the same time he was one of the most modest men, in regard to his own personal merits, that I ever knew.' For instance, with regard to the command of the frontier force, 'Nicholson told me that when he heard of Chamberlain's being in the field for it, he immediately wrote to say he would never think of putting himself into competition with Chamberlain.'

'In course of conversation,' adds the same officer, 'he

---

[1] Raikes, *Notes on the Revolt in the North-Western Provinces of India.*

said, " There is one thing in life I have failed in, and which
I wished to attain ; that is, to be popular with my brother-
officers.   I know I am not."   That he was not popular in
the ordinary use of the word, is quite true ; but there was
no dislike.   He was graver than most of us, with a stern,
rather haughty air when transacting business, but no sign
of arrogance.'

Some of his methods of transacting business were none
the less effective for their bold defiance of set rules.   'Not
long after he came to Bannu,' says General Younghusband,
'he met a jirga[1] of petty native chiefs from beyond the
border.   They had been so accustomed to rather a weak
rule on the frontier that their insolence in speech and
behaviour was very marked.   Nicholson listened to what
they had to say.   At last one of them hawked and spat
out between himself and Nicholson.   This was a dire
insult, and meant as such. " Orderly !" said John Nicholson,
" make that man lick up his spittle, and kick him out of
camp."   The orderly seized him by the back of his neck,
ground him down, and held him there until the deed was
done.   This lesson in politeness had a most marked effect,
and, curiously enough, was thoroughly appreciated by the
trans-border men themselves, the hero being unmercifully
quizzed for his share in the transaction.'

One day, after Nicholson had thoroughly established
himself, Younghusband was speaking about him to a trans-
border chief. 'Nikalsain !' he exclaimed ; 'he *is* a man.
There is not one in the hills who does not shiver in his
pyjamas when he hears his name mentioned.'   Some
twelve years after his death, Younghusband was in the
Shahpur district, south of Rawal Pindi, talking to a towâna,

---

[1] A council or deputation.

or chief, about John Nicholson's doings in that district during the second Sikh war. He said, 'To this day our women at night wake trembling, and saying they hear the tramp of Nikalsain's war-horse.'

Nicholson never brooked the faintest show of insolence towards an officer of the ruling race. The same kind of grim humour which marked his requital of insults offered by a rude hill-chief comes out in his mode of punishing an insolent Muhammadan mullah. He was riding one day through a Bannuchi village with his escort of mounted police and a few of the local maliks. As he passed along every villager saluted him except one, a mullah, or Musalman priest, who sat in front of the village mosque. Instead of salaaming he sat on, looking at the hákim with a scowl of open hatred. As soon as the cavalcade had passed out of the village, Nicholson asked one of his orderlies if he had noticed the mullah's behaviour. Yes, he had noticed it. 'Then go and bring him to my camp.' The village barber was sent for at the same time. When the mullah appeared, his replies to Nicholson's queries were tantamount to a confession of guilt. Whereupon Nicholson ordered the barber to shave off the man's beard—the direst ignominy known to a true Muhammadan. He was then allowed to return to his village, where the sight of a beardless mullah made a lasting impression, and became the talk of the whole district [1].

Racily humorous also, and substantially true, is a story which Mr. S. Thorburn heard told by the greybeards of a Bannuchi village. 'In the old Sikh days one Alladàd Khan, who was guardian of his orphan nephew, seized the child's inheritance for himself, and turned the boy out of

[1] Letter from Colonel H. B. Urmston.

the village. Arrived at man's estate, the youth sued his uncle in Nicholson's court; but Alladâd Khan was the strongest man in the village, so no one dared for his life give evidence against him. Whilst the case was pending, one of the villagers, when walking to his fields at dawn of day, was spell-bound at seeing Nicholson's well-known white mare quietly nibbling the grass just outside the village entrance. When he had got over his fright, he ran back and communicated the news to Alladâd Khan and others.'

Ere long the whole village turned out to gaze at the awe-inspiring mare. At length Alladâd Khan advised them to drive her on to the lands of some other village, else 'they would certainly be whipped or fined all round. They began doing so, but had not gone very far when they saw Nicholson tied to a tree. After the first start of surprise and inclination to run away *en masse*, some of the bolder spirits advanced with officious hands to release their dreaded hâkim.' But John Nicholson, bidding them stand back, inquired wrathfully on whose land he was standing. Every one pointed silently to Alladâd Khan, who came tremblingly forward and said, ' No, no! the land is not mine, but my nephew's.' Nicholson 'made him swear before all the villagers that he was telling the truth, and then permitted himself to be unbound. Next day the nephew was decreed his inheritance, and the whole village rejoiced that the wronged boy had come to his own again. But the wicked uncle, cursing his own cowardly tongue, and his stupidity in not suspecting the ruse, went off on a pilgrimage to Mecca, as he found home too hot for him [1].'

[1] Thorburn, *Bannu.*

' I need say little of Nicholson's personal characteristics, which are well known,' writes Sir Richard Pollock. ' He was gifted with a powerful physique, a commanding figure and manner, and at once impressed those who had to deal with him as a man of indomitable energy, a very terror to evildoers. His mind was concentrated on the particular matter in hand, and his sense of duty and devotion to his work never relaxed. Edwardes found Bannu a valley of forts, and left it a valley of open villages. Nicholson found it a hell upon earth, and left it probably as wicked as ever, but curbed to fear of punishment.'

' His powers of investigation were great, and his methods severe, and people who wanted to kill an obnoxious cousin learnt that they could only do so by running a very considerable chance of being hanged. Nothing seemed to tire him ; a ride of twenty or thirty miles before breakfast, to visit a boundary or scene of a crime, in no way interfered with his working on in court through a long summer day with the thermometer over 90.'

' Though very prompt when quick action was required, he could be very patient when patience was needed ; his judgement was excellent, and his knowledge of character great, and he could bear with fools and even criminals when they were useful to him. His saying used to be, " Never remove a native official unless you know that you can replace him by a better one, otherwise you will get an equally stupid or corrupt man, minus the experience of his predecessor." '

' His wonderful activity and endurance made a great impression on the border people. Edwardes has recorded what a Peshâwari said of him, that " you could hear the ring of his horse's hoofs from Attock to the Khaibar." '

'If he knew when it was good to be severe in aid of the repression of crime, he also knew when to pass over an offence lightly.'

'One characteristic should not be overlooked—his generosity. Caring nothing for ostentation and little for money, he spent a great deal on others and very little on himself. In official matters he was wisely liberal in rewards, and would on fit occasion let a man put his hand into a bag of rupees and take all he could grasp.'

'In society Nicholson was hardly ever seen at his best. Naturally shy and reticent, he found it difficult to converse freely in a mixed company, especially if there was a single person present whom he disliked or mistrusted. With those he really liked he would unbend; with Henry Lawrence he was at his best, and doubtless with the Edwardeses, but I had no opportunity of judging. He had a great liking for Sir Harry Lumsden, who passed away last year He was also greatly attached to Arthur Cocks, as to whom he made the quaint remark to me that " he was the only man about whom he felt, that if Cocks were to kick him, he could hardly feel angry!" He had a great sense of humour, and I can remember his enjoyment of Leech's masterpieces. I am sure that he had more religion than he was commonly given credit for, and, with a horror of cant, a very great respect for the scruples and opinions of people whom he had learned to esteem. I have heard him speak rather bitterly of the enforced strictness of his ante-school days, mentioning the dislike it gave him to the Sunday observances of those days[1].'

We have seen how fiercely John Nicholson resented all plundering of the people by an army in the field. General

---

[1] MS. Notes by General Sir F. R. Pollock.

Younghusband relates a typical instance of his frequent onslaughts on the peaceful plundering which many of his countrymen passed by as a matter of time-honoured use and wont. The incident happened early in 1854, during the chief commissioner's progress along the Trans-Indus frontier. Captain Younghusband commanded the body of frontier police which formed his escort. ' I was walking,' he says, ' with John Lawrence, when Nicholson came striding along with his head well in the air, as it always was when he was very angry. Behind him came his orderly, leading a gold-laced, scarlet-coated jemadar of chuprassies. " Lawrence," said Nicholson, " this infernal scoundrel has been taking *dastúri* (percentage on goods sold) for the supplies brought into this camp. I am going to flog him. You have no objection, have you ? " '

The jemadar was flogged accordingly, for all his fine feathers and his official rank ; and the people of that district knew that the white chief who ruled them with a rod of iron was sure to protect them from the greed and tyranny of their own countrymen.

CHAPTER XVI

On Christmas Day of 1855 a brilliant company of soldiers and civilians with a few ladies came together in the Peshâwar Residency to enjoy the good Christmas cheer provided by Colonel and Mrs. Edwardes. John Nicholson was there of course; and there too were the fiery Major John Coke from Kohat, and the kindly Major John Becher from Hazâra; the quiet, keen-eyed Robert Montgomery from Lahore, who would one day succeed John Lawrence in the government of the province he helped to save; Captain Hugh James, the active deputy commissioner at Peshâwar; and Major George Jacob, who was ere long to die the soldier's death at the head of his Bengal Fusiliers. 'Little could any of us have guessed,' writes Colonel Urmston, who was also present as one of Edwardes's assistants, 'that within two years from that bright and happy gathering such a storm as the Mutiny would have swept over India, and that two of our fellow-guests, Nicholson and Jacob, would be numbered with the dead.'

'Nicholson's handsome face and commanding figure,' continues Colonel Urmston, 'made an impression upon my mind, and doubtless upon others who had not met him before, which could never be effaced. No pictures that I have ever seen do him justice. His face was full of power, and no one could look on him without feeling that he was a man of mark, and no ordinary character. . . . The monument at the Margalla Pass, and the fountain for thirsty travellers, raised to his memory after his death, attest his heroic deeds during the second Sikh war. Every traveller to and from Peshâwar passes through the defile, or now looks at it from the railway carriage, and none can do so without recalling the noble exploits of this gallant soldier.'

'He spent only a few days, if I remember rightly, with his dear friends, the Edwardeses, that Christmas, and then returned to his work at Bannu, which, being a frontier district, and much exposed to hostile tribes, could not long be left without its chief civil officer. Shortly afterwards it was rumoured that he was about to succeed Captain James as deputy commissioner of Peshâwar, who was required to officiate for Mr. Richard Temple, then secretary to the chief commissioner. I can remember the interest, not to say excitement, which the report caused in the minds of the natives; for Nicholson's stern character and vigorous action had already become known amongst the better-informed classes and the officials of the courts, while those of the baser sort—the "badmâshes"—feared him greatly, and justly dreaded his rule.'

Nicholson reappeared at Peshâwar in the spring of 1856, 'not, however, as deputy commissioner,' says Colonel Urmston, 'but *en route* to Kashmir, where he had been appointed by the Government as "officer on special duty." He was our guest for a few days, owing, I think, to the absence of the Edwardeses at Abbottabad: and we felt it a great pleasure to receive him and give him a most hearty welcome. One of his first acts of kindness was to give our children a splendid magic lantern and slides, which I took to England two years later, and kept for many years, till the young people became too old for such an amusement.'

Nicholson had also brought with him the band of a police battalion, which he commanded in addition to his civil duties. This band he purposed taking on for the summer to Kashmir, for the entertainment of the English visitors to that country. 'During his stay with us,' says Colonel Urmston, ' the band played every evening in our garden, and gave much enjoyment both to natives and Europeans. It was thus I became more intimate with the distinguished soldier-civilian, and learned to regard him with deep respect.'

The same informant relates one of those incidents which illustrate the gentler side of Nicholson's character. ' Sitting one day at our dinner-table, opposite to our little girl, he fixed his gaze upon her, and watched her for some moments, quite unconscious of what effect it would produce. She suddenly burst into a flood of tears, and being rather a nervous child, cried most bitterly and could not be pacified. Feeling that he had been the unintentional cause of her paroxysm of grief and fear, and all parental efforts having failed to soothe her, he came round the table, sat himself in her high chair with the child in his arms, and soon quieted her. Smiles came to her face at once, as she found the tall, handsome man sitting in her own chair ; and from that moment till he left our house, no shadow of fear crossed her brow. The effect of his action was magical upon the little tender heart which could

not withstand the piercing look of his dark and lustrous
eyes when fastened upon her face [1].'

Between that Christmas gathering at Peshâwar in 1855
and the visit to Captain Urmston in the spring of 1856,
John Nicholson had again 'run rusty' with his long-
suffering chief, who went down to Calcutta in February
to exchange a sad farewell with the great marquis, whose
eight years of strong and beneficent rule had just been
crowned by the decree annexing Oudh to the dominions
of the East India Company, and in whose frail body the
seeds of an early death were already sown.

John Lawrence had at last consented to ask Lord Canning, the new Governor-General, to transfer his troublesome
lieutenant from Bannu to Bhurtpore. Happily for Upper
India this was not to be. Temple's departure homewards
cleared the way for a compromise which satisfied the lieutenant without displeasing the chief. Captain Hugh James
took Temple's place with Sir John Lawrence, who had
just been made a K.C.B.; while Nicholson was appointed
Deputy Commissioner of Peshâwar. During the six
months of his absence on special duty in the Happy
Valley, Captain Urmston had temporary charge of the
Peshâwar district.

For Nicholson himself such an arrangement left little
to desire. After four years of strenuous work in a wild
border district, peopled mainly by ruffians of every shade,
he had fairly earned the sort of holiday which his temporary mission to Kashmir betokened. He felt that
Bannu could now get on without him, while the change
from a very trying climate to the cool breezes of the
glorious Himalayan valley, which he knew so well, would

[1] Colonel Urmston's *MS. Recollections.*

brace him up for the work which lay before him in Peshàwar. Nor was he going to Kashmir on six months' leave, like those of his countrymen who resorted thither in yearly increasing numbers since the annexation of the Punjàb. The Government had at length resolved to depute yearly a special officer empowered to deal with the disputes which often arose between the Maharajah's subjects and the European or native visitors from India. His term of duty was limited to the six months during which European visitors were allowed to stay in the valley. On this errand John Nicholson was the first to go.

How efficiently he discharged it, the officer who next year succeeded him in the same post shall tell us. 'Many young officers,' writes Colonel Urmston, 'found their way every year to this beautiful country; some for sport, of which there was abundance in those days, both of large game and small; others for mere pleasure and amusement. Amongst the latter there were some few who, being themselves free from the influence of English society and all military control, indulged in larking, often of a most immoral kind. Nicholson's high moral tone and innate purity revolted against such conduct. Ordinary larking by high-spirited youngsters would never have called forth his reprehension; but when English ladies were scandalized by the scenes on the river and in the gardens and orchards about Srinagar, in which foolish young officers and the native women of the town played the chief part, he felt that the good name of his countrymen was at stake, and that these things must be put down. To report the conduct of these offenders to their commanding officers was one mode of punishing them, but prompt and vigorous action would be more to the purpose. From the Punjâb Government he obtained authority for dealing with gross cases in a more summary fashion. He was empowered to order such offenders at once out of the valley. By the exercise of this authority in a few cases he dealt a successful blow at these flagrant breaches of good manners and public decency.'

Nicholson had also received the full powers of a Court of Requests to try cases of debt between British subjects in Kashmir, over whom in criminal causes he possessed full magisterial authority. Before the summer season was over, the valley had become a more decent place of abode for English ladies. 'The result of all this,' says Colonel Urmston, ' was that in the following year, when I succeeded him on the same "special duty," and when many more ladies than usual were wending their way to Srinagar, I had no difficulty in dealing with one or two similar cases of gross misconduct, and I found the moral atmosphere much purified by his vigorous and timely action. Nicholson in truth was honoured and respected by all classes, except those whom he had to call to order and punish. His hospitality and generosity were proverbial in Kashmir [1].'

In May of this year, 1856, John Nicholson's younger sister, Lily Anna, was married to the Rev. John Seymour, afterwards Canon Seymour, then curate of Lisburn, and incumbent of St. Matthew's Church, Broomhedge, in Lisburn parish. Mrs. Seymour was tall and stately and fine looking, like her elder sister; equally clever and good-hearted; a charming talker; and an earnest Christian in deeds as well as words. Six years later, in August, 1862, she died, leaving a daughter, Clara, and a son, John Nicholson, to

[1] Colonel Urmston's *Recollections.*

the care of her bereaved husband. The son took high honours at Trinity College, Dublin, served for a few years as a surgeon in the Royal Navy, and is now doing good educational work in Japan.

Meanwhile our John Nicholson had been watching from Srinagar the course of events which resulted in war with Persia later in the year. Writing to Herbert Edwardes in July, 1856, with reference to the Persian advance on Herât, he doubts whether the Government is duly alive to the importance of preserving that city from Persian rule. 'We were madly anxious on that subject some years ago, but I fear we have now got into the opposite extreme; and that, because we burnt our fingers in our last uncalled-for expedition into Afghanistan, we shall in future remain inactive, even though active interference should become a duty and a political necessity. The Russians talk much about the exercise of their " legitimate influence " in Central Asia. When we cease to exercise any influence in a country so near our own border (and which has been correctly enough called the gate of Afghanistan) as Herât, I shall believe that the beginning of the cessation of our power in the East has arrived. And if our rulers only knew it, how easy the thing is! We don't require a large army, which in those countries it is always difficult to feed and protect the baggage of. Five thousand picked men, with picked officers, and armed with the best description of weapon (such as the revolving rifle, with which the Yankees over-threw the Mexicans), would roll the Persians like a carpet back from Herât, and do more for the maintenance of our influence and reputation than a year's revenue of India spent upon treaties and subsidies. We have a right to infer from the experience of the past that a select body of troops, however small, could achieve *anything* in Central Asia. . . . I fear, however, that while our people will bear in mind the disasters occasioned by incompetence without a parallel, they will ignore the lessons taught by the successful advance of Pollock and Nott in the face of the whole Afghan nation through as difficult a country as any in the world, and with no loss to speak of, though our infantry in those days had neither percussion-locks nor rifles [1].'

If the Government intended to make Persia withdraw from Herât, Nicholson would ' be glad to go in any capacity under a competent leader.' Go, however, he did not, although war with Persia was proclaimed on November 1, and a competent leader for the troops assembling in Bombay was found in Sir James Outram, who was hurrying back from sick leave in England to win fresh laurels on the banks of the Euphrates.

Before the 'Indian Bayard' reached Bombay, John Nicholson had taken up his new duties under Herbert Edwardes at Peshâwar. ' The two friends,' says Lady Edwardes, ' rejoiced exceedingly at being once more together. Little did they then know the full importance and value of the move they had so long struggled to accomplish, for they could foresee nothing of the terrible times that were so near, in which their united strength would be of such value [2].' On November 6 Nicholson had crossed the Indus at Torbela on his way to Peshâwar. ' From this time,' says Colonel Urmston, ' I was brought into close and regular official correspondence with him, and found him, as I expected, a truly great master in the art of ruling a frontier district. The very look of the man

____
[1] Kaye.   [2] *Life of Sir H. Edwardes.*

seemed to inspire confidence in him, and I could well understand how the old Sikhs described in Charles Raikes's *Revolt in the North-West Provinces*, when showing visitors over the battlefield of Gujarât, began their narrative by saying, " Nikalsain stood just *there!*" '

The same informant goes on to tell how one day in the court-room of Nicholson's cutcherry at Peshâwar he found some of the Nikalsaini fakirs, who had come from Hazâra, intending to worship him as before. Once more, forgetful of past rebuffs, the devotees fell down at Nicholson's feet; and once more he ' sternly resented their acts of adoration, ordered one or two of their leaders to be whipped by the court sheriff's men, and sent them back to their homes with a solemn warning never to molest him again. That they did not do so is due, not to their obedience to his wishes, but to the fact that within a few months of this time he left the Punjâb for the seat of war at Delhi, never, alas! to return [1].'

The capture of Herât by a Persian army in October turned men's thoughts in India to the expediency of making common cause with the Amir of Kâbul against a common foe. At Herbert Edwardes's earnest recommendation the treaty of March, 1855, was now followed up by fresh negotiations for the closer alliance which Dost Muhammad himself desired. On January 1, 1857, in the British camp at Jamrud was held the first of those conferences between the stout old Amir and Sir John Lawrence, which issued some weeks later in a second treaty fraught in that same year with the happiest consequences to our Indian rule. ' I have made an alliance with the British Government,' said Dost Muhammad, when he had signed

[1] Colonel Urmston's *Recollections*.

the new compact, ' and, happen what may, I will keep it faithfully till death.' And Edwardes, who was standing by, to whose agency the result was mainly owing, knew how loyally he would keep his word.

But where was John Nicholson, who ought to have been present on this occasion ? Instead of attending the chief commissioner's darbar, he wrote Sir J. Lawrence a request to be excused from such attendance, or from having anything to do with those Afghan visitors. Having thus relieved his mind, he went off into camp at the furthest end of his district, towards Yusafzai. Colonel Urmston, who was then on duty in the camp of Sir John Lawrence, finds ample reason for his friend's waywardness in his ' intense feeling of hatred for the Afghan nation,' a feeling of which he made no secret, a feeling which brooked no kind of intercourse with the countrymen of Muhammad Akbar. How much he himself had suffered at their hands, the readers of this book have seen already. But his bitterness against the Afghans undoubtedly sprang from a worthier source than mere resentment of wrongs inflicted on himself or others. We have seen how, in a letter to Edwardes, he spoke of the Afghans as utterly false, treacherous, and faithless even among themselves ; and his inborn truthfulness of word and deed revolted from all intercourse with a nation incapable in his eyes of telling the truth, or of keeping the most sacred promise. Happily for British India, Nicholson's indictment of a whole nation was not to be sustained in the case of its masterful and enlightened ruler. It was Herbert Edwardes who proved the truer prophet.

Meanwhile, at Nicholson's request, Captain Urmston had undertaken to attend upon his chief, and to make all due arrangements for the great meeting of New Year's Day,

1857, in the camp by Hari Singh's Tower. A brigade of troops under the brave old Sydney Cotton was also encamped near at hand, to furnish the guard and escort for the chief commissioner and his Afghan guests.

' John Nicholson,' says Colonel Urmston, ' breathed more freely, and returned to Peshâwar as soon as the camp broke up, and the Afghans had cleared out of the district. He used to say that he " could not trust himself if he met them, and might even be tempted to shoot one." Hence his absence during the whole of January, with some forty or fifty miles between him and them.'

Early in the following month Nicholson officiated as commissioner in the Peshawâr division in the room of Herbert Edwardes, who had obtained three months' leave of absence, that he might accompany his ailing wife as far as Calcutta on her way home. Captain Urmston ' had the good fortune to act as deputy commissioner, and thus learned more of John Nicholson's character and ability for ruling frontier tribes, ' an object-lesson which proved most useful to me when I became, in 1862, a *pucca* Deputy Commissioner of Bannu [1].'

On March 9 Nicholson wrote to a friend from the frontier post of Mardân, ' Old Coke [2] writes me that the Bannuchis, well tamed as they have been, speak kindly and gratefully of me. I would rather have heard this than got a present of £1,000, for there could be no stronger testimony of my having done my duty among them. I hear that, in an assembly the other day, it was allowed that I resembled a good Muhammadan of the kind told of in old books, but not to be met with nowadays. I wish with all

---

[1] Colonel Urmston's *Recollections.*
[2] Afterwards Sir John Coke, K.C.S.I.

my heart that it were more true, but I can't help a feeling of pride that a savage people whom I was obliged to deal with so sternly should appreciate and give me credit for good intentions[1].'

On March 20 he sent off a telegram to Edwardes at Calcutta, followed next day by a letter which emphasized and enlarged upon the few words flashed through the lightning-post.   Nicholson was 'very sorry indeed' to have been driven to the conclusion that it was better for him to leave the Punjàb at once, while he could do so quietly.   He was 'not ambitious, and would be glad to take any equivalent for a first-class deputy commissionership.' He would like to go to Oudh if Sir Henry Lawrence, the chief commissioner of that province, would like to have him.   'It would be a pleasure to me to try and assist him ; but if he would rather not bring in Punjàbis, do not press it on him.   What I should like best of all would be if we could get away together anywhere out of this[2].'

Herbert Edwardes lost no time in pleading his friend's cause before the new Governor-General.   He enlarged with earnest eloquence upon Nicholson's great qualities and just claims to any preferment which might be open to 'one of the very best district officers in the Punjàb, and one of the finest soldiers in the army.'   And he enforced his arguments on a not unkindly listener by some such words as these :—'If your lordship should ever have anything of real difficulty to be done in India, I give you my word that John Nicholson is the man to do it.'   To which Lord Canning replied, with a smile of approval, 'I will remember what you have said, and I will take you for Major Nicholson's godfather[3].'

---

[1] Kaye.   [2] Ibid.   [3] Lady Edwardes.

On this occasion it appears that Lord Canning would have appointed Nicholson to some command under Outram in the Persian Gulf, but for the fact that Outram's officers all belonged to the Bombay Presidency. Nicholson, in fact, was weary of civil duties which involved obedience to the orders of so masterful a ruler as John Lawrence, and gladly would he have exchanged his official trammels for the command of an irregular brigade either on 'this frontier' or at the seat of war. Meanwhile the time was very near when all his best efforts would be needed to save not only the Punjâb, but all Northern India from a foe far more dangerous than the Shah of Persia.

Five years later, in February, 1862, when Nicholson's name had become a glorious memory, and Lord Canning was about to retire from the scene of his hardest trials and noblest achievements, he received Edwardes once more at Government House. 'Do you remember, my lord,' asked Sir Herbert Edwardes, 'our last conversation about John Nicholson?' Lord Canning answered with much feeling, 'I remember it well[1].'

[1] Kaye.

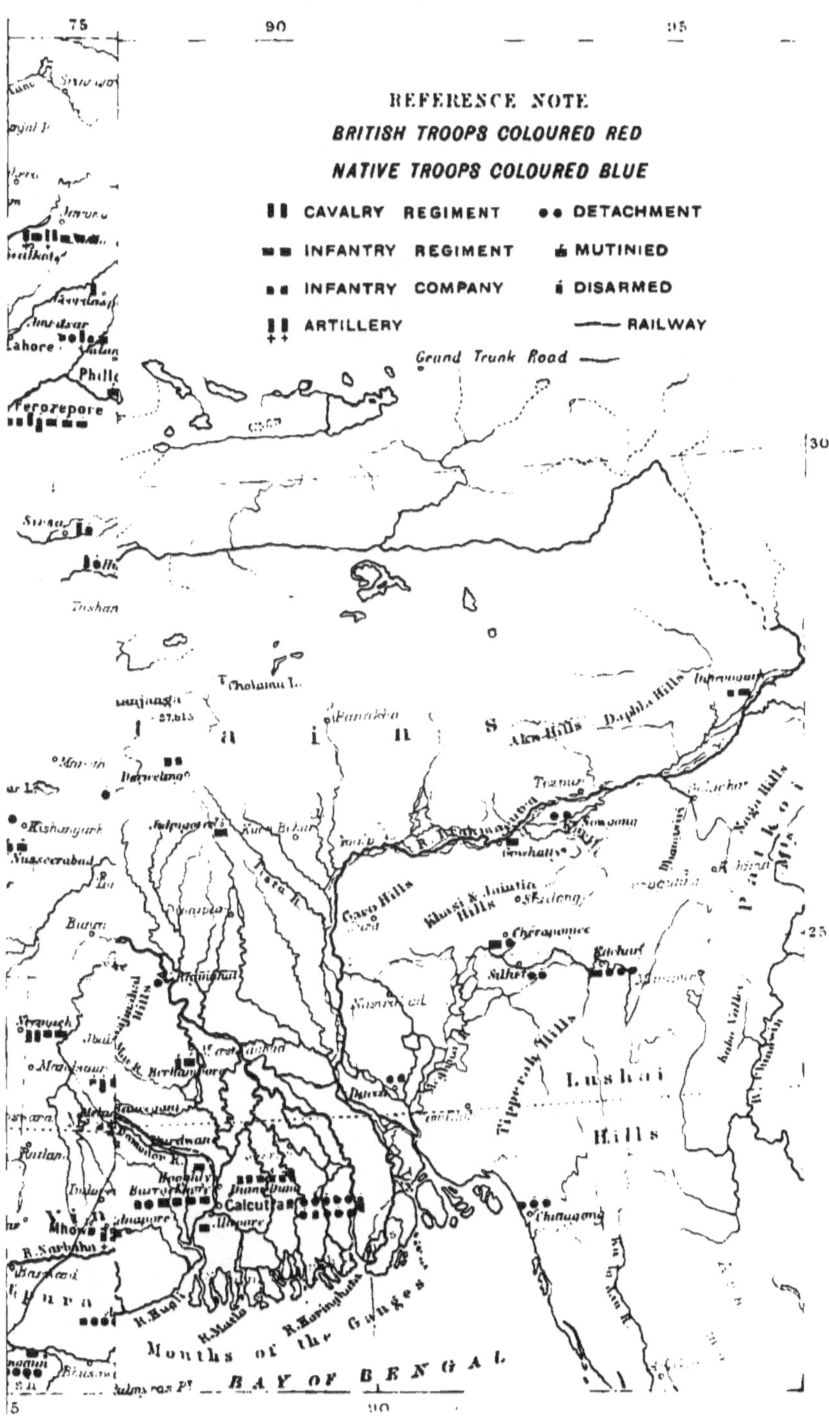
REFERENCE NOTE
BRITISH TROOPS COLOURED RED
NATIVE TROOPS COLOURED BLUE
CAVALRY REGIMENT
INFANTRY REGIMENT
INFANTRY COMPANY
ARTILLERY
DETACHMENT
MUTINIED
DISARMED
RAILWAY
Grand Trunk Road
Lahore
Phill
Ferozepore
Sirsa
Delhi
Tushan
Cholamu L.
27,815
Kishangurh
Nusseerabad
Assam
Aka Hills
Daphla Hills
Tezpur
Nowgong
Gowhatty
Garo Hills
Khasi & Jaintia Hills
Shillong
Cherrapunjee
Silhet
Kachar
Naga Hills
Patkoi Mts.
Julpigoree
Kuch Behar
Tista R.
Berhampore
Hooghly
Burdwan
Calcutta
Mhow
R. Soobun
Chittagong
Tipperah Hills
Lushai
Hills
Months of the Ganges
R. Hugli
R. Matla
R. Haringhata
BAY OF BENGAL

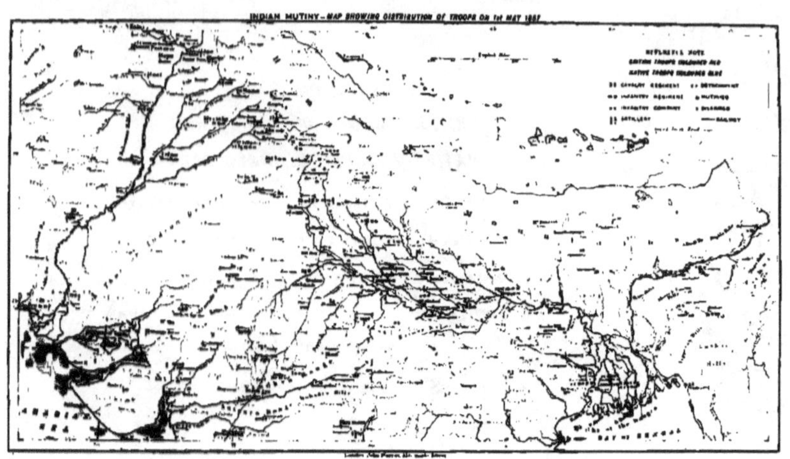

INDIAN MUTINY — MAP SHOWING DISTRIBUTION OF TROOPS ON 1st MAY 1857
REFERENCE NOTE
BRITISH TROOPS COLOURED RED
NATIVE TROOPS COLOURED BLUE
CAVALRY REGIMENT
DETACHMENT
INFANTRY REGIMENT
MUTINIED
INFANTRY COMPANY
DISARMED
ARTILLERY
RAILWAY

CHAPTER XVII

THE CRISIS IN PESHÂWAR, MAY, 1857

ON May 5, 1857, Edwardes found himself again at Peshâwar, and received a smiling welcome from the friend who had been acting for him during his absence. 'Nicholson is looking much better than when we left him,' Edwardes wrote to his wife. 'He has been in camp, moving round the district, and this has done him good. Nicholson's society in the house is a great comfort to me.' Edwardes had much to tell his friend about mutinous outbreaks in more than one station of Bengal, about his interview with Lord Canning, the parting from his wife, and the few happy days he had spent with Sir Henry Lawrence at Lucknow, whose look was much graver than of yore, and whose good grey head was already turning white, while in his newly-awakened zeal for work he seemed 'like a war-horse, ever ready for the battle [1].'

For a clear and befitting retrospect of the work which John Nicholson had been doing in Peshâwar during the past six months, I may quote the following passage from Herbert Edwardes's Administration Report for 1857 :—

'I cannot close this year's Report without a tribute to

[1] Lady Edwardes.

Colonel John Nicholson. Had he been spared he would very shortly have brought the Peshàwar district, as he had before brought Bannu, to the minimum of crime and its every official to the maximum of exertion. Even in one half-year (as Captain James has honourably pointed out) he made an impression not easily to be effaced. It is generally supposed that he was a severe ruler. In some senses he was. A criminal had no chance of long escaping him; for his police investigation was the most extensive, painstaking, able, and determined I ever saw. And an incorrigible official had no chance of ultimate impunity; for to stop corruption and do justice was his vocation: but I have never known any judicial officer so deliberate in his punishments. He warned repeatedly before he struck. He gave the worst offenders an opportunity of turning over a new leaf, and was generous in overlooking the past when a man set himself to recover his character. Malpractices in the courts disappeared before him, but it was seldom an official lost his place. The very first day he entered the district he suspended a thanadar[1] whom he caught in an act of oppression, and he committed a tahsildar[2] to the sessions; but I do not remember that any other examples were necessary, and both cases were forced on him by the people. In business he was most laborious, he worked from morning till night—he went everywhere and judged for himself. He was often at the scenes of crime or dispute, realizing the rights of cases, and hearing the people as well as the police. He was rapid in settling trials in his own court, and prompt in hearing appeals;

---

[1] *Thanadar*, head constable.
[2] *Tahsildar*, native collector of revenue.

he used the lash freely to vagabonds and petty ruffians instead of loading the jails and hardening men in crime. The tahsildars, the police, the whole executive machinery, was alive under his supervision, and each man felt that there was a master-hand upon the district. The people and the neighbouring mountain tribes all felt it too. As a native well expressed his influence, "The sound of his horse's hoofs was heard from the Attock to the Khaibar." '

I mention these points not in eulogy, but for the right understanding of the great colleague we have lost. It is no disparagement to those who survive that such an administrator leaves no equal. Nature makes but few such men, and the Punjáb is happy in having had one.'

To this tribute of sorrowing friendship Mr. Edward Thornton, Judicial Commissioner of the Punjáb, appended the following comment :—' To the strict accuracy of the foregoing delineation I can bear personal testimony, having been in official connexion with Colonel Nicholson in 1849, when he was Deputy Commissioner of Rawal Pindi. His sterner qualities and his high sense of duty are generally known, not so, perhaps, the remarkable deliberation which preceded his infliction of punishment : his justice as well as his vigour have taken deep hold of the minds of the Sind-Ságar population, and he remains fresh in their memories, though eight years have passed since his official connexion with them has entirely ceased.'

But the shadows of a dread catastrophe were already sweeping over the parched plains between the Ganges and the Satlaj. On the night of May 11, 1857, within a week of his return to Pesháwar, Edwardes received the telegram which told him that the mutineers from Meerut had come over to Delhi, burnt the bungalows there, and 'killed several Europeans.' This was 'serious news' indeed; and next morning came a telegram which had been dispatched from Meerut at midnight on the 10th. 'Native troops in open mutiny; cantonments south of the Mall burnt; several European officers killed. European troops under arms defending barracks. Electric telegraph wire cut.'·

Edwardes saw at once the true meaning of these two messages from the old imperial city on the Jamna and the wide military cantonment which lay only forty miles east of Delhi. 'We must expect the mutiny to spread to every station,' he wrote to his wife, 'if not put down with the bayonet at some one cantonment. If it comes here, we shall, please God, make short work of the mutineers; for we have three European regiments in the valley, and all the artillery is European.' What he and Nicholson must have thought of the sad paralysis which had seized our military leaders at Meerut, may be inferred from the foregoing passage in Lady Edwardes's book. When the news of a murderous outbreak at Meerut first reached the hill-stations on the road to Simla, it seemed to many of us incredible that such things could have been allowed to happen in a cantonment guarded by two strong European regiments and several batteries of artillery.

At the frontier station by the Khaibar such things were not likely to happen under such leaders as Herbert Edwardes, John Nicholson, and the stout-hearted veteran Sydney Cotton, who commanded the Peshàwar Brigade. To these three was quickly added the like-minded Brigadier Neville Chamberlain, who rode over from Kohat in prompt answer to Edwardes's call for help. Nicholson's first thought in so grave a crisis was the imperious need of forming a movable column of picked troops, which should march about the Punjâb to overawe the disaffected and strike swift and hard at open mutineers. His next thought was to raise a strong levy of Multâni horse from the Derajât. Both these proposals were heartily seconded by Edwardes, who hastened in company with his friend to lay them before ' our fine old brigadier.' Sydney Cotton approving, they proceeded to impress their views upon Major-General Reed, commanding the Peshâwar division. That officer at once consented to organize a movable column, and issued for that end the order which summoned the trusty Guide Corps to Naushéra, in the room of the doubtful 55th Sepoys, who were to take their place on the frontier at Fort Mardân.

One of the Sepoy regiments at Peshâwar, the 64th, had more than once in the past twelve years displayed a mutinous spirit. Nicholson arranged with Brigadier Cotton for their swift removal from cantonments where they lay nearest the guns to the forts on the Mohmand frontier, as if to repel a threatened attack from that quarter. Edwardes himself, as the chief civil officer, kept up a brisk correspondence by telegraph and letter with the chief commissioner at Rawal Pindi. ' There is no time to be lost,' was the burden of all his messages. ' What you do about the movable force,' he writes on May 12, ' do *at once*. There is no time to be lost in getting to the struggle which is to settle the matter. . . . If you wish for the Multânis, let us know by telegraph.' In the same letter he urged the need of ' bringing the matter without further delay *to the bayonet*. This disaffection will never be talked down now. It must be put down [1].'

Edwardes spoke as much for John Nicholson as for

---

[1] Lady Edwardes.

himself. The two men were of one mind on the best way of encountering the storm, whose wide-wasting fury they had been quick to foregather from the first hurried messages that reached Peshàwar. Nicholson had offered through his friend to command the proposed levy of Multàni warriors; and Edwardes, speaking for both, had placed their services at the disposal of their toil-worn chief, whose journey to the Marri Hills had been cut short at Rawal Pindi by the dismal tidings flashed on from Lahore.

'Depend upon it, there will be plenty of work, and you cannot act too promptly,' Edwardes had written to his chief on May 12. On the forenoon of the 13th, Cotton, Chamberlain, Edwardes, and Nicholson met together in a council of war convened by its president, General Reed, to decide on the first steps to be taken for ensuring the safety of the Punjàb. Edwardes himself had just received a telegram from Sir John Lawrence, which told how, early on that same morning, the Sepoy regiments at Lahore had been quietly disarmed. Thanks to Robert Montgomery and Brigadier Corbett, prompt action wisely guided had saved the capital of the Punjàb. And for prompt action of the kind proposed by Nicholson and Edwardes the council at Peshàwar gave its unanimous vote. Its decisions were recorded by two staff-officers, one of whom was a young lieutenant of Bengal Artillery, now widely known and honoured as Lord Roberts of Kandahar, whose *Forty-one Years in India* has shown that he wields the pen as skilfully as the sword. During that momentous meeting young Roberts was 'greatly impressed by the calm view of the situation taken by Edwardes and Nicholson.'

It was little more than a fortnight, by the way, since Frederick Roberts had come to know and admire the

Deputy Commissioner of Peshâwar. He was out surveying in the hill-country at Cherât, with a view to ascertain the best site for a sanatorium greatly needed by English troops at Peshâwar. One day he found a camp pitched quite close to his own tent. It was that of Nicholson making a tour of inspection. 'Very soon I received an invitation to dine with him, at which I was greatly pleased. John Nicholson was a name to conjure with in the Punjâb. I had heard it mentioned with an amount of respect—indeed awe—which no other name could excite. I was all curiosity to see the man whose influence on the frontier was so great, that his word was law to the refractory tribes amongst whom he lived. . . . Nicholson impressed me more profoundly than any man I had ever met before, or have ever met since. I have never seen any one like him. He was the beau idéal of a soldier and a gentleman. His appearance was distinguished and commanding, with a sense of power about him which, to my mind, was the result of his having passed so much of his life among the lawless tribesmen with whom his authority was supreme. Intercourse with this man among men made me more eager than ever to remain on the frontier ; and I was seized with ambition to follow in his footsteps. Had I never seen Nicholson again, I might have thought that the feelings with which he inspired me were to some extent the result of my imagination, excited by the extraordinary stories I had heard of his power and influence ; my admiration, however, was immensely strengthened when, a few weeks later, I served as his staff-officer, and had opportunities of observing more closely his splendid military qualities, and the workings of his grand simple mind[1].'

[1] *Forty-one Years in India*, by Field Marshal Lord Roberts.

The council of war decided among other things that General Reed, as senior officer in the Punjáb, should act as commander-in-chief for that province, while Brigadier Cotton commanded all the garrisons beyond the Indus, and Chamberlain was selected to lead the movable column. That same evening the 39th, 55th, and 64th Native Infantry were marching towards the frontier, as if for active service, from their respective quarters at Jhilam, Naushéra, and Peshâwar. Next morning General Reed set off for Rawal Pindi, where he could take counsel with his civil colleague, and be trusted to issue no orders of which John Lawrence might disapprove. Thither also went Colonel Chamberlain to consult with Lawrence about the movable column which was soon to be assembled under his command at Wazirabad.

Edwardes himself had cheerfully seconded Reed's proposal that Nicholson should go with the column as civil and political officer. To his thinking, Nicholson's unrivalled knowledge of the country, his conversance with both regular and irregular armies, 'his rare talent for acquiring information in the field, and the general force and ability of his character,' all marked him out as 'the fittest officer he knew of for that duty.' But Sir John held that, for the present at least, John Nicholson could not be spared from Peshâwar; and even 'talked of going himself[1].'

'At Peshâwar all is quiet,' Edwardes wrote to his wife on May 16, 'and we have taken all reasonable precautions. . . . Nicholson is well, and deeply interested, as you may suppose, in all that is going on.' The Guides under Captain Daly had made 'surprising efforts,' and the whole of that fine corps would soon be massed at Rawal Pindi,

---

[1] Lady Edwardes.

ready to go wherever they might be needed. General Anson, the commander-in-chief, had gone down from Simla, to march against Delhi with the troops already mustering at Umballa. At Firozpur the rebellious 45th Native Infantry had been utterly routed, and the 57th Native Infantry had been disarmed by the 61st Foot. The Sepoy garrison of Attock was replaced by trustworthy Pathâns from Kohat. Edwardes and Nicholson are 'deeply anxious about dear Sir Henry Lawrence,' whose position in Oudh is 'the weakest in India.' They can get no news 'from those parts, but suppose the Delhi magazine to be in the hands of the mutineers;' and hope that General Anson 'has done in Upper India what we are doing in the Punjâb.' The supposition was better founded than the hope; for the heroic nine who held the magazine on that woful May 11 succeeded in blowing up only a portion of its contents, while circumstances fought at first against prompt action in the country between Umballa and Delhi.

On the same day Nicholson sends his mother a few lines viâ Agra, to say that he is quite well, and that the Punjâb is perfectly quiet. 'I hope this will find you enjoying yourself at some sea-bathing place. There have been disturbances among the native troops in the North West Provinces, but they have not extended to the Punjâb, and I trust are not likely to do so. Charles also is well. . . . Love to Lily [Mrs. Seymour], who I hope has got safely over her confinement.'

Meanwhile, as Edwardes had predicted, there was plenty of work for him and his colleagues to do in their own part of the Punjâb. Edwardes and Nicholson made daily raids upon the native correspondence that passed through the post-office; and the secrets thus revealed to them were not revealed in vain. Nicholson had brought off some twenty-four lakhs of treasure, £240,000, from the cantonments to the fort containing the magazine, and guarded thenceforth by white troops. At Nicholson's request Brigadier Cotton fixed his headquarters at the old Residency, which, as Edwardes declared, was 'centrical for all military orders, and close to the civil officers for mutual consultation.' As a strong two-storied building, very capable of defence, the Residency was to become the place of refuge for all our women and children, whenever an alarm occurred; and often was it crowded during the anxious months that followed[1].

It was not until May 15, when Edwardes was starting for Pindi, on a few days' visit to the chief commissioner, that he got permission to raise 1,000 Multâni Horse. Leaving Nicholson to issue the needful orders in their joint names, 'for the Khans in the Derajât were as much his friends as mine,' he went his way to Pindi, where he very soon persuaded his chief to sanction the raising of another 1,000 horsemen, and 2,000 foot.

To return for a moment to the memorable May 13. An hour or two after the council of war had broken up, Nicholson called on Captain Roberts, and told him that, somehow or another, the proceedings of the council had become known, and it was thought that he might have been guilty of divulging them. 'I was very angry,' says Lord Roberts, 'for I had appreciated as much as any one the immense importance of keeping the decisions arrived at strictly secret; and I could not help showing something of the indignation I felt at its having been thought probable that I could betray the confidence reposed in me.'

[1] Edwardes, *Official Narrative*; Lady Edwardes.

Roberts 'denied most positively' that he had done anything of the kind. At Nicholson's suggestion they went together to the telegraph office, to see 'whether the information could have leaked out from there.' The signaller was 'a mere boy, and Nicholson's imposing presence and austere manner were quite too much for him. He was completely cowed, and after a few hesitating denials he admitted having satisfied the curiosity of a friend who had inquired of him how the authorities intended to deal with the crisis. This was enough, and I was cleared. The result to me of this unpleasant incident was a delightful increase of intimacy with the man for whom, above all others, I had the greatest admiration and the most profound respect. As if to make up for his momentary injustice, Nicholson was kinder to me than ever, and I felt I had gained in him a firm and trustworthy friend [1].'

At Rawal Pindi Lawrence, Reed, Chamberlain, and Edwardes held much earnest colloquy, for 'matters were growing worse each day, and it was now clearly understood by us . . . that, whatever gave rise to the mutiny, it had settled down into a struggle for empire under Muhammadan guidance, with the Mughal capital for its centre. From that moment it was felt that at any cost Delhi must be regained [2].'

On May 19 Nicholson telegraphed to Pindi that the irregular cavalry at Mardân showed signs of disaffection. On the same day he imprisoned the Persian editor of a native newspaper for publishing false and incendiary reports of a murderous outbreak at one of the frontier posts. On this day also Mr. Wakefield brought before Nicholson a fakir, on whose person was found a purse

____

[1] Lord Roberts.   [2] Edwardes, *Narrative.*

full of bright new rupees, with a seditious letter hidden
under his armpit. Such evidence of criminal intent could
not be explained away. Fakirs do not abound in silver
money, nor did the treasonable paper show any marks
either of age, or of the snuff it was said to have enwrapt.
The allusions in the letter to a great Muhammadan festival
then near at hand, left no doubt in Nicholson's mind that
the letter was sent by Muhammadan conspirators in cantonments to their fellow-worshippers at the outposts, inviting
them, as Edwardes put it, ' to come in with a few English
officers' heads, and join in a rising on May 26[1].' The
fakir was duly tried and hanged. From the treason thus
discovered, and the intelligence brought by his spies,
Nicholson saw that the plot was thickening about Peshâwar.
He lost not an hour in trying to raise the levies which
Sir John Lawrence had so tardily ordered. But very few
of the chiefs in the Peshâwar valley responded to the call
for help in a cause which by that time seemed so desperate.
Most of them felt that our Râj was coming to an end,
when Delhi had passed into the hands of successful
mutineers, and a Sepoy revolt was growing fast into
a dangerous rebellion. One old Afghan chief who had
been our good friend for some years past, told Nicholson
that this was a crisis in which the sahibs must rely upon
themselves[2].

Things were looking ugly enough when Edwardes
returned to Peshâwar in the early morning of May 21.
He found Nicholson ' immersed in cares and anxieties . . .
the regiments talking big, and the natives of the district
wearing that consciousness of impending difficulty to their
European rulers, which is so sure a herald of a crisis. All

---

[1] Edwardes, *Narrative.*　　　　　　　[2] Lady Edwardes.

that day Nicholson and I were engaged in using our influence with small maliks in the district to raise men.' Recruits were sorely needed to meet the growing danger in cantonments, and Edwardes wrote off to Captain Henderson to send him all the men he could from Kohat.

That night Edwardes and Nicholson, who were living together, lay down to sleep in their clothes, convinced that something would happen to break their slumbers. At midnight they were aroused by news of a Sepoy mutiny at Naushéra, about thirty miles east of Peshâwar. In a moment the two friends were in close and anxious counsel over this new disaster. The rising at Naushéra was pretty sure to involve a similar outbreak at Mardán. To send a trustworthy force from Peshâwar against the mutineers would gravely imperil the safety of that important station, while the news from Naushéra would soon become known to the Sepoys at Peshâwar, who would hail it as the signal for their revolt. There was one thing only for brave men to do. The Sepoys at Peshâwar must be disarmed at the earliest possible moment.

What had happened at Naushéra was told in Edwardes's letter to his wife. The 27th Foot had been called away thence to join the movable column, and some companies of the 55th Native Infantry with the 10th Irregular Cavalry remained in charge of the station, and of all the women and children of their absent comrades. At the first signs of open mutiny, Alexander Taylor[1], a lieutenant of Bengal Engineers, 'like Horatius of old, cut away the bridge of boats [over the Kâbul river] and thus prevented the mutineers from being joined by the rest of the 55th Native

[1] Now Sir Alexander Taylor, K.C.B.

Infantry from the fort of Mardán, of which they were in charge during the absence of the Guide Corps.'

Edwardes and Nicholson went over to the brigadier's quarters, and urged him to disarm the greater part of his Sepoys. Their arguments soon convinced him that no other course was possible as things stood. When the commanding officers were all assembled before their brigadier, 'a most painful scene,' says Edwardes, 'ensued. The commandants of those regiments which were to be disarmed, unanimously and violently declared their implicit confidence in their men. One advised conciliation, and another threatened us that his men would resist and take the guns.'

Many an angry look and word were thrown at Nicholson and Edwardes by old colonels, each of whom honestly believed in the perfect loyalty of his own Sepoy 'children.' At last Sydney Cotton cut short all further remonstrance. 'No more discussion, gentlemen! These are my orders, and I must have them obeyed.' It was six in the morning when the council broke up. An hour later the troops were quietly forming up in front of their respective lines for the parade which their brigadier had ordered [1].

Three regiments of Sepoy infantry, including Nicholson's own, the 27th, and one of cavalry, were to undergo the sentence from which their loyal brethren of the 21st were declared exempt. Two Queen's regiments, the 70th and the 87th, with twelve guns ready loaded, were drawn up at either end of the cantonment, within sight of the paraded Sepoys, but not so near as to provoke resistance. Edwardes rode beside the brigadier-general, while Nicholson from the other end accompanied Brigadier Galloway. A troop of

[1] **Lady Edwardes.**

Multâni Horse, and a body of wild Afridi volunteers, just sent in by Henderson from Kohat, served as escort to the military commanders.

The doomed regiments, taken completely by surprise and unable to act in concert, obeyed, each in turn, the order to pile arms. 'It was a painful and affecting thing,' says Herbert Edwardes, ' to see them putting their own firelocks into the artillery waggons—weapons which they had used honourably for years. The officers of a cavalry regiment, a very fine set of fellows, threw in their own swords with those of their men, and even tore off their spurs. It was impossible not to feel for and with them; but duty must be done, and I know that we shall never regret the counsel that we gave[1].'

The effect of that morning's masterstroke, as John Lawrence rightly called it, was magical. The air, as Edwardes said, ' was cleared as if by a thunderstorm. We breathed freely again. On our return from the disarming parade, hundreds of Khans and Urbabs, who stood aloof the day before, appeared as thick as flies, and were profuse in offers of service. They had not calculated on our having so much pluck.' Edwardes received them ' very coldly indeed.' Henderson's succours from Kohat kept hourly flocking in, Afridis, Momands, Yusafzais, were hurrying across the border to fight for the manifest masters of Peshâwar. 'Men,' wrote Edwardes, ' are coming from Miranzai, which we were subduing last winter. Miranzai is now as quiet as a Bayswater tea-garden.'

----

[1] Lady Edwardes; Edwardes, *Official Narrative,* &c.

CHAPTER XVIII

NO time was lost, to use Edwardes's own phrase, in
' picking up the fragments of the mutiny.' By sunrise, on
May 23, the forethoughtful Commissioner of Peshâwar had
thrown a chain of his levies and police round the rear
of the cantonments, to forestall any mutinous outbreak of
disarmed Sepoys. This done, the Subadar Major of the
51st Native Infantry, who had been condemned to death as
a proved deserter, was marched round the whole paraded
garrison. When his crime and sentence had been carefully
explained to each regiment in turn, he was led off to the
scaffold prepared for him, and hanged in view of the
assembled troops. ' It shows them,' as Edwardes wrote
to his wife, ' that we will maintain discipline, and are
strong enough to enforce it.'

That night some 300 of the 70th Foot, 250 Irregular
Cavalry, a squadron of Multàni Horse, with a battery of
eight light guns, marched off for Mardàn under the command of Colonel Chute. Colonel John Nicholson, with a
small body of his mounted police, accompanied the column
as political officer. Vaughan's Punjàbis and a wing of the
27th Foot, which John Lawrence had sent back in hot
haste from Rawal Pindi, were marching from Naushéra

towards the same goal.   A warning message from the civil officer at Mardân had in fact reached Peshâwar on the heels of Taylor's message from Naushéra.   Baffled by Taylor's promptitude and the bold front shown by a handful of European invalids, and alarmed at Vaughan's near approach from Attock, the Naushéra mutineers had gone off to join their like-minded comrades on the Momand frontier.   Their arrival at Mardàn heralded a burst of wild commotion, in which only 120 Sepoys ranged themselves on the side of their English officers.   Happily for these last, their men, though defiant, were still respectful, and forbore from clinching mutiny with murder [1].'

Before the two columns joined hands at Mardàn on the morning of the 25th, the mutineers had marched off with drums beating and colours flying towards the hills of Swàt. They had gained so long a start that pursuit with our tired infantry under the fierce May sun was out of the question, while Brougham's guns could make but slow progress over the broken ground.   The irregular cavalry had no heart for the work that lay before them.   But John Nicholson was there on his great grey charger, longing only to hunt down and cut up the retreating enemy.   At the head of his own ' Sowàrs,' stoutly seconded by Lind's Multânis, he dashed forward on his death-dealing errand, like an eagle swooping on his prey.   Mile after mile, and hour after hour the chase continued ; Nicholson's great sword felling a Sepoy at every stroke.   The mutineers, as he himself admitted in a private note to Edwardes, fought stubbornly ' as men always do who have no chance of escape but by their own exertions.'

The retreat erelong became a rout.   The rebels, says

[1] Rev. J. Cave-Browne, *Punjâb and Delhi.*

Edwardes in his official report, 'were hunted out of villages, and grappled with in ravines, and hunted over the ridges all that day from Fort Mardán to the borders of Swát, and found respite only in the failing light.' It was near sunset ere the hunters turned their horses' heads towards Mardán. By that time 120 Sepoys had been slain outright, many of them by Nicholson's own hand; while 150 had been taken prisoners, forty of whom were afterwards blown from guns before the assembled garrison of Peshàwar, while the rest were doomed to a life of hard labour in jail or on the public roads. Of the 400 who got clear away, many were handed over to Edwardes's police by the people with whom they had hoped to find refuge, and many more were hunted down by the levies of Major John Becher[1].

The 55th Native Infantry had now ceased in fact to exist. The regimental colours and 200 stand of arms were among the trophies of that long day's ride under a scorching sun. Nicholson himself was twenty hours in the saddle, during which he must have covered at least seventy miles of very rough ground. Now too it was becoming clear that the border tribes would not side against us with our mutinous Sepoys[2].

Mardán thus rescued in the nick of time was handed over to the care of Vaughan's trusty Punjàbis. But there were other forts on that frontier, at Abuzai, Shabkadr, and Michni, for whose safety Chute and Nicholson had yet to provide. Each of these posts was garrisoned conjointly

---

[1] The mutineers were tried by court-martial under the orders of Brigadier Cotton. Edwardes and Nicholson had of course nothing to do with the punishments inflicted.

[2] Lady Edwardes; Cave-Browne; Kaye.

by the loyal Kailât-i-Ghilzai regiment and the disloyal
64th Native Infantry, who had been vainly trying to infect
their new comrades with the mutinous spirit. At Nicholson's suggestion the disarming of the tainted regiment was
entrusted to the Peshâwar column, which kept the field
for nearly a fortnight, marching under Nicholson's guidance along the Swât border, with a view to thwarting the
attempts of a noted outlaw, one Ajun Khan, to stir up
strife against us in that quarter. ' The game,' wrote
Nicholson from Mardân to Edwardes on May 26, ' is
becoming nicer and more complicated. . . . There is no
doubt that for some time past emissaries, chiefly mullahs,
from the hills, had been going backwards and forwards
between the 55th Native Infantry here, and certain parties
in their own country.'

The question of disarming the 64th Native Infantry was
still for a few days in suspense. On the morning of the
30th Nicholson promised to let Edwardes know that evening
what he himself would advise. ' I am strongly inclined to
believe that we should not merely disarm but disband that
corps and the 10th Irregular Cavalry. There is no doubt
that they have both been in communication with the
Akhund of Swât. . . . I believe we did not pitch into the
55th one day too soon. That corps and the 64th were all
planning to go over to the Akhund together. I have got
a man who taunted my police on the line of march with
siding with infidels in a religious war. May I hang him [1]?'

On the same day, May 30, the column reached Abuzai,
where Nicholson found the Sepoys of the 64th ' looking
very villainous but of course perfectly quiet.' They had
been talking treason both to the Ghilzais, who at once

[1] Kaye, *Sepoy War.*

ceased to associate with them, and to the people of the country, who were 'rather hoping for a row, in the midst of which they may escape paying revenue.' The needful permission to draw the teeth of such traitors was not long in coming from Rawal Pindi. In the first days of June the 64th Sepoys at Abuzai, Shabkadr, and Michni, were quietly disarmed by separate portions of Chute's brigade. To the 10th Irregulars no such process was then applied; for Nicholson himself had counselled forbearance, so long as Delhi remained untaken. Like most of our country-men in the Punjàb, he looked upon the recapture of the imperial city as a thing to be accomplished in a few days, or at the latest in a very few weeks. To make short work of Delhi was then the common cry from Peshâwar down to Calcutta, taken up and repeated alike by the Governor-General and the Chief Commissioner of the Punjàb. Only in the camp of the dying commander-in-chief, as it drew near the rebel stronghold, did the cry sound like a cruel mockery [1].

On June 10 Nicholson was back again at Peshâwar, a march or two ahead of Chute's little force, which had done its work nobly under the most trying conditions. 'Nicholson,' wrote Edwardes to John Lawrence, 'came in this morning from Abuzai, looking rather the worse for exposure.' Once more the two friends were at work to-gether in strenuous concert with brave old Sydney Cotton, for the maintenance of order in the Peshâwar valley, until the time came only too soon, when John Nicholson's services were required elsewhere. Well might Edwardes congratu-late himself on having secured 'such a noble coadjutor as Nicholson,' and on the 'entire harmony' which prevailed

[1] Kaye.

between them and the brigadier. And well might Sir John Lawrence, to whose dauntless courage in ' steering his province through the storm ' Edwardes himself bore hearty witness, declare in a public letter to Lord Canning his firm assurance ' that, with three such officers at Peshâwar as Brigadier Sydney Cotton, Colonel Edwardes, and Lieut.-Colonel Nicholson, everything that is possible will be done to maintain order and security [1].'

Sir John's own biographer, Mr. Bosworth Smith, has told us with what self-denying energy the chief commissioner had complied with the appeals of Cotton and Edwardes for timely succour in the hour of their sorest need. His arrangements for safeguarding Attock and strengthening Peshâwar were crowned by the dispatch of 200 police from Rawal Pindi. ' We have not kept,' he wrote to Edwardes, ' a single soldier worth anything here. We are very anxious for your safety. I cannot fail to see how precarious your position may prove [2].'

By this time Edwardes knew that one supreme danger to our cause had in fact been turned aside by the treaties he had helped to make with Dost Muhammad. ' How valuable,' Edwardes wrote to his wife in June, ' is now our friendly policy with Afghanistan.' And again, a few months later, he tells John Lawrence that ' the policy we have adopted with Kâbul has proved a perfect Godsend to us. It keeps all above us quiet in a wonderful way. . . . It is clear that, if we had been on *bad* terms just now with Kâbul, we should have lost, first Peshâwar, and then the Punjâb, and all India would have reeled under the blow [3].'

This indeed was the simple truth. One shudders even

---

[1] Kaye ; Lady Edwardes.   [2] Bosworth Smith.
[3] Lady Edwardes.

now at the thought of what might have happened, had the wise Barakzai prince cared less for his plighted faith than for the clamours of those Afghan fanatics who continually urged him to proclaim a holy war against the infidel masters of Peshâwar.

Upon this question of an Afghan alliance, Nicholson himself, in spite of his old prepossessions, was now in hearty agreement with his friend. He could not close his mind to the logic of accomplished facts. He owned one day to Herbert Edwardes that ' he never thought we should live to derive such solid advantage from our alliance with Dost Muhammad as we are doing at this crisis, in the perfect peace of our border ; so that we are left at liberty to contend with our own Sepoys [1].'

On June 12 Nicholson wrote to his mother from Peshâwar : ' I just write a few lines to tell you that we are quiet here, and have made ourselves secure by disarming all the disaffected native regiments. Charles is with a wing of his regiment in the neighbourhood of Lahore. Do not be under any apprehension about either of us. I consider that we are stronger in the Punjâb at this moment than in any other part of the Bengal Presidency [2].' Two days earlier he had written with like brevity to his good friend Mrs. Edwardes to assure her ' that dear Herbert and I are well, and have made ourselves very strong here. In fact I believe that at this moment we have the best position in the Bengal Presidency. Do not therefore be uneasy about us. We have no fears for the result ourselves. With God's blessing we shall emerge from this crisis stronger than we have ever been in India before [3].'

Across the Indus, in Hazâra, Major John Becher was

---

[1] Lady Edwardes.   [2] MS. Letters.   [3] Lady Edwardes.

doing his best, with the aid of his faithful highlanders, to intercept parties of fugitive Sepoys heading towards Sitâna and Kashmir. ' I am proud,' he writes to Edwardes, ' to see you and Nicholson in this grand storm masters of your work; right glad that Nicholson did not leave. There was work for his war-horse, and he is in his element; the first who has struck the death-blow. . . . Here I am tranquil, only that of course there is excitement among the people. Chiefs and people flock in. They are in the most loyal spirit, desirous only to be employed more than I can employ them. If I ask for two horsemen I get ten supplied.'

Everywhere indeed along the trans-Indus frontier our officers were working heart and soul together in aid of the ruling spirits at Pindi and Peshâwar. On May 21 Major Henderson had written to Edwardes from Kohat, telling him what was done and doing there for the safeguarding of the fort and treasure. ' From to-morrow I will also mount strong pickets over the guns, and then, come what may, we need not fear for the result. If you want *more* men, tell me, and you shall have them at once.' And about the same time Major Richard Pollock, then deputy commissioner in the Derajât, assures Edwardes that ' nothing could really have been better than the feeling exhibited by the headmen of this district. They could hardly conceive that any one would dare perpetrate the enormities they heard of, but begged to be employed if they could be of use.' Of Sydney Cotton's zeal and helpfulness Sir John Lawrence said everything when he pronounced him to be ' an old trump [1].'

Edwardes himself, like Nicholson, felt perfect confidence in the issue of that tremendous struggle which still lay before his anxious countrymen until help could reach them

[1] Lady Edwardes.

from England. Meanwhile, as he tells his wife, 'we shall have as much as we can do to hold India, . . . but, if we are true to ourselves and act vigorously with God's help always, we shall do it; and however anxious and harassed I may be, I never for a moment admit the possibility of ultimate failure.'

Not all his countrymen, however, were true to themselves in their hour of trial, even in the Punjâb. For want of timely vigour, three native regiments at Jalandhar were allowed one night in June to rise in open mutiny, and march off unhindered to swell the numbers already mustered within the walls of Delhi, to whose northern front Sir Henry Barnard's little force had successfully fought its way on the morning of June 8. How long that heroic force was to lie sweltering behind the historic ridge, through the heat and steam of an Indian summer, wasted by daily fighting and disease, waiting for reinforcements which only the Punjâb could send—for even Agra could do nothing to help them, and Henry Lawrence had his hands full in Oudh—was now a question to which the most sanguine could give no reassuring answer. Even John Lawrence fell for the moment into a desponding mood. Events were showing him that Delhi would be a harder nut to crack than he had foreseen. The untoward delay in massing and equipping troops at Umballa and Karnâl had given the rebels time to prepare for a determined stand in a great walled city whose defences had been strengthened by our own engineers. Their numbers too were being steadily recruited by fresh contingents of disciplined Sepoys and armed villagers.

Sir John's change of mood betrayed itself in a fashion which took both Edwardes and Nicholson completely by surprise. In a letter received by Edwardes on June 11, the great chief commissioner proposed to 'look ahead and consider what should be done in the event of disaster at Delhi.' In that case, he held that 'we must concentrate. All our safety depends on this.' In order to retain our hold on Lahore and Multân, we must make up our minds to abandon Peshâwar and the trans-Indus frontier. But the withdrawal from Peshâwar should take place 'early in the day,' for 'at the eleventh hour it would be difficult, perhaps impossible.' Sir John therefore would 'make a merit of necessity' by inviting the Amir of Kâbul to take charge of the Peshâwar valley as our friend, and promising to leave him there in full possession, if he remained true to us throughout the crisis. He would keep the Derajât for the present; but even this he was prepared, if necessary, to give up.

'Unless this had been in his own handwriting, I would not have credited it,' was Edwardes's first remark on a proposal which seemed to him the child of mere panic. At Sir John Lawrence's request he at once proceeded to consult Cotton and Nicholson upon the fitting answer to this unwelcome proposal. All three concurred in scouting the notion of abandoning the frontier province, and falling back behind the Indus. Edwardes's answer, dispatched the same day, insisted strongly on the absolute need of holding on to Peshâwar—'the anchor of the Punjâb, and if you take it up, the whole ship will drift to sea.' The Peshâwar valley and the Mânjha—the country about Lahore and Amritsar—were the two vital points on the holding of which must depend our mastery of the Punjâb. Whatever disasters might occur at Delhi, so long as we held Peshâwar and the Mânjha with an adequate force, we could keep our footing in the Punjàb until troops arrived from England. To retreat from the frontier would only tend to renew the disasters of our retreat from Kâbul. 'We earnestly hope,' continues Edwardes, 'that you will stand or fall at Peshâwar. It must be done somewhere; let us do it in the front, giving up nothing.'

John Lawrence still clung to his own idea, and harped at times to Edwardes on the same cracked string. He applied to Lord Canning for full powers to act in this matter as he might deem best. Lord Canning's answer, when it did come in August, was decisive; ' Hold on to Peshâwar to the last. Give up nothing[1].'

The bravest men may have their weak moments, and the only wonder is that any man in John Lawrence's position should, at his age, have kept his head at all during those months of physical and mental strain which he had to endure, as the one man upon whose shoulders rested the burden of saving not only the Punjàb, but all Northern India from the horrors of a successful revolt. Amidst all the cares, anxieties, and toils of his high office, he was in a very low state of health ; the wife whom he loved so deeply was not far off at Marri, within the circle of ever-impending danger ; and he lived in daily fear of what might happen in the province where his beloved brother Henry was trying so manfully to steer his bark through the rush of a wide-wasting deluge. What wonder if his mind misgave him as to the temper of the Sikhs in the Mânjha, their original home, or if he feared that the growing disaffection would soon upset the loyalty even of his best Punjâbi troops? Edwardes and Nicholson, on the other hand, were young, hopeful, audacious,

---

[1] Lady Edwardes.

and their womenkind were all safe in their far-off island homes.

At last the hour came when Nicholson and Edwardes were to part, as Fate decreed, for ever. The death of Colonel Chester in the fight of June 8 at Badli-ke Serai left vacant the post of adjutant-general to the army before Delhi. It was soon arranged between Sir John Lawrence and General Reed, who had left Pindi for the front, that Chamberlain should go to Delhi as adjutant-general, while Nicholson should take command of the Punjâb movable column. On the 14th a telegram from John Lawrence requested Nicholson to start that evening for Rawal Pindi. 'So there goes dear fine Nicholson—a great loss to me,' writes Edwardes, 'but a still greater gain to the State at this crisis. . . . A nobler spirit never went forth to fight his country's battles.' At ten o'clock that night the two friends clasped hands together for the last time on this earth, and John Nicholson rode off into the darkness, followed by his escort of Pathân sowârs.

CHAPTER XIX

On his arrival at Rawal Pindi John Nicholson held much earnest and sometimes passionate talk with his chief on subjects nearest to both their hearts. On the burning question of the abandonment of Peshâwar he spoke out for Edwardes and himself with all the vehemence of one who felt strongly what he saw so clearly, the mischievous futility of pulling up the anchor that held the ship. After a somewhat stormy interview with the much-enduring chief commissioner, he pursued his journey that same evening across the Punjâb, whilst Sir John's able secretary, Major Hugh James, was sent off at Edwardes's request to take Nicholson's place at Peshâwar.

The night brought with it for Nicholson a kindlier feeling towards the master who had once more placed him on the road to new achievements in his country's service. Next morning, June 18, he wrote from Jhilam to Sir John Lawrence, 'I forgot before starting to say one or two things I had omitted saying. One was to thank you for my appointment. I know you recommended it on *public* grounds, but I do not feel the less obliged to you. Another was to tell you that I have dismissed old grievances, whether real or imaginary, from my mind, and, as far as I am concerned, bygones are bygones. In return I would ask you not to judge me over hastily or harshly[1].'

Several changes had meanwhile taken place in the composition of the force which Brigadier-General Chamberlain was waiting to make over to his old friend John Nicholson, promoted by Reed to the rank of Brigadier-General. The Guides, for instance, under Captain Daly, had started a month before from Jhilam on that wonderful series of forced marches which brought them down to Delhi almost as soon as Barnard himself. From time to time other troops were detached to points of danger within the Punjàb, or hurried off to reinforce Barnard before Delhi. The gaps thus made in the column were filled up from Sialkôt by the 52nd Queen's Light Infantry, Dawes's troop of Horse Artillery, and Bourchier's Light Field Battery, with a wing of the 9th Bengal Cavalry and the 35th Sepoys. On May 28 Chamberlain began his march from Wazirabad, and encamped near Lahore on June 1. The timely presence of his white troops had a quieting effect upon the people, and enabled his countrymen to relieve the disarmed cavalry at Mianmír of the horses they had hitherto been allowed to keep[2].

On June 9, at Anarkalli, two Sepoys of the 35th were blown from one of Colonel Bourchier's guns for having tried to stir their comrades up to open mutiny. Full tidings of the Jalandhar outbreak now reached Lahore, and Chamberlain, scenting possible mischief, made a forced march to Amritsar, where he arrived on the morning of

[1] Bosworth Smith.

[2] On this occasion a number of horses, purposely let loose by some of the dismounted troopers, charged down upon Captain Charles Nicholson's irregulars, causing for the moment much confusion in their ranks. Young Nicholson himself was lamed by a severe kick.—Cave-Browne.

the 11th.   That evening a vast crowd thronged out of the
populous city to witness the hanging of a fakir who had
been caught tampering with some of Colonel Coke's Pun-
jabis, then forming part of the movable column.   Three
days later, leaving all quiet about Amritsar, and seeing all
safe in the fort of Govindgarh, the column marched on
leisurely towards Jalandhar, where it halted on the 20th,
waiting for its new leader, who arrived on the following
day.   About the same time the column received a welcome
reinforcement of 700 Multáni horse and foot, whom
Edwardes had promptly dispatched after his friend from
Pesháwar.   On June 22 Chamberlain made over the command to John Nicholson, and hurried off by mail-cart for
Delhi, along a road which some loyal Sikh Rajahs, in ready
answer to John Lawrence's summons, were keeping safely
guarded by their soldiers and police [1].

Before leaving Jalandhar Nicholson played a characteristic
part in a curious little drama, of which the future Lord
Roberts was an amused eye-witness.   The faithful Rajah
of Kapurthalla had placed in Jalandhar a body of his own
troops, to protect the station and discharge the duties
formerly reserved for our Sepoys.   As commissioner of
the province, Edwardes's old comrade, Major Edward Lake,
desired to pay a befitting compliment to the Rajah's officers
and sirdars.   At his request Nicholson consented to meet
them at a darbar in Lake's house.   Lord Roberts, who
was present as one of Nicholson's staff, shall tell us what
happened at the close of the ceremony.

' General Mehtáb Singh, a near relative of the Rajah, took
his leave, and as the senior in rank at the *darbar* was

---

[1] Sir G. Bourchier, *Eight Months' Campaign*; Cave-Browne; Lady
Edwardes.

walking out of the room first, when I observed Nicholson stalk to the door, put himself in front of Mehtâb Singh, and, waving him back with an authoritative air, prevented him from leaving the room. The rest of the company then passed out; and when they had gone Nicholson said to Lake, "Do you see that General Mehtâb Singh has his shoes on?" Lake replied that he had noticed the fact, but tried to excuse it. Nicholson, however, speaking in Hindustani, said, "There is no possible excuse for such an act of gross impertinence. Mehtâb Singh knows perfectly well that he would not venture to step on his own father's carpet, save barefooted; and he has only committed this breach of etiquette to-day because he thinks we are not in a position to resent the insult, and that he can treat us as he would not have dared to do a month ago." Mehtâb Singh looked extremely foolish, and stammered out some kind of apology; but Nicholson was not to be appeased, and continued, "If I were the last Englishman left in Jalandhar, you (addressing Mehtâb Singh) should not come into my room with your shoes on." Then politely turning to Lake, he added, "I hope the commissioner will now allow me to order you to take your shoes off and carry them out in your own hands so that your followers may witness your discomfiture."

' Mehtâb Singh, completely cowed, meekly did as he was told. Although, in the kindness of his heart, Lake had at first endeavoured to smooth matters away, he knew the natives well, and he readily admitted the wisdom of Nicholson's action. Indeed, Nicholson's uncompromising bearing on this occasion proved a great help to Lake, for it had the best possible effect upon the Kapurthalla people; their manner at once changed, all disrespect vanished, there

was no more swaggering about as if they considered themselves masters of the situation [1].'

On June 23 the movable column, weakened by the
departure of Coke's staunch Punjábis for the camp before
Delhi, marched off under its new commander towards
Philúr, on the right bank of the Satlaj. The 33rd Native
Infantry at Hoshiarpur had been ordered to join the line
of march at the point where the Hoshiarpur road fell into
the main road from Jalandhar. John Nicholson's real object
was a mystery to all outside his own staff, but the whole
movement had been carefully planned by a master in the
art of war. Nicholson knew that the 33rd were ripe for
mutiny, while the 35th, in spite of Chamberlain's sternly
eloquent appeal to their loyalty after the lesson read them
on June 9, were only waiting their opportunity to rise.
Both these regiments he intended to disarm at Philúr. If
they resisted, or tried to cross the Satlaj, he was prepared
to punish or forestall them. Mutiny, he declared, was 'like
smallpox; it spreads quickly, and must be crushed as soon
as possible.'

The desired junction was effected at Phagwára on the
night of the 24th. As the column moved on, the 33rd
Sepoys fell in behind their brethren of the 35th Light
Infantry. Both regiments seem to have fancied that the
general was leading them on to Delhi, the place they
wanted, for private reasons, to get near. At the head of
the column marched Dawes's troop and Bourchier's battery,
followed by H.M. 52nd Light Infantry. After them came
the two tainted regiments. The rear-guard was formed by
a wing of the 9th Bengal Cavalry, the other wing of which
was doing duty at Sialkôt.

<hr>

[1] Lord Roberts, *Forty-one Years in India.*

Meanwhile two of Nicholson's staff-officers, Captain Farrington the deputy commissioner, and Lieutenant Roberts of the quartermaster-general's department, had been sent on to Philúr, to examine the ground within range of the fort's guns, to make a show of examining the bridge of boats, and to collect waggons, as if for the passage of troops across the river. During the night Nicholson himself rode on ahead to examine the ground near the fort. Finding the space there too small for his purpose, he fell back upon the usual camping-ground for the crowning proof of his daringly resourceful genius. While he himself was carefully revising the details of his scheme, Mr. Ricketts, the bold and zealous magistrate of Ludhiàna, instructed the police who guarded the bridge of boats to cut the boats adrift on the first sound of firing from Nicholson's camp.

In the early morning of the 25th the head of the column marched up to the point where Nicholson had prepared his trap for the false-hearted Sepoys. In a few moments the 52nd Queen's were resting at ease on the open ground beyond the right of the road, with half a dozen nine-pounders unlimbered on either flank. Briefly and clearly the brigadier-general revealed his purpose to the European troops. 'Well do I remember,' wrote the future Sir George Bourchier, 'as he was leaning over one of my guns, the coolness with which he gave every order. His last was, " If they bolt, you follow as hard as you can; the bridge will have been destroyed, and we shall have a second Subraon on a small scale." '

A few minutes later the 35th Native Infantry came up, little dreaming of the surprise in store for them. They were ordered to turn to the left and pass round the rear of a serai which lay at the corner of the camping-ground.

When they had wheeled again to their right and formed in close column, they found themselves face to face with an English regiment standing to their arms, and twelve guns limbered up for action within easy range for grape. Their colonel was told by Nicholson that his men 'must give up their arms.' The order to pile arms was given, and the Sepoys, scared and crestfallen, obeyed it without a murmur. Their arms were promptly gathered up and carted off to the fort in the waggons which Nicholson's forethought had provided.

Then came the turn of the 33rd Native Infantry, who, tired with their long march from Hoshiarpur, had lagged some way behind their comrades of the 35th. It is not unlikely that for this piece of good fortune the column was indebted to its wise commander. To deal with the two corps separately was quite in keeping with his previous practice at Peshâwar. Had these two regiments been nearer each other at the critical moment, the attempt to disarm them might have provoked a struggle in which the Sepoy officers would have been the first to fall beneath the weapons of their own men. As things fell out, however, the 33rd were disposed of quite as easily as the 35th. Thanks to Nicholson's masterly precautions, a very ticklish business was carried through without a hitch. Not a shot was fired nor a drop of blood spilt in the process of luring some 1,500 armed mutineers into the trap so artfully contrived for them. Among the many native spectators of that morning's work was an old Sikh colonel who had fought against us at Gujarât. 'You have drawn the fangs of 1,500 snakes,' he remarked to Captain Farrington. 'Truly your ikbâl (good fortune) is great[1].'

[1] Cave-Browne; Bourchier.

Just before the disarmed Sepoys were marched off into camp, Nicholson rode up to warn them that any attempt at desertion would be punished by death. The fords, he added, were all watched, so that escape would be impossible. Eight men, however, says Sir G. Bourchier, 'tried their luck: all were caught and executed after trial by drum-head court-martial.' Had the wing of the 9th Cavalry got their just deserts, they also would have been disarmed as fellow-plotters with the Sepoy infantry. But Nicholson's hands were tied by a fear lest the other wing at Sialkôt might be driven to work sudden mischief in a station where the brave but over-trustful Brigadier Brind had refused to disarm his native troops while the means for disarming them were still within his grasp.

The complete success of Nicholson's manœuvre taught some few croakers in his camp the unwisdom of prejudging any movement which such a leader might choose to undertake; a leader who, in Roberts's expressive words, 'seemed always to know exactly what to do, and the best way to do it.' These words, as true of Nicholson as of Wolfe, or Wellington, or Charles Napier, may be said to sum up all the essential qualities of the greatest soldier who ever led an army in the field. Nelsons and Wellingtons are, like great poets, usually born, not made; and Nicholson, as I have said, was a born soldier, who had turned his opportunities both in peace and war to the best account, before the Mutiny opened out to him a yet wider and loftier sphere of achievement. His genius for command, to quote again from Lord Roberts, 'was felt by every officer and man in the column before he had been amongst them many days.' Roberts, however, was soon to part from his new chief. A few hours after the disarming, he was in the

Philúr fort with Nicholson, when the latter received a copy of a telegram from Sir Henry Barnard to the Punjâb authorities, begging that every artillery officer employed on non-regimental duty might be sent down at once to Delhi. Nicholson was loth to part with the ablest of his staff-officers, and Roberts himself was divided between his longing to reach the front and the growing attachment which closer intercourse with a man of Nicholson's quality had brought about. The victor of Kandahar is 'proud to remember' that his chief did not wish to part with him. Both of them felt, however, that Roberts's first duty was to his regiment. Nicholson only stipulated that Roberts should find a man to replace him as deputy-assistant quartermaster-general, as he himself knew none of the officers with the column. A successor was soon found in Captain Grindlay of the Bengal cavalry. That same evening Nicholson and Roberts dined quietly together, and at dawn next morning Roberts left Philúr by mail-cart for Delhi.

In the very first days of his command, Nicholson devised an effective system of intelligence, whereby he was kept informed of all that was going on in the neighbouring districts. To secure prompt and speedy action in any sudden emergency, he had also formed a part of his brigade into a flying column, ready to move anywhere at the shortest notice. While three guns of Dawes's troop were to keep their full equipment, the rest of his men were to be mounted as cavalry. Twelve empty ammunition waggons were to carry supplies for a certain number of days, as well as nine European riflemen to each waggon [1].

On June 28 the column retraced its steps towards Amritsar. For the moment all was quiet in the Punjâb;

---

[1] Lord Roberts; Sir G. Bourchier.

but the presence of armed Sepoys at Rawal Pindi, Jhilam, Kangra, and Siálkòt was an abiding source of anxiety to the chief commissioner. Once back at Amritsar, Nicholson would be able from that commanding watch-post to strike hard and swiftly at any evil thing that stirred within reach of his long, strong arm. But his cares for the Punjàb never blinded him to the need of succouring the brave men who held the ridge in front of Delhi. Before leaving Philúr he had written to General Gowan, then commanding the Punjàb division, a letter urging the immediate withdrawal of the troops at Pindi to Lahore. A copy of this letter was forwarded to Sir John Lawrence, followed by one from Nicholson himself. 'If I considered the question of slight or even moderate importance, I should,' he wrote, 'out of deference for you, have refrained from expressing publicly an opinion at variance with yours. But I think the matter one of the very greatest consequence, and that, entertaining the decided opinion upon it that I do, I should be wanting in my duty if I neglected every means in my power to get what I think right done. I consider the retention of the 24th [Queen's] and the Horse Artillery at Rawal Pindi as the most faulty move we have made in the game here, and one which I think you will repent should any check occur at head-quarters. Montgomery writes me that the feeling among the Muhammadans is not good; and I do not think it is good here either. I wish I were commissioner or deputy commissioner for a week [1].'

On the bank of the Biàs, which the column had to recross slowly in boats, for the rising river had now broken up the floating bridge, Nicholson bade farewell

<hr>

[1] Bourchier; Kaye.

to Captain Farrington. 'You'll soon see me back again,' he added significantly, as he turned away.

Meanwhile Nicholson wrote again to Sir John Lawrence: ' The movable column as at present constituted is no doubt strong enough to put down any rebellion or disaffection which may show itself in any locality at this end of the Punjâb. But suppose a rise in two places at once; suppose, before I had disarmed, that the 33rd had broken out at Hoshiarpur, the 46th at Sialkôt, and the 59th at Amritsar. I should have been awkwardly situated then. My position since I have got the 33rd and 35th off my hands is much better. But I think that there is still great reason why the 24th should come down from Pindi. Suppose the commander-in-chief to send an urgent application for more reinforcements. If the 24th were here, either it or the 52nd could move off at once. As it is, a delay of at least ten days would have to elapse [1].'

Neither Sir John Lawrence nor General Gowan would view the matter with Nicholson's eyes, and circumstances were soon to decide that question in their own rude way. The movable column reached Amritsar on July 5. The disarmed 33rd had been dropped at Jalandhar, while the 35th were in camp halfway between the Biâs and Amritsar. Two days later Nicholson learned that the Sepoys at Rawal Pindi had just been disarmed, not without bloodshed, while the attempt to disarm the 14th Native Infantry at Jhilam was proving a disastrous failure. Next day the further tidings of a desperate fight at Jhilam decided Nicholson to disarm the 59th Sepoys at Amritsar. On the morning of the 9th a punishment parade was held on the plain between the city and the fort of Govindgarh, for the execution of

[1] Kaye.

a rebel sentenced to be blown from a gun. After the sentence had been carried out, the 59th were ordered to lay down their arms. Astonished as men would be, who only the day before had been complimented on their loyalty, they obeyed the order at once without a murmur.

It was a wise precaution to take at such a time. But Nicholson took it with very great reluctance. In his public letter of the 10th to Neville Chamberlain, the adjutant-general, he declares himself 'bound to place on record my belief that both in conduct and feeling this regiment was quite an exceptional one. It had neither committed itself in any way, nor do I believe that, up to the day it was disarmed, it had any intention of committing itself; and I very deeply regret that, even as a precautionary measure, it should have become my duty to disarm it [1].'

His regret could not have been lessened on learning that the disarmed Sepoys had gone straight from the parade to their belts of arms, and of their own accord made over to their officers several hundred muskets belonging to their sick or absent comrades [2].

Before he wrote that letter to the adjutant-general, John Nicholson knew that the time was come for sterner and more desperate work than disarming regiments or holding punishment parades. About dawn of the 10th two special messages, one from Montgomery at Lahore, the other brought by a young bandsman of the 46th Native Infantry, who had galloped his ponies all the way from Sialkòt, reached the commander of the movable column within half an hour of each other. They told him, in few words, of the murderous outbreak which had taken place the morning before at the northern station of Sialkòt. The

[1] Kaye, *Sepoy War*.　　　　[2] Cave-Browne.

few hurried lines which young McDougal, the bandsman, had brought in from McMahon, the civil officer at the station, spoke for themselves as to the need for urgency. ' The troops here are in open mutiny : jail broke. Brigadier wounded. Bishop killed. Many have escaped to the fort. Bring the movable column at once if possible. $6\frac{1}{2}$ a.m. July 9 [1].'

It was the story of many an Indian station, where a handful of our people lay at the mercy of rebels and mutineers. The 46th Native Infantry and the wing of the 9th Cavalry had risen at last, and murdered every white man who crossed their path, from the brave old brigadier himself—for his wound was mortal—to the two Doctors Graham and the Rev. J. Hunter, whose fate was shared by his wife and child. Several gentlemen and all the other ladies found shelter in Rajah Tej Singh's old fort, while many of the Sepoy officers made off betimes for Gujrànwàla. Between the Sepoys and a mob of ruffians from the jail and the bazârs, the work of pillage and destruction went merrily forward all that day. About four in the afternoon the mutineers marched away towards the Ràvi laden with plunder, and taking with them the old station-gun, which had long been wont to signal the daily recurrence of sunrise, noon, and sunset in Sialkôt.

[1] Cave-Browne ; Kaye.

CHAPTER XX

PUNISHMENT OF THE SIALKÔT MUTINEERS, JULY, 1857

NICHOLSON'S first move, on hearing of the Sialkôt disaster, was to draw the fangs of his regular cavalry, whose comrades of the other wing were the first to rise in the great military station below the mountains of Kashmir. Soon after sunrise of July 10, their commandant was taking a roll-call of his men in 'Hindustani dress,' that is, without arms or uniform. Before them drew up into line a company of the 52nd Foot, with rifles loaded and bayonets fixed. Major Baker explained to his troopers the circumstances which compelled the general to disarm them. A party from each troop was then ordered to collect the arms left piled as usual outside the tents. In the marching orders issued that afternoon, '*the horses* of the 9th Cavalry' were to accompany the column; the disarmed and dismounted troopers being left behind under guard of a company of the 52nd, and three of Bourchier's guns[1].

All through that blazing July day the road between Lahore and Amritsar was alive with ponies, *ekkas* or pony-cars, and *bylies* or bullock-coaches, secured betimes by Montgomery's officers for the difficult errand which

[1] Cave-Browne.

Nicholson's soldiers were about to undertake. The camp itself was all astir with preparations for the coming march. From later reports of that day it seemed clear to Nicholson that the Sialkòt force would make for Gurdàspur, midway between the Ràvi and the Biàs, in hopes of raising Jackson's irregulars there, and of making a junction with the 4th Sepoys from Kangra and Nurpur. The mutineers had probably lost some hours in waiting for their comrades from Jhilam, many of whom had been slain by Ellice's troops on the 8th, while the rest were now being hunted down by parties of Punjàbi infantry and police.

A mutiny at Nurpur or Kangra might herald a general rising of the hill-people in those parts. In a warning note, forwarded through Nicholson to Reynell Taylor, then Commissioner of Kangra, Montgomery urged him 'at all risks' to disarm the Sepoys in both those garrisons. How to do it, Taylor, Younghusband, and Wilkie, commanding the 4th Native Infantry, could decide for themselves. 'I send this,' he adds, 'through Brigadier Nicholson, whose experience may suggest something.' The desired experience came out in Nicholson's postscript to the note he had to forward: 'I can suggest nothing. You and the officers on the spot are the best judges of how you should act. God prosper what you do!' On the morning of the 11th, Taylor read the note, and, in concert with Major Younghusband, then at the head of the district police, proceeded to disarm the wing of the 4th at Kangra. Next day, before Taylor and his bodyguard reached Nurpur, the other wing at that station had quietly given up their arms[1].

The object of the mutineers, as set forth by Nicholson himself in a letter to the adjutant-general, 'was evidently to

[1] Gambier Parry, *Reynell Taylor.*

plunder the station of Gurdàspur, and get the 2nd Irregular Cavalry there to join them. They would then have proceeded *viâ* Nurpur and Hoshiarpur to Jalandhar, whence they could have made the best of their way to Delhi.' 'It was evident,' he went on, 'that, as the mutineers had two days' start, and as Gurdàspur was something over forty-one miles from my encampment, no time was to be lost. I therefore decided on reaching that station in a single forced march.' To attempt such a feat with European infantry in one of the hottest months of the Punjàb year would have seemed to most men like attempting the impossible. But for John Nicholson, as for Napoleon, the word 'impossible' did not exist. He 'was born,' as Kaye has well said, 'to overcome difficulties which would have beaten down other men.' The ponies and *ekkas* brought by scores into his camp were meant for the use of his precious Europeans, and with their aid the long march was to be successfully accomplished in less than twenty hours.

At 9 p.m. of July 10, Nicholson led out of camp a force consisting of Dawes's Troop, three guns of Bourchier's Battery, the 52nd Light Infantry under Colonel Campbell, 184 men from the 3rd and 6th Punjàb Infantry, a company of armed police, and two troops of newly raised police levies. Next morning the column halted for two hours at Patàla, after a march of twenty-six miles. Bread and rum, with an abundance of milk, were served out to the troops. About 10 a.m. the column started again on a march of eighteen miles to Gurdàspur. The fierce July sun was already beating down upon the heads of man and beast. 'All were aware,' says General Bourchier, 'what a terrific sunning we might expect, none knew it better than Nicholson, but he knew also the value of the stake.' In spite of his *ekkas*, ponies, and the horses taken from the 9th Cavalry, some of his devoted infantry had to take their turn of trudging on foot under a sun which sorely tried the endurance even of their mounted comrades. Now and then some poor fellow lay prone from sunstroke, or faint from sheer exhaustion. But the rest of our men pushed on with unflagging spirit, as if they were out on a holiday excursion in their own country.

Songs, jokes, and laughter enlivened that terrific march. The good humour was infectious. Like Mark Tapley, every one did his best to be jolly in the most trying circumstances. Of the humours of the march we get some glimpses from Bourchier's narrative. Branches of trees served as awnings for the gun-carriages and waggons that bore his men, reminding them of 'carts got up for a day at Hampstead.' Officers crowned with wreaths of green leaves ' were chaffed by their comrades for donning head-dresses à la Norma.' At one moment a soldier on a rampant pony would desire a companion similarly mounted to ' keep behind him and be his " edge-de-camp." ' Another hero, mindful perhaps of Epping on Easter Monday, bellowed out his inquiries as to who had seen the fox. Privates never intended for the mounted branch here and there came to grief, and lay sprawling on mother-earth; while ever and anon some mighty Jehu in his *ekka* dashed to the front at a pace a Roman charioteer would have envied.

During the hottest part of the afternoon a halt was sounded beside a grove of trees, in order that our overworn soldiers might snatch an hour's rest beneath its cool shade. Nicholson, eager to press on, had taken this step with manifest reluctance. One of his officers, on awaking from his brief slumber, inquired for the general, but could not find him among the sleepers. At last he saw Nicholson in the middle of the hot dusty road, sitting bolt upright on his horse in the full glare of that July sun, waiting, like a sentinel turned to stone, for the moment when his men should resume their march. Was it, as some thought, a silent protest against the delay to which he had consented?

At last, however, the long march was over. The artillery halted outside Gurdâspur about 3 p.m., having covered the forty-four miles in eighteen hours. It was near 6 p.m. before the whole column reached its ground. ' Longer marches have been made,' says General Bourchier, ' but none severer, or attended with more satisfactory results.' Thus far, indeed, Nicholson's plans had prospered up to the hilt. Gurdâspur had been saved, as well as the Kangra district; and the enemy were still fifteen miles off beyond the Râvi, little dreaming that the movable column had left Amritsar. So strict a watch was kept on the fords and ferries of the Râvi, that the mutineers knew nothing as yet of Nicholson's whereabouts. At the moment, however, of his arrival, the danger which he most dreaded was close at hand.

On the evening of the 11th, Nicholson was passing through the camp of the 52nd on his way to see Colonel Campbell, when, among the villagers who had thronged into camp to sell their little stores of milk, eggs, fruit, and vegetables, his keen eye detected two men whose bearing was not as that of harmless village folk. He called at once for the sergeant-major of the regiment. ' Sergeant-major, these two men are Sepoys of the 46th. Have them secured.' This was done forthwith. The men confessed that they were Sepoys, who had been sent to raise the 2nd Irregulars at Gurdâspur. But for that opportune discovery, the disguised mutineers would have got away from Gurdàspur in time to warn their comrades of the Nemesis awaiting them if they crossed the Ràvi [1].

Early next morning, July 12, Nicholson learned through his spies that the enemy had begun crossing the river by a ford at Trimmu Ghàt, nine miles from Gurdàspur. This was welcome news indeed for the commander of the movable column. He must have felt with Cromwell on a like occasion, that the Lord had delivered them into his hands. He had feared to oppose their passage of the river, lest they should 'break southwards,' and so escape him [2]. But once fairly landed on the left bank, they could not escape him, do what they might.

About 9 a.m. of the 12th, after a night's rest and a good breakfast, the column began its march in the best of spirits towards the Ràvi, burning to wreak its vengeance on ' the mutinous scoundrels who had so recently shed the blood of our friends at Sialkòt [3].' The 52nd pressed on as if nothing in the world could tire them. It was noon before the blue-grey jackets of cavalry videttes revealed to Nicholson the nearness of his quarry. The mutineers had crossed the river with all their baggage, the plunder of Sialkòt, and were now drawn up in line about a mile from the left bank, with the 9th Cavalry on either side of the 46th Sepoys. Their right rested on a serai and an empty old mud fortlet; their left on a small village and a clump of trees. Their front was covered by a deep narrow nullah spanned by a single bridge. Nicholson delivered his attack in two lines. The first line was formed by 300 of the 52nd, armed with the new Enfield rifle, marching in loose

<hr>

[1] Cave-Browne.   [2] Nicholson, *Official Report*, July 19.
[3] Sir G. Bourchier.

order on either flank of Bourchier's three guns, while the six guns of Dawes's troop guarded the outer flanks of that regiment. The rest of the 52nd and the companies of Punjâb Infantry formed the second line. The advancing batteries were masked by the new levies of mounted police; the only thing in the shape of cavalry which the force could boast of [1].

Hardly had our men crossed the nullah when some of the mutineer cavalry, maddened, it was said, with *bhang*, made a sudden dash upon Dawes's guns of the left wing, scattering the mounted levies, and making straight for the battery before the 52nd could come to the rescue. If the miscreants hoped to seduce our native drivers—of whom, indeed, their own officers had felt somewhat uncertain—they soon paid dearly for their misreckoning. The drivers did their duty as zealously as the English gunners, and not one of the attacking party returned to his camp [2].

Nicholson had ordered his troops to reserve their fire until they came within 300 yards of the enemy's line. Then both guns and rifles were to open together a deadly fire upon the Sepoys, whose smooth-bore muskets could do little harm at such a range. At about that distance, however, the mutineers led off with continuous file-firing, which at closer quarters might have been deadly enough. 'We lost no time,' says Nicholson, 'in replying, and for about ten minutes they stood up very well indeed against the great odds opposed to them; many of them advancing boldly up to the very guns. Meanwhile the cavalry had made several rushes in detached parties on our flanks and rear; but had always been repulsed by the file-firing of our infantry.'

[1] Nicholson, *Report*; Bourchier.　　　[2] Bourchier.

The mutineers had fought stubbornly; but, in General Bourchier's own words, ' a well-directed pounding of grape and shrapnel from nine guns, aided by the rifles of the infantry, soon told its tale.' Within half an hour they were speeding back to the river, leaving 120 dead upon the field. Nicholson followed them up with his artillery and Boswell's Punjàbis: for the gallant 52nd could hardly drag one foot after the other. Even the artillery horses were so spent that they could hardly get up a canter to the river bank [1]. The guns, however, inflicted some further loss upon the mutineers as they fought their way through the swollen current towards an island in mid-stream, on which they had planted the old 12-pounder station-gun. The Ràvi was already in flood through the melting of the Himalayan snows, and many a Sepoy who escaped the fire of our guns was swept away in the turbid torrent.

A few rounds from our batteries silenced the fire from the 12-pounder. The whole of the enemy's baggage and camp-furniture was in our hands. Had Nicholson possessed a squadron or two of good cavalry—for his raw police levies were but a sorry makeshift—the victory of that day would have been crowned by the annihilation of the Sialkòt mutineers. As things stood that afternoon, to use his own words, ' The want of cavalry (which crippled us sadly during the action), the depth of water in the ford, and the fatigue the troops had undergone on the previous day, all conspired to prevent me from attempting to pursue the enemy across the river.' Leaving the Punjàbis under Lieutenant Boswell in the Serai to watch the enemy and guard the captured baggage, Nicholson marched his

[1] Bourchier.

Europeans quietly back to Gurdâspur, where he meant to await further tidings of the enemy's movements.

He knew that they could not move far. They were caught in fact between the devil and the deep sea. Their isle of refuge was surrounded by a deep, unfordable river. Of those who tried to swim across the river to the further bank, very few escaped death by drowning. The rest of the Sepoys, still numbering 400 or 500, resolved apparently to take their chance of life or death on firm ground. They threw up a breastwork for the 12-pounder gun, of which Brigadier Brind's *khansamah* had undertaken the management. Their main body entrenched themselves about a village at the northern end of the island.

Among the wounded in that day's fight was Nicholson's orderly officer, Lieutenant Baillie of the 35th Native Infantry. Disabled for a time from active service, he was left behind at Gurdâspur, when the victorious column marched back towards Amritsar. Nicholson, however, had not forgotten him. On the 25th, from the left bank of the Biàs, he wrote to the sufferer—

'Just a line to say how sorry I am to hear that your wound is more severe than was at first supposed, and that I came away without seeing you. Make haste and get well, and I will (if in my power) find something to your liking for you before Delhi.

Yours sincerely,

J. Nicholson.'

'He did not forget me,' writes General Baillie, 'for, when called upon to nominate officers for the newly raised Punjâb levies, he sent in my name for the adjutancy of the 7th Punjâb Infantry, the first of the new regiments; and this appointment I held throughout the remainder of the mutiny campaign.' Baillie was never to see his kind commander again, for the corps of which he erelong became second-in-command was serving in the Meerut district, on the flank of Wilson's army [1].

Our own losses in the fight itself had been very small. But the unwonted hardships of the last two or three days told once more upon our jaded countrymen during the return march on the evening of the 12th. A sergeant in Bourchier's battery died by his captain's side from sheer exhaustion, and several of the 52nd succumbed to the effects of exposure and fatigue. Bourchier probably saved one poor fellow's life by offering him the tumbler of beer which he had just poured out for himself. A grateful ' God bless you, sir ! ' was for the giver an ample reward. The 13th was a day of much needed rest for the force at Gurdâspur, while Nicholson waited for the information which Captain Adams, the assistant commissioner, had gone off to collect for him at Trimmu Ghât.

The reports received from Adams and from Boswell, who had gone with a company of police to watch a ford higher up the river, soon determined Nicholson's plans for completing what he had so brilliantly begun. Towards evening of the 14th the artillery and the 52nd Foot marched off again for Trimmu Ghât. The next day was spent in careful preparations for the crowning stroke. On the evening of that day two large boats were quietly brought down from ferries higher up the river, for every boat that plied near Trimmu Ferry had been sunk by our district officers on the first tidings of the Sialkôt disaster. At daybreak of the 16th, the infantry were ferried over to the southernmost end of the island, where a thick screen

---

[1] Letter from General J. C. Baillie.

of brushwood parted them from the enemy's pickets. Meanwhile Bourchier's three guns and four of Dawes's troop—the other two being placed on elephants ready at need to wade across the river—kept blazing away at the old 12-pounder, nearly hidden by tall grass and a protecting earthwork, in order to 'draw off Pandy's attention from the real game[1].'

The 52nd were soon moving forward, skirmishers in front, while Nicholson himself, with a few of his staff and a small escort, rode on ahead to reconnoitre, and sent a cavalry picket flying in wild haste before his sudden onset. The alarm soon spread, and the mutineers slewed their only gun round to bear upon the advancing infantry. But the men who worked it could not get its rusty old screw to act properly at short notice, and the shot flew harmlessly over the heads of our men. A rush upon the battery was led by Nicholson himself, whose keen sword, impelled by a singularly nervous arm, crashed down with cut No. 1 upon the shoulder of the man who worked the gun, and clove him literally in two[2]. In another moment not a man was left alive beside the gun.

'It was now helter-skelter,' says an eye-witness, quoted by Mr. Cave-Browne. 'They ran to the head of the island, were followed up by our fellows, and took to the water. Many of them must have been drowned; numbers were like mud-larks on sand-banks and small islands.' The real business, according to Nicholson, 'was over in a few minutes without any check, and with a loss

---

[1] Bourchier. 'Pandy' was then a common nickname for the Sepoy rebels, with many of whom it was a real surname.

[2] Bosworth Smith. 'Not a bad sliver that!' he remarked to his aide-de-camp.

to us of only six wounded.   A few resolute men among the mutineers died manfully at the gun ; the rest fled, and were either slain on the bank or driven into the river.' The few who escaped across the river were given up by the village people to Commissioner Roberts's police.   Thus within eight days from their murderous outbreak, the mutinous half of the Sialkôt brigade had been hunted down and destroyed by their late comrades, marching under a leader who knew exactly what to do, and the best way of doing it.

From his camp at Gurdàspur, whither the column returned on the evening of that eventful July 16, Nicholson next day issued the following order to his troops—

'The last remaining party of the Sialkôt mutineers was yesterday morning destroyed, and its gun captured.

'The object of the forced march of the column from Amritsar to this place having been thus successfully accomplished, the brigadier-general desires to return his sincere thanks to officers and men of all arms and grades for the cordial and valuable assistance he has received from them throughout these operations.

'The brigadier-general considers that the column has reason to feel proud of the service it has rendered the State within the last few days.   By a forced march of unusual length, performed at a very trying season of the year, it has been able to preserve many stations and districts from pillage and plunder, to save more than one regiment from the danger of too close a contact with the mutineers ; and the mutineer force itself, 1,100 strong, notwithstanding the very desperate character of the resistance offered by it, has been utterly destroyed or dispersed.

'It will be the pleasing duty of the brigadier-general

to bring prominently to the notice of Government, in detail, the services rendered by officers and men on this occasion, and he entertains no doubt but that those services will be appreciated and acknowledged as they deserve.'

Sir John Lawrence was not slow to proclaim his satisfaction at the brilliant feat of arms by which, at an aggregate loss of forty-six fighting men, Nicholson had given 'practical evidence of what can be accomplished by a really efficient commander.' Its beneficial effect in the Punjâb is of course acknowledged. But its main result, thinks the chief commissioner, 'consists in the loss which has been directly or indirectly inflicted on the general cause of the mutineers in Hindustan as well as the Punjâb.' But for Nicholson's prompt soldiership, the force which he entrapped and destroyed at Trimmu Ghât 'would probably have reached Delhi with 3,000 or 4,000 good native soldiers, to the infinite encouragement of the insurgents in that city.' And, pointing to the incalculable mischief caused by the mutinies in Jalandhar and Rohilkhand, John Lawrence might well avow his belief 'that Delhi would long since have fallen into our hands, had the commanders in those places acted with the energy shown by Nicholson in dealing with the mutineers from Sialkôt [1].'

On the morning of July 22 the column was once more encamped at Amritsar; its commander having stayed behind at Lahore to take counsel with the chief commissioner who had just come down from Rawal Pindi, bent upon reinforcing the camp before Delhi with his last available troops and guns. That evening orders were issued to prepare for a march next morning towards the Biâs. The camp was full of speculation as to the meaning of this new move.

[1] Bosworth Smith.

Few dared think of Delhi as their destined goal; for in that case how many white soldiers would be left to guard the Punjáb and keep watch on thousands of disarmed Sepoys? All doubts, however, were to be dispelled on the 24th, when Nicholson rejoined his column near the Biás, and the glad tidings spread among his men that they were really marching down to Delhi. They learned that the self-sacrificing policy which had nearly stripped the Punjáb of troops was to be carried still further, and their only fear was that Delhi might fall before they could reach it. Every one, however, felt certain that it would not be the general's fault if his troops should not arrive in time [1].

On the 25th the column once more crossed the Biás, on whose bank, about three weeks before, Nicholson had spoken to Captain Farrington those parting words, ' You'll soon see me back again.' The column now consisted of Dawes's troop of horse artillery, Bourchier's battery, the 52nd Queen's, a wing of the Amritsar Police Battalion, and about 240 Multáni Horse.

Nicholson had been ordered to leave Dawes's troop behind, unless General Wilson, who had commanded the troops before Delhi since the death of Sir Henry Barnard, should make an urgent demand for more guns. But he felt that the column had special need of so good an officer as Colonel Dawes in the event of anything happening to himself; and Sir John Lawrence, with a monitory grumble, let him have his own way. On the 27th, when his troops were nearing the Satlaj, Nicholson wrote to the chief commissioner: ' I have telegraphed to General Wilson about the artillery. Twelve or even eighteen guns is not a large proportion of artillery for the reinforcements going down.

[1] Bourchier.

Moreover the European troops coming up from below will be very weak in artillery, and it is better we should have it on the spot than be obliged to send for it. Unless General Wilson should say ' No,' I should recommend either Paton's troop or the battery which has come from Peshâwar to Rawal Pindi being sent down when the Punjàbi Infantry Corps goes for Peshàwar [1].'

With the same heroic disregard of orders, Nicholson carried off a body of European gunners from the Fort of Philúr. ' I fear you are incorrigible,' wrote John Lawrence on August 4, ' so I must leave you to your fate. But depend on it,' added that experienced mentor, ' you would get on equally well, and much more smoothly, if you worked *with* men rather than against them [2].' Wise counsel indeed for ordinary men, but thrown away perhaps on this incorrigible Titan !

[1] Bosworth Smith ; Kaye.   [2] Bosworth Smith.

CHAPTER XXI

On August 2, as the column was pushing on from the Satlaj towards Umballa, Nicholson heard from General Wilson that the enemy had restored the broken bridge over the Najafgarh canal, for the purpose of 'moving on Alipur and our communications to the rear.' He was therefore earnestly entreated to push on with all possible speed, ' both to drive these fellows from our rear, and to aid me in holding my position.' When the column reached Umballa by forced marches on the 6th, its commander wrote to John Lawrence : ' I am just starting post to Delhi by General Wilson's desire. The column should be at Karnâl the day after to-morrow.'

In the same letter he replies to his chief's half jocular remonstrance quoted in the previous chapter : ' I am very sorry to hear that General Gowan has taken offence again. I don't wish to ignore him or any other superior. I dislike offending any one, and except on principle would never have a disagreement. You write as if I were in the habit of giving offence. Now I cannot call to mind that since my return to India, upwards of five years and a half ago, I have had any misunderstandings except with —— and ——. The former I believe is conscious that he did me wrong, and

I trust the latter will eventually make the same admission. I fear that I must have given offence to you, too, on the Rawal Pindi question. I can only say that I opposed my opinion to yours with great reluctance, and had the matter been one of less importance, I might have preserved silence. But when in a great crisis an officer holds a strong opinion in any matter of consequence, I think he fails in his duty if he does not speak it out, at whatever risk of giving offence [1].'

One may imagine the smile of amused impatience with which John Lawrence read this very characteristic revelation of a nature as masterful and more stubbornly self-reliant than his own.

A night's jolting on the mail-cart brought Nicholson next morning to the head-quarters camp before the great strong city which for two months past had given our soldiers no rest from daily fighting and frequent alarms. He had come on ahead of his troops to confer with Wilson about matters of grave moment, and to see for himself what chance there was of bringing the siege to a swift conclusion. As the news of his arrival spread through the camp, every one felt that stirring times were at hand for the Delhi Field Force, and that the great soldier of whose prowess they had lately heard so much was come to lead them, as no one else could do, over the ramparts of the rebel stronghold. 'Nicholson has come on ahead,' wrote Hodson on August 8, 'and is a host in himself, if he does not go and get knocked over as Chamberlain did. The camp is all alive at the notion of something decisive taking place soon.'

Only to a few of Wilson's officers was the new-comer

<hr>

[1] Kaye, *Sepoy War*.

personally known. His old friend Neville Chamberlain had been badly wounded in the sharp fighting that took place on July 14. Roberts also had received a wound which still kept him on the sick list. Coke and Hodson and Taylor of the Engineers had been doing conspicuous service in their respective ways. But those who now saw Nicholson for the first time were not slow to recognize the advent among them of a new and all-commanding force. A competent eye-witness tells how about this time 'a stranger of very striking appearance was remarked visiting all our pickets, examining everything, and making most searching inquiries about their strength and history. His attire gave no clue to his rank ; it evidently never cost the owner a thought. . . . It was soon made out that this was General Nicholson, whose person was not yet known in camp ; and it was whispered at the same time that he was possessed of the most brilliant military genius. He was a man cast in a giant mould, with massive chest and powerful limbs, and an expression ardent and commanding, with a dash of roughness ; features of stern beauty, a long black beard, and deep sonorous voice. There was something of immense strength, talent, and resolution in his whole frame and manner, and a power of ruling men on high occasions which no one could escape noticing. His imperial air, which never left him, and which would have been thought arrogance in one of less imposing mien, sometimes gave offence to the more unbending of his countrymen, but made him almost worshipped by the pliant Asiatics [1].'

On the evening of the 7th, Nicholson dined at the head-quarters mess, where his grave, stern face and quiet manner acted as a damper on the gaiety of some who sat around

---

[1] *History of the Siege of Delhi,* by an officer who served there.

him. In one of his bright 'Letters from the Camp,' for instance, the civil commissioner, Mr. Harvey Greathed, describes him as 'a fine, imposing-looking man, who never speaks if he can help it; which is a great gift for a public man. But if we had all been as solemn and as taciturn during the last two months, I do not think we should have survived. Our genial, jolly mess-dinners have kept up our spirits.' Nicholson was always shy and reserved before strangers, and there was much at this time that might well make him unusually grave. He had just heard of the death of his old master and dearest friend, Sir Henry Lawrence, and must have felt with Sir Henry's brother, that the loss of such a man at such a moment was a national calamity. The Residency at Lucknow was closely besieged by swarms of rebels and mutineers. Havelock and Neill had reached Cawnpore too late to avert the dreadful massacres which capped the prolonged sufferings previously endured by Wheeler's luckless garrison. For a month past a British regiment and a battery of guns had been locked up in the fort of Agra, together with a body of civil officers and hundreds of refugees from the surrounding districts. Outside Agra, the whole country between Delhi and Cawnpore was given over to anarchy and rebellion. Beyond the Ganges, nearly all Rohilkhand and all Oudh, except the fortified Residency, had slipped out of our hands.

Even in the Punjâb there was cause for disquietude. The sudden rising of a disarmed regiment at Lahore in the last days of July was promptly quelled by the pursuit and slaughter of nearly all concerned. But what if similar attempts should be made elsewhere with better chances of success? The sickly season was setting in over the

Peshâwar valley, and fever and dysentery would soon thin the ranks of our European soldiers at a time when their help was most sorely needed.   Sir John Lawrence was sending down to Delhi his last man and his last gun.   Wilson still pressed him for more Europeans, but was told in answer that he had no more to spare, and that everything, even in the Punjâb, depended upon the speedy capture of Delhi by the troops already placed at Wilson's disposal.

On the morning of the 8th, Nicholson started on a round of inspection among the batteries and pickets that guarded the front and flanks of our position along the ridge.   In company with Colonel—now Sir Henry—Norman, he paid his first visit to the great post at Hindu Rao's house, which Major Charles Reid and his sturdy little Gurkhas had defended so stubbornly against all assailants for two months past.   Baird Smith, the chief engineer, was present at the meeting between the gallant commander of the picket and the haughty-looking stranger who questioned him so closely on every detail connected with his charge.   After Nicholson's departure, Reid complained to Baird Smith of his late visitor's lofty manner and overbearing style of address.   'Yes,' assented the chief engineer, ' but that wears off.   You'll like him better when you have seen more of him.'   And it turned out as Baird Smith predicted, for not many days were to elapse before Reid's dislike changed into admiration, and the two men became excellent friends [1].

What time Nicholson could spare from examining our line of outposts, watching the enemy's counter-attacks, and holding conference with General Wilson, was devoted to looking up his particular friends.   To please Roberts rather

[1] Kaye.

than himself, he told his young admirer all about his fight with the Sialkôt mutineers at Trimmu Ghât, and the various marches and counter-marches which he had made since they two parted at Philúr [1]. Chamberlain was slowly recovering from his wound, and Daly was still disabled from active duty at the head of his Guides. But to both of them John Nicholson's kindly visits gave earnest of a speedy and triumphant issue to the long-drawn struggle between the rebels and the hard-pressed guardians of the ridge.

There was much sickness at this time in camp, and Wilson himself had been one of the sufferers. 'Our general, since his illness,' writes Hodson, 'has got a still greater dread of responsibility, and ceased to be nearly as vigorous as heretofore [2].' He had a certain amount of backbone as well as soldierly skill, and appeared even to John Lawrence 'a vast improvement upon his predecessors.' But he was not an ideal leader for such a crisis, and his waning energy, coupled with a growing dread of responsibility, had made the chief commissioner all the more anxious that such a man as John Nicholson should be at hand to keep General Wilson up to the right mark.

> 'If we fail, we fail;
> But screw your courage to the sticking-place,
> And we'll not fail '—

was the burden of many a letter from Sir John Lawrence to the perplexed commander of the Delhi Field Force.

On August 8 the rebels contrived to erect a battery at Ludlow Castle, the fire from which presently began to annoy our pickets about Metcalfe House, on the left of our line. At Nicholson's request, Wilson agreed that the task of clearing away this new obstruction should devolve

---

[1] Lord Roberts.   [2] *Hodson of Hodson's Horse.*

upon the movable column as soon as it arrived in camp. On the morning of the 12th, Nicholson rejoined his troops at Rhai, two short marches from Delhi.   He told his excited hearers that the tide had turned at last, but that some tough work still lay before them.   'General Wilson promised our column a little job by way of getting our hands in: to dislodge a body of troops who have planted themselves with some guns about Ludlow Castle[1].'   The little job, however, had been accomplished by other hands in the small hours of that very morning.   So troublesome grew the fire from Ludlow Castle, that a column of mixed troops under the bold Brigadier Showers sallied forth in the darkness, and by dawn of the 12th swooped down upon the obnoxious battery.   The rebels, taken by surprise, fought hard but vainly, and in a few minutes Ludlow Castle was cleared of every living Sepoy.   Four of the enemy's guns were brought into camp as trophies of a success somewhat dearly earned by the loss of more than a hundred slain or wounded.

On the 13th the movable column was encamped at Alipur, whence through his glasses a man could see the flag-staff tower on the top of the historic ridge; while his ears were filled with the roar of a ceaseless cannonade, and the moist hot air reeked with foul odours from the rear of Wilson's camp.   At night the frequent flashes from the guns told of a struggle that knew no rest.   Nicholson had been warned to expect an attack from the enemy, but none was attempted.   As Sir G. Bourchier remarks, 'our greatest safety from surprise was the state of the country. Five yards on either side of the road, except exactly the ground on which we were encamped, was a swamp, imprac-

<hr>

[1] Bourchier.

ticable for artillery or cavalry; but on this occasion, as on most others during the Mutiny, when head and combination were necessary, the enemy signally failed to take advantage of their position.'

Along the seven miles of road between Alipur and the camp before Delhi, the signs of a deadly and desolating warfare grew more and more visible as Nicholson rode on at the head of his brave and eager troops. The trees by the wayside had been lopped and stripped of their foliage to feed the camels and supply fuel for our troops. Badli-ke Serài, the scene of Barnard's first encounter with the rebels, was now strongly fortified and garrisoned by the followers of a loyal Sikh chief. An hour later in the morning of August 14, the Punjàb column, 3,000 strong, headed by its glorious leader, marched into camp with bands playing, amid hearty cheers from the force it had come to succour in the nick of time [1].

It was not quite the same column as that from which Nicholson had parted at Umballa. Greatly to his regret, Colonel Dawes and his six-pounder troop had to stand fast until further orders. On its way down through Sirhind the column had picked up nearly 400 of the 61st Queen's from Firozpur, and 700 of Green's Punjàbi Rifles. Not far behind them were Wilde's Punjàbis, a company of recruits for Rothney's Sikhs, and three strong companies of the 8th Foot. The whole of these reinforcements from the Punjàb amounted to 4,200 men, of whom nearly 1,300 were Europeans [2].

Thus in a few days Wilson's numbers would be nearly doubled. Meanwhile the arrival of Nicholson's column brought Wilson's soldiers a timely respite from 'the

[1] Bourchier.　　　　　　　　　[2] Cave-Browne.

pressure,' in Wilson's own words, ' of the severe duties imposed on them by the constant attacks of the insurgents[1].' For some days after the 12th the enemy remained unusually quiet, and ' the morning and evening game at long bowls was,' says Bourchier, ' our only occupation.' But the rebels were planning mischief elsewhere. On the 14th Wilson learned that a party of armed men had left Delhi by the road to Rohtak, forty miles away on his right rear, and Hodson was at once instructed to look after them. With 230 of his newly raised horse and 100 of the Guide Cavalry, Hodson started on one of those daring reconnaissances which won for him the unfeigned admiration of the whole camp. At the end of a week Hodson reappeared, having discharged a hazardous errand in a manner which delighted Wilson, and enhanced his own fame as a consummate cavalry leader[2]. The rebels had been heavily routed and the Rohtak district saved from pillage, with a loss on our side of only seventeen officers and men wounded.

A few days later a task of still greater importance was entrusted to Nicholson himself. On August 10 a powerful siege-train had left Firozpur under a weak escort, and was dragging its ponderous length of five or six miles along the great Trunk Road that led towards the ridge. The rebels in Delhi were quite aware of its approach, and knew what awaited them if once it entered the British camp. On the 24th Wilson learned that a large force of mutineers, with sixteen guns, had marched out of Delhi towards Najafgarh for the purpose of cutting off our supplies, worrying our rear, and intercepting the siege-train. Nicholson

---

[1] Forrest, *Indian Mutiny, Selections.*
[2] Forrest; *Hodson of Hodson's Horse.*

was ordered to go out and intercept the enemy. The column which he had to lead consisted of three troops of horse artillery under the dashing Major Tombs, a squadron of the 9th Lancers under Captain Sarel, 200 of Lind's Multâni Horse, a squadron of the Guides under Sandford, a troop of the 2nd Punjâb Cavalry under Charles Nicholson, Colonel Rainer's wing of the 61st Foot, 200 of the 1st Bengal Fusiliers under Major Jacob, 400 of Coke's and as many of Green's Punjâb Infantry, with 30 sappers and miners [1].

At daybreak of the 25th, in a drenching rain, Nicholson rode away at the head of 2,500 good troops and sixteen guns. He would gladly have kept a place on his staff for two such men as Hodson and Roberts, and gladly would they have served under such a leader. But both of them were on the sick list, and neither could persuade his doctor to take him off it. Hodson, who was down with dysentery after his Rohtak raid, was told by Dr. Mactier to stay at home and nurse himself, and let some one else have a chance of doing good service [2].

'It proved,' says Lord Roberts, 'a most difficult march. The rain fell in torrents, and the roads were mere quagmires.' In the first nine miles the troops had to struggle through two difficult swamps, in which the guns sometimes stuck fast up to their axles, before reaching the village of Nanglui. Nicholson decided, as his own dispatch tells us, to push on, attack, and rout them, 'if possible, before night.' Sir Theophilus Metcalfe, who as magistrate of Delhi knew the whole district well, had volunteered to act as guide to the column. During the halt at Nanglui he rode on ahead

---

[1] Forrest; Cave-Browne.　　　[2] Rev. G. Hodson.

with two officers to examine a nullah which crossed the road some five miles off. They found the nullah fairly practicable, and saw beyond it the enemy's outposts. The news carried back cheered all hearts, and braced up our men to fresh feats of soldierly endurance [1].

By 5 p.m. the whole column had got across a broad and rather deep ford over a branch of the great Najafgarh *Jheel* or marsh, near the village of Basraula. The time which his troops took in crossing was spent by their leader in a rapid reconnaissance of the enemy's position. For want of guides, he had to trust entirely to his own re-searches; but these served him well enough. The enemy's line extended for nearly two miles, from the town of Najafgarh on their left to the bridge over the Najafgarh canal on their right. 'Their strongest point,' he wrote, ' was an old serai on their left centre, in which they had four guns; nine more guns between this and the bridge.' While his troops were yet struggling through the ford, Nicholson had made up his mind to ' force the left centre, and then, changing front to the left, sweep down their line of guns towards the bridge [2].' There was no time to lose, he knew, on that August evening, and he was going to attack the strongest point in the enemy's position. But with such troops as his he could safely risk something for a great and far-reaching issue. He formed up the 61st Queen's, the 1st Bengal Fusiliers, and Green's Punjàbi Rifles for the attack, leaving 100 of each corps to act as rear-guard and reserve. Four guns were to cover the right and ten the left flank of our advancing infantry, while the 9th Lancers and the Guide Cavalry were to support the attacking line. Charles Nicholson's cavalry and a

---

[1] Cave-Browne; Forrest.　　　　　　[2] Forrest.

troop of Multâni Horse with two guns remained behind to guard the camp-stores in the village at the ford.

The rebels had opened a smart fire on our men as they crossed the ford. After our infantry had formed line on the other side, they lay down by Nicholson's order while our guns began to answer those of the enemy. Before sounding the advance, Nicholson rode along the line of his eager infantry, and spoke a few warning words to each regiment in turn, bidding them reserve their fire until they had got within thirty or forty yards of the serai. 'Then pour in a volley and charge straight upon them.' 'Remember,' he added to the 61st, 'what Sir Colin Campbell said to you at Chilianwâla, and you have heard that he said the same to his gallant Highlanders at the Alma.' To the 1st Fusiliers he said, 'I have nothing more to say to the men of the 1st Fusiliers; they will do as they have always done [1].'

After some well-delivered rounds from our guns, the bugles sounded the advance. Nicholson's infantry sprang to their feet and swept forward, Nicholson leading the way under a heavy fire of guns and musketry, over the two hundred yards of mud that lay between them and the enemy. In a few minutes the serai was stormed and the battery taken, after a fierce but short struggle with its resolute defenders, scores of whom were slain on the spot. Emerging from the serai, our victorious infantry formed up to the left, and, sweeping along the rear of the position, drove the rebels in swift retreat across the canal bridge, and captured all the guns they were trying to carry off [2].

---

[1] Forrest; Cave-Browne; Innes, *History of the Bengal European Regiment.*

[2] Cave-Browne; Kaye.

Meanwhile Lieutenant Lumsden, who commanded Coke's Punjábis in the room of their gallant leader, wounded in the attack on Ludlow Castle, had been equally successful in driving the enemy out of Najafgarh. But just as the day's work seemed over, Nicholson learned that a small body of mutineers were lurking in a hamlet between the serai and the canal. Lumsden was ordered to drive them out. But they fought so desperately for their last chance of life—being like rats in a cage—that Lumsden himself and many of his men were killed, and the 61st Foot had to turn back and help their luckless comrades in achieving a task of unforeseen difficulty [1].

But for that one mishap, the victory of Najafgarh would have been almost as bloodless as it was brilliant and complete. In less than one hour at the end of a day's long and toilsome marching through a flooded country scarcely practicable even for light guns or lightly laden camels, Nicholson had routed 5,000 or 6,000 disciplined Sepoys, strongly posted and covered by the fire from thirteen field-guns. He had cut through the strongest point of their line, rolled up their right, captured all their guns, ordnance stores, baggage, and camp furniture, and driven them with heavy slaughter across the bridge on their way back to Delhi. The bridge itself was blown up by Lieutenant Geneste and his sappers. And all this, including the capture of the small village, had been accomplished with a total loss of two officers and twenty-three men killed, two officers and sixty-eight men wounded. 'Our loss,' writes Hodson, one of Nicholson's warmest admirers, 'was small for the gain. The victory is a great one, and will shake the Pandies' nerves.'

[1] Forrest.

The victors passed the night without food or shelter on the ground they had won; Nicholson faring no better than the rest. Happily the night was fine and warm. Soon after daybreak of the 26th the troops began their march homewards, bringing with them the captured guns and some other trophies of their success. Nicholson's aide-de-camp, Captain Low, rode on ahead to acquaint Wilson with the happy issue of yesterday's operations. Some elephants were at once sent out from camp to bring in the wounded and footsore men. But it was late that evening before the whole column marched into camp.

There was great rejoicing in Wilson's army over the hardest blow which had yet been struck at the Delhi mutineers. Every one was loud in praise of the regimental captain of thirty-four summers who had once more proved his fitness for high command. The gallant Coke gave voice to the general feeling when he declared that 'there was not another man in camp, except perhaps Chamberlain, who would have taken that column to Najafgarh. . . . An artillery officer told me that at one time the water was over his horses' backs, and he thought they could not possibly get out of their difficulties. But he looked ahead and saw Nicholson's great form riding steadily on as if nothing was the matter, and he felt sure that all was right [1].'

Wilson himself in an order of the day tendered his 'most hearty thanks and congratulations to Brigadier-General Nicholson and his troops, on the very successful issue of the operations they were engaged in.' For the 'glorious result of these operations' he declared himself 'indebted to the judgement and energy displayed by the commander; the steadiness and gallantry of the troops in action; and

[1] Kaye.

the cheerfulness with which they bore the fatigue and hardships they were called upon to undergo.' In his dispatch to General Gowan, the same officer declares that 'they all most richly deserve my highest praise'; and he begs 'that Major-General Gowan will bring to the favourable notice of Government the name of Brigadier-General Nicholson, as well as all those officers mentioned in his report [1].'

In his own report Nicholson had expressed his 'extreme satisfaction' with the conduct of his troops. 'No soldiers ever advanced to the attack of a position with greater gallantry and steadiness than H.M. 61st Regiment, the 1st Fusiliers, and the 2nd Regiment Punjâb Infantry. No infantry was ever more ably assisted by artillery.' Nor did he fail to testify to the cheerfulness with which his troops had borne the hardships of a long and very trying march, followed by a night passed 'on the field, without food or covering of any kind.' Among the officers deemed worthy of mention, the first place is given to Major Tombs, whose merits 'are so well known to the major-general that it is unnecessary for me to dwell upon them [2].'

To the chief commissioner Nicholson forwarded a rough draft of his report. 'The field was of such extent,' he writes, 'that it was not easy to estimate the mutineers' loss. I think, moreover, that they suffered more severely from the fire of our artillery after they had bolted across the bridge than they did on the actual battle-field. According to all accounts the Nimachh brigade (the one I dealt with) only musters 600 men now. Many of those who fled would appear never to have returned to Delhi. Most of the officers with me in the action rated them at 6,000, 7,000,

---

[1] Forrest.   [2] Ibid.

and 8,000. My own idea is that they were between 3,000 and 4,000. Except when poor Lumsden was killed, they made little attempt to stand. Most of the killed were Kotah Contingent men. We took the Nimachh troop of artillery complete, three light field battery guns, and four of the King's Own. I wish sincerely they had had as many more, as after their flank was turned they could not have used them, and must have lost them all. An old subahdàr [native captain] who stuck in a *jheel*, begged for mercy on the ground that he had eaten the Company's salt for forty years, and would never do it again! The 13th and 14th Irregulars, who were in the action, are talking of asking pardon. I feel very thankful for my success, for had these two brigades succeeded in getting into our rear, they would undoubtedly have done much mischief[1].'

One of the brigades to which he referred was the Bareilly brigade, which had borne no part in the fight of the 25th, being either unable or unwilling to push on a few miles further to the front. Nicholson learned too late how near he had come to striking at this force also on his way back. 'Had I had,' he wrote afterwards to his chief, 'a decent political officer with me to get me a little information, I might have smashed the Bareilly brigade at Pàlam the next day. As it was, I had no information, not even a guide that I did not pick up for myself on the road; and had I obeyed my instructions and gone to Bahàdurgarh, the expedition would have been a fruitless one[2].' The Rohilkhand mutineers, however, had learned their lesson, and made the quickest of their way back to Delhi.

From that time forth the Delhi insurgents ceased from troubling us either in front or in rear. When the ubiquitous

<hr>

[1] Kaye.   [2] Cave-Browne; Kaye.

Hodson rode out on the 29th over the battle-field won by 'the general after his heart,' he 'found no enemy, and everything quiet in the direction of Najafgarh.' After the rout of Najafgarh the King of Delhi, according to Major Norman, 'felt that all chance of success against the British force was at an end [1].' Hodson tells us how a messenger from the palace came into camp on August 30, 'with much assurance and great promises; but he was sent back rather humbler than he came, for he fancied he should make terms, and could not get a single promise even of bare life for any one, from the king downwards.' 'All is quite quiet here,' he writes on the 31st, 'only a few occasional shots from the batteries. The Pandies are quarrelling among themselves, and are without money.'

On September 1 Hodson speaks of everything as 'stagnant, save the hand of the destroying angel of sickness. We have at this moment 2,500 in hospital, of whom 1,100 are Europeans, out of a total of 5,000 men (Europeans).' The whole force at this time hardly exceeded 8,000 fighting men, and the sickly season was in full swing. But the siege-train was nearing Rhâi, and the camp was already astir with preparations for the actual siege; for thus far it was the rebels in the city who had been besieging the heroic guardians of the ridge.

[1] Major Norman's *Narrative*.

CHAPTER XXII

FROM the friends he had left behind in the Punjàb John Nicholson received the warmest congratulations on his latest exploit. None wrote with keener appreciation than Sir John Lawrence, who well knew the sort of ground which the column had to struggle with in the height of the rainy season. 'Though sorely pressed with work,' he wrote on August 27, 'I write a line to congratulate you on your success. I wish I had the power of knighting you on the spot. It should be done. I hope you destroyed no end of villainous Pandies.' 'Many thanks for your kind letter,' was Nicholson's answer on the 30th. 'I would much rather earn the good opinion of my friends than any kind of honorary distinction.' Careless of honours and rewards for himself, he was always ready to help in procuring them for others. Young Gabbett of the 61st had fallen some way in front of his men in the act of capturing a gun at Najafgarh. Had he lived, Nicholson would have recommended him for the Victoria Cross [1].

Just after his return from Najafgarh, Nicholson received from Edwardes a letter filled with loving reminiscences

[1] Kaye; Cave-Browne.

of their common friend Sir Henry Lawrence, who had
died of his wound at Lucknow on July 4, having not
only 'tried to do his duty,' but succeeded in doing it
to the best of his power. Nicholson replied on September 1 : 'I have your kind, good letters of August 20
and 23 before me. I do so wish I could have seen dear
Sir Henry under the circumstances you mention. If it
please Providence that I live through this business, you
must get me alongside of you again, and be my guide
and help in endeavouring to follow his example ; for
I am so weak and unstable, that I shall never do any
good of myself. I should like to write you a long letter,
but I cannot manage it. God bless you, dear Edwardes.
Ever yours affectionately, J. Nicholson[1].'

A few days earlier he had written to the same friend :
'Our position is a perfectly *providential* one. We could
not have found one better suited to our requirements.
Had the ground been of an ordinary character, we must
have abandoned it long ago ; but the ridge, with the
strong buildings on it in front, and the river and canal
protecting our flanks and rear, has saved us. I think
Wilson has hitherto had considerable cause of anxiety.
Had the enemy had the enterprise to detach a strong
force to his rear, we could not have sent more than five
or six hundred men against it. It is too late for them
to try that game now, and they know it, and are at their
wits' end to devise some new plan of action. When the
second siege-train from Firozpur arrives, I believe we shall
be able to go in[2].'

---

[1] Nicholson showed his friend's letter to Chamberlain and Daly, and
promised the former a copy of it. The promise was never to be fulfilled.

[2] Lady Edwardes.

There were many Sikhs at this time in the ranks of the Delhi garrison, who might, it was hoped, be induced to return betimes to their old allegiance. On August 27 Nicholson writes to Sir John Lawrence, ' We have been trying to get over the Sikhs, but without success. They have been formed into a battalion at their own request, and seem inclined to stand their chance. They may possibly think better of it as the crisis approaches. Some of the irregular cavalry regiments have indirectly hinted that they are anxious for forgiveness. Now, though I should not pardon a single Pandy in a regiment which had murdered its officers or perpetrated any other atrocities, I do think that these are corps which it would be neither just nor politic to refuse pardon to. The irregular cavalry have, as a rule, everywhere taken a much less active part in this Mutiny than either regular cavalry or infantry. They have no love or fellow-feeling with the Pandies. Several of these corps are still serving with arms. We are in great want of cavalry, and are likely to be in still greater. All accounts from below state that want of cavalry prevents Havelock from completing his victories. My own opinion is that we ought to forgive all regiments which have not committed murder, or played a prominent part in the mutinies. Some, like the 29th at Moradabad, were positively the victims of circumstances, and could not have held out longer. We cannot, if we would, annihilate the whole force now in arms against us in this Presidency; and it is not wise, all things considered, to make *every* man desperate. . . . I spoke on this subject yesterday to both Wilson and Chamberlain, and they agreed with me; but Wilson thought his hands were

T

tied by the Government proclamation, prohibiting pardon. I do not think we should allow that notification to be actually binding on us. We cannot now communicate with the supreme Government, and the state of affairs is different now to what it was when the order was issued [1].'

Here we are listening to the voice of the same John Nicholson who, at the close of the second Sikh war, had pleaded for mercy to all who played no prominent part in a revolt which opened with the murder of British officers at Multán.

Writing to Edwardes on September 1 he said, 'The siege-train will probably be here in four or five days, and I trust we shall then go in without delay. I doubt if we shall attempt a breach, or anything more than the demolition of the parapet, and silencing the fire of such guns as bear on this front. We shall then try to blow in the gateway and escalade at one or two other points. I wish Chamberlain, Coke, Showers, Daly, and many other good men were not *hors de combat* from wounds.' On the 4th he wrote again: 'I think we have a right to hope for success, and I trust that, ere another week passes, our flag will be flying from the palace minarets. Wilson has told me that he intends to nominate me Military Governor, for which I am much obliged, but I had rather that he had told me that he intended to give me command of the column of pursuit [2].'

From Nicholson's correspondence with the chief commissioner it is easy to see that neither of them looked for prompt and vigorous support from the commander of the Delhi Field Force. 'In Chamberlain and John

<hr>

[1] Kaye.   [2] Ibid.

Nicholson I rest my main hope,' wrote Sir John Lawrence to Ross Mangles, then Chairman of the East India Company. General Wilson seemed to him 'too undecided for such a task,' whereas Nicholson was 'an officer of great force of character and resolution.' 'Wilson says that he will assume the offensive on the arrival of the heavy guns,' Nicholson wrote in August to his chief, 'but he says it in an undecided kind of way, which makes me doubt if he will do so, if he is not kept up to the mark. Do you therefore keep him up to it. He is not at all equal to the crisis, and I believe he feels it himself.'

Writing a few days later on the incompetency of certain political officers in camp, he says, 'Should I escape the storm and have to go out with a column afterwards, I must—unless you can supply a competent man—be my own political agent. I would rather have 2,000 men and be so, than 4,000 and hampered with an incapable. If you agree with me, you must authorize it, however, for Wilson will take no responsibility on himself, and it seems to me that he is becoming jealous of me, lest I should earn more than my share of *kudos*. He will not even show me the plan of assault now, though I feel pretty sure his nervousness will make him do so before the time comes [1].'

The reference to Wilson's jealousy need not be taken too seriously. In all likelihood that officer merely resented the tone and bearing of his masterful lieutenant, who found fault with some of his arrangements, and wanted him, against all rule and precedent, to stake everything at Delhi on a gambler's throw. But the friction between these two men on matters of military detail did not prevent them from working loyally together for the common good.

[1] Bosworth Smith.

Sir Neville Chamberlain, whom the younger man visited regularly to talk over the events of the day around Delhi and in camp, 'is not aware that John Nicholson was not on good terms with General Wilson in the ordinary sense of the words, or that he had any important difference of opinion with him, although their views on many matters connected with the military operations were not in accord[1].'

At last on September 4 the long train of heavy guns and mortars drawn by elephants, and of bullock waggons loaded with shot, shells, and ammunition of all kinds, was conducted safely into camp by Bourchier's battery and two squadrons of the 9th Lancers. The arrival of these grim, slow-footed messengers, preceded or followed by a few hundred fresh troops from the Punjàb, Firozpur, and Meerut, filled every heart in camp, except perhaps Wilson's, with proud anticipations of a swift and glorious ending to the toils, struggles, and anxieties of the past three months. No one exulted with fiercer joy than John Nicholson. 'Poor Pandy,' he wrote to Edwardes, 'has been in very low spirits since then [the rout of Najafgarh], and, please God, he'll be in still lower before the end of the week[2].'

'The Engineers,' he wrote to John Lawrence on September 7, 'have consulted me about the plan of the attack, though Wilson has not. They tell me they proposed to him that I should be consulted, and that he maintained a chilling silence. I imagine it is as I supposed, that he is afraid of being thought to be influenced by me. I care little, however, whether he receives my suggestions direct, or through the Engineers. Like Barnard, he talks about the "gambler's throw!"' In another note he says, 'I just write a line to confirm what you will have heard from

<hr>

[1] Letter from Sir N. Chamberlain.   [2] Kaye.

Wilson. We break ground with No. 1 heavy battery at 650 yards to-night, Nos. 2 and 3 to-morrow night at 550 and 350. Batter on the 9th, and go in on the 10th. I can't give you the plan of attack, lest the letter should fall into other hands. Wilson's head is going : he *says* so himself, and it is quite evident that he speaks the truth. . . . Poor Pandy is in very low spirits, and evidently thinks he has made a mistake [1].'

Amidst the bustle and excitement of that busy time, Nicholson took care to bespeak the good offices of friends in the Punjàb for those who had served him faithfully in the field. ' A poor orderly of mine, named Sàdat Khan,' he writes to Edwards, ' died here of cholera the other day. He has a mother and a brother, and I think a wife, in the Yusafzai country. Should I not be left to do it, will you kindly provide for the brother, and give the women a couple of hundred rupees out of my estate [2] ?' Captain Randall had served him well as aide-de-camp with the movable column. Nicholson offered him, as he tells John Lawrence, ' the adjutancy of Stafford's corps ; but he wishes to serve here, though on his bare subaltern's pay. Bear this in mind if anything happens to me ; for it is not every man who declines staff employ, that he may serve in the trenches on his regimental allowances and without increase of rank. Randall is, moreover, a very steady, intelligent, conscientious fellow.' The chief commissioner did bear his friend's request in mind, and when he himself became Governor-General, Colonel Randall was appointed one of his aides-de-camp [3].

In the camp before Delhi all men were now looking to Nicholson as the Joshua who should lead them into the

<hr>

[1] Bosworth Smith.   [2] Kaye.   [3] Bosworth Smith.

promised land. ' He was a grand fellow,' wrote Daly after his death. ' He had a genius for war. He did not know his own powers, but he was beginning to find them out. His merits were recognized throughout the camp. Between the 6th and 7th he rose higher and higher in the minds of all, and when General Wilson's arrangements for the attack were read out, and the post of honour was given to Nicholson, not a man present thought that *he* was superseded [1].'

During the first week of September the greater part of Wilson's force was employed in various ways in making all ready for the attack which our heavy guns were to open against the doomed city. Wilson had yielded a grudging consent to the plan of operations which Colonel Baird Smith had set before him. On the shoulders of his dauntless chief engineer he laid the whole responsibility for the success or failure of a scheme which he would neither criticize nor reject. Between the cross-fire of John Lawrence's letters and the plain speaking of Nicholson and the Engineers, he felt himself committed to a course of which he heartily disapproved. He would still, it seems, have waited for those reinforcements from below, which the chief commissioner warned him not to expect for months to come. If Delhi, urged Sir John Lawrence with perfect truth, were not speedily taken, the whole of Northern and Central India would be lost to our rule. ' Every day's delay,' wrote Sir John, ' is fraught with danger. Every day disaffection and mutiny spread. Every day adds to the danger of the native princes taking part against us. In the Punjâb we are by no means strong.' Out of three European regiments and a strong force of artillery only 1,000 men were now fit for service, the rest being down with fever. And

---

[1] Lady Edwardes.

they had 8,000 Hindustáni troops to guard. The 51st Sepoys had just broken out at Pesháwar. And if anything happened to Dost Muhammad, the Afghans would certainly come down and swell the number of our foes [1].

Between September 7 and 11 the work in the trenches went briskly forward beyond the ridge, which served as our first parallel of attack. A second parallel offered itself in a ravine which ran between the ridge and the northern face of the city. Night after night a fresh battery was traced, erected, and armed with its due proportion of heavy guns, howitzers, and mortars. Each day a new battery began to pound the walls or hurl its shells among the outworks. On the night of the 11th, another battery, in the planning of which Taylor had surpassed himself, rose up silently from the custom-house compound within 160 yards of the Water or Mori Bastion, under a furious musketry fire which the native workmen bore with unflinching coolness. The heavy battery of the right attack was covered by a light field-battery planted by an old Hindu temple known as the Sammy House [2].

Nicholson meanwhile was growing fiercely impatient of Wilson's incapacity for the task that lay before him. Writing to Sir John Lawrence on the 11th, he says, ' The game is completely in our hands. We only want a player to move the pieces. Fortunately, after making all kinds of objections and obstructions, and even threatening more than once to withdraw the guns and abandon the attempt, Wilson has made everything over to the Engineers, and they, and they alone, will deserve the credit of taking Delhi. Had Wilson carried out his threat of withdrawing the guns, I was quite prepared to appeal to the army to

---

[1] Kaye; Bosworth Smith.　　　　[2] Bourchier; Kaye.

set him aside and elect a successor. I have seen lots of useless generals in my day; but such an ignorant, croaking obstructive as he is, I have never hitherto met with; and nothing will induce me to serve a day under his personal command after the fall of this place. The purport of his last message in reply to the Engineers ran thus: "I disagree with the Engineers entirely. I foresee great, if not insuperable, difficulties in the plan they propose. But as I have no other plan myself, I yield to the urgent remonstrances of the chief engineer." The above are almost the very words used by him, and yet he never even examined the ground on which the Engineers proposed to erect the breaching batteries. I believed the Meerut catastrophe was more his fault than Hewitt's; and by all accounts he was driven into fighting at the Hindan, and could not help himself. The same may be said now. He is allowing the Engineers to undertake active operations, simply because the army will not put up with inactivity [1].'

This was strong language; but John Nicholson's wrath had been justly aroused by the manner in which his commander shuffled off upon Baird Smith's shoulders the responsibility for an enterprise which he himself regarded as resting on ' the hazard of a die.' Yielding to the judgement of the chief engineer, he was ' willing to try this hazard, the more so because I cannot suggest any other plan to meet our difficulties.' ' This,' remarked the chief engineer, ' places on my shoulders the undivided responsibility for the results of a siege,' a burden which Baird Smith cheerfully accepted. As for Wilson's share in the Meerut catastrophe of May 10, Nicholson only forestalled the verdict of history, which divides the blame between General Hewitt

---

[1] Kaye; Bosworth Smith.

and his brigadier[1]. Wilson's backwardness in the hour of our need at Meerut gave little promise of bold and resolute action in the commander of the Delhi Field Force.

By September 12 the whole of our heavy guns and mortars, some fifty in number, were in full play upon the walls and bastions of the rebel stronghold. Three days earlier one tall bastion, facing our right attack, had been reduced to silence and utter ruin. On the 11th the Kashmir Bastion to the right of the Mori was in much the same plight. The enemy still kept up a vigorous fire of guns and musketry from every point of vantage within or beyond their walls. But our guns were well served, though volunteers from the cavalry had to help in fighting them ; and the Water Bastion near the Jumna was soon knocked into a heap of shattered masonry, while broad gaps became visible in the parapets of the long curtain walls. Day and night, for some days past, nearly all our effective infantry had been serving in the trenches, to cover the construction of the batteries, and to keep down the musketry fire from the enemy's outposts.

In spite of the Pandies' attempts to repair the breaches and bring more guns into play, it became clear by midday of the 13th, that the hour for assaulting the great city was close at hand. Captain Alec Taylor, under whose personal direction the heavy batteries had been constructed, assured Wilson that the breaches were now practicable. On the 13th all the chief officers in camp had been summoned to a meeting in the general's tent, to hear the plan of assault read out, and to learn what part was assigned to each. Nicholson alone was absent. He had gone down at an early hour, according to Chamberlain, ' to see the opening

[1] Kaye.

salvos of the great breaching battery within one hundred
and sixty yards of the Water Bastion, and the Engineers
had been behind their promised time.' That evening he
accompanied Chamberlain on his tour, in a doolie, along
the ridge as far as Hindu Rao's house. On their return
he insisted, adds his old friend, ' on my going to his tent
and dining with him. After dinner he read out the plan
of assault, . . . and some of the notes then made by him
I found afterwards among his papers [1].'

From the first days of his appearance in camp Nicholson
had taken infinite pains to study our position and make
good all serious defects. ' Not a day passed,' says Chamberlain in the same letter, ' but what he visited every battery,
breastwork, and post ; and frequently at night, though not
on duty, he would ride round our outer line of sentries, to
see that they were on the alert, and to bring to notice
any point not duly provided for.' After the arrival of the
siege-train, he ' was the only officer, not being an engineer,
who took the trouble to study the ground which was to
become of so much importance to us ; and had it not been
for his going down that night, I believe that we might have
had to capture at considerable loss of life the positions
which he was certainly the cause of our occupying without
resistance. From the day of the trenches being opened to
the day of the assault he was constantly on the move from
one battery to another ; and when he returned to camp he
was constantly riding backwards and forwards to the chief
engineer, endeavouring to remove any difficulties.'

The plan of the assault had been imparted to Wilson's
leading officers, but the day and hour had not yet been
fixed, when Roberts came over to Nicholson's tent for a few

---

[1] Letter to Herbert Edwardes, quoted by Kaye.

minutes' quiet talk with one who always treated him as a friend. After some confidential chat upon 'personal matters,' Nicholson told Roberts of 'his intention to take a very unusual step, should the council fail to arrive at any fixed determination regarding the assault. Delhi must be taken, he said, and it is absolutely essential that this should be done at once. If Wilson hesitates longer, I intend to propose at to-day's meeting that he should be superseded.' Roberts, 'greatly startled,' ventured to remark that, 'as Chamberlain was *hors de combat* from his wound, Wilson's removal would leave him, Nicholson, senior officer with the force.' He answered, smiling, that he had not overlooked that fact, but, under the circumstances, he could not possibly accept the command himself. 'I shall propose that it be given to Campbell of the 52nd. I am prepared to serve under him for the time being; so none can ever accuse me of personal motives.'

The two walked together to the head-quarters camp. Roberts waited 'in great excitement' while the council of war was sitting. At last Nicholson came out of the general's tent, and Roberts learned, to his intense relief, that Wilson had agreed to do what Nicholson desired [1].

There is no doubt that Nicholson would have carried out his purpose had Wilson hesitated any longer; nor can any sane man doubt that the circumstances of the moment would have amply justified the breach of military use and wont. It is pleasant to find Lord Roberts, the field-marshal, still holding on this point to the opinion formed by Lieutenant Roberts of the Bengal Artillery.

In his last chat with Daly on the 13th, Nicholson expressed his pleasure at receiving the commissionership of

[1] Lord Roberts.

Leia. 'Oh! you won't take it,' interjected Daly, 'now that you are likely to remain a general and get a division.' 'A general,' he said, laughing haughtily; 'you don't think I'd like to be a general of division, do you? Look at them! Look at the generals!'

Talking with Edwardes a few months later at Peshâwar, Daly said, 'How the two brothers [John and Charles] loved each other! The great one used to come down and see me when I was wounded, and the little one found out the hour, and used to drop in, as if quite by accident, and say, "Hullo! John, are you there?" And John would say, "Ah! Charles; come in." And then they'd look at each other. They were shy of giving way to any expression of it, but you saw it in their behaviour to one another [1].'

September 13 was a busy day for all in camp; but Nicholson rode over two or three times to Chamberlain's tent, to tell him his news and beg him to use his influence with Wilson in favour of certain measures advocated by the Engineers. On returning from his evening tour along the ridge, Chamberlain found his friend in the head-quarters camp, 'whither he had come to urge upon the general the importance of not delaying the assault, if the breach should be reported practicable.'

Chamberlain begged his friend to stay and dine with him, but Nicholson 'said he could not, as he must be back in his camp to see his officers and arrange all details for the coming assault.' On his way home he passed once more along the batteries, to see for himself whether our gunners had done their work so thoroughly as to warrant an assault being made on the morrow. 'He was evidently satisfied,' says Lord Roberts, 'for when he entered our battery he

---

[1] Kaye.

said, " I must shake hands with you fellows, for you have done your best to make my work easy to-morrow." ' To Nicholson had been assigned the post of honour in the crowning struggle on whose issues the life of every Englishman in Northern India might be said to hang. He was to lead the first of the storming columns and to direct the general development of the assault.

Half an hour later he was back in his tent, explaining to his officers in clear detail what part they and their men were to play in the coming venture, and the best way of advancing after they had carried the breaches in the wall and the Kashmir Bastion. On this latter point Sir John Lawrence, who knew Delhi thoroughly and had a soldier's eye for its internal defences, had sent Wilson full and precise information, of a kind which very few in camp could have supplied. Nicholson's last words on this occasion were words of wisdom :—' Don't press the enemy too hard. Let them have a golden bridge to retire by [1].'

By this time Nicholson had gained his heart's desire, for, besides the post of honour in the assault, he had at last been selected to command the column of pursuit after the fall of Delhi. His request that Hodson might join the column was also granted. And if he survived the perils of the morrow, he had the further satisfaction of knowing that John Lawrence had just promoted him to the post of Commissioner of Leia in the Punjàb. Nicholson, however, had little time to think of anything but the immediate future. The night had long closed in, when four young engineer officers stole down in pairs to the moat, and examined the breaches near the Kashmir and Water

[1] Colonel Innes.

Bastions. Their reports were not wholly favourable ; but Baird Smith, impatient of further delay, sent Wilson a message calling for immediate action. Thus it happened that the final orders for the assault were issued only a few hours before its actual delivery [1].

[1] Rev. G. Hodson ; Cave-Browne.

THE STORMING OF DELHI, SEPTEMBER 14

BEFORE daybreak on the eventful September 14, 1857, some 3,000 of Wilson's infantry were drawn up in three columns on the ground between the ridge and Ludlow Castle, awaiting the signal for an advance. Nicholson himself was at their head, and every one felt that under such a leader the victory was certain, against whatever odds. As Roberts stood 'on the crenellated wall which separated Ludlow Castle from the road,' he wondered, naturally enough, what was passing through Nicholson's mind. 'Was he thinking of the future, or of the wonderful part he had played during the past four months? ... At Delhi every one felt that during the short time he had been with us, he was our guiding-star, and that, but for his presence in the camp, the assault which he was about to lead would probably never have come off. . . . Any feeling of reluctance to serve under a captain of the Company's army, which had at first been felt by many, had been completely overcome by his wonderful personality. Each man in the force, from the general in command to the last-joined private soldier, recognized that the man whom the wild people of the frontier had deified, the man of whom Edwardes had said to Lord Canning, " If ever there is a desperate deed to be done in India, John Nicholson is the man to do it," was one who had proved himself beyond all doubt capable of grappling with the crisis through which we were passing, one to follow to the death '.'

The storming columns were ready for the work before them ; but they had to wait until our batteries had cleared the breaches, which the enemy during the night had partially repaired.   The first column, 1,000 strong, commanded by Nicholson himself, and made up from the 1st Bengal Fusiliers, the 75th Foot, and Green's Punjâbis, was to carry the main breach and to scale the face of the Kashmir Bastion.   On its left stood the second column of 850 men, from the 8th Foot, the 2nd Bengal Fusiliers, and Rothney's Sikhs, with Brigadier Jones of the 60th Rifles in command. Its first duty was to storm the breach in the Water Bastion. The third column, on the right and rear of the first, was commanded by Colonel Campbell of the 2nd Light Infantry, and consisted of the 52nd, the Kamaon Battalion, and the 1st Punjâb Infantry, 950 men in all.   This column was to rush in at the Kashmir Gate as soon as it had been blown open by our engineers.

These three columns, covered by the 60th Rifles, formed the left attack.   A fourth column, under the gallant Major Reid, was to advance from the right of the ridge, and force its way through the Kishnganj suburb towards the Lahore Gate.   It numbered about 860 men, from Reid's own Gurkhas, the Guide Infantry, and the pickets left in camp ; beside several hundred of the Kashmir contingent, which had come in a few days before.   Three engineers accompanied each column.   A fifth or reserve column of 1,500

' Lord Roberts.

under Brigadier Longfield was formed out of the 61st Foot,
Wilde's Punjâb Infantry, the Bilúch Battalion, the troops of
the brave old Rajah of Jhind, and the 60th Rifles.

Nicholson's own column now marched on into the Kudsia
Bagh, while Jones's column turned off into the custom-house
garden, and Campbell's men passed up the high road to the
Kashmir Gate. At the head of this column moved the
explosion party of two young engineer officers, Home and
Salkeld, three sapper sergeants, Carmichael, Burgess, and
Smith, and Bugler Hawthorne of the 52nd, who was to
sound the advance when the gate had been blown in.
Eight native sappers under Havildar Madhu carried the
powder-bags with which their white comrades were to
assay their perilous task [1].

The sun had risen some way above the horizon when
our heavy guns suddenly ceased firing. They had done
their work, and the breaches were once more clear.
Nicholson gave the signal for an advance. The 60th
Rifles, with a loud cheer, dashed forward in skirmishing
order, followed by the ladder parties of the first two
columns. As our troops emerged from the low brushwood which lay between the Kudsia Bagh and the open
slope of the *glacis*, they encountered a furious storm of
musketry from front and flanks, which laid many a brave
man low. But Nicholson strode on unhurt and unheeding,
as if death itself could not stand against him. In a few
minutes the leading stormers were in the ditch with
Nicholson, planting their ladders on the heaps of fallen
masonry which nearly filled it. In a few minutes those
who escaped the bullets and stones showered upon them
clambered over the breaches in their front, and, with

[1] Cave-Browne; Forrest.

U

a wild exultant cheer, drove the Pandies before them in momentary rout [1].

While the first two columns were clearing the ramparts from the Water Gate to the Kashmir Bastion, the explosion party under Home and Salkeld had succeeded, by force of sheer self-sacrificing heroism, in bursting open the Kashmir Gate after four of their number had fallen dead or wounded into the ditch. Once inside the shattered gate, Campbell's column drove the rebels from the main guard, and pushing on past the English church and along the broad Chàndni Chauk—the street of silversmiths—found its progress stayed by a heavy fire from Delhi's great mosque, the Jamma Masjid, and the adjacent buildings. Nothing remained for Campbell but to fall back on the police station and the line of the church. Here, in the open space around the church, Longfield's reserves were already posted. They, too, had come in through the Kashmir Gate; and, clearing the rebels out of the college gardens, had occupied the neighbouring houses, and with two guns commanded all the approaches to the Kashmir Gate [2].

Meanwhile a party of the 1st Fusiliers under the brave young Gerard Money had been ordered by Major Jacob to advance along the ramparts to their right. Money hastened on, fighting his way at times against heavy odds, driving the enemy out of the Shah Bastion, turning their own guns against them, and finally halting at the Kàbul Gate. He had expected to be joined by the rest of his regiment on the way. But Nicholson had carried them off to the attack and capture of various buildings held by the enemy along the line of his advance. By this means

---

[1] Bourchier; Innes; Cave-Browne.   [2] Norman; Cave-Browne.

he enabled Jones's column to push on before him towards the Kâbul Gate, and hoist the British colours on the spot which Money had been the first to reach[1].

An hour later Nicholson himself, with the toil-worn remnant of his troops, appeared at the point beyond which no further advance was that day to be made. For the murderous repulse of Reid's column on its advance through Kishnganj had sadly diminished our fighting strength, and was now encouraging the mutineers to renewed resistance within the city. It had been part of Wilson's plan that the storming columns should clear and hold the ramparts as far westward as the Lahore Gate. Nicholson was bent on fulfilling his instructions to the last letter. But what would have been possible an hour or half an hour earlier on that sultry day could not, in the opinion of those around him, be prudently attempted now.

Beyond the Kâbul Gate ran a lane which skirted the ramparts leading up to the Burn Bastion. Its left side was lined by the backs of mud huts, and further on by a few houses. No doors or windows opened into the lane. On the other side there was only a line of broad recesses surmounted by the rampart itself. Up this lane a few of the 1st Fusiliers had already ventured as far as the Burn Bastion, when the returning tide of mutineers constrained them to fall back[2]. A little later the fearless Jacob caught his death-wound in leading his Fusiliers against some guns which swept the rampart and the lane below it with showers of grape and shrapnel. A few brave fellows who spiked a gun or two were struck down

---

[1] Kaye; Innes.

[2] Colonel Graydon's MS. Letter to Sir N. Chamberlain. Lord Roberts speaks of houses beyond the huts.

the next moment, and Captain Greville withdrew his men from what seemed a hopeless task [1].

It became clear, indeed, that the only way to win the bastion and the gateway beyond was to break through the huts and houses along the lane. Our men, in fact, had little strength or spirit left for another call upon their courage and endurance. They were utterly spent and worn out by the strain which that morning's work had placed upon energies severely tried by a week of open trenches and the poisonous air of the camp. The fierce excitement of the assault was over. They had 'stormed the gates of Hell,' had done their duty like good soldiers, and felt that, for the present, they could do nothing more.

But Nicholson, who had worked as hard as the meanest soldier, failed to realize the true condition of things. He called upon the 1st Fusiliers to 'charge down the lane,' while the 75th were to 'charge along the ramparts and carry the position above.' Once again his men rushed forward, only to be driven back by the deadly hail of rifle-bullets and grape. Still, Nicholson would not give in. He had been reconnoitring the field outside the walls from the top of the Shah Bastion, and he longed to reach the Lahore Gate in time to secure an entrance for the fourth column. Collecting his men for one last effort, he marched proudly forward, waving his sword above his head and pointing it towards the foe in front. Two or three officers came close after him, one of whom, Captain —afterwards Colonel—Graydon, was doing duty with the 1st Fusiliers. But the men behind were slow in moving— too slow for their impetuous leader, who was by this time halfway up the lane [2].

---

[1] Innes.　　　　　　　　　[2] Cave-Browne; Kaye; Innes.

What followed must be told by Colonel Graydon. 'He found his troops checked; and it was while again encouraging the men, with his face towards them and his back to the enemy, that a shot, evidently fired from the Burn Bastion, struck him in the back, causing him to reel round. Luckily the recess before alluded to was close by. Indeed, he was partly inside it, but not sufficiently sheltered from the enemy's fire. Fortunately also for him, a sergeant was at hand—probably an orderly—who immediately caught him, and laid him on the ground inside the recess, and tended him. I happened to be on the opposite side of the lane, and went across to Nicholson, and did what I could, giving him some brandy, which seemed to revive him. Thus we remained for some little time, when it occurred to me that the enemy would most likely gain confidence, and move down the lane, when Nicholson would fall an easy victim to their fury.

'I therefore suggested to Nicholson that he should let the sergeant and me remove him to a place of safety. He however declined, saying he should allow no man to remove him, but would die there.' Finding persuasion fruitless, Graydon 'judged it best to bring up assistance to him. So, leaving him in charge of the sergeant, I returned down the lane, meeting an officer and some men, to whom I mentioned Nicholson's state and the place where he was, and advised their hurrying up to his help; which I believe they hastened to do.' Shortly after, he met Nicholson's aide-de-camp, Captain Trench, who on hearing the sad news immediately went in search of assistance. About half an hour later Nicholson was brought back to the Kâbul Gate, and Graydon learned from the faithful sergeant that his wounded commander wished to see him. 'I went across to him, found him in great suffering, and gave him a little brandy, which evidently did him good. This was the last I saw of this gallant soldier, who was taken to the hospital in camp, where he lingered, I think, for a week before death put an end to his sufferings.'

At the moment of Nicholson's fall, several officers of the 1st Fusiliers had just been struck down, so that none but Graydon and the sergeant were at hand to help him. Graydon was now told that soon after his departure several others came up to assist the sorely wounded hero. But no one was allowed to touch him, except Captain Hay of the 60th Native Infantry, with whom, says another informant, he was not upon friendly terms. 'I will make up my differ- ence with you, Hay,' he gasped out; 'I will let you take me back.' And so, under Hay's direction, John Nicholson was borne slowly back to the sheltering gateway, whence he was presently removed in a doolie to the field hospital below the ridge.

But his native carriers had small regard for the safety of their precious burden. By this time General Wilson, who had taken up his quarters in the church, was growing seriously alarmed about the issue of that morning's work. The failure of Reid's column, and the news that Reid him- self had been badly wounded, were disheartening enough for a man of his temperament. But the sad tidings of Nicholson's fall, coupled with false reports about the death of Hope Grant and Tombs, drove him to the verge of despair, and he began to talk of withdrawing his troops from the positions they had already won. Roberts, who had now resumed his place on Wilson's staff, was sent off to 'find out the truth of these reports, and to ascertain exactly what had happened to No. 4 column and the cavalry on our right.'

On his way through the Kashmir Gate, Roberts noticed by the roadside 'a doolie without bearers, and evidently a wounded man inside.' Dismounting to see what help he might render, he found to his 'grief and consternation that it was John Nicholson, with death written on his face. He told me that the bearers had put the doolie down and gone off to plunder; that he was in great pain, and wished to be taken to the hospital. He was lying on his back, no wound was visible, and but for the pallor on his face, always colourless, there was no sign of the agony he must have been enduring. On my expressing a hope that he was not seriously wounded, he said, " I am dying; there is no chance for me." The sight of that great man lying helpless and at the point of death was almost more than I could bear. Other men had daily died around me, friends and comrades had been killed beside me ; but I never felt as I felt then—to lose Nicholson seemed to me at that moment to lose everything [1].'

With no small difficulty, for the doolie-bearers and other camp-followers were busy plundering the nearest houses and shops, Roberts hunted up four men, whom he placed under charge of a sergeant of the 61st Foot, bidding him see that Brigadier-General Nicholson was taken direct to the field hospital. This was the last that Roberts was to see of John Nicholson ; for though he managed several times to ride over and inquire after the dying hero, he was never admitted to his bedside.

It was late in the afternoon when John Nicholson was brought into the field hospital. Beside the doolie in which he awaited his turn for surgical inspection, another doolie was presently set down. Its occupant, Charles Nicholson,

---

[1] *Forty-one Years in India.*

had been badly wounded in leading Coke's Punjàbis to the assault, and the shattered arm had since been amputated at the shoulder.   Surgeon H. Buckle, who had assisted in this operation, had since gone to see John Nicholson and ask what he could do for his old acquaintance.   He found the poor sufferer 'as collected and composed as usual, but very low, almost pulseless.'   What struck him was Nicholson's face. ' It was always one of power; but then, in its calm, pale state, it was quite beautiful [1].'

It was piteous to see the two brothers lying there so helplessly side by side in the prime of their stately man-hood, looking sadly into each other's eyes, and exchanging their last words on this earth. ' Last words, I fancy, they must have been,' writes Dr. Mactier, ' for, as far as I can remember, they never saw each other again, both being too severely wounded to be moved from their respective tents [2].'   From a child, indeed, Charles Nicholson had been John's favourite brother, and the letters he wrote to a friend after his own recovery show that in losing John he had lost his heart's idol and guiding-star.

A little later John Nicholson was borne away to the camp on the ridge, where Dr. Mactier as staff-surgeon attended to him till within a day or two of his death. He at once called in Dr. Campbell Mackinnon of the Horse Artillery, a friend of Chamberlain's in the old Afghan days, in whom many besides Chamberlain had the greatest confidence. Nicholson's case, says Dr. Mactier, ' was from the first a hopeless one, and it was a matter of surprise to his medical attendants that he survived even so long as he did. The nature of his wound—a shot through the lung—necessi-

---

[1] Buckle's Letter to John Becher, quoted by Kaye.
[2] MS. Letter from Dr. Mactier.

tated absolute quiet of mind and body ; and we would fain have enforced complete silence upon him. All this it was impossible to carry out, for he would insist upon hearing how matters went on in the city, and would excite himself terribly over the news that was brought in from time to time.

' Not only did he make comments and criticisms to friends about him, but he sent them to Sir John Lawrence and others at a distance, I had myself to act as amanuensis in conveying his views to Sir John. Professionally speaking, all this was of course wrong, and the cause of grave anxiety to his medical attendants. Still, we could only admire the man who seemed to think little of his own sufferings, and whose whole thoughts were absorbed in the success of the military operations [1].'

Lieutenant Montgomerie of the Guides had helped to lift Nicholson out of his doolie on to a bed prepared for him in his own tent. As he kept on bathing the sufferer's temples with eau-de-cologne, Montgomerie saw that he ' was in fearful agony.' He had been shot through the body, and the blood was flowing from his side. ' It was terrible,' he wrote, ' seeing the great strong man, who a few hours before was the life and soul of everything brave and daring, struck down in this way. . . . I could have followed him anywhere, so brave, cool, and self-possessed, and so energetic, you would have thought he was made of iron. The shot that killed him was worth more to the Pandy than all the rest put together [2].'

On the evening of that memorable day Chamberlain came over to see his poor friend from his post at Hindu Rao's, whence with Daly and a few other disabled comrades

<hr>

[1] Letter from Dr. W. Mactier.   [2] Kaye.

he had watched the fortunes of the fight, and prepared to hold the ridge with a handful of soldiers scarce fit for any sort of duty. Thanks, however, to the heroic steadiness of Hope Grant's cavalry brigade, and the desperate courage displayed by Tombs's gunners in covering the retreat of Reid's infantry, Chamberlain was free at last to go forth on his sorrowful errand. He found John Nicholson 'lying stretched on a charpoy [native bed], helpless as an infant, breathing with difficulty, and only able to jerk out his words in syllables at long intervals, and with pain. . . . He asked me to tell him exactly what the surgeons said of his case; and after I had told him, he wished to know how much of the town was in our possession, and what we proposed doing. Talking was, of course, bad for him and prohibited, and the morphia, which was given him in large doses, to annul pain and secure rest, soon produced a state of stupor [1].'

About 11 p.m. Chamberlain saw his friend again, before he himself returned for the night to his post of command at Hindu Rao's house. 'He was much the same; but feeling his skin to be chilled, I suppose from the loss of blood and two hand-punkahs going, I got him to consent to my covering him with a light Rampore blanket.'

What Wilson himself proposed to do on the evening of that momentous September 14 is well-known. When Roberts made his report of what had really occurred, his general seemed for the time a little happier. But presently, when he learned at how heavy a cost—1,170 killed and wounded out of 5,000 engaged—a part only of that day's programme had been accomplished, Wilson returned to his croaking, and talked once more about retiring to the ridge. Lord Roberts thinks that he would have carried

---

[1] Letter to Sir Herbert Edwardes, quoted by Kaye.

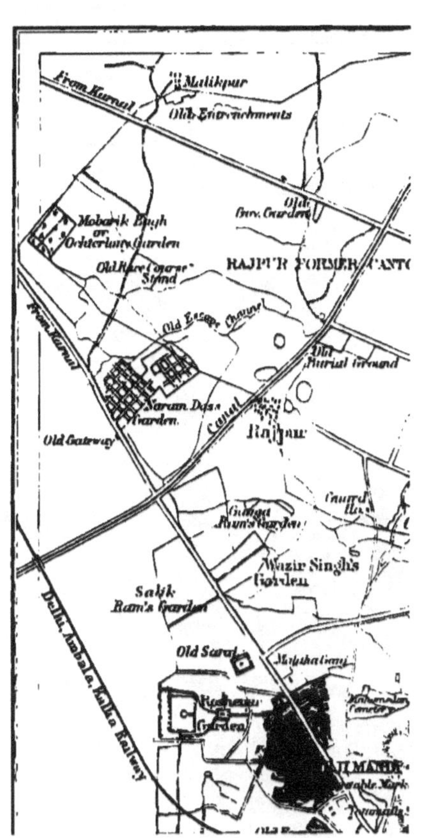

From Karnal
Malikpur
Old Entrenchments
Old Gov. Garden
Mobarik Bagh or Ochterlony Garden
RAJPUR FORMER CANTO
Old Race Course Stand
Old Escape Channel
From Karnal
Narain Das's Garden
Old Burial Ground
Canal
Rajpur
Old Gateway
Ganga Ram's Garden
Wazir Singh's Garden
Salik Ram's Garden
Delhi-Ambala-Kalka Railway
Old Sarai
Malaka Ganj
Kishanu Garden
Mahomedan Cemetery
JI MANDI

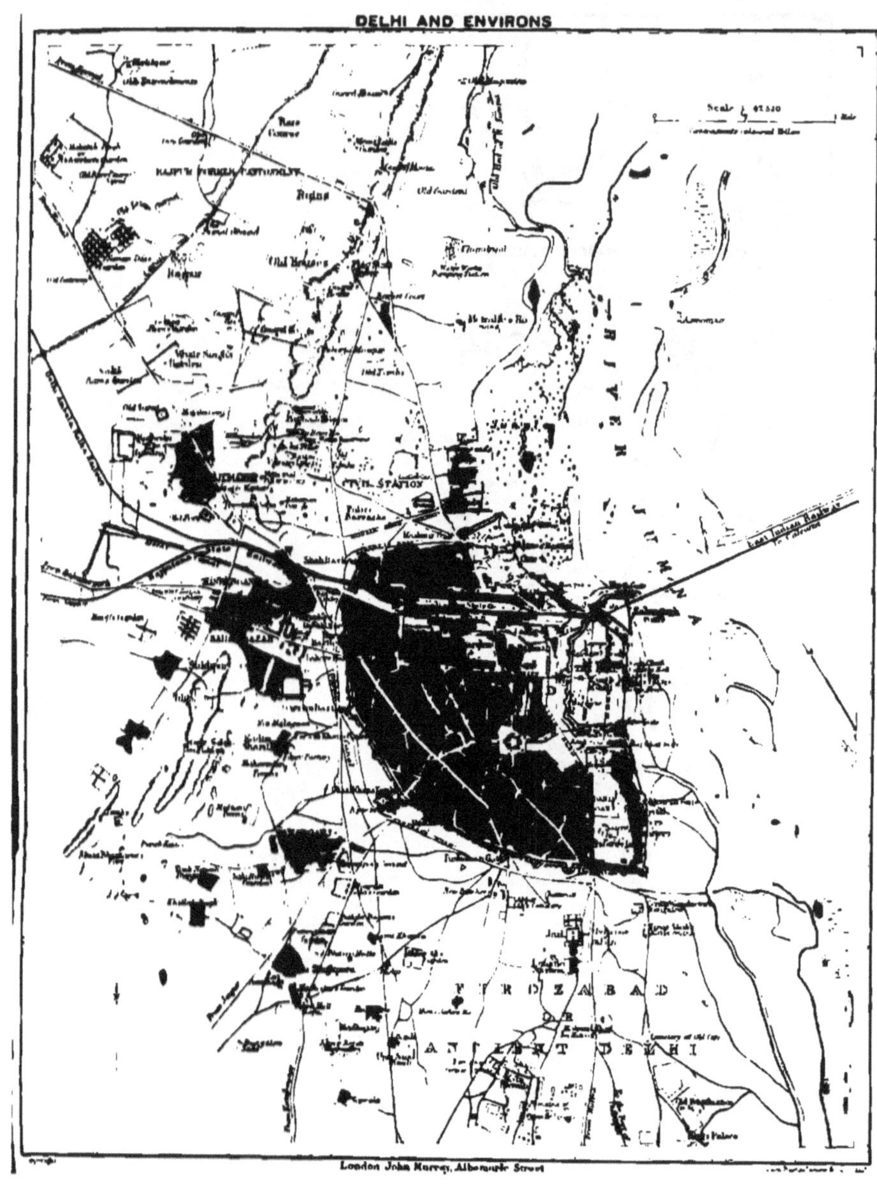
RIVER JUMNA
RAIL STATION
FIROZABAD
OR
ANCIENT DELHI
Scale
East Indian Railway

out this 'fatal measure,' to which every officer on his staff was utterly opposed, and against which Chamberlain firmly protested, had not Baird Smith been at his elbow in front of Skinner's House, when Wilson asked him whether we could hold what we had won. 'We *must* hold on,' was the laconic answer of the chief engineer, whose indomitable spirit had borne him up through the pain of a recent wound and the weakness caused by a wasting disease[1].

To fall back indeed at such a moment would have been sheer madness, while everything could be gained by holding on. Our success, however partial, was really decisive, for our men had won a footing inside the walls, from which nothing but their own folly or their leaders' blundering could dislodge them. To hold on was to go forward, until the last mutineer had been driven out of a stronghold whose fate was sealed on that September 14, 1857.

'Poor Nicholson was most dangerously wounded,' writes Hodson next day to his brother; 'at a time, too, when his services were beyond expression valuable.' His grief was shared by Wilson himself and the whole army. It was soon known throughout the Punjáb that John Nicholson, 'our best and bravest,' had been badly wounded; and men's hearts were chilled in the midst of their rejoicing by fears for the safety of their wounded hero. For some days yet they tried to hope against hope that a life so precious might be spared for the service of his country in her great need. 'What a time of suspense it is,' wrote Herbert Edwardes on the 16th, 'until more news can reach Peshá-war.' He had already heard through John Lawrence that 'both the Nicholsons were severely wounded,' and with un-speakable anxiety he longed, yet dreaded, to hear more[2].

---

[1] Kaye; Lord Roberts.　　　　　[2] Lady Edwardes.

CHAPTER XXIV

'TRIUMPH WEEPS ABOVE THE BRAVE,'
SEPTEMBER 23, 1857

ON September 15 the struggle within the city was maintained chiefly by our engineers and artillery; the former sapping their way from house to house, while our guns played from various points of our line upon the palace, the magazine, and the old riverside fortress of Salimgarh. That evening Chamberlain was again at Nicholson's bedside. His poor friend ' breathed more easily, and seemed altogether easier—indeed, his face had changed so much for the better, that I began to make myself believe that it was not God's purpose to cut him off in the prime of manhood. . . . On this evening, as on the previous, his thoughts centred in the struggle then being fought out inside Delhi; and on my telling him that a certain officer had alluded to the possibility of our having to retire, he said, in his indignation, " Thank God! I have strength yet to shoot him, if necessary [1]." '

The natural man broke out in that fierce denouncement of a commander who could talk thus openly of abandoning a field already half won. Such conduct seemed to John Nicholson at least as criminal as that of an officer deserting

[1] Chamberlain's Letter, quoted by Kaye.

his post in the face of the enemy. How strongly he felt
on this subject came out in the message sent at his dictation
to Sir John Lawrence, begging him by his own authority
to depose Wilson and appoint Chamberlain in his stead [1].

Among the ruins of the cantonment was a small bungalow, a part of which had escaped destruction by the
mutineers on May 11. Hither John Nicholson, who had
complained of the heat in his tent, was removed next
morning under his good friend's careful supervision. The
bungalow was not far off, and his removal was effected
without causing him much pain. He expressed his thank-
fulness for the change, and said he was ' very comfortable.'
He dictated to Chamberlain the following message for
Herbert Edwardes : ' Tell him I should have been a better
man if I had continued to live with him, and our heavy
public duties had not prevented my seeing more of him
privately. I was always the better for a residence, however short, with him and his wife. Give my love to
them both.'

' Up to this time,' writes Chamberlain, ' there was still
a hope for him, though the two surgeons attending him
were anything but sanguine. He himself said he felt
better, but the doctors said his pulse indicated no improvement ; and notwithstanding the great loss of blood from
internal hemorrhage, they again thought it necessary to
bleed him. . . . One of the surgeons attending him used
to come daily to the town to dress my arm, and from him
I always received a trustworthy bulletin. From the 17th
to the 22nd he was sometimes better and sometimes worse ;
but he gradually became weaker, and on the afternoon of
the latter date, Dr. Mactier came to tell me that there was

[1] Bosworth Smith.

little or no hope. On reaching him I found him much altered for the worse in appearance, and very much weaker —indeed, so weak, that if left to himself he fell off into a state of drowsiness, from which nothing aroused him but the application of smelling-salts and stimulants. Once aroused he became quite himself, and on that afternoon he conversed with me for half an hour on several subjects as clearly as ever. He, however, knew and felt that he was dying, and said that this world had now no interest for him.'

Nicholson regretted that he had been unable to make his will the day before the assault, and was anxious to get that business done without more delay. But feeling tired just then with so much talking, and too weak to keep his senses collected, he begged his good friend to come again that evening, and arouse him for the purpose in view. And then he dictated another message for Herbert Edwardes. ' Tell him that, if at this moment a good fairy were to grant me a wish, my wish would be to have him here next to my mother.' When these words had been written down, he said, ' Tell my mother that I do not think we shall be unhappy in the next world. God has visited her with a great affliction ; but tell her she must not give way to grief[1].'

Chamberlain at once telegraphed to Edwardes that Nicholson was worse. ' He has directed a few kind words to be said to you. I fear a letter from Peshâwar may not reach in time. Send me any message you wish given to him. He talks much of you both.' Feeling that the worst was come, Edwardes telegraphed back, ' Give John Nichol-son our love in time and eternity. God ever bless him !

[1] Kaye.

I do not cease to hope and pray for him as a dear brother[1].'

It comforted the dying hero to know that he had not fought and bled in vain. Day after day our troops had carried one strong position after another, until, on the morning of the 21st, a grand salute from our guns proclaimed that the whole of Delhi was once more in British keeping. Later in the same day the capture of the fugitive king by Hodson gave fresh significance to the achievements of the previous week. It was a marvellous feat of arms which its foremost hero had lived to see accomplished, a feat which broke the neck of a wide-spreading rebellion, and ensured the safety of our countrymen in the Punjàb. Thenceforth they could breathe more freely, as men awaking from a hideous nightmare.

But their anxiety for Nicholson had not been allayed. 'It did not sound like a victory,' Edwardes wrote, when the news of our success in the opening assault was coupled with the tidings of General Nicholson's fall. And each day, as fresh news from Delhi travelled up the Punjàb, the question still was, 'Is Nicholson any better?' On the 20th it was known that Delhi had fallen, and 'there seemed a hope that Nicholson might live.'

Late in the evening of the 22nd, when asked if he could dictate his will, Nicholson replied that he felt too weak to do so, and begged that it might be deferred until the morrow, when he hoped to be feeling stronger. 'But death,' says Chamberlain, 'had now come to claim him. Every hour he became weaker and weaker, and the following morning his soul passed away to another and a better world.'

---

[1] Lady Edwardes.   [2] Edwardes, *Official Report*.

'Throughout those nine days of suffering,' says Chamberlain, in his touching letter to Edwardes, 'he bore himself nobly; not a lament or a sigh ever passed his lips, and he conversed as calmly and clearly as if he were talking of some other person's condition, and not his own. . . . I wish you could have seen him, poor fellow, as he lay in his coffin. He looked so peaceful, and there was a resignation in the expression of his manly features that made me feel that he had bowed submissively to God's will, and closed his eyes upon the world, full of hope. . . . It is a great consolation to think that he had the most skilful medical attendance, and was waited upon as carefully as possible. Nothing was left undone that could be done to allay suffering and prolong life.' It had been to Chamberlain a source of much regret that his duties prevented him from being oftener with his dying friend. He had the comfort, however, of knowing that Nicholson clearly understood the cause of his frequent absence. 'When, the afternoon before his death, I said to him he must have thought me very neglectful, his reply was, " No ; I knew that your duty to the service required your being at head-quarters, and I was glad to think that you were there to give your counsel." '

At half-past nine on the morning of September 23, ' the heroic Nicholson,' as all his friends and brother-officers were wont to call him, breathed his last, in the thirty-fifth year of his age, at the moment when his greatness seemed a-ripening. As he lay there in his last sleep, one might truly say of him what Walter Scott had said of the younger Pitt,—

> 'Now is the stately column broke;
> The beacon light is quench'd in smoke;
> The trumpet's silver voice is still;
> The warder silent on the hill.'

During the last hours of that long death-struggle General Wilson officially recorded his deep regret that the services of 'that most brilliant officer, Brigadier-General J. Nicholson, whose professional character and qualifications are so well known and appreciated,' were ' for the present lost to the State[1].' A few hours later the whole army knew that those services were lost for ever.

The sirdars of the Multâni Horse and some other natives were allowed to take a last look at the dead leader, for whose life they would have given their own. ' Their honest praise,' wrote Chamberlain to Becher, ' could hardly find utterance for the tears they shed as they looked on their late master. The servants and orderlies also who were in attendance on him, when the fact flashed across their minds that he had left this world for ever, broke out into loud lamentations ; and much as all the natives feared to displease him, there could be no question that he commanded their respect to an extent almost equal to love[2].'

In India burial soon follows death. On the morning of the 24th the remains of John Nicholson were borne to the grave prepared for them in the new burial-ground near Ludlow Castle, opposite the Kashmir Gate and the breach which he had been among the first to crown. A small company of sorrowing friends and followers, headed by Neville Chamberlain, followed the body to its last resting-place, but a few yards from one of the breaching-batteries which had cleared the way for our storming-columns. As the coffin was lowered from the gun-carriage into the grave, the solemn funeral-service was read by the Reverend Mr. Rotton, the Chaplain to the Force. Nothing of pomp or show marked the obsequies of India's greatest soldier.

---

[1] General Wilson's Dispatch of September 22.   [2] Kaye.

No cannon saluted the dead; no band played solemn music; no volleys of musketry rattled over his open grave [1].

The truth was, as Sir N. Chamberlain tells me, that our small army had too much work on hand, both inside and outside the captured city, to pay the customary honours to the dead.

Among those who attended the funeral was Captain Lind of the Multáni Horse, who had marched and fought with Nicholson from Hoti Mardán to Najafgarh, and had watched his last moments, as he 'turned once on his side, and died without a sigh.' In his letter to Edwardes he goes on to say, 'I went to his funeral with Naurang Khan and Atta Muhammad [Nicholson's orderlies], and the latter wept with me, and we felt that we had lost one of our dearest friends on earth. . . . His active mind was never quiet, and his constant inquiries were—what steps we were taking to pursue [2].'

Another of the mourners beside that open grave was the wise and kindly Charles B. Saunders, then Commissioner of Delhi, afterwards Chief Commissioner of Mysore. One of Nicholson's warmest admirers, he had vainly sought admission to the bedside of his dying friend; and now that all was over, no claims of duty within the captured city could stay him from rendering the last poor tribute of love and silent reverence to the dead.

But John Nicholson had never cared for mere show and ceremony; and the most splendid tribute to his worth was the general sinking of heart with which men read the news that Delhi had fallen, and that Nicholson was no more. The last flicker of hope was extinguished by the tale which the telegraph flashed on from station to station in the

---

[1] A chaplain's narrative of the siege of Delhi.   [2] Lady Edwardes.

Punjâb, and ' with a grief unfeigned and deep, and stern and worthy of the man, the news was whispered, *Nicholson is dead*[1].'   Sir John Lawrence, the man of iron, burst into tears as he read the telegram addressed by Chamberlain as Adjutant-General to the Chief Commissioner, to Colonel Edwardes, and others.   It reported the death of Nicholson, in whom ' the Bengal army has deeply to deplore the loss of one of its noblest and bravest soldiers.'   No wonder that Herbert Edwardes was down again with fever, the day after he had learned that all was over with his dearest friend.   The fall ' of Delhi lifted a load of care from our minds,' wrote Younghusband of Reynell Taylor and his assistants in Kangra, ' but it was with little gladness we heard of it, for Delhi had been dearly won with the loss of so many of our best, and amongst them the foremost man in India—John Nicholson[2].'

It was ' with heartfelt and unaffected sorrow ' that General Sydney Cotton announced to his troops the death of ' this daring soldier and inestimable man.'   ' England,' he added, ' has lost one of her most noble sons ; the army one of its brightest ornaments ; and a large circle of acquaintance a friend warm-hearted, generous, and true.'   In a General Order deploring the loss of his great subaltern, Sir John Lawrence said of him, ' brave, sagacious, and devoted to his profession, the Bengal army contained no nobler and no abler soldier.'   And a year later, in his Mutiny Report, he affirmed that, ' so long as British rule shall endure in India, his fame can never perish.   He seems especially to have been raised up for this juncture.   He crowned a bright though brief career by dying of the wound he received at

---

[1] Edwardes, *Official Report*.
[2] Bosworth Smith ; Lady Edwardes : Gambier Parry.

the moment of victory. The chief commissioner does not hesitate to affirm that without John Nicholson Delhi could not have fallen.'

'He was a glorious soldier,' John Lawrence wrote to Chamberlain; 'it is long before we shall look upon his like again.' Talking a few weeks later at Delhi to his secretary, Richard Temple, who had just returned from his furlough, John Lawrence said that in Nicholson 'were combined ardent energy, lofty aspirations, indomitable will, unswerving perseverance, unfaltering coolness, unflagging zeal, and to these moral qualities was added the advantage of enduring strength. But he had an imperious temper, and was hardly tolerant of even reasonable and necessary control.' And he held that few commanders, save Nicholson, could have achieved that swift forced march from Amritsar to Gurdàspur, but for which the mutineers 'would have passed on to light a flame in the heart of the Punjâb[1].'

As true an appreciation of the dead hero may be found in one of Hodson's letters to his brother. 'I mourn deeply,' he wrote, 'for poor Nicholson. With the single exception of my ever-revered Sir Henry Lawrence and Colonel Mackeson, I have never seen his equal in field or council. He was pre-eminently our " best and bravest," and his loss is not to be atoned for in these days.'

Writing to condole with Edwardes on ' the loss we have all sustained in John Nicholson,' Colonel Macpherson, Military Secretary to Sir John Lawrence, said, ' 'Tis hard to think that he should have been cut off just as a fair field was opening out for the exercise of the great talent and sagacity he possessed, and from which so much might have been gained to the cause of his country. We have none

---

[1] Sir R. Temple, *Men and Events of my time in India.*

like him left, and notwithstanding the incalculable advantage of the fall of Delhi, one is almost inclined to say it has
been too dearly purchased with the loss of such a man, at
such a crisis as the present [1].' In January, 1858, Sir John
Lawrence, writing to his old friend and master, Lord Dalhousie, declared that if Wilson's troops had retreated, ' all
must have been lost. Had indeed the storming not succeeded, all must have gone. To Nicholson, Alexander
Taylor of the Engineers, and Neville Chamberlain, the
real merit of our success is due. . . . John Nicholson, from
the moment of his arrival, was the life and the soul of the
army. Before he went down, he struck the only real blows
which the mutineers received in the Punjâb; he led the
assault, and was the first man over the breach [2].'

' It is a matter of the deepest regret to the Governor-
General in Council,' ran Lord Canning's General Order of
November 5, 1857, ' that the mortal wounds received by
Brigadier-General Nicholson, in the assault to the success
of which he so eminently contributed, have deprived the
State of services which it can ill afford to lose [3].' In every
station, where a salute was fired for the fall of Delhi, the joy
of a great victory was overclouded by the sense of a great
national loss. Nor was that feeling confined to his own
countrymen. In the great frontier province which he had
helped to subdue and govern, thousands of Sikhs, Punjâbis,
and Pathâns bewailed the death of a master, whose like,
while living, they had never seen before.

Over his grave was placed, under Chamberlain's direction,
' a solid slab of marble [4], resting upon a basement of two

---

[1] Lady Edwardes.   [2] Bosworth Smith.   [3] Forrest.
[4] This white marble slab had long served as a garden-seat for the Kings
of Delhi.

perfectly plain steps of gray or stone-coloured limestone.' The monument would thus, in Chamberlain's words, be ' simple, and chaste, and solid, and such, I hope, as his relations and friends would desire[1].' On its surface were chiselled these words :—

THE GRAVE

OF

BRIGADIER-GENERAL JOHN NICHOLSON

WHO

LED THE ASSAULT AT DELHI

BUT FELL IN THE HOUR OF VICTORY

MORTALLY WOUNDED

AND DIED SEPTEMBER 23, 1857

AGED 35[2].

Fewer words would have satisfied Chamberlain himself. ' Our hero,' he wrote to Edwardes when the tomb was finished, ' needs but to have his name engraved upon his tomb, for it to be respected by all ranks.'

Writing to Edwardes from Lahore, on October 2, Sir Robert Montgomery bewailed the loss of ' the two *great men*, Sir Henry Lawrence and John Nicholson. They had not, take them all in all, their equals in India. . . . Had Nicholson lived, he would as a commander have risen to

---

[1] For this inscription I am indebted to Major G. A. Keef, Royal Scots Fusiliers.

[2] Lady Edwardes.

the highest post.   He had every quality necessary for a successful commander: energy, forethought, decision, good judgement, and courage of the highest order.   No difficulty would have daunted him, and danger would have but calmed him.   I saw a good deal of him here, and the more I saw the more I liked him.'   Nicholson's discernment of native character, Montgomery writes to Kaye, ' was remarkable, and he selected and had around him the most faithful and devoted followers.   He was as swift to punish as he was quick to reward.   He had truly a hand of iron in a silken glove [1].'

Edwardes's love for Nicholson had been like the love of David for Jonathan.   Besides the personal and the national loss, ' I feel,' he said, ' as if all happiness had gone out of my public career.   Henry Lawrence was as the father, and John Nicholson the brother of my public life. . . . How is one ever to work again for the good of natives?   And never, never again can I hope for such a friend.   How grand, how glorious a piece of handiwork he was!   It was a pleasure even to behold him.   And then his nature so fully equal to his frame!   So undaunted, so noble, so tender, so good, so stern to evil, so single-minded, so generous, so heroic, yet so modest.   I never saw another like him, and never expect to do so.   And to have had him for a brother, and now to have lost him in the prime of life—it is an inexpressible and irreparable grief.   Nicholson was the soul of truth [2].'

' Nicholson,' wrote a young officer, who had marched with him to Mardàn and Trimmu Ghàt, ' was a man in whom the troops had the most unbounded confidence, and whom they would have followed anywhere cheerfully. . . .

---

[1] Kaye.   [2] Ibid.

I never heard so much anxiety expressed for any man's recovery before, and the only term I know that is fully adequate to express the loss we all felt, is that in each of our hearts the victory that day had been turned into mourning. He was a man whom all would have delighted to honour, and was beloved both for his amiability and kindness of disposition, and for his more brilliant qualities as a soldier and a ruler of the people. . . . When it was known that he was dangerously wounded, every one's first inquiry was, " How is Nicholson ? Are there any hopes of his recovery ?" ' And another spoke of him as ' without exception the finest fellow I ever saw in the shape of a soldier; handsome as he was brave, determined, cool, and clever. I knew him well at Peshâwar, and I feel his loss to be one which the country cannot replace¹.' ' His loss is a national misfortune,' Sir John Lawrence wrote in November to John Nicholson's still suffering brother. ' None of his friends have lamented that loss more deeply or more sincerely than myself. . . . I wish I could say or do anything to give you comfort.' The kindly Chief Commissioner knew how bitterly poor Charles Nicholson was grieving for his lost brother, with a grief which nothing human could for the present allay.

By that time Charles had been removed from Delhi to the cooler, purer air of Umballa, whence on November 1 he wrote with his left hand quite a long letter to his uncle, Sir James Hogg, the true parent of John Nicholson's brilliant career. After recounting his brother's exploits during the Mutiny, Charles begs his uncle ' not to imagine that my respect or affection for my brother has led me to exaggerate his services. It is not necessary for me to

---

¹ Kaye.

do so. I have said nothing but what is acknowledged universally to be fact. I write to you because it was you who placed him in a position where he had so many opportunities of distinguishing himself, a fact which he never lost sight of, and I thought you would like to know everything connected with his final career. Of all the men sent out to India since 1839, not one was a better soldier, and not one proved himself to be so good.'

Charles went on to state that ' by an old will made on the eve of the last campaign he left everything to his mother. After her he liked and respected, as I have often heard him say, Lady Hogg better than any woman in the world[1].'

' Foremost in all brave counsel,' wrote John Becher to Lady Edwardes, ' in all glorious audacity, in all that marked a true soldier, so admirable was our dear friend, John Nicholson. From the beginning of the great storm his was the course of a meteor. His noble nature shone brighter and brighter through every cloud, bringing swift and sure punishments to rebellion, wherever it raised its front in the Punjâb, carrying confidence and new vigour to the walls of Delhi, triumphant in the greatest fight that preceded the assault; the admiration of all the force. His genius foresaw the sure success; his undaunted courage carried the breach. He fell, the greatest hero we have had, loved and mourned through all India. Glorious fellow! Would to God he could have lived to hear the praise he had so earned from lips that he loved; to have seen the end of his great work! . . . How proud must his mother feel that God gave her such a son, even though he was so soon taken away! . . . In him I have lost a great friend and a great example[2].'

<hr>

[1] MS. Letter from Charles Nicholson.
[2] MS. Letter from Colonel J. Becher.

The *Lahore Chronicle* swelled the chorus of praise and lamentation over the departed 'Lion of the Punjâb.' 'His loss is deeply felt by the soldiers he had led to victory, and by all who can appreciate devoted gallantry and talents of a high order. The loss of such men makes victory very dearly bought.' And at a great meeting held that winter in Calcutta, in honour of three great soldiers who had lately died in their country's service—Nicholson at Delhi, Neill and Havelock at Lucknow—Mr. Ritchie, the Advocate-General, made an eloquent speech in praise of the 'young general,' the 'heroic Nicholson,' who 'fell, a youth in years, a veteran in the wisdom of his counsels, in the multitude of his campaigns, in the splendour of his achievements.' And the speaker went on to compare his hero with 'another youthful general, the immortal Wolfe—like him in the number of his years, like him in his noble qualities and aptitude for command, like him in the love and confidence he inspired in all around him, and like him in the wail of sorrow which told how his death marred the joy of a nation in the hour of victory [1].'

How deeply the death of Nicholson touched the imaginations of his Nikalsaini worshippers in Hazâra, may be seen from a letter written in October, 1860, by Sir Donald Macnabb, afterwards Commissioner of Peshâwar, to Sir James Hogg. 'When they heard of his glorious death, they came together to lament, and one of them stood forth and said there was no gain from living in a world that no longer held Nikalsain. So he cut his throat deliberately, and died. Another stepped forward and said that was not the way to serve their great *Guru*; that if they ever hoped to see him again in a future state, and to please him whilst

[1] Kaye.

they lived, they must learn to worship Nicholson's God. The rest applauded, and off started several of them, and coming to Peshâwar, went straight up to the missionary there, and told him their desire. He gladly offered to instruct them, seeing these men were religious enthusiasts, anxious to worship the Unknown God, and not mere lazy vagabonds like the common fakirs of India.

'After a year's teaching they expressed so strong a wish to be baptized, and the missionary was so satisfied that they now understood what they asked for, that he baptized some of them; and Captain James, the commissioner of Peshâwar, who told me of it, said he believed the feeling was spreading. I wonder if Nicholson's mother knows of this [1].'

When Mrs. Nicholson came to know of it, her heart was gladdened by such a revelation of her dead son's influence for good, even with those whom he had been wont to chastise for what seemed to him their criminal adoration of a mere man. On such occasions she would raise her eyes to heaven, 'with that grand lifting of the head which all who knew John Nicholson can remember in him [2].' The same witness from whom I have just quoted, speaks of her as 'a grand and noble woman; with a Spartan heroism about her, that showed the root of much that sprang up so gloriously in John Nicholson's nobility of soul.'

In the second volume of his delightful autobiography, Lord Roberts tells how in 1863 he was at Hasan Abdâl, the scene of Nicholson's exploits in 1849, looking out for a site for Sir Hugh Rose's camp. 'The people of the country were very helpful to me; indeed, when they heard I had been a friend of John Nicholson, they seemed to

---

[1] MS. Letter, copied by Miss Hogg.   [2] Lady Edwardes.

think they could not do enough for me; and delighted in talking of their old leader, whom they declared to be the greatest man they had ever known.'

In the *Gazette* containing the list of honours conferred by the Crown upon the heroes of Delhi, it was expressly notified that Brigadier-General Nicholson, had he lived, would have been made a Knight Commander of the Bath. The East India Company acknowledged the debt they owed to one of their most illustrious servants by bestowing on Mrs. Nicholson a special pension of £500 a year.

His friends in India set up to his memory, in the church at Bannu, a tablet bearing an inscription worthy of himself and of the friend who wrote it.   After referring to Nicholson's latest deeds and death in the hour of victory, Edwardes speaks of the man himself.

'Gifted in mind and body, he was as brilliant in government as in arms.   The snows of Ghazni attest his youthful fortitude; the songs of the Punjàb his manly deeds; the peace of this frontier his strong rule.   The enemies of his country know how terrible he was in battle, and we his friends have to recall how gentle, generous, and true he was[1].'

Nicholson's friends would have raised a tablet to his memory in the parish church at Lisburn, where his mother still dwelt.   But Mrs. Nicholson determined to undertake that loving duty at her own cost, leaving Sir Herbert Edwardes to supply the inscription.   The result was a beautiful work of art, designed and executed by J. H. Foley, R.A., whose equestrian statue of Sir James Outram ranks among the masterpieces of modern sculpture.   On the upper part of this memorial tablet, carved in

[1] On this memorial Nicholson's age is rightly given at 34, not as the tombstone gives it, '35.'

clear relief on the white marble, is a scene which represents the storming of the breach in the Kashmir Bastion by John Nicholson and his Fusiliers.

In the spring of 1862 this monument was placed in the parish church of Lisburn, the cathedral church of the diocese of Connor. Beneath the carved work runs the following inscription :—

' The grave of Brigadier-General Nicholson, C.B., is beneath the fortress which he died to take. This monument is erected by his mother to keep alive his memory and example among his countrymen. Comrades who loved and mourn him add the story of his life:—He entered the army of the H. E. I. C. in 1839, and served in four great wars — Afghanistan, 1841–42; Satlaj, 1845-46; Punjàb, 1848·49; India, 1857. In the first he was an Ensign; in the last a Brigadier-General and Companion of the Bath; in all a hero. Rare gifts had marked him for great things in peace and war. He had an iron mind and frame, a terrible courage, an indomitable will. His form seemed made for an army to behold; his heart, to meet the crisis of an empire; yet was he gentle exceedingly, most loving, most kind. In all he thought and did, unselfish, earnest, plain, and true; indeed, a most noble man. In public affairs he was the pupil of the great and good Sir Henry Lawrence, and worthy of his master. Few took a greater share in either the conquest or government of the Punjàb; perhaps none so great in both. Soldier and civilian, he was a tower of strength; the type of the conquering race. Most fitly in the great siege of Delhi he led the first column of attack and carried the main breach. Dealing the death-blow to the greatest danger that ever threatened British India, most mournfully, most gloriously, in the moment of victory, he fell mortally wounded on the 14th, and died on the 23rd of September, 1857, aged only 34[1].'

Meanwhile Nicholson's friends in India had decided to honour the dead hero by erecting a plain obelisk on the crest of the Margalla Pass—the scene of his sublime daring in 1848—with a small tank of water in the pass below. In Edwardes's opinion no more befitting or suggestive spot for such a monument could have been found in the whole Punjâb. Before 1857 a broad English road had superseded the old Muhammadan causeway, and the road has now given place to a line of railway. But the tall stone obelisk still challenges the notice of the railway passenger, and now and again some thirsty native traveller may refill his *lotah* from the neighbouring tank[2].

But of all the honours paid to John Nicholson's heroic memory, none perhaps struck so deep a chord of popular sentiment as the ballad which, within ten years of Nicholson's death, Captain Newbery heard some wandering minstrels chanting in the streets of the city which their hero had died to take. The ballad was in Punjâbi, which Captain Newbery afterwards rendered, as closely as he could, into spirited English verse. In April, 1867, Colonel J. Younghusband, Director-General of Police in the Punjâb, forwarded a copy of the English version to Sir John Lawrence, then Viceroy and Governor-General of India. It struck the sender as ' a remarkable testimony to the power Nicholson had over the warlike classes,' and he pointed to

---

[1] *Illustrated London News,* May 10, 1862.

[2] The building of this monument was supervised by Colonel A. Taylor, the Engineer of whom Nicholson had said to Chamberlain, 'If I live, the world shall know who took Delhi. The work was completed in 1868 by Mr. J. H. Lyons, Executive Engineer.

'the extraordinary fact that such a ballad should have been sung in the city of Delhi by men singing for their livelihood, and therefore unlikely to sing any but popular songs.'

Sir John thought the translation 'admirable and most creditable' to its author. He would have liked to publish the verses, but perhaps Lieut. Newbery might 'wish to dispose of them himself.' He will send a copy, however, by that day's mail to Nicholson's mother. 'Poor woman! How great is her loss! Nicholson was a wonderful fellow, and I really believe that but for him we should not have taken Delhi on September 14, 1857[1].'

He was right of course in so believing. But for the victorious march to Najafgarh, in happy disregard of Wilson's orders, the siege-train might never have reached the camp before Delhi. While the breaching batteries were doing their work upon the city, it was Nicholson's Titanic energy which drove his reluctant chief to fix upon the earliest possible moment for the crowning assault, according to a scheme prepared by its destined leader. The ballad on ' The death of Nicholson ' strays sometimes off the line of ascertained fact, as when we are told that—

> 'His cannons pour'd unceasing storm full on the Kashmir Gate ;
> And gazing at the combatants, he swore 'twere mortal sin,
> With food or drink to break his fast, until his troops should win.'

And there is more of fancy than of truth in the lines which tell how the Queen wept in sympathy with Nicholson's mother, and

> 'from her royal neck,
> Weeping, a priceless necklet took, her sobbing guest to deck.'

But the ballad, as a whole, is not unworthy of its high theme. It contains some of those touches of nature which

[1] For copies of the Letters here quoted I am indebted to Miss Hogg.

make the whole world kin, and it may fitly claim a place in the Appendix.

What more can I say of John Nicholson than has been said before in these pages? Both as soldier and administrator he had made his mark in the great days of Lord Dalhousie, and his name was a word of awe and wonder from the Jhilam to the Suliman Hills. In the sharp crisis of 1857, so fruitful of heroes, no grander or more heroic figure meets our gaze than that of the young general, who, after crushing two great mutinies in the Punjâb, marched down to Delhi to show his countrymen how the central stronghold of the rebellion could be won. To what heights he might have reached had he lived, it were waste of time to consider. At the age of thirty-four John Nicholson had already passed through many a 'crowded hour of glorious life'; and the capture of Delhi, which crowned his public career, was in itself one of the very greatest achievements of modern warfare. So long as Englishmen care to read the story of that wonderful siege, the memory of its foremost hero must remain green.

APPENDIX A

DEATH OF NICHOLSON

Brigadier-General John Nicholson received his mortal wound when storming Delhi, September 14, 1857, from the effects of which he died on the 23rd of the same month, aged 34 years.

The following is an attempt to convey to an English reader an idea of a Punjábi ballad recently sung in the streets of Delhi; some of the monotonous repetition has been omitted, but the translator considers it incumbent on him to follow as far as possible the disjointed sentences of the original.

WHEN Nicholson addressed Sir John, right quickly came reply,
To Delhi haste with armèd host and make the rebels fly.
With joy brave Nicholson advanced, to meet a warrior's fate,
His cannons pour'd unceasing storm full on the Kashmir Gate;
And gazing at the combatants, he swore 'twere mortal sin
With food or drink to break his fast, until his troops should win.
Oh, brother! 'twas an awful sight, the stormers' vengeful tread;
Then fired the caitiff Kâleh Khan. brave Nicholson was dead!
A soldier of Towana race upbore his dying frame,
Expiring Nicholson exclaim'd, 'Lawrence shall know thy fame—
'He'll make thee lord of Pindee's lands, of Pindee Gheb a chief,
'And give thee noble heritage, with many a smiling fief;
'When the glad news of Delhi's fall to Britain's Queen is told,
'She'll deck my troops with guerdons rare and necklets red
    and gold.'

Y

When Nicholson to Delhi came, right solemnly he swore,
If God will only spare my life, her name shall be no more;
Proud Jumna's flood shall wash her streets, her battlements
    I'll raze,
And nought but blacken'd mounds shall meet the wond'ring
    traveller's gaze.

Oh, brother! see the English charge, the Chândni Chauk is won,
In the red palace of the kings their bloody work is done;
The quaking Pourbeahs hear the tale and curse their losing fate.
Now magic peace the conqu'rors bring where carnage reign'd
    so late,
While merchants vend again their goods 'neath British arms
    secure,
The warriors lay aside their hate to feed the hungry poor.
Oh, Lion-hearted Nicholson! couldst thou but live once more,
We'd slay, and leave each Pourbeah dog to welter in his gore!

But British hearts are merciful, and vengeance is forgot,
E'en injured serfs obtain their rights, and bless their happy lot;
Where erst a vicious emperor sat, an honest ruler sways,
Aiding the ruined citizens, who murmur grateful praise.
Oh, Nicholson was bravest brave that English Chief could be;
My brother, such a gallant man seems very God to me.
And thus the dying hero wrote, to Lawrence at Lahore,
'Thou art lord of the Khâlsa's land, my brother chief of yore;
'List to my pray'r for Hyât Khan, my brave Towana guard :
'Make him a noble of the land, with him my all is shared.
'Write, and let India's Viceroy hear, a childless Captain's prayer,
'Regard my troops as dearest sons, make them my country's care,
'To recompense my children's deed the choicest gifts I crave.'
Oh, brother! we can ne'er forget John Nicholson the brave.
Oh, dearest spark of chivalry, let a Punjâbi cry
All shame that British soldiery left Nicholson to die!
Upon our father's honoured grave, thy Khâlsa soldiers weep,
Towanas brave and stout Pathâns lament thy lifeless sleep;
Mourning we say, hadst thou but lived, what riches were in store
For us, who war for stranger chiefs, since thou canst fight no
    more!

John Lawrence sent a missive sad to Britain's gracious Queen,
Recounting first proud Delhi's fall, and the great hero's mien,

How gallantly he stormed the breach, above the Kashmir gate,
And ever foremost in the van, had met a soldier's fate.
The Queen, with gentle sympathy, in tears this letter read,
And then her chieftain's mother called, whose only son was dead.
She soothed the mother's bitter grief, and from her royal neck,
Weeping, a priceless necklet took, her sobbing guest to deck :
'Oh! mother's heart, be comforted, nor mourn thy soldier son :
'God owns thy child, in England's Queen thou hast a mother won.'

Oh! foremost in the deadly breach, no foe could make thee halt,
Slain by the dastard Kâleh Khan, the traitor to his salt.
We ceaseless pray the warrior's God, with all a soldier's love,
That he would make brave Nicholson a prince in heaven above.
Oh! Godlike chieftain Nicholson, our children lisp thy name,
Thou'lt not forget the Khâlsa's prayers, their babies prate thy
 fame.

APPENDIX B

HYÂT KHAN.

SIRDAR MUHAMMAD HYÂT KHAN, C.S.I., whose name appears
in the foregoing Ballad, was John Nicholson's Native Orderly
during the campaign of 1857. From information supplied by
Colonel Urmston, and Colonel J. Johnstone, he seems to have
been a son of Fathi Khan, the brave Pathân chief who fell by
Nicholson's side in the attack on the Margalla Tower in 1848.
Fathi Khan's people dwelt at Wâh, about a mile from Hasan
Abdâl. Some years later, at Nicholson's request, Edwardes gave
Hyât Khan the post of Police Darogah (Superintendent) at
Peshâwar. After the outbreak of the mutiny he served as Nichol-
son's Native Orderly through all the enterprises which marked
his chief's victorious progress from Peshâwar to Delhi. For
several years after the mutiny he served as Assistant to successive
Deputy Commissioners of Bannu and Kohat.

During the Afghan War of 1878-80 Hyât Khan served as political assistant to General, now Lord Roberts. For some years
past he has been a divisional judge in the Punjâb.

APPENDIX C

CHARLES NICHOLSON survived his famous brother only by five years. Early in 1858 he left India on sick leave, and rejoined his mother at Lisburn, whence from time to time he paid a series of visits to relatives and friends in the north of Ireland. In the summer of 1859 he visited the United States. In October of that year Captain Nicholson married in Staten Island Miss Elizabeth Gillilan, a distant cousin, whose father had long been settled in New York. In November Charles Nicholson brought his wife home to Lisburn. Soon, however, it became clear that one of his lungs had been affected by the amputation of his arm. He appears to have passed the next two winters in the north of Africa, and in the valley of the Nile. In the summer of 1862, Sir Hugh Rose, afterwards Lord Strathnairn, offered him the command of a Gurkha regiment in Northern India. With the sanction of his medical advisers, Charles Nicholson accepted the offer.

In company with his wife he reached Calcutta; whence on Dec. 12, 1862, they began that journey up the country which ended abruptly five days later in the dawk-bungalow at Domri on the road to Almorah. A broken blood-vessel had caused his death, at the age of thirty-three. His body was taken back to Raniganj, where it received a soldier's funeral, under the care of his cousin Charles Hogg, who conducted the childless widow back to Calcutta. About six months afterwards she also fell a victim to the disease which had slain her husband. John Nicholson's mother died in 1874 at the age of 88, having survived by many years the whole of her seven children, except Mrs. Maxwell, who lived on until 1889.

APPENDIX D

The following lines may be quoted from *Delhi and other poems*, by Charles Arthur Kelly, M.A., Bengal Civil Service. (Longmans, Green & Co., 1872.)

With brand up-raised, and white plume flashing far,
What haughty chieftain holds the front of war?
Well knows the foe that warrior in the fight,
Stern as the storm, and terrible as night;
Not his to dread the battle's blood-red waves,

Nor the wild rush of Heaven-detested slaves,
Though from the thundering bastion burst the cloud,
And the thick war-smoke clothes him like a shroud.
On towards the gate of Death, he pressed, and fell,
The proud stern man they feared, yet loved so well ;
Quenched by the death-shot, lie for ever still
That iron spirit and that master will,
The princely heart of steel that would not yield,
But, like the Spartan, died upon the shield.
Say not such earnest toils were borne in vain ;
Who wins the glory first must feel the pain.
Champion of right, the noblest aim of man,
He lived, and died when vengeance led the van.
May loftier harps record his glorious youth,
His love of honour, and his living truth ;
We only mourn for him whose work is done,
And wish the world had more like Nicholson !

THE NICHOLSON MONUMENT AT THE MARGALLA PASS.
From a photograph copied by R. Hennell, Esq.

INDEX

THE END

www.ingramcontent.com/pod-product-compliance
Lightning Source LLC
Chambersburg PA
CBHW031127120726

47905CB00006B/1590